Envoy of the Black Pine

By Clio Gray

Guardians of the Key
The Roaring of the Labyrinth
Envoy of the Black Pine

Types of Everlasting Rest

Envoy of the Black Pine

Clio Gray

headline

First published in 2008 by
HEADLINE PUBLISHING GROUP

1

Cataloguing in Publication Data is available from the British Library

ISBN 978 0 7553 4353 9

Typeset in Bembo by Palimpsest Book Production Ltd,
Grangemouth, Stirlingshire

Printed and bound in Great Britain by
Clays Ltd, St Ives plc

Headline's policy is to use papers that are natural, renewable and recyclable
products and made from wood grown in sustainable forests. The logging and manufacturing
processes are expected to conform to the environmental regulations of the country of origin.

HEADLINE PUBLISHING GROUP
An Hachette Livre UK Company
338 Euston Road
London NW1 3BH

www.headline.co.uk
www.hachettelivre.co.uk

To Louise, my mother, for everything

A quick but heartfelt thanks to Flora Rees at Headline for her intuitive editorial support, and to Yvonne Holland, whose tweaks and turns have made the text tighter and more fluent and eliminated the odd anachronisms and mistakes. Any left are certainly my own responsibility. Also, many thanks to my agent, Laura Longrigg, at MBA, for her unstinting encouragement and hard work.

And thank you, Melissa, for entertaining Quigley and Mrs B on all those long, long walks.

Contents

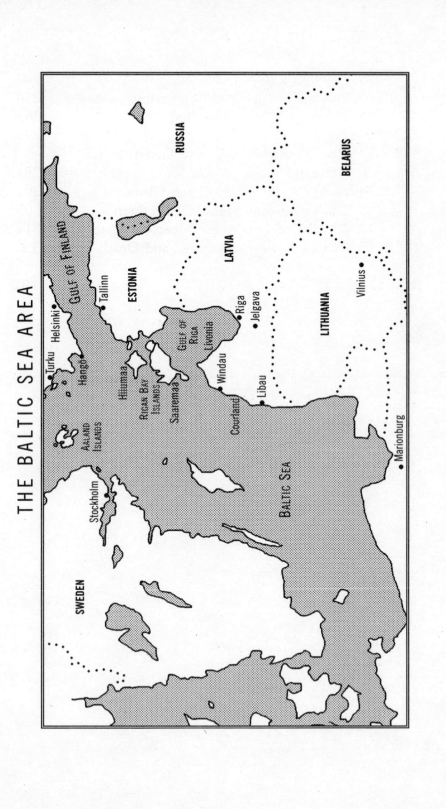

THE BALTIC SEA AREA

SWEDEN

Stockholm

ÅLAND ISLANDS

BALTIC SEA

Marionburg

Turku
Helsinki
Hangö

GULF OF FINLAND

Tallinn

ESTONIA

Hiiumaa

RIGA BAY ISLANDS

Saaremaa

Gulf of Riga

Livonia

Windau

Courland

Libau

Riga
Jelgava

LATVIA

LITHUANIA

Vilnius

RUSSIA

BELARUS

Preface

Early Spring, Early Warning: 2 February 1808

DAWN BREATHED A line of light the colour of quinces across the sea's grey and slumped horizon, bled a little red towards the east, where the sun would soon-time rise, spread the sandstone cliffs with gold and shadow. Almost to the top, a stick insect seemed to twitch its legs and move. It was a boy, his thin body spread-eagled against the rock, fingers clinging to their holds, heart beating fast as stoats amidst the clap, clap, clap of pigeon wings that spiralled about his head in half-asleep alarm, disturbed from their roost by his climb.

Steffan felt the prickle of sweat on his forehead, at the roots of every hair, wanted more than anything to brush it away, fought off the reflexive itch of his muscles which tried to make him lift his hands. He breathed hard, touched his head to the rock, felt the drip-wet dew of it, the stink of foul-smelling oil that came from the fulmars' nests, and knew he did not have far to go.

Only a few yards, he thought. Surely I can do this.

1

The birds bred soonest here, were the only ones to have eggs this early in the season. His grandfather had told him they were like troubadours without the singing, spent their whole lives adrift and alone upon the sea, until the milder weather came and they headed for land. It had been so very mild this year, and by the middle of January they were already circling about the edges of the cliff, cackling on their bare rock ledges, clacking beaks and winding necks. His grandfather had taught him all this, though could not be here with him to collect the early eggs; had been six spades deep these past few weeks, with Steffan blinking away the tears over the cold, frost-hardened ground, giving the old man one last promise: that he would go in his stead.

And so here he was, spooked by a pack of rock doves, and only a few yards to go. He hoped the lifting of the birds would not disturb the big grey gulls which were his aim, though felt a little calmer now the doves had risen, could hear his grandfather's voice telling him which way to go, loosened his left hand and moved it up a pace, found another grasp-hole, hauled his feet up below him, just as he had been taught to do. Slowly now, trying to remain invisible and without sound, he got himself ready for the next move, knew he was close, heard the gentle cackling of the birds just above him, knew that it was almost sunrise and the time when the fulmars would stretch their long grey wings and set out across the sea, leaving their eggs for him to steal.

The slip and slide of sheep guts came at him from nowhere, landed with a slap against his upturned face, the slither-green sack that had contained them becoming a mask of stink and blood. He lifted his hands involuntarily to wipe the shit-smelling, grass-fermenting coils from off him, and felt the cold of air rush past his body as he left the sand-stone of the cliff, recognised the panic that he had sweated through so often in his dreams of falling, went over once, then twice, his sheep-splattered head shattering on the outlying precipice of rock from which the doves had so recently departed, mewling like a seal pup that has been long abandoned upon the sand. Two seconds later, and Steffan hit the cove floor, every part of his young body breaking, the water sucking at his wounds, the tide already snatching at his clothes and rolling him out into the breakers, swirling him with the spume between the outcrops and bouldered arches that lay scattered about the base of the cliff like bones; a single splash of colour in the scroll of rolling grey that was the uncaring sea.

Up above, gaunt strands of heather began to lift as the sun warmed the frost from off their tips, stretched a silent hand down the sandstone to tease up from their nests those last few fulmars sleeping. Only a scrape of time since Steffan had fallen, and already he might never have been, and the man who had unburdened himself of his sack was already a quarter-mile distant, running like a wolf across the moor, his shadow lengthening over the newly budded shoots of bilberry with the growing sun, making it hard for him to see his steps, made him stumble into bog-fringed pools and over clumps of cotton grass, made him curse the cold and cramp that twisted the muscles within him, torqued the skin upon his skeleton as upon a rack.

Eyvind Berwald was neither young nor small, as Steffan had been, and yet the fear he felt tightened his lungs just the same, brought the goose-bumps up on his hard, soldier-man's skin, made his close-cropped beard prickle amidst the grey. It was the same fear he'd felt as when Gunar Torrensson first spoke of his schemes to his specially elected crew, the strong wrapping of each one's hands within his own as he passed amongst them, boasting of the days of thunder and strike to come, marking each date out upon the calendar with the black swirl of his thumb. The weeks of worry that had followed had hammered like wood-peckers at Eyvind's heart, made it harder than ever for him to think, which had never come easy, the constant tick and tick inside him as he tried to hatch a plan to get him off this wagon he had hitched to Torrensson so long ago. Then, it had carried him strong and screaming through each battle at his brother, Onni's, side, feeling braver with each survival, the ever-growing possibility of victory within his sights. Now he realised the battles would never end, that Torrensson had no other life but to lead, and needed this band of men at his back to do so, needed their shouts behind him to push him on, would rather die and take every last one of them with him than live in any other, more ordinary, way.

Throwing down that bag of guts, Eyvind knew again the same jig and jump of his heart as that morning when he'd knocked on Torrensson's cabin door, made his poor argu-ment, his voice pale and trembling, his fingertips twitching at the seams of his pockets, the tic of blood throbbing beneath his temples, the sickly rise of hope and bile within his throat as Torrensson sat and smoked and thought, left him hanging in the doorway like an outsized strip of arsenic paper used to catch the flies, swaying slowly, waiting for whatever was to be thrown at him to hit and stick.

And then Torrensson had rolled his shoulders, rubbed his neck, turned his flat grey face towards him, and Eyvind had known from the twist of his captain's lips that his contribution to the cause had been approved, and Eyvind had won his way out of the mutiny and off the boat, and had to put his hand out to the doorframe to keep himself from sinking to his knees with relief. He felt again that same paroxysm of giggling that had accompanied his slow release from the deep, dark pool of war and death and duty that had weighed upon his shoulders like a grindstone; felt and savoured the gradual lightening of his conscience as it rose towards a better life, the growing hope that one day soon he would break the surface, and step out clean and without blood and be able to live his last few years as a blameless man.

Eyvind thought these thoughts as he took his uneven way back across the moors, having thrown his sack of sheep guts down and over the cliff, wiping his hands again and again upon his trousers to remove the blood he knew must still be there. He could feel it hardening beneath his fingernails, in the skin about his knuckles, and the loose wrinkles rippled around the callused pads that ridged his palms. The sweat was pouring down his back, and his skin felt slack and wet against his bones, but the knife was still heavy in the inner pocket of his jacket, pricking at his side with every step, so that when he finally reached the abandoned byre he now called his home, it was with a certain satisfaction that he stripped away his stinking shirt, and found a pipped and purpled bruise the size of a fist against his side, gained comfort from its presence. Prodding at it with his thumb, he found satisfaction in the pain it gave him, a hidden penance for all the things he had done, and those he would yet be forced to do.

He would have sicked his stomach inside out to see the dead boy, Steffan, rolling in the surf and know it was his doing, would have understood then that the clouds he saw were only reflections and that the dark waters were already gathering above his head, that the self-disgust and sorrow he felt had only just begun.

On top of that cliff, he had turned for a moment, stared at the rising sun until he had to close his eyes, could still see the burning disc of it upon his eyelids, sparks splintering all about it like a devil in the fire. He had opened his eyes then so that he could see again to walk, saw instead the dark and terrifying circle of the sun riding ramrod through his vision, the black and dirty marks of Torrensson's thumb inked upon his calendar, and dreaded the times he knew were about to come.

At matins that morning, the priest who had so recently buried Steffan's grandfather, and who would so soon have to bury a coffin of stones approximating the boy's weight, crossed from his reed-hatted cottage the one hundred yards to his wooden church. He rubbed and blew into his hands to keep them warm – had always had problems with his circu-lation these cold winter months, would find his fingers waxy and white and completely without feeling when he awoke. It was a condition that often persisted the whole day through, and had forced him to devise a system of strings and weights with which to turn the pages of his books and Bible. He glanced at the pink midriff of sky, which glowed so serenely between the sea and the orange-bellied clouds above it, shivered as the wind cudgelled at his cassock, recognised its direction, and that it meant to stride across the sky towards the islands, bring those clouds with it, and obliterate the earth beneath its snow.

It had been a strange year, a start of warmth that had misdirected the willows to roll out their buds before their time, bring up the butterbur two months early from the soil, eased the odd mining bee or butterfly from its hole. But he was not a man for signs and miracles, and knew his God, knew without doubt or rancour that what was given with one hand would always be taken away with the other. He shook his head and watched his breath hang there like a mist, tried to get back to the sermon he had been working on, knew he would have to remember it without his notes, that once again his fingers could not be relied upon, even with their tags and weights. St Blaise's Day, he reminded himself, feast day of the crippled and diseased, always a big turn-out, no matter the weather.

He paused his step a little as he approached his church, could see a shape hunched on the deck of the porch. He crossed himself with the frozen hooks of his fingers, hoped to God it was not another child, remembered the last one, blue as a cornflower and dead, despite the blanket that had been so carefully cosseted around her shoulders. But the next step told him that this was no child, no human form, could smell it too clearly as he closed upon it. It was an animal, a lamb, or at least a small sheep: small, and curled into a comma

7

upon the church steps, a faint glisten of blood iced about it in a pool. It had been crudely shorn, and beside it lay a woolcomb. His fingers hurried to the sign of God's comforting cross about his neck, but as ever, his fingers disobeyed him, could not find what they sought beneath his cassock and caught instead at the throat of his long-johns. His words of pre-emptive blessing were leaves in a frozen waterfall and, like them, he stopped. There was something else about St Blaise, delivered up so early to his martyrdom in AD 209, something that called the priest right back to his seminary days and his early teachings: St Blaise, his flesh torn from his body by an iron woolcomb, right down to the bone, until he had died like an animal where he lay.

Just like the one that had been left for him here, still bloody, abandoned next to the corpse that lay upon the steps of his church.

PART 1

LOST VALLEYS AND MISSING LIBRARIES

1

The Coprological Museum that is Everyman's Home: April 1808

'So what's this you've been doing, Jack?' asked Whilbert Stroop, leaning down low over the papers laid out on the table.

Jack moved slowly and deliberately, sucking the end of his pencil in the same manner Stroop always did – though neither of them was aware of it – carefully laid the tip of his index finger to the edge of the drawing he had been working at, then retreated from the table, wanting to let Stroop make his judgement in peace.

Thomas was in no such mind of reverence, and spoke up for both.

'So what do you think, Mr Stroop? Will it do?'

Stroop looked at the page of painstaking work, knew his word would be taken more seriously than anyone else's, excepting perhaps for Mabel's. He leant forward, studied the picture and its notes carefully for a full minute to emphasise how seriously he was taking their task.

'Excellent notes,' he said as he straightened, looked at the lanky lad who had subsided into the furthest, most shadow-ridden corner of the room. 'Jack and Thomas, you have done wonders, and you are both welcome to become Members of the Institute of Stroop Studies.'

Jack catapulted out of the chair that had barely been containing him, and shouted out at the top of his voice, which wasn't loud, muted by the strictures of scar tissue that wrapped around his throat like a second, thicker skin. 'I told you he'd like it! Didn't I tell you?'

Thomas, all fourteen years of him, was bound to agree. 'We done just what you said, Mr Stroop, and a bit more. See when we went to that museum place? We been chasing it up ever since.'

'So I see,' said Stroop, and didn't wonder at it. He'd taken them to Coffer Byng's Coprological Entertainment a week last Wednesday. It offered a complete diagnostic of tracking the spoors and excrements of animals they were highly unlikely to encounter during their everyday lives, and included the exotica of giraffe and lion droppings, fresh from the King's zoo at the Tower, but both Thomas and Jack had been adamant this was a trail they chose to follow, and Stroop had been pleased to encourage them.

'Look for the different things we might find near rivers, or barns, or various work establishments,' he'd advised. 'Let's see if we can't find patterns in what is dropped and where.'

Thomas and Jack had taken him quite literally, and found otter spraint by the river, bat droppings near barns and churches. Owl pellets. Excrement of dog, cat, fox, vole, rat, whatever they could find. Thomas had taken notes in a scrawl decipherable only by himself, spent long laborious hours transcribing those notes into wobbly lines of capitals in a spare ledger Stroop had provided. Jack had done the drawings, astounding everyone with how meticulous he was, how steady his hand. He'd invented a little code, just as he knew Stroop would have done: a sign to denote the colour of the collected specimen, another for where it had been found – wiggly lines for water, sticks for trees, blocks for walls.

Stroop felt an immense, if slightly ridiculous, pride that they were proceeding with their experiment just as he would have done, and with as much dedication. They'd gone out into the field, collected their spoors, taken samples where they could, and made drawings where they could not, taken notes of each and every find. It all helped to fill out another little part of Stroop's Sense Map of London. And also helped to fill the void left by Mabel, since she had been invited to the site of last year's adventure, exploring the catalogues of Astonishment Hall.

'If only Mabel could see you now,' Stroop said, and wished immediately that he hadn't.

They all missed her in so many different ways. Stroop missed her careful copying of all the notes he had made on his own latest forays. He'd spent a lot of time with glass-blowers and bellfounders, and with the makers of prosthetic limbs. But each night he got home, he knew she would not be there to go through them all again with him, to be so evidently excited at each new discovery made, each interesting fact, her enthusiasm to get them catalogued and cross-referenced, pointing out any holes and gaps. He missed the home-baked smells of the meals she made, still stopped every time he put his hand out to the latch of the gate to try to guess what would be on the table waiting, had to remind himself she would not be there to greet him, had to stop himself shouting out every evening for more coffee or more wine when he was working at his desk.

He knew that Thomas missed her guiding hand at almost every turn, missed her little lectures on how not to be a street boy any more. That he had taken to stealing from the markets again, but left his prizes to rot on the table, not knowing what to do with them now she was not there.

But mostly it was Jack who quietly grieved, who had grown so silent and thoughtful, though no one ever knew what he was thinking. Only Mabel. Jack was a boy who had never grown older than his boots, and he never had those for very long, not unless Mabel was there looking after him.

Stroop couldn't say how much he longed to have her back with them all, knew she would return in a moment if only he would ask. Knew also that she needed time to get over the things that she had seen and suffered, both at Astonishment Hall and before. And that it was there that she had realised other horizons might await her, different parts of herself she might explore, and, God knew, he did not begrudge her that.

Still, there it was. He missed her, and he wanted her back, and so did Jack and Thomas. She was the ribbon that plaited them all together, and without her they were all just strands of horsehair tangled in the same tail, though with no guiding pattern.

Stroop heard a tap-tap-tapping at the door. Knew it would be the street vendor come to dispense his ladles of stew. Sighed, because it was Friday, and inevitably the stew would involve some kind of fish, which he hated. He had found lamprey suckers in the last Friday bowl he had gingerly explored; had given it to Bindlestiff, Mabel's old dog, who had somehow managed to wheeze on in his corner of the kitchen, despite being apparently older than the hills and having feet that smelt of cheese. Even the dog missed Mabel, had twice this week neglected to haul himself to his stinky feet and woof to be taken to the garden to have his pee. Stroop remembered coming in the night before last and seeing the old dog on its blanket looking up at him, the soft waft of warm urine coming up from his blanket, the awful look of resignation in the old dog's eyes.

'Thomas,' he said, as he unbent his back away from the chair in which Jack was now sitting, still poring over his drawing, his pencil in his fingers. He placed his hand on Jack's head a moment as he straightened. 'Thomas,' he repeated, and had a shiver of Christmas about to unwrap itself as he spoke out loud the words he had thought so many times to say but not yet said, 'go and get my writing kit from the desk. I think it's time we asked Mabel to come home.'

2

False Lights, False Hopes

A STRANGE PLACE IS the island world of Saaremaa, spread low like freckles across the long arm of the Baltic Sea as it swims the one hundred and fifty miles between Sweden and the Estonian Bay. Throughout the long months of winter, the salt waves froze into a crust about the islands, stopped up ships like corks caught in its ice, squeezed at the crews stranded upon the wooden-backed boats on which they spent their days, sent them sometimes crawling out over the ice like sprays of pebbles, bludgeoning seals hauled up through their blow-holes until the snowy surface was stained black with blood, sucking the blubber to keep them alive on the ship that shadowed behind them, or loading whatever they could onto sledges, which they hauled the long walk back to land.

Strange are the names of those islands: Abruka, Hiiumaa, Kassari, Prangli, Vislandi . . . More than a thousand of them, almost two, if each rocky outcrop and reef were known, or counted, by any but the few who wedged their boats into bays too small to beach a whale-bone, to cast out their nets and lines and drag in their catch, boots jacked into crevices to halt their fall when the wind changed direction, or a wave loomed up behind them like an anvil, brutal, unexpected and three times the size of the ones that had gone before.

Tamas Swarthaar knew nothing of those other islands, knew only this small part of the bay that stretched out from Hiiumaa, and looked out now across the mist-shivered causeway that linked him to his home. He knew he would have to speed his work, saw the storm clouds lift from off the mainland as the sun began to sink, as if a vast blue heron had drawn its wings across the sky. He'd been stranded here once, a few years before, having misread the signs of the sky, and the petrels and puffins that had huddled back into their holes. The wind had swept so swiftly across the bay it had scoured the surface of the sea clean over his narrow pathway, left him cleaving to the rock with his bare hands, the spray drenching his back, filling his mouth, the fish creel ripped from his shoulders and almost taking him with it. The few seals that had wallowed on the spare yard of shingle below him had flumped and galumphed back into the rising waves, popped up their heads a bit way out and stayed there, staring up at him, their brown eyes full of pity, wondering why he didn't follow. He'd spent that night in cold and terror, the storm rising so suddenly it snatched the breath from his throat, stole the light from his eyes, left him like a piece of sodden kelp, straggle-backed against his rock, clinging on and on, crying to think he might not live to see another dawn.

He had never made such a mistake again. No man would, or wouldn't survive it if he did. And so he wondered a little

17

at what he thought he could see now, thought he could make out a man, pinch-backing himself and his lantern up the side of a distant rock. He held his hand to his eyes, tried to make things out a little clearer, for ever since that long and lonely night his eyesight had been bad. The salt had sucked out the centre from his vision, left him only a circle of world frayed at its edges. He tilted his head, was sure he could see a lantern flickering, hoped for a wild moment it was his lost son Steffan's spirit lingering on though almost three months dead, the grief still raw as butcher's meat within him.

But no, whatever might have been on that ziggurat of rock was lost now to the mist, and Tamas concentrated on his line, unhooking the mackerel one by one into the creel which rode upon his back like a shell, then set himself back across the causeway, picking his way like a crab across the stones.

Out on that other rock, Eyvind Berwald hauled himself up from the sway of his boat by a grapple-hook, the slight glow-worm of his light wobbling in the jar he'd slung about his neck, the heavier sack upon his back constantly slipping to one side and impeding his climb. Cursing, he gained the top of the talon-splintered reef, his hands torn by the sharp cuts of barnacles, pricked red and ringed with anemone stings, and slimy from the bursting of their guts.

He panted, patted at the rock to find a flattish place to sit, and wiped his hands upon the sacking of his bag. He flexed his fingers free of the pins and needles caused by his climb, took out his rations from the sack, and, more importantly, the lamp that was the purpose of his struggle onto his pinnacle of rock. He didn't want to do this, had been dreading it, had been counting off the days one by one, hoping the message would not come. He found a crevice and jammed the lamp in so that it stood steady, made sure the shuttering of the door was oiled and easy to move, that the wick was trimmed and ready.

He saw the long worm of wind stretch across the surface of the sea, sink down into every trough, and back up to the white tops of the breakers, gathering the scent and scale of deep-living things and the brine that moved upon them. He saw the truncated outline of the lighthouse away to his right, built only to its neck and no further, still lacking its light, as was integral to Torrensson's plan. Eyvind checked his lamp, made sure of its wick and oil, tried to be calm, to breathe in the exhalations of the dim and dying day, that drift of wet and wind that falls upon every rock and boulder, on every house and tree and blade of grass, on every man, and every night, in Saaremaa.

Anto Juusa ordered the men of the *Pihkva* to slacken the sails, close-haul them into the wind. He needed to turn the boat about, stop it running so hard before a broken sea, felt the rise of wind beginning to push the boat too quickly towards the shore. The *Pihkva* was sluggish with the weight of its cargo, though they were hardly fully laden, only the huge sacks of grains and sugar hugging at its boards down below, casks of wine and spirits rolling slightly in the cradle of their wedges, rocking with the play of the sea. Juusa and his crew had plied over from Sundsvall to drop off supplies to the islands before heading on for Tallinn. They'd been planning to dock in at Körgessaare on Hiiumaa, took each island turn by turn on every pass, but the sky had darkened too soon, making it difficult to navigate the thousands of reefs and islets that surrounded Hiiumaa's shores. It was here they had meant to swap most of their cargo for the short, stocky workhorses bred by the so-called barley-heads who lived here, which sold so well on the mainland. He was thinking now they might have no choice but to go on. The winds were pushing the waves out from Sweden behind them, and when the storm hit from the other side, they would be caught in the middle, and the waves would begin to boil in angry swirls about the reefs, hiding them, making of them maelstroms, unnoticed until they started to scratch at the bottom of the boat, and rip at its planks.

His first mate came up behind him. 'Thinking to go on, sir?' he said, one hand flat on his head to hold down his cap.

'Ay, thinking so,' replied the captain, not taking his eyes from the dirty-yellow clouds that lay like scum over the sea to the east, narrowing them against the hard dash of spray that slapped against the boat-sides, threw up and over them like spittle. 'Men be all right with that, will they, Valk?'

Johann Valk nodded grimly. 'Better skin on their bones than gold in their pockets. I'll talk 'em round, though they'll not be best pleased. Lost a bit of a packet last time and this'll not help back home.'

Valk's captain screwed up his mouth as he ran his tongue along the inside of his teeth. He was still angry at the pallets of tea-bricks found spoilt by mould and ballast that last return to Sundsvall, was going to give that bastard Russki merchant something to chew on when he caught him up. They'd lost good money from that rotten sale, and it had cut the boys' profits to practically nothing. They'd been meaning to make it up again this trip, take on more horses, had deliberately kept the cargo weight light so they could take more than usual to make up the gap. Horses were good tender in these parts, none better. Island horses, said every man in Estonia, despite the barley-head slur, lasted twice as long for twice the labour as those bred on the mainland.

Both Valk and the captain were startled by a crew boy coming scuttling across the boards towards them, arms splayed out to take the dip and yaw of the boat as it came along-side the wave-roll, turned through it, moving away from the island.

'Quarter man's seen lights off to starboard!' he shouted excitedly, the large gap in his front teeth making him whistle with every exhalation, with the hiss of a slow-boiling kettle.

Captain Juusa and his first mate exchanged glances, thought they'd piloted the vessel too far from the shore to be able to see any lights, at least from the main ports.

'Could be the peninsula at Ristnaneem,' shrugged Valk. 'Heard they're building lighthouses there and all along the shore.'

Juusa was doubtful. Last time they'd passed close enough to see, the tower was barely halfway built, and that had only been a few months back. He rolled his lips together, tasted the salt that had grown from his beard, the spit and cut of blood from his cold sores, wanted to ease himself out of the constant dampness of his clothes, thought about the log fires that would be awaiting them at the inn of Körgessaare, shivered as another blast of wind sliced the collar from his neck. He lifted his head slightly at Valk, who understood, strode off quickly with the boy to check out his story, make sure it was signals they were getting to help them in, and not some light from a fire on a hovel-rock where a man might be cooking up some soup from seaweed and sand-gritted oysters. He was as keen as the captain to get beached and dried and preferably drunk, which is every sailors' duty when he first hits shore. Juusa watched them disappear into the shrouds of sail and spray and night and storm, and hoped the boy was right, hoped there was someone out there who had seen them, who would guide them in from the storm. Nobody knew like a sailor did how precious such a light could be in the dark night of the sea. Knew that if anyone shorewise had seen them, they'd be eager to get them in safe, be first to greet them and their cargo and see what barters might be made. Knew also that no one on the island could have known they were coming in right at this moment, that only a rough agreement had been made the last time they had visited as to when they would come by again.

A few minutes later, and he saw Valk waving a lantern above his head, confirming the boy's tale, that the lights and the messages they gave out had been properly sent and received and responded to, so down he went to the wheelhouse to send them tacking inwards like one firefly towards another, sending signals, being answered, one flash, two gained, then three repeated on either side. They went slowly still, didn't know the waters, had to trust to the signaller the way they must go, sending them to the left or the right. And so it went, and they went well, and they rounded a dark headland with relief, saw it loom out to starboard, saw more lights flashing their staccato greetings from what Juusa assumed must be the stub-headed cliffs, knew then they were safe and would soon be out of the reaches of the storm.

The barrage of cannonballs hit them like thunder, split through their bows like fire-headed hail. Broadside on broadside came roaring down upon them, set the sails into sheets of flame, bonfires of burning oil skittering out across the decks where the canvas drooped and fell, volley after volley of musket shots spitting down upon them, splintering the wood from the masts and the sides of the *Pihkva* and the edges of the wheelhouse, stopping the men who were trying to escape from the burn of the sails, holing out the stomachs of the first mate and the boy as they tried to weave an unseen path to safety, sent them screaming into the sea with their guts spilling out of them, eyes wide and white with shock as the water dragged them under, skinny arms waving like pale, moon-struck weeds above the surface for just a second, before they both disappeared, and Valk and the hissing boy were no more.

Juusa saw nothing except a night torn asunder by fire and smoke, was horrified by his incomprehension, was screaming into the wind for his first mate to drag his men to order, heard instead the confused crew of the *Pihkva* yelling and calling for help, their thin black silhouettes spread-eagled across the deck-boards as they tried to reach the wheelhouse and the pistols they knew were stockpiled there in case of the emergency no one had seriously thought would come; saw instead the boulder of the unlit boat that had drawn alongside, the sharp, spider outlines of grappling hooks backlit

23

by the fires that spread out across the boards in their rainbow pools. And then came the screech of wood on wood as gang-planks were thrown from the enemy ship to the *Pihkva*, and Captain Juusa could only watch as the invaders began to spill over the sides of his boat like beetles, grinning and shouting and firing indiscriminately into the air, into the deck, into anybody who had the courage to run at them with their empty hands and threats.

'Hold fast!' commanded the last man to board the pirated ship, stood with his feet anchored to the deck as if he were made of iron. 'Hold fast and surrender!'

Juusa felt the sweat and salt spray streaming down his face, his hands shaking with fury, his legs numbed by fear, but he took his way from the back of the wheelhouse, went out and onto the upper deck, screamed out his rank and called for his men to get into line, to cease their commotion, wanting to stop any more of them being killed than had already been. And up beside him came the foreign captain, took over his charge, gave out his own orders, knowing there would be no dispute.

Quick and brutal went the action after that. The wheel-house was overrun and robbed of every last firearm it had stockpiled, and the cargo doors were torn open, the crew of the *Pihkva* forced to disgorge its holdings at musket-point. The few who refused were given no second chance, were slung about their necks with ropes and flung over the boat's sides, heels kicking against the boards as they choked in a slow and horrid death, or fell into the cold arms of the sea as the ropes were cut.

Juusa's own throat felt hard and bitter as unripe almonds

as he scanned his shivering crew for first mate Valk, who had always been his strength, wanted Valk to cry out in the voice he could not himself muster for his men to stay calm and obey. Better skin on their bones, was all he could think, in an echo of Valk's voice, but he could not see him anywhere, and never would again. Not even a rag of bones and bloated flesh upon the next day's shore.

He waited out his impotency as the marauders took what they would and went, streaks of ruined grain strewed out across the decks where the sacking had been dragged and snagged upon the boards of the deck, spilling out their entrails to soak and burn in the thin glimmer of flame that licked and lapped at its feeble fuel, aided by the tar that caulked its planks.

The attackers disembarked as suddenly as they had come, and left the *Pihkva* limping loosely, wagging without anchor in the slack waters of the bay, the wind screaming over-head and plucking at what little was left of the topmost sails as if they were flags spelling out their despair. There was nothing the crew could do then but wait, and soon enough came the horrid caterwaul of strangling boards as the base of the *Pihkva* finally ground to, caught the last of its wooden life upon the reefs below the watery surface of the sandy bay, and ceased its toil.

Juusa remembered only dimly the hard climbing over the rocks behind the *Pihkva*, the tears in his eyes as he heard his first and last command being dismembered plank from plank, nail from nail, mast from board, side from side; the scram-bling of his men down to the skirt of shingle at the head

25

of the bay, trying, in darkness, to salvage the last few crates that floated free, looking harder for the bodies of their comrades, of which they found but a few, and one they wished they hadn't, which was the boy who had been in the crow's-nest when the sail-fires had taken, and the odd smallness of his blackened body which seemed to have flown free from his high home and out into the sea, and curled and burnt itself into a cinder upon the shore.

Juusa remembered the smell of wet tar-paper from the cover of the logbook as he clutched it tightly to his chest, the drag of his clothes against his skin, the scratch of salt and sand in every seam, the desultory walk over the clumps of crowberry and heather into the morning, the swearing of his men at his back, the constant clicking of their tongues as if there was something else they thought he should have done.

But how could he have known those welcoming lights were luring them into ambush under perfect cover of the storm? Did they suppose he would have responded to them if he had known?

He didn't want to answer his own questions because, beneath it all, like them, he blamed himself, because, yes, he should have known, and taken evasive action, or anchored the *Pihkva* out in open seas and ridden out the waves and the wind, which surely they could have done; waited until morning to take harbour.

The guilt of his loss consumed him without the added accusations of his crew, and he tried instead to concentrate on what they would do now, how things would go, the tasks he would need to complete, the letters he would need to write. But over and over in his head, the words shook inside him like knuckles in a counter-cup — how could he have known? How could he have known?

Most likely he could not have, just as he could not have known that this same storm, now spiralling on to the North Sea and a thousand miles to Juusa's west, would soon start its ruination of far more lives than he had ever been responsible for, and that two of those lives would wash up on these same shores, and one of them take the same path that he was taking now, tread upon the shingle of this same bay, and take a little piece of the wreck of his beloved *Pihkva* away with him in his hands.

3

The Fading of Astonishment

MABEL WAS SITTING with her own little piece of wood, the splinter embedded into the heel of her hand a full half-inch. She had been crow-barring off the lid of yet another crate when the battered old slats had suddenly given way, and she had sat back, tears of frustration and pain rising in her eyes. She had gazed up then at the domed windows above her head, saw the soft drift of blown cherry blossom mingling with a brief late fall of snow that had gathered there overnight, and wished she were up there with them, ready to blow away with the wind. She had been happy at Astonishment Hall, had enjoyed the trust that had been given her to do what she had been asked to do; she had opened crate after crate of books, tingling with excitement at each levering up of their lids, each careful exploration of the piles of manuscripts and papers that lay within. Had done her absolute best to catalogue the extraordinary knowledge that each book held, had tried her hardest to get as much of it down in the tiny but legible writing she knew was expected of her, filling out stack after stack of catalogue cards with titles, authors, notations, cross-references; the huge satisfaction that came with each completion of her task as she filed the finished cards into the cataloguing drawers and moved on to the next book and the next stack of cards.

And yet, and yet, she could hardly bear to say it, could hardly even admit it to herself, had kept at her work the harder to try to push the feelings away, and had managed it well enough until this one morning when she had just sat there, the splintering bulk of the unexplored crate beside her, the tears trickling down her face, the horrid, empty feeling of unhappiness washing over her. She longed to be back with Jack and Thomas and Mr Stroop, could feel it more with every minute that passed. She had sworn she would take her post of secretary for the spring and summer seriously, yet after only a few weeks she had felt the pull of home so strongly she had almost thrown down her pen and papers there and then, and started off for the nearest road that would take her there. She had quelled those first feelings of homesickness, had persevered, had seen through the weeks as they came and went, one by one. But always there was that nagging little tapping out of all the scenes she might be missing, her eyes constantly flicking to the big clock above the fireplace in the library, trying to imagine what Jack and Thomas were doing at that moment, if they would be sitting down to breakfast or tea, and if they were, what they would be eating now she wasn't there to prepare their meals for them. Or if maybe Thomas was out at the marketplace pinching handfuls of spring greens, worried as always, that one day he would be caught; could picture Jack in his always-filthy trousers, leaning too far over the enclosures of Smoke

29

Street, trying to comfort each and every animal that was due for slaughter. Saw Mr Stroop hunched over his desk in the study, adding a little bit more to his Sense Map of London, had a sudden panic that she would not recognise the map when she got home, that it would be too different; had nightmares that finally she had come home and nobody had recognised her either, and woke up sweating, wondering for a moment where she was, why the windows of the room looked different, why the bed was so soft, why the wardrobes were not standing in their usual crooked way.

She had been so excited when she had started out, had been assured by Mr Stroop that she could stay as long as she wanted, wished now that he had demanded, no! One month and no longer! Wished he had voiced his need of her, that he had not told Jack and Thomas to stop their begging that she would not go. She couldn't understand now how she could have been so eager to leave them all behind, and at that moment, with the splinter sharp in the heel of her hand, the drops of blood falling and soaking into her dress, she felt the letter Stroop had written her several days before, crumpled in her skirt pocket, and knew now she would answer. He had finally asked her home, and she would go.

She looked up again to the domed window above her, saw the clear blue sky beyond where the sun had melted away a little patch of snow, and the wind had swept the glass almost clean of fallen blossoms and leaves, and felt a warmth growing within her bones that she would soon be looking out of other windows, for other things. Would soon be scouring the streets for Jack and Thomas and Mr Stroop, could almost smell the big pot of stew she would have waiting for them, and the cheesy whiff of old Bindlestiff's feet as he snuffled about her, tripping her up, felt like the swallows and swifts must feel after their long flight over the sea, to spy the first footfall of land at last before them and know that within days, they would be back to the very nest they had first flown from, and where they knew they truly belonged.

4

The Slaughter of Lower Slaughter

THE STORM THAT had done for the *Pihkva* came in slowly from the sea, had been a smaller and less greedy thing by then and almost spent, but had bided its time, swirled itself around a while in the Atlantic, and come back at the valleys of England with new strength. It came light enough at first, a dancer alone in its ballroom, a few days of sleet, a little hail, the wind swirling slowly about the dour hills of Wales, gathering its stamina, sending out dark blusters into the valleys below and away to the east, building slowly, settling snow then setting it to thaw, swelling the waters at the head of the valleys, getting ready to send its fist flying with the full force of its wind.

The snow fell in silence upon Griselda as she hurried across the millpond bridge. She had done everything she could do to make safe her home, had loaded down the thatch with stones and sealed every window tight with straw. It worried her that she could not do more, that the bakery building, onto which her little house was tacked like a kid to the teat,

32

could not be strengthened any more than had already been done, that only moments had passed before it was rain that had fallen and now it was snow, had never known a thing could change so quick from one skin to another.

Her boot spanned the missing spar without losing pace. A sprinkle of snow fell and disappeared where the mouths of mullet sucked the belly of the ice skinning the water below. She slowed at the downward steps, not wanting to slip, the suede of her gloves darkening with damp, skimming the guiding rails like skis down the slope of the valley. She crossed the miller's kailyard, bolted cabbages frozen into sentries, fennel stalks fallen-waisted in the wind, bayonets abandoned amidst the battlefield, crossing blades with broccoli spears, purple and pimpled with the cold. She reached the door, stubbed her toe on the crouched iron boot-scrub, which could not be seen beneath the little nubs of snow growing all around it, started to hammer at the wood. The stiff breeze coloured her cheeks, pulled strands of hair from her bonnet, strengthened as she raised her fists and went at the dark planks again and again. The wind sighed around the barn and set the water wheel scratching at the thin ice, rocking in its paddles. The sentries shivered and whispered in the garden, the moon a silver penny balanced upon the hump of the hill, haloed with ice, the threat of dark and heavy clouds slowly sinking down upon it, crowding out the last of its pale light with their heavy-shouldered hunch.

The miller sat by the fire, wreaths of smoke being blown back by the wind from the hearth, the steady puffing of his pipe further obscuring the accounts book at which he had been working. He reached the bottom of the page and flipped the lid closed on the inkwell, laid aside his pen, cocking his head as the wind whipped at the cottage that enclosed him and his book and sent showers of old soot down upon his fire. It flared and floozied with black-shadowed demons as he stood to poke it back from the hearth, and only then did he hear the arrhythmic thumping upon his door break through the years of dust and husks that had dulled his ears. He replaced the poker, put his pipe on the mantel, led the lamp to the door.

They're not using the bell, he thought as he made his way down the hall, clapper must've frozen. Means another month till proper spring.

He tapped at the weather-glass as he passed it by, watched the mercury shiver and drop, felt the draught around his ankles where his stockings parted company from his trousers, watched the flame's reflection flicker in the rusty flakes that were all that was left of his mother's mirror, heard another barrage of fists hitting at the door, setting it shivering in its frame.

'I'm bloody coming, aren't I?' he grumbled half out loud. 'Keep yer blinking hair on.'

When he opened the door to Griselda, her hands were lifted to strike again, her gloves soaked, her hair flat and wet against her pale face, bonnet blown and gone.

'Well, well—' he began to say, but she cut him off, shouting against the wind.

'It's the river.' She pointed wildly up past the millrace where the banks had been widened and weired to lead the water down to the wheel. Her breath froze a cloud about her head like the cold arc around the now hidden moon.

'The river!' she mouthed so he could read the words he could not hear. 'It's taken Upper Slaughter, and it's on its way down here!'

The church bell tolled in Lower Slaughter, water dragging at the ropes. The heavy church door groaned upon its iron clasps but did not give, yet still the water filched a way through every crack and gap and would not go, lifted the coarse-haired, boot-cleaning mat from the flagstones, wended a slow way through hymn sheets and books of psalms, made a path through apse and bay, tugged at rope and hassock, sat itself at every pew, eased the candles from the tenebrae hearse, left their tang-spikes bare and sharp as the tines of a newly sharpened fork. It dragged the verger's gown around his legs, sucked at the seams, layered them with silt. He struggled through the swirling mud, hands slapping at the brown scum as he tried to reach the altar. The water was up to his waist when he'd gained his goal, the altar cloth already lifting gently from its table, trying to trip the thurible that held it down. He saw the monstrance in its niche behind; he struggled to gain the aisle steps, reached out his hand.

But before his fingers could grasp its stem, the monstrance eased gently over with the rising water, and scattered the Sacred Body onto the scum. Pale penny wafers, blind eyes gazing up at painted stars, soaked and sinking, melted into the flood. The verger wept to think his God would curse him for his negligence, but the brown owl in the gallery cared nothing for his despair, only shrieked at her disturbance, set the bats to spin and slap their leathery wings about the turret, turned her head to the belfry openings, where the sounds of the softly ringing bells escaped into the storm. Her wings unfurled and she disappeared into the snowy night, oblivious of the watery world below her, caring nothing for the low-lying houses, whose tie beams broke, their ancient gable-ends collapsed, thatch turned into duck-raft as it was swept off on the broad, black back of the flood.

Scrambled up on the hill, the villagers huddled and cried and swore; they held their silent children's hands and sat and watched their pots and pans, their beds, their homes, their farms, their fences, their goats and cattle, their stacks of salt and sacks of peas, their pillows and blankets, Bibles and bath-tubs, carts and tools, all snaking away into the approaching night. They tried to stop their ears, but could not halt the roar and crack, the mewls and bleats, the howls of dogs still tied to their chains, bolted to walls that were torn and borne away on the boiling black back of the river, the awful moans and terrible cries that seemed to ring on and on and on, far after the vicious tumult of water had flooded every field they had spent their lives tilling and passed on the rest of itself down the valley. They sat there, everything they still owned in sodden sacks about their feet, saw the heavy brown streak of water headed down towards the baker's and the miller's, knew it was too late to run and help, and that all they could do was sit here and wait and listen to the wind and the sighs of broken buildings, and the soft step of the snow as it padded on down as it had before, cradling the ruins of Slaughter.

In the barn, Griselda and the miller hoisted sacks of grain into the grinding room. A whole valley's supply of what was left of the winter's corn and pea-flour to be shifted to safety. They couldn't do it all, but they could do some of it at least. The dust choked them as they tried to move with urgent speed, the miller's back cracking as he turned the crank-arm of the winch, spilling hot oil and wax over the ropes to make them slide the quicker. Then it was straight away back to his house to grab at the accounts book, the hoarded bag of coins. He took his pipe from the mantel, carefully tapped it out and stowed it in his pocket, added his bottle of ink, stuffed some breeks and shirts into a bag, called for the cat, who did not answer. He bolted the door tight, dragged snow-draped sacks of sand across its foot, stowed his bag into the barn. Without words, they both ran back across the bridge and the millpond to Griselda's, to lift all the trays and bake-pans from the village oven they could manage. They worked quick and quiet, cocked their heads to listen for the sounds they knew would come: the river racing down the valley, the roar and splinter of the water as it took what it would take.

The miller heard nothing in the wind but felt the ground begin to tremble, called for the woman to hurry. They grabbed the few sacks they had packed and headed back to the barn, up the steps, past the grain store and into the attic space. There was a swirl of bats as they pushed up the hatch and the miller went first, hauled Griselda after him, into the small space. He called for the cat again, thought he saw a ginger streak stalk behind the grain sacks and was relieved. They closed the hatch and sat squashed up, the single lamp taking all the room between them, heard the wind tearing at the boards outside, the wheel groaning in the ice, flurries of snow coming in through the open window, lacing their backs, melting into bat droppings, which had frozen hard and green upon the floor.

Griselda thought briefly back to when she had first come here with her father – twelve years old then, thirty-nine now – and all the years she had spent here in between, and how it had become her home. She didn't want to leave as they had done before, her father trying to find the way to Painswick so he could work again with his inks and prints, following the vague map he had been given upriver, clutching his child to him as a tramp hugs his bag, fearing that the cord would break and all his rags fall out in a banner behind him, and that what little he had would be lost. She tried to remember those times when her father was so alive and filled with hope, wished more than anything that he was here to clutch her to him once again, protect her, keep her from harm, but could only feel the growing dread as she heard the waters hurtling down the valley towards her and this mouse-hole of the mill.

It was only minutes since they'd gained the attic when the lamp began to flicker wildly and the wind to scream, and they felt the body and boards of the barn begin to shake. The flood hurled down the valley floor, willows weeping in its wake, torn-up tree trunks gouging at the sides of a river risen many yards above its banks, planks and roofs and bits of wall and cob coming hurtling down.

It gained the weir and then the millpond, overwhelmed the bridge in a moment, snapped its back, swallowed it whole, took the planks and the traveller, so near his destination, as if they had not been there at all. The layer of ice splintered and cracked and flew like broken glass through the air; the water battered at the miller's door; the bell, unfrozen by the movement it was forced to take, clanged and clanged and clanged like a ship lost in a fog at sea, until it too was torn from its crooked iron stem.

Inside the barn, Griselda wrapped her arms about her knees, eyes wide open, heart ringing within her. She felt the river spate hit the wall, heard the creak and groan of the water wheel as the seethe and swirl relieved it of its icy brake, heard the metal sleeve that held the wheel to the wall loosen its grip on the spindle with the friction and force of its spin, the terrible sound as the paddles began to smash from side to side within the narrow well of the wheel-brace, battering the sodden bodies of sheep, which clogged its passage, eyes glazed and uncomprehending, their wool heavy, dragging them drowning into the depths. It was thunder and roil and thumping and noise, groans and rivets, squealing planks, writhe and rip. Griselda put her hands to her ears, waited out the terrible time it took the storm-bore to sweep down through their valley and on, with its gathering fury, to the next.

And then it was all over, and the river, with its rage, was at least half gone. And so too, was Lower Slaughter.

The monks in the monastery at the head of Stroud Valley were as silent upon their hill as the villagers, although they were several miles distant. Like them, they had been stopped in their prayers. They'd seen the water running high and huge beneath them, had seen it rising, rising slowly through the weeks of early spring. So had everyone in the valley seen it just like they had. But they hadn't known, as no one had, that it could come as hard and fast as this, that the brief thaw they had greeted with such pleasured and measured surprise could end by sending the snows of every tributary and stream to melt and pour down upon them with such anger as it had done, that it could race with such weight through the valley like a demon. They weren't ready for the charity they knew would soon be asked of them, knew their vows had not been made with this kind of disaster in mind, had already posted guards upon their storehouses with instructions to restrain any man by force if he tried to take what was not his own. They abandoned their rule of contemplation and hours, and hauled up as many blankets as they could find, piled them high in one of the barns, got the kitchens fired and readied, brewed soup from the thinnest vitals they could conjure, made ready as best they could for the testing of their faith, and the several hundred refugees they knew would soon be at their doors.

They didn't for a moment think of the traveller who had so recently left them, nor the burden that he had carried so far to show them, nor what might have happened to that man or his wares on his way from one place to another, from the monastery to the baker's house to give to Griselda the letter written by her father just one small day before he had died.

5

How to Lose a Library

'THIS IS VERY strange,' said Stroop, as he sipped from the rather foul cup of tea Jack had just made. He wondered if the lad had swilled out the old tea leaves before adding the new. Thought that probably he hadn't, but was not going to mention it. He saw Thomas sitting over from him at the kitchen table making the same grimace. Knew Thomas would say nothing either. 'We've had a letter.'

'Hooray!' shouted Jack, who was beginning to throw eggs into a pan, having neglected to remove the shells. 'Mabel!'

Stroop looked at the letter. It was certainly not from Mabel, though they expected to hear from her any day now. When she had not answered immediately to his earlier request that she come home, he had worried that he was coercing her into doing something she did not want to do. But eventually she had replied, and he still remembered what she had written almost word for word – about how terribly she missed them all and would come as soon as she could, needed though a few short weeks 'to finish my duties', as she had put it, and that the thought of coming back to them had given her the strength not to let Violena and the major down. He had smiled to realise how grown up she had become and with how much responsibility she felt herself to be burdened, and so he hadn't hurried her, had been proud of her and told her so, had written to say that they would wait until she wrote again with details of her return. He had been proud also at the way Jack and Thomas had taken the news, having read out Mabel's letter to them, and yet each day Jack still went out to the mail stop to see if she had written yet, to find out if she was already on her way home from Astonishment Hall.

'Not from Mabel,' Stroop supplied, somewhat sadly to his expectant audience. Jack immediately slumped lower on the stool he was kneeling on to massacre the eggs, which were beginning to burn within their pan. A few more moments of smoke and charcoal elapsed before Thomas managed to say a few words, as keen as Stroop to halt Jack in his culinary activities by whatever means.

'Who's it from then, Mr Stroop?' was his simple question.

'Well,' said Stroop, 'it's a little unusual.' His mind was already wandering to his study, recalling the books laid out upon their shelves, mentally fingering each of their spines as he tried to find the precise ones that would give him the correct information and bearings he might need.

Thomas gave him a short jab in the shin with his boot.

'Sorry,' Stroop apologised, held out the letter at arm's length, though neither Jack nor Thomas would be able to read the convoluted spirals of the writing. 'As I said, it's come from somewhere rather strange, and its contents are even stranger. It's from a Baron Von Riddarholm.' He looked around him for recognition and found none. 'He lives somewhere called

Hiiumaa. He wrote a short while back asking if we would be prepared to look for one of his employees over here in England.' Neither Jack nor Thomas remembered, which was hardly surprising. The only letters they had been interested in were the ones from Astonishment Hall. Stroop himself remembered the name only vaguely, hadn't extended any effort other than to write back to say he would certainly accept the offer on the proviso that further details, and a retainer, be forwarded forthwith. And here, now, were both.

'Apparently,' said Stroop, with an unaccustomed sense of the dramatic, 'this baron has lost an entire library.'

Jack gaped, and the smell of burning eggshells was more than Stroop could bear. He stood up, started to lift the pan from off the stove, saw with slight dismay that the bottom was already completely black beneath the slime of half-mixed whites and yolks, thought that even lamprey might be preferable, suckers and all.

'An entire library,' he repeated, to take his mind from the smell that was seeping up his nose, making his mouth involuntarily turn itself down at the corners. He put the pan hopefully by the bundle of Bindlestiff, where he lay as usual on his pile of blankets. The dog turned his nose away, and Stroop couldn't help but admire his discretion. 'An entire library,' he elaborated, as he opened the back door and threw out the eggs, pan and all, 'contained in the size of a suitcase. And we've been asked to find it.'

Stroop and Thomas spent the rest of the afternoon finding out all they could about Hiiumaa and the baron who lived there who had lost his books, which was not much.

Jack was sent surreptitiously out of the way, ostensibly to find a decent pie-shop, and also to dispatch a further missive to Mabel from whichever post stop was due the most imminent pick-up of mail to be taken north. Jack went at this with such evident enthusiasm, and was gone for so long, that Stroop felt his own heart droop a little to realise how much Jack must want Mabel back. They found out later that he had visited every coffee shop and ostler within a mile's radius before making his choice and returning to the one that would provide the fastest passage for a letter dispatched to Astonishment Hall, telling Mabel where they were going, and that they would meet her in London on their return.

Thomas also surprised him, proved himself an able assistant, had obviously spent more time studying Stroop's library than Stroop had realised, was able to find almost every title Stroop asked for within moments.

'Mabel taught me,' Thomas said once as he delivered a book to the desk, saw Stroop's raised eyebrows at the quick return of his request. 'I know all about how your stuff is numbered. She told me about the cards too.'

Stroop reddened a little to think that his secrets had been shared, his revolutionary cataloguing system unmasked, how he had used to send long epistles to great libraries suggesting they label their books on their shelves as he did, instead of the absurdly random system of placing titles by author, or the vagueness of their subject, or even by their height or colour. Remembered also the time before Thomas and Mabel, and was ashamed for the pride he had taken in such things.

'Look at this, Mr Stroop!' Thomas was excited, had just descended the ladder of twine and wood that he needed to reach the topmost shelves of Stroop's library. 'It's all about making tiny books!'

Stroop looked at the manuscript Thomas had deposited on the desk before him, shocked to realise he had forgotten completely about its existence. He always had one special shelf for his latest acquisitions, things that he had purchased and meant to go through, which needed to be listed in his catalogue and have the label put upon their spines to spell out their final homes upon his shelves. He had been so used to Mabel being with him, going through these latest findings, creating the cards for the catalogues as he dictated them, that he had neglected its existence. He remembered it now, as he looked at it: it had been after the Lucchese affair when he had taken a sudden interest in printing and its workings, after Castracani had introduced him to Golgafoni the printer, knowing Stroop was cataloguing the crafts and industries of London town. Stroop had been fascinated by the details of how a broadsheet or book was actually produced, the machines that had been invented to shift the plates of moveable type to be inked and pressed, the different ways of stamping out pictures, the intricacies of woodcut, etching and engraving that needed to be employed.

And then here was the manuscript Thomas had put before him, a very recent inventory of miniature books for children, alerting potential customers to the illustrated *Gigantick Histories* created by Thomas Boreman in the 1740s, books no more than two and a half inches high and bound in flowered Dutch boards, which included *The History of Cajanus The Swedish Giant*, and *Curiosities in the Tower of London*. There were thumb Bibles containing equally miniature engraved plates of Old Testament scenes, and finger Bibles, which were slightly taller and thinner than the thumbs; a description of *The Infant's Library* in all its sixteen volumes, illustrating ice-skating, ships, castles, how to go hunting, and the 1800 issue of *People of all Nations: a Useful Toy for Girl or Boy*.

Stroop rested his fingers upon the manuscript, closed his eyes, tried to think what else upon his shelves he might have missed. He had been charged with finding a miniature library, and before he set off on the search he knew he would have to find out more about the nature of what he was looking for. There was a person to look for too, one Jarl Eriksson, and if he had been a man who lived locally, Stroop would have talked to everyone that person had contact with: family members, servants, if they had any, co-workers, the people any one of these last might have met in the street, at work, in the market, at church. But the man Eriksson was an enigma, had no base excepting Hiiumaa, spent his time here travelling as a representative of Hiiumaa's work. And then there was the search for the miniature library itself, which Eriksson had been carrying. For Stroop it was a search far more sacrosanct, a need to discover how such a treasure was made and distributed. He already knew from his employer that the library was housed in a suitcase, that it was an exemplar of the specialist skills Von Riddarholm's own print and ink shops offered. He knew also that it was highly valuable, and offered potential customers not only a range of differing inks and type styles, but also of paper, made from different resources. And that it was unique. Not unlike a person, Stroop thought, as he recalled the description he had been given of Eriksson, which had been sketchy, and then that of the library, which had been so detailed; had to remind himself that this was not just any old suitcase housing any old library of a print shop's wares. That this was the exemplar of what could be achieved by the very best of the best. That it was nothing less than a work of art.

They had been hunched over the table so long that both Stroop and Thomas felt they might be solidifying into gargoyles, their shoulders pinched and gutted to take the rain that had been falling outside their home without cease for the past two hours. Jack had returned a while back, a mud-spattered, wind-tattered scarecrow, and was now sizzling and steaming before the open fire. He had brought mutton-and-veal pies, with far more mutton than veal, and a greenness soaking through the pastry that spoke of too many peas being added to the sauce to thicken it up and eke out the meat. Thomas and Jack had been too excited to notice, and Stroop didn't care, so intent had he been on their plans. He looked at the itinerary that he had laid out before him, carefully sharpened his blunted pencil one more time, scratched out the last part of the line he had been tracing, dotted it with a finality that made them all unlock their shoulders and start to stretch. Jack's whole body widened out in one vast yawn, skinny limbs cracking, mouth cavernous and outlined with a thin line of dried pea green that he had tried, unsuccessfully, to brush away with his hand.

'That's it then,' said Stroop, blinking, trying to stop the tiredness that had begun to water down his vision. 'To bed, boys. We've a lot to do in the morning.'

Both lads creaked up from their chairs, Jack in a strange

47

sort of jiggle as he unlocked his knees and went to stand, Thomas scraping his chair onto two legs and leaning back, hands outstretched and wedged against the table's edge, wiggling his toes in his boots, realising how cold they had become.

'We can't go to bed now,' he remonstrated, and heard Jack's echoes coming from the kitchen into which he had just vanished, the sound of him peeing into the pail by the side of the door.

'Not likely,' Jack was saying as he came back into the study. 'Can't we do all the packing now? I'll not get a wink of sleep, even if I tried.' He yawned again, tried to turn it into a grin behind his hands, but did not succeed.

Stroop realised that, tired as he was, he didn't feel like turning in either, felt the old tingle of excitement to be back on the trail of something lost, wanting to know how and where and if it could be found.

'Another adventure,' Thomas laughed, landing his chair back to the floor with the sound of grinding teeth, lacing his fingers into a cat's cradle.

'Tell us again where we're going,' Jack begged, beginning to trace a grubby finger along the big map that lay stretched out beneath all their books and notes, up the rivers, along the tracks that led out from London like the wobbly spokes of a wheel.

Stroop smiled. 'All right then, one more time,' and Jack hurled his arm around Stroop's neck and dragged his head so close to the table he could see nothing more than the end of his nose where his eyes crossed. Stroop untangled himself, poured the boys each a glass of tepid beer and another of brandy for himself. 'All right then,' he repeated, and all three heads leant down low as Stroop's pencil pointed to the maps that straddled and overlapped one another across the face of England.

'Up the river until we reach the new Kennet Canal at Newbury, and then on west towards Bristol as far as we can get, and after that, away from the water and up country towards Cheltenham . . .'

The only thing that doused his spirits slightly was that Mabel would not be going with them. The only thing that lifted them again was knowing that by the time they got back to Eggmonde Street, so too would she.

6

The Swan, the Baker
and the Miller

GRISELDA AND THE miller at last lifted the hatch, and descended the grain-store ladder on shaking legs. The last lamp guttered as they opened the door below and they stared across the wreckage of the millpond. The wheel wagged at a bad angle, still catching at the wind, limping from side to side as it tried to stay its accustomed course, jammed by the clog of tree branch and the corpses of sheep and goats and dogs that had been caught below the broken paddles or swirled still in the detritus of the millpond. The bridge was no more than four splintered boles splayed out on either side of the water-burst banks, the pond engorged with mud and leaves and branches, unidentifiable pieces of household items bumping against the semi-denuded, stone-clad sides of the millpond, and far over its edges into the scum that spread a full seven or eight yards distant, which told how high the flood had been. The water, sated now and calming, reached over and lapped at the mill cottage door. The bakery building might never have been, was only a few heavy beams scattered above a mass of tumbled stones, the huge iron range torn a full twenty yards from its place of ages, its doors hanging off at their hinges or gone, their fires, which had burnt without ceasing for the many years of life that Griselda had spent at their feeding, and for so many, many years before, turned into a mess of sludge and muck and twig. Griselda and the miller stood cold beneath the pale circle of the moon, which revealed itself from a dark afternoon of not caring, and the hard black brush of storm cloud that soon made its pallid face shiver and hide.

They stood there, side by side, nothing for them to say. The miller took off his cap, heedless of the newly falling snow, held it open in his hands. He squinted at the wheel as the water sucked and puckered against the bruise of its battered paddles. Saw a mat of orange hair, a tail round-ringed with brown and ginger, and he started to weep for all the things in his long life that he had seen and lost.

Griselda looked for the bridge that was no longer there, the building that no longer stood on the other side. Turned from the loneliness of not belonging, saw the remnants of the miller's cottage up to its knees in silt and spate, its four walls miraculously still standing, sparred over with half a skeleton of roof, its beams ripped free of thatch. She took the miller's arm, steered him towards what little remained of his home. The sandbags had gone, as had the door, and they made their way down the sodden hall, gently, gently paddling their way towards the parlour, past the bell that was no longer there, and the mirror, and barometer that had told the miller all his life that a storm was coming, and that now it had, had gone. The chairs and chests had been swirled about and heaped broken-limbed against the furthest wall. The mantelpiece remained, six foot of sycamore above the flagging, and on it still stood the silver cup, miraculously shining, the miller's grandmother's bridal gift from her father, its two handled arms rearing up like angry geese against the dull, dark brown of mud that was everywhere else, that still swirled about their feet like a swamp.

The miller waded through darkness. Saw the unstoppered jar of crude corn brandy, from which he had so recently drunk, still sitting on the sycamore ledge above the fire as if nothing had ever happened, the empty bookcase against the cottage wall where all the old ledgers had used to stand, which had been his father's and his grandfather's, and held the name of every family and every farm for five miles distant hereabouts for more than two hundred years. The miller could not move, didn't even feel the water at his ankles, and it was Griselda who took the bottle from the mantel and wiped it clean, and together they stood, and together they passed that bottle between them, staring at the water as it seeped slowly away from their boots, and the floorboards, and the furniture, the patch of sodden, still-singed carpet, so empty now of ginger cat, enclosed by a house that had its walls but could no longer be called a home. Tried not to think of tomorrow and the awful things that it would bring. Tried not to imagine what must have happened further up the valley to the village and the river that had run through it, for here at least they'd had the small protection of the flood plain, the flatness of the land that led out to the right, into which the irrigation dykes ran out into the barley fields. But there would be nothing left of those fields now – they knew it already, without waiting for the morning to look.

All the topsoil would be gone with the water, and what use would next year's harvest be without a mill to grind it, or a bakery to turn it into bread? And what use anyway, with every house and home of Lower Slaughter gone?

The miller and Griselda stood clammy and frightened within their skins, passing that rough corn brandy between them, said not a word. The miller thought on all the years that had come and gone, the generations of his family who had lived and died here, could not help but cry to know that this was the last of it all, wept silently with shame to know that mostly what he would miss would be the ginger mouser who had kept him company for almost eighteen years. Couldn't look at the baker's woman who had risked her life to save him, couldn't bear that she stood so erect and dry eyed before him, as if she had already known disaster and knew what came after, who looked across towards the bridge that was no longer there and the bakery that no longer stood on the other side of the still-racing millpond. He had spent his whole life here within the bailiwick and green arms of the valley, and wanted nowhere else, had always known that however things went, they would always end here.

And up on the hill sat Oravo Tallista Swan, apart from the main huddle of villagers, separated from them even in disaster, just as for him it had always been. It seemed only minutes and not hours since the morning, when, just like them, he had been securing his house, looking at his double-skinned windows: cheap, village-made glass on the one side, shutters of rough-hewn elm for the other, made from the big tree that had fallen last autumn. The same tree that had gone into the making of the cages for his linnets, erected directly above the gorse so they could nest in safety from the merlins, which sped in dark, harpooned streaks along the ditches and lines of hedges, and again for the tight crate for the cock-roaches he bred. Minced up, they made good liniments for the gout and always sold well, as even the surliest of his neighbours agreed.

He thought of those shutters now, and the way he had pulled them to, had slid the pins in to secure them. Felt that same feeling – that shutting of himself off from his past, and from the rest of the villagers. They'd never liked him anyway. Always a foreigner to them he'd been, though his hair was the same colour of thin earth the rest of them had, and his eyes the same restless shade of blue. He'd been born to the same soil the rest of them had been born to, spoke the same words in the same way, paid the same taxes on the same land; but always he'd been different, though he'd tried to be the same. Yet always there was the name. All that parted him from them, but it had been enough.

Oravo thought of the bakery woman he'd seen a while past, flying down the track and off the two miles to her home to rescue what she could. She was a stranger too, with her thick, straw-coloured hair, speaking some foreign language easier than their own when first she'd come, but they'd taken to her right enough. He'd tried to make her his own when she was old enough – two strangers exiled together, he'd thought. Knew it could be good, that they would have made fine children together and worked hard. Maybe worked hard enough to get out of this place and leave it all behind. But then she'd up and married Woolgar, the baker's lad, had a bit of fine-standing, with her father working over the valley at Painswick, in the big print shop, that bit of learning she'd had over them all.

He remembered Woolgar, and the thumping the man had given him when he'd found out about Oravo's little bit of courting, though it had been no more than a few stuttered words, before Woolgar had taken the girl for his own. And then old Wheatwhiskers, the father, had died, and Woolgar the son had, years later, gone the same way too, both to the same disease that had made them shake and creak like aspens in high winds. And Oravo knew about aspens. Knew how they could crackle like a fire starting low and quick, or sound oddly like a stream stumbling over stones. Fire and water, all at the same time. It was something about trees that always made him smile.

He knew a lot about wood, did Oravo, just as his father had done, or so he had been told by Grandmother Swan. Knew every tree by its bark and buds, even by its shape in winter, when all the leaves were gone and all you could see was an old man's stoop of branches outlined upon a hill with the wind pushing through them.

Oravo knew too, but he knew nothing about people, had found that out the moment he'd knocked on the baker's widow's door a year or so back, to hand over the bunch of new-sprung daffodils a few decent months after her man had died. Still smarted at the stiff way she had taken them from him, thanked him with her foreign-hinting tongue, and closed the door. Shut him out. Just like everyone else had always done. Like they'd always done his father. Spanish scum, they'd called his father, never mind that he could break bones to dust for fertiliser like they'd never been able to do, work any piece of wood better than they'd done for a hundred years, and still cursed Oravo for the sins he knew his father must have done.

Oravo had wondered briefly, when he'd seen her running, if he shouldn't have helped the baker's widow. Thought again. Knew better than to poke a wild cat in a barn that has already scratched and spat at the hand you'd offered with food. Remembered her own hands when she had accepted his posy: pale and soft as cherry blossom, the small scatter of freckles at her wrists, neat-clipped nails clouded with flour-dust beneath their tips. He blinked to stop himself having thoughts about the other secret freckles that might be hidden about her body that she would never give him leave to find, that just like everyone else in the valley, he would always be a stranger to her, and nothing would change.

Some things are not made for stopping, and Oravo Swan was one of them. At least that's what he told himself that day the flood came, vowed that if the waters chose to take away his home then he would leave the way that it went. And so he had walked one last time across the miller's bridge and climbed the steep sides of his valley, and sat there waiting, waiting for the waters and the storm to do their worst. But there was something else that he was waiting for, though he did not admit it to himself, that if there was any one person in the world he needed to see again, he knew that it was her.

And so he sat that wild night through, staring intently down at the bakery and the mill, his bones already shuddering with the oncoming passage of the flood waters through the soil and the rocks of the upper valley, regretting only that he had forgotten to take the cage from off his linnets to let them fly, to take their chance. He chided himself for this negligence, thought he heard their voices, thought perhaps they had escaped and come to him upon the wind. Knew at the same time that this was nonsense, that they would no more come to him than would the villagers. He saw Griselda and the miller take their safety in the miller's barn, barely registered the other man who appeared out of the storm-heavy darkness of the afternoon and looked up towards the river. Oravo Swan saw him and yet did not see him, was only waiting for things to pass, felt a lightness in himself that he had not felt for years, a slight discomfort about the face, and it took him some time to realise the cause, and that he was smiling.

And so the storm passed from one day to the next, a blind man searching for his settlement; sinking the *Pihkva* in the Estonian Bay, destroying the valleys of Slaughter.

The last man it took was crossing the bridge to the bakery, bent like a fish-hook by the wind, his suitcase clutched in one hand, his foot caught in the hole left by the missing plank. The water came down like a bad-shot bear and swept the bridge away beneath him, folded him up like a piece of paper, and carried them both away.

The very last man it did for was Captain Anto Juusa, three weeks later, stripped of his command and his position, a swallow of water-hemlock burning upon his lips, the trembling of his heart as his diaphragm spasmed and went still, the slow squeezing of his ribs against his lungs. His last thought was of First Mate Valk, his friend and companion for more than fifteen years, and of the *Pihkva*, and how proud he had been to stand as first captain on its newly white-washed decks, with Johann Valk ever at his side. Heard the one last creak of his breath as it left him, still struggling against his useless sacrifice, just as the *Pihkva* had done upon the rocks and the sand.

7

Leaving London

JACK WAS THE undisputed captain of the barge on which they rode the river up, his shirt smudged black with the carved piece of coal that hung about his neck like an anchor, given him by the wheel man, who had thought his human cargo amongst the strangest he had ever seen. Normally he just carried coal, bellied down into the hold like a great dark cloud, sometimes taking steel for upstream works, or the flat stone flags that bore the imprint of fish no one had even seen, that came down from Scotland and were so highly prized by the upmarket builders that they didn't mind a bit of coal dust about their edges.

It was rare he carried people, who mostly preferred the more luxurious accommodations of those barges decked out to take them. But the man who had hired him had asked for him specifically by name. Had asked about another passenger he had ferried a little while back at the start of April, whom he had taken upriver several times before, the man who had travelled with his fine suitcase, who had hopped off here and there and then joined back up with Isaac's barge a few villages or towns upstream, waving at him from along the towpath.

He guessed his select passengers had picked him because he went the same way, was unusual amongst his barge-faring fraternity in that he went the whole passage from London docks to Bristol, in a straight-through journey, his other mates going only part-way from one place to another and then returning. They'd always laughed at him for this long way he had chosen, for the lesser profits they knew he must make, knew also they sometimes envied him for his knowledge of the water and the ways he took his barge from canal to river and back again. But he liked it, the continual procession from one place to another, had organised his horses well to get the best speed without tiring them, saved the money he spent on ostlers by not having to spend it at a procession of inns and wasting his time on beer and chat with the other bargemen. He knew he was always a little apart from them, would rather be alone with his *Matilda*, had named his barge after the woman he had spent so little time with, and would gladly have given up the whole universe to be with again. Still ached with sadness to think of the twin children she had tried to bear him, and died with the effort, taking them with her, hoped they were all in a better place than with himself, a man who was black as the coal he carried, and still too poor to give her the care she had needed.

For a man who was used to being alone for the two weeks it took him to cross upcountry, he was oddly at ease with this company he had taken on against his better judgement. But the thin man with the crisscrossed hands had been so insistent, had offered him more money than he would make for the entire trip, that he had agreed, and now was glad of it. He particularly liked the gangly boy with his neck so scarred it looked like his head had once been torn from off his shoulders and badly put back on again, the lad called Jack, who was helpful to a degree that would have been irritating in any other person, but not with this boy, who plainly had a head filled with noodles, and was amused at every turn the river revealed, asked innumerable questions about why the water looked the way it did, and what were those ducks over there? And that tree? And why didn't he ride the horse that was pulling the barge? And why was he carving all that coal into tiny figures?

It was a pastime of Isaac's, this carving; had started when Matilda began to grow, so that their children would have toys aplenty to play with when they came, had instead had to sell them for tuppence a piece at the Bristol markets he had made so many, and could not stop, and had no place to put them, and no children to give them to. Had devised a way of setting the figures into varnish so they would not bleed their black tattoos into everything they touched.

And then this gangle of a boy came on board and watched him with a fascination he had once hoped to see in the sons and daughters he would now never have; and he worked with a self-consciousness he had never known before, and carved an otter to such a black life that even its tail seemed to switch as he ran the glasspaper about it.

Jack laughed, and took it from his fingers when he offered it up for inspection, and straight away put it around his neck on a piece of string he apparently had waiting, even though Isaac told him the little carving would need setting first.

And he himself laughed out loud to see the boy string it about his neck, already ruining what little was left of the cleanness of his shirt, but making little impress on the scarred scarf of his neck; watched him dance up and down along the deck boards, shouting, 'Mr Stroop! Mr Stroop! Look at this!'; laughed, in fact, so loud that he alarmed the horse along the towpath, made it turn its head within its blinkers, made the barge swerve a little and set a raft of golden-eyed ducks into rising and flapping an ungraceful way into flight. It occurred to Isaac then that he had hardly even smiled since his Matilda had died, had certainly not laughed out loud, not until this moment.

And so Jack became the boatmaster, and the boatmaster became the crew, and Isaac freely answered every question the man Stroop asked him, no matter how peculiar those questions seemed.

That night he gave the coal talisman to Jack, the boy with the neck that looked like it had been roasted in an oven, he sat at the tiller of his barge, while the rest of them slept below decks on the sparse cushions that softened his small home, and supped at his bottle of unstoppered wine, looked up at the bright stars that seemed everywhere about him, glittering with the intensity of quartz crystals scraped by his knife into the impure coal, and thought, for the first time since Matilda, that maybe life could get better, and that maybe, just maybe, the ache she had left in him might yet be healed.

Down below, in the cabin, warmed on each side by the ballast of coal and the small fire that burnt in its grate, Stroop took out his little notebook. He wrote down everything the bargeman had told him about where the man with the suit-case had been, and where he was going, appended these to the notes he had already taken of how he had found this particular bargeman going this particular route. It hadn't been difficult, only tedious, to track him down. Von Riddarholm had already told him that Jarl Eriksson, the missing print merchant, had decided on a route followed by the barges up to Bristol and the large established print houses that city afforded, and, whilst en route, seeking out as many smaller ones as he could find. From there, it was only an arduous search of the docksides, questioning innumerable bargemen about a man with a suitcase enquiring for passage, until finally one man remembered referring such a man on to another, whose name was Isaac, who ferried coal from the docksides straight on up to Bristol.

Stroop had had a small map draughted of the route they were taking and where it might lead. He marked out the path from London to Bristol, and a line from Bristol to Cheltenham, which was the way the print merchant had told the baron he intended to take. He also drew a dotted line of the places he knew the man with the suitcase – as Isaac always referred to him – actually to have been, and the last place Jarl Eriksson – as Stroop knew his proper name to be – had been seen by Isaac. The bargeman had told Stroop that Eriksson had decided to go upcountry first, before heading back down to Bristol, had even arranged to meet Isaac again so that he could call at all the same places on his return back to London, presumably to secure any sales he might have made on the outward journey. Although obvi-ously a methodical man, Jarl Eriksson had not made that meeting, and the last communiqué the baron had received from him had been dispatched from the town of Stroud, detailing several visits made to bookshops on the way there from Bath. After that, Jarl Eriksson had vanished. And right now, according to Stroop's map, the most likely place he might have made for was another of the baron's allied English firms, the small but prestigious printworks at Painswick.

And so Stroop struck a bargain with Isaac the bargeman, just as Jarl Eriksson had done before him. This time, the arrangement was to meet up again, not at Bristol, but at Bradford-on-Avon, where Stroop and his entourage disembarked on Isaac's recommendation, and engaged a post-carriage to take them to Stroud, which would lead them the quickest way to Painswick.

Isaac watched them as they went, saw Jack turn and wave at him with his little black icon, watched in alarm as his companion, Thomas, stroked the stolid shire horse, which towered above him, before making a leap at its back. He made the landing, his small legs horizontal across the horse's broad back, his weight scarcely making the large animal twitch. Thomas then leant right over the huge head, and whispered in its ear before sliding off again, feeding it something from his pocket and taking off after Stroop. Isaac envied the familiarity with which the two boys clapped each other's backs in congratulation of their jape, before running on to catch up their Mr Stroop, hoped that they would find what they were looking for, hoped, for the first time since Matilda, that so too would he, had already decided that if they were late for their appointment, he would wait as long as it took.

8

Leaving Lower Slaughter

GRISELDA LEFT THE miller's cottage soon after the storm had passed, stared with shock at the devastation that was all that was left of the millpond and the bakery, unable for a few moments to move, didn't know which way to go now that the bridge was gone. Then she struggled along the edges of the submerged riverbank until she finally found a place she thought she could ford, its turbid brown waters made sluggish by the long stretch from bank to bank, hindered by rafts of weeds and fallen trunks. Her boots slung about her neck, tied together by their strings, her skirts dragged up about her waist, she stepped in. The current almost immediately took her off her feet and she had to return, find two strong branches to use as sticks, then plunged back in again, determined this time to cross. It was hard, but the stones beneath the water had been turned by the storm and the slime that had grown over them stripped away, leaving small scoured-out pockets that gave her bare feet purchase.

When at last she reached the other side, she sat a while to get the trembling from her legs, dry her skirts a little, and

then she made her way back down to what little was left of
the bakery buildings and raked through the mud and sludge
to find anything that might be salvageable. She found nothing,
nothing at all. Even the old chest, where her husband had
kept their few valuables, was cracked like a cobnut and lay
in splinters against the menacing lean of the single remaining
gable wall, the rest stoved in by roof beams, bracketed all
about with the fallen masonry of what had once been her
home. She sorely regretted not having had the wit to take
the bag of coins from the hidden corner of the smokehouse,
saw now that the bricks had been loosened and lost, and
though she scrambled in the coal-blackened sludge, she found
only a few of the several hundred sovereigns that had been
stored there, and knew that whatever wealth she once
possessed was now gone. She stood there a while, the water
still pooled in the detritus of stones and branches and toppled
chimneys and walls, their stillness reflecting the turbulence
of a troubled, cloud-ridden sky. She looked about and about
in case there was something she had missed, saw only dinted
kitchen coppers and the caved-in cauldron she had used for
the washing, the tin bath keeled over, flat as a boxer's nose,
the few books she had owned de-paged, and with only a
curl of cardboard to show for the knowledge they had once
possessed. She found a couple of ragged dresses torn apart
on the blackcurrant bushes that bounded the little garden of
which she had been so proud, the roots of the plants she
had tended with such care upended and sheared, like those
of the docks and the dandelions after the plough has furrowed
its way through the field, the strangely human figures they
made, with arms and legs akimbo, small knobbles for heads,

looking like battlefield corpses, drowned in the mud and left to die where they lay.

She looked over at the millpond and the bridge that was no longer there, saw the miller hacking away at the sails of the water wheel with his shovel, could almost hear the creak of his back as he went at it with the same sad resignation she carried like a stone within her own chest, saw him tug gently at a small mat of ginger to release it and knew it would be his cat. She watched as he laid down the crush of skin and bone that had been his companion, could hardly bear it as he picked up his shovel and began to excavate a hole, yet stayed there like a mourner at the graveside, unable to move, while he dug the pit and laid the remains of the poor creature in, and patted down the mud upon it. The miller stood then, swiping fiercely at his eyes with the hand that held his hat, let fall the shovel, which subsided slowly into the suck of mud that surrounded its half-buried blade. He looked up then, saw her watching on the other bank, straightened himself as much as he was able, but could not hide his defeat. He raised his hat to her, and she lifted her own pale, freckled hand, but did not wave. It was too solemn a time, this awful loss that had overtaken them, and she couldn't bear the small smile he gave her before he unwound a rope from about his waist, then bent again to work the fallen shovel free. She wondered what he would do now, knew he wouldn't leave, even as she made her own small decision, and had no doubt about where it was that she was going now.

And so she turned from him, moved away from the bank and towards the small path that led up from the bakery to the hill beyond. The path was gone, a vicious, stone-straddled gully left in its place by the water, which had torn down from the top any way that it could find, felt the wet rub of sodden boots against her ankles, realised that she was leaving just as she had come, with nothing but the clothes upon her back and a couple of coins in her pocket, wondered if this was how her father had felt when he too had been forced to leave his home in '81, just as she was leaving now. She remembered him telling her that if only you had life and legs, there was always someplace you could go and make your own.

The thought of her father and his recent death brought the guilt back to her like a thorn in the foot, and the anger at the letter she had received from Painswick telling her he was already dead and done, and that it was too late for her to take charge of his burial. And the shame she had felt that she had not taken the time to trek once more over the moors to visit him, that she had used the excuse of the bakery and Woolgar dying to keep herself bound to this little piece of land.

No more, she thought, and blinked away the useless tears; all that was past now, and there was only one place left for her to go. She took one last look back at the ruined bakery, and then she turned and struggled her pathless way up the hillside, crawling at it, pulling at the boulders that had doubled in size since the water scraped the soil and fill from their bases.

She reached the top, and sat panting and trying to get her breath, when she was near startled out of her skin by a figure suddenly emerging from the thicket of birches bent down to the ground since striplings, and she put her hand to her heart in fear as she scrambled to her feet. And then she recognised him.

It was Oravo Swan, the man who lived up the valley a

way, between the mill and the village, the sack strapped to his back hiding the small hump that had grown these past few years between his shoulder blades, the man who had brought her daffodils a few weeks after her man had died, who had looked at her so strangely when she had thanked him, and then closed the door in his face.

They stood for a moment on the brow of that hill, her freckled hands still trembling, his own unwavering upon the straps of the bag that weighed down upon his shoulders, the low leant birches limping slightly in the wind that had not ceased since before, nor after, the flood, the sky above them heavy and dark and waiting for its release to rain or snow. Oravo was the first to lose his nerve, and shifted his gaze down to the flattened sedge and the early purple orchids that had sprung too soon in the false promise of spring. Griselda relaxed a little, let her arms drop, clutched her hands to each other across the wet line of her hips, which the waters of the river had so recently breached.

'Nothing left,' said Oravo, neither a question nor a statement, his eyes drifting sideways towards the valley; didn't want to say that he had seen that latest small drama unfold, had stood there watching whilst Griselda watched the miller. Had seen, as she had seen, the silent burial of what was left of his ginger companion, and the salute, and the slow unwinding of the rope from around his waist. Knew, as she must know, that the rope would soon be lifted to the miller's neck, wondered briefly if the deed was already done. Knew the futility and unkindness any intervention would have brought.

'You heading to the monastery?' Oravo asked. He didn't want to seem presumptuous or too inquisitive, yet had a tremble in his heart as if his bones had set themselves on fire and were clawing at his skin just to be near this woman, and to speak to her.

Griselda stood a few yards distant, was embarrassed by the cold cling of her clothes as they stuck to her limbs and belly, the hair that had been flattened against her head and neck, her skirts wrapping around her legs to show the contours of her knees and thighs. She felt absurdly naked, and had no words to say, and could only stand like the miller's shovel stuck in its mud, while Oravo lowered the bag he carried from his misshapen back, eased open the strings that tied its neck and removed a cloak.

'You look cold,' was all he said, as he handed over the poorly woven garment that had been about his own body so often it seemed to hold its contours. Griselda took it from him and unfolded it into the wind.

'Thank you,' she said tying it around her shoulders, drawing its edges about her, covering her vulnerability. She moved a few steps towards him and put a hand on his arm for a moment before drawing away.

And Oravo Swan kept his own hands upon the draw-strings of his bag as he pulled them closed again, and felt her fingers on his sleeve as if they had gone right through the cloth and touched his skin. He forgot the loss of his house and the shutters and the linnets and the cockroaches, and instead thanked God that these things had passed, and that he had perhaps been given another chance.

'What will you do?' he said, and looked helplessly down the valley at the mess of sticks and stones that covered the space where the bakery had been. Griselda hesitated a moment, shivered as a sharp gust of wind raked over the cotton grass at her feet, made her pull the cape close about her and hid her hands inside its folds.

'I'm off to the printworks at Painswick, where my father used to work.'

Oravo nodded slowly, still wouldn't look at her. 'Heard he'd died already,' was what he said, knew like everyone in the valley knew that she'd had prayers said in his memory, had lit candles in the church and stuck them onto the wax-covered feet of St Luke, who looked down upon them all with his frown and the slight squint given him by the slip of a mason's chisel, which had always made Oravo deeply suspicious of that stone saint, ever since his youth. Remembered sitting by those same feet, picking bits of wax off with his thumbnail, until his grandmother noticed and whacked him smartly about the ear with her hymn book.

He looked up, saw Griselda staring at him, noticed for the first time that she wasn't carrying a bag or a sack or possessions of any kind at all.

'I could go with you a bit,' he tried to say, wasn't sure if the words actually came out of his mouth, cleared his throat. 'I've bread and cheese, and a blanket.' He stopped, wondering if he had said too much, if she would think he meant something he didn't mean at all. He moved his eyes away from her again, this time to the sky. Saw the angry slump of it above them, a deep purple anvil heaving up from the horizon, pushing at the smaller, paler clouds until they were engulfed, leaving only dark and fractured bruises in their place. She too lifted her eyes, saw the light being wrung out from every corner of the sky and harrowed into a single harsh and yellow band about the enormous thundercloud, watched it carve its whale-back over the low hills, wondered what else it hid behind. She thought briefly that perhaps she should return, go back down to the miller's cottage and the barn, where at least there would be some shelter, thought also of what she might find there if she did, and did not want to go, saw no other way but forward, and the long, bleak walk through night and day that awaited her, the miles and miles of mud and moor and snow over which she must pass.

And she saw Oravo, his hunched and hesitant form standing like a monolithic servant before her, and knew she could have worse companions, and probably no better protector.

She had known who he was since first she had come here, just turned twelve years old, hired as assistant to the baker whose son she had finally married; had seen nothing then or since but the brutal gruffness everyone in the valley had told her to see, knew nothing of him but the stories that must have trailed him since his early days: of a father who had murdered his mother and then taken his own life by sitting in the snow until the cold had taken them, who both now lay outside the churchyard wall with nothing but a blank stone to mark their passing. All those tales, sticking to him like burrs, keeping him prickling from his neighbours and they from him, all those tittle-tattling tongues that knew a boy could be no better than his father, and that what a father did, so too would do his son.

And yet here she was, standing not two yards from him, and all she felt was his loneliness, the same loneliness she had felt the first few years she had spent in this valley, before Woolgar had made her his own. Remembered also the nosegay of early daffodils that this Oravo had given her, realised how he must have scoured the fields to find them, for they had not yet bloomed in her own small, well-tended garden. Thought of those last awful months when Woolgar had sickened on his bed and finally left her, how he had been so light a weight at the time of his death that she had been able to lift him in her own two arms and carry him across the bridge to the miller and his dray to take him to the churchyard, not wanting the intrusion of strong village men at such a time. Realised the kindness this one man had shown her, had tried to bring some brightness into her days of mourning, the same kindness he was showing her now, despite the contempt with which she had treated him then.

'I could go with you a way,' he said again, as if he'd not already said it, and Griselda smiled, felt her lips crack with the cold and the wet and the weight of sadness and loss they had both endured, saw that he still could not bring his eyes to meet hers, that they were fixed somewhere in the dark menace of storm that lay across the valley like a bear that has stretched itself full length and is lying still, waiting for the right time to flex its claws.

'I'd be glad of it,' she said, and if he was surprised, he didn't show it.

Together they turned their backs to the valley and set their faces to the wind. He never touched her, and she never touched him, and they spent the worst of the night together in a half-timbered cattle byre, burning the few stalks of bracken and broken branches blown in and dried by the winter within the cold stone walls, toasted the bread he had brought with him on the meagre flames of the fire he made, sleeping on a soft floor of rotting planks, which he had swept clear of excrement and dead bones, sleeping under the same blanket, she rolled to the wall in his cloak, thinking of how her thirty-nine years had never prepared her for any of this, he gazing out at the whirl of snow, watching it settle lightly on the crumbling bricks of the empty windows, building the few small inches of white castellations that seemed to him to separate them both from the rest of the world.

He walked with her through all the next day until they reached the printworks at Painswick. They did not speak much, or rather he didn't. Griselda found herself telling him all about her life before she had come to these valleys, before she had even come to England. Maybe it was because she had already made up her mind what she would do: that she would collect what little her father must have left her, and go back the way she had come as a child, take her father's memory home to the place he had told her he meant to go that very same summer.

She told the stiff-lipped, silent, humpbacked Oravo all about her island; the miles of cliffs that wrinkled about the bays, which shone like nacre above the shell-white sand, the rows of angled wooden fences that racked the rough ground into fields for the barley and the rye, the crops of cabbages and beets that kept their stomachs quiet throughout the winter; the rarer, more exotic lines of linseed, flax, fennel, jute and hemp that went into the paper factories; the groves of different trees that were used for the same purpose. He showed some interest at the mention of these trees, even asked a question or two, but she was unable to give him the answers he required, only the impressions she still had of their varying scents and barks and the way the light fell in different colours through their leaves, so you thought you were walking through a tapestry instead of a forest.

She told him of the great meteorite that had once fallen from outside their world and left a crater lined with stone that was black and sharp as glass, made the deep water within it shine even in its depths. She told him lastly of the place near her village where the old burial grounds had been, where families had once burnt their dead on pyres and buried their bones beneath low cairns of stones, of the great red boulder at its centre where their names were carved, so that it was covered almost to the top with centuries and centuries of the details of her ancestors' lives. And of the tree-chapels. How they had been woven into the glade of ancient cypresses and evergreen elms and yews and holm oaks that grew in a great circular glade about that rock, each one reached by steps carved into trunks, or ladders set against their boughs, or branches copsed out for a staircase.

She told him of those childhood days she had played in the bays around Ristnaneem, feeling her toes sink into the tide-soaked sand, so wet that when you pressed your foot upon it, the sand changed its colour as the water was pushed away beneath its weight, how the waves unfurled a continuous ribbon all across the bay, and rolled and broke at once so the dunes seemed to ring, and you could feel the singing of it through the sand and your feet, and right up into your bones.

9

Leaving Astonishment

FAR UP NORTH at Astonishment Hall, Mabel received another letter, or rather, two. Violena handed her the first, which she had already recognised as being from Mr Stroop. Her eyes dropped when she read the latest news, that he and Jack and Thomas were off on some trip to the West Country, but not to worry, that they would soon be back and would see her on their return. It perplexed her, and hurt her, that they should be off on some sally without her, knew also how irrational this was, that there was no reason they should postpone any missing person's case until she returned, that it was she who had left them, and not the other way around. And yet she could not hide her disappointment, and the harder she tried, the more she felt like she would cry. She turned away from Violena, did not want any witness to her distress, nor any comfort. But as always Violena pre-empted her, putting her hands upon Mabel's shoulders, and turning her firmly back towards her.

'We've had another letter,' she said.

'From Mr Stroop?' Mabel knew her voice sounded like a

whimper, but didn't much care, knew also it could not be so, that it was hardly likely she would receive two messages from the same person on the same day.

'Not from Mr Stroop,' Violena answered, releasing Mabel, watching her small protégée drying her eyes, trying to rub the redness from them, trying to be brave, 'although it does concern both him and you.' That caught Mabel's attention, and Violena went on. 'It was addressed to me primarily, as your employer.' She could not help but smile to see a small flush of pride replace the tears on Mabel's cheeks. 'And within it comes a letter to yourself, which I shall now read, if you will give me leave.' Mabel nodded an assent, and Violena began. '"My dear Miss Flinchurst,"' said Violena, going on to the introductions made by one Baron Von Riddarholm, and a brief explanation of the task he had set for Mr Stroop, '"to recover my representative and the miniature library with which he was travelling."' He went on to say that he had requested Mr Stroop's services for certain other more obscure 'adverse matters' that had been happening upon the island where he lived. Violena continued:

Whether he recovers said library and its carrier or not, there have been certain developments on the estate for which we require his help. To such an end, we have arranged his passage here forthwith. He has, however, not yet been apprised of this circumstance, but should he accept the offer, we have no doubt that he should require your presence with him. And so, on behalf of the Riddarholm Estate of Hiiumaa, we extend our welcome to you now, and have provided your employer

with all the necessary details of the journey, along with
the provision for expenses . . .

Mabel was too excited to question anything, was up and
packed within the hour, frustrated at having to bide the
night to wait for the barge that would take her on a round-
about way to the east and then to the west, to meet the
boat that apparently awaited her arrival at Carlisle, to take
her down to Bristol.

Mabel kissed Violena goodbye on the morning of their
parting, expressing her sincere regret that she could not fulfil
her part of the bargain they had agreed. But Violena had
already known that Mabel would not be able to stay so long
away from her adopted family, and only raised that single
eyebrow, as Mabel had never been able to do despite the
months of trying.

'Another adventure, Mabel,' Violena said. 'Never ignore
that.'

And Mabel nodded, could hardly get out her words of
thanks, found her head was too wound up to say any of the
words she had practised. But Violena only pointed to the
extra small crate, packaged and ready at Mabel's feet.

'This is for you,' Violena said. 'All adventurers need supplies,
as I well know, and I have put everything in there that I
think you might need.'

It did not occur to Mabel to wonder what was in that
package, at least not then, for the barge was already powering
up its steam, and she was already being helped on board with
her bags and booty, stood looking at the straight-backed,
grey-clad form of Violena waving, waving, could think

nothing else about this strange turn of events, except the gratefulness she felt to know that in just a few days, she would be seeing Jack and Thomas, and Mr Stroop.

Jack and Thomas, she thought, and Mr Stroop. And Mabel cried again as the barge pulled away from the station that was Astonishment, couldn't believe she had thought she could ever have been happy without them, couldn't believe how happy she was now to know that in just a few days, she would be with them again.

10

The Secrets of Quaritch and his Printworks

IT WAS A pity that telepathic thought had no place in Stroop's life, or any other, else enduring his journey to Painswick might have been the easier, knowing that Mabel was on her way towards them. It had taken Stroop a succession of three carriages to transport him and the boys the thirty miles upcountry from the canal, though the last delivered them with its other packages directly to, and through, the gates of the printworks at Painswick.

It hadn't been hard to spot: two great towers rising like mammoth tusks from the flat green fields, the slope of a cavernous, round-backed barn tapering away behind them, arched between the slight undulation of two eskered hills.

'Blimey,' said Jack, as usual getting another person's complicated admirations into a single word.

'Indeed,' Stroop replied, his eyes widening, scanning the lines of the building as they closed upon it, wondering at the immense wooden structure that stretched a full quarter-mile away from the towers like a gigantic upturned boat, its supporting ribs visible between the lines of thatch, which seemed to grow into the ground. It was such an oddity amidst the pear orchards and hop fields through which they had so recently passed, the neat white cottages, the low lines of hedges and stone-walled dykes, he wondered if perhaps the architecture had not come from some other place, some other country. From Hiiumaa, for instance.

He had already established early on in his enquiries that the world of print and ink and book, and all the arcana that went with it, seemed to hold itself a little apart from every other industry. Print shops and booksellers sprang up side by side, or were one and the same business, and often many of the same businesses conglomerated around one spot, along one street, as if they could not bear to be apart. In London, the booksellers of the Strand and the Churchyard of St Paul's were centuries established, Type Street an upstart that challenged, but could not overcome. The buildings of such places hugged each other back to back and side to side, their tenants vying for the same custom, the same advantage above their neighbours, would sooner cut their own throats than reveal the secrets of their inks, or the composite nature of their papers, whether woven from cabbage leaves or bark or beaten vellum, the guts and glue they used for binding, the sources of the leather that enclosed the printer's part of the work, the dies that cast the tools and types, the ways to scroll the patterns and gilded titles onto the outside skin of every book.

He knew that there were other places that stood apart from the general puggerment of the crowd and were not so many, gave themselves over to experiment and innovation, were as far above the average print-and-page shop in their art as the termite hill is above the woodlice that hide together beneath

their stones. Places such as Hiiumaa were at the very top of
that pile – this much Stroop knew from his research – and
now, on seeing Painswick, he thought perhaps that he had
come across another. He was more intrigued than most upon
his arrival at the printworks of Painswick, though perhaps not
more so than Griselda's father had been his first time here,
nearly thirty years before, almost two months after the expulsions of 1781 that had turfed him from the island that had,
until then, been his home.

Unlike Stroop, Kustin Liit had not been welcomed through
those huge iron gates, but had been left on the other side,
locked out and uninvited, gazing up at the behemoth before
him, knowing that his daughter was too tired to be impressed
by its grandeur, too cold to feel surprise, too grateful to have
finally arrived to do anything other than murmur a quick
prayer. Griselda's father had wavered beside her, squinting
through his clouded spectacles and the scrollwork of metal that
yet barred them from their goal. Towering above them, in
squared Gothic script, the words 'Painswick Printworks' spelled
out their destination, but would not let them in, and they had
waited there, feet sore and blistered in their rag-stuffed clogs,
the short shoe-tacks pinching through the wood into their toes
where the sides and soles had worn too thin. It was raining,
and they had sat huddled together against the lee-side of the
enormous granite gate columns.

It was growing dark, and they had almost given up hope of
anyone appearing, but then a bell rang sharp and high, from
one of the towers, made the mist around it hover and shift a
little way from the stone, counted out the hours and end of

shift. Griselda pulled herself to her feet and peeped through the bars, across the wet, turtle-backed cobbles of the courtyard, watched as the side of the barn split open and grinned, two doors the height of houses being drawn into its sides, and out came the light from the inside workshops, and the silhouettes of machines already groaning as they cooled, and a tumble of men spilling out across the yard, handing their tally-sticks to the foremen as they passed, the rain glittering down upon them as the lamps were lit about the door sides, splintering the rain into shards of glass.

The first men ran out, sprinting and splashing upon the cobbles, came up level with the gates that separated Griselda and her father from their aim, started to haul at hidden winch-wheels not two yards from where they stood drenched and waiting on the other side. Slowly, as the wheels were turned, the height and weight of the iron gates shifted, set gliding in the arc of the trammels buried into the cobbles, until they were almost fully opened. At once their workmates hurried across the yard in noisy knots, caps and collars pulled against the rain, clogs ringing upon the stones as they pushed and jostled, eager to be the first into the pub for pies and beer, or home to the hearth and the wife and the table already laid.

Griselda and her father waited, almost waited too long, didn't see the last of the men release the levers that began to pull the gates closed by some unseen mechanism of weights and cogs, dashing through the closing mouth behind their mates, leaving only a slim gap after their passing for her father to push himself through, dragging his daughter behind him, almost squeezing her like a lemon in a press. And then there they were, all alone in the yard and the rain. Before them lay the shrinking entrance to the printworks, the sliding doors being pushed back together beneath the thatch. Her father grabbed at her hand and started to slip and trot along the cobbles, calling out, panting, for them to stop. A large red arm appeared and caught the door to a halt moments before it closed, heaved it open enough for the arm's owner to step out, already shouting them away, slapping at his dirty leather apron, no workers needed, he was saying, and no beggars allowed.

Griselda marvelled at her father's patience and persistence as he had stood there with the rain seeming horizontal in the strange light that came from inside the doors, his breath a thin halo about his head. He apologised politely, said he had business, brought out the waxed packet from his inside jacket pocket, removed from it a calfskin wallet and from that took the letter he had carried and protected, all the long way from Hiiumaa.

'We've an appointment,' her father said as he removed his hat, his hair just as wet as the felt that had been upon it, and the man in the leather apron finally stopped, looked them properly up and down, saw a pair of gutted crows that might have been draped on a fence to keep away the foxes.

'You don't look like no sort of appointment to me,' he said critically, but leant his neck down anyway and studied the front of the letter, finally took it from her father's hand and turned it over, examined the seal. He looked at them again with no more enthusiasm than before, but shouted out behind him into the depths of the barn, crooked his arm to another man, who came swiftly towards them, his head cocked upon his neck, one still, green eye gazing back into the barn, the other sharp and serious upon the stamp of the letter as he took it from her father. And after what seemed an age of scrutiny, of both them and their letter, he told the leather-aproned man to get back in and close the doors, and then, with some distaste appearing in his down-turned mouth, he took them back out across the courtyard, led them round the building, the water dripping from each reed and jut of thatch, led them to a door sewn into the wall of the first tower, opened its wooden battens, stepped across the six-inch threshold and led them in. And in Griselda went behind him, out of the chill and rain and the months of tramp-and-travel that it had taken them to get themselves to just this place, to here. She stepped over the doorjamb onto a calm, blue floor, saw a passage leading to her left to some vast hall, felt the draught of wind catching at the door, slamming it closed behind her, cutting her away like a stencil from her childhood and her past.

Jack and Thomas had no such past from which to tread, had only the bits of baggage they were already picking out from the parcels just thrown down from the carriage roof by the postmaster. Stroop, wincing to wonder what was in those packages being so roughly treated, realised now why Von Riddarholm had dispatched his most precious goods only into the protective custody of men he knew and trusted. One of the last parcels to be thrown down landed in the fountain that stood at the centre of the courtyard, made a large splash as it hit the water, brought a man running from a tall split in the thatched overhang of the barn as the doors were pulled away, giving Stroop a glimpse of what lay beyond, as had once been given to Griselda: large machines, huge frameworks of iron, great flatbeds of metal, for what purposes he could not guess. The man who emerged from this glimpse was encumbered by a large leather apron, which was speckled all over with mackles and splats of ink.

'Hie aye!' he started yelling at the postmaster, who was now standing unconcerned to one side, smoking his pipe, looking at an untidy sheaf of paperwork clipped to a ramshackle splinter of board. 'What's with all this, Hieronymus?' the aproned man persisted as he slowed his approach, drew level with the fountain and leant over to retrieve the package, bobbing below the shadow of the large stone bird and the curtain of water that was released from the tips of its wings. A scurry of workers had come out behind him and even before they'd begun loading the boxes and packets onto trolleys that shook their joints right up to the elbows, the aproned man had come back exasperated, with the wet package under one arm, water from the fountain dripping from his head.

'Hie, you lot!' he shouted. 'Take a care. You know this stuff's precious and don't want breaking. And as for you . . .' he tried to roll up his sleeves with menace as he stamped up close, but the carriage man smoked on.

''Tain't Hieronymus this trip, guv, told you that last time. He fell off at Oxford somewheres, and got his back broke.'

The man in the leather apron tutted, shook his head, his anger spent before it had properly begun, reduced itself to concern for a fellow workman. 'Aye, aye,' he said. 'I forgot. How is he?'

The postmaster puffed again at his pipe. 'Don't look good. In the alms hospital right now. Got a birch blanket, if you know what I mean.'

Stroop grimaced, knew well what a birch blanket was, had

seen its practice diminish the life of many a patient in the hospitals he had visited, seen them strapped between a rigid set of boards for several months, turned on their backs one day, and on their fronts the next, knew that any shepherd could have told them it was harmful to treat an animal in such a way, that its guts would just have settled and would need careful moving to let its insides shift again without harm. Knew that these men had it worse, that they would also be bled, enemaed and catheted and most probably cupped. Felt a surge of rage and pity that he could not intervene.

The postmaster was unconcerned, tapped out his pipe, handed a couple of tatty bits of paper to the foreman for his signature and got back on his carriage, began to turn his horses round.

'That all then, is it?' he asked without stopping, whipped up his horses and headed to the gates, and without another glance at anyone, including Stroop, jagged off with his carriage out of the courtyard, through the open gates and back out onto the track going north.

'Hie!' shouted Stroop, whose arrangement with the man had been for him to wait until he had made his enquiries, found out if he needed to stay or no. But it was too late, and Stroop stood there in the yard, saw that Jack and Thomas had already deserted to help the other men take in their packages and sacks to the big barn, held up his hands in exasperation and turned to look at the leather-aproned overseer, who stood impotently by his side, mumbling out curses that placed the postmaster at the bottom of a well with no rope, and the lid already being lowered and hammered into place for all eternity.

Stroop was about to introduce himself when they were interrupted by another man, who had scuttled across the yard towards them from the tower. He too had obviously wanted words with the postman.

'He can't have left, Oakley,' he was saying as he reached them. 'I specifically told you to tell him to wait. I have orders! Orders, man. Mr Quaritch was most particular. You should have kept him here.' He turned to Stroop suddenly, his hands fiddling with a large watch he had taken from his suit pocket, though plainly the time to use it had gone. 'And who are you?'

'My name is Whilbert Stroop, sir, from London.'

The man stopped his fidgeting, blinked several times, his neck swivelling at an uncomfortable angle, as though some great weight pressed down upon his neck and made it hard to turn. Stroop could not help but notice that one of the man's eyes was slotted like a marble towards its outward edge, and moved even less than did his neck, moved, in fact, not at all, made one half of him seem to gaze off at some other quarry.

'Stroop,' Stroop repeated, and made a small bow. 'I've come on behalf of a Baron Von Riddarholm.'

The name made the wall-eyed man's head wobble slightly from side to side, brought his one mobile eye to rest on Stroop's face.

'You'd best come in, then,' he said. 'And you,' he jabbed at Oakley with the hard-nailed point of his finger, 'I shall have words with you later.'

He took a last squint at the iron gates through which the postmaster and his carriage had disappeared, saw they had already closed behind him, tutted loudly and led Stroop towards the conjoined towers and the great oak doors that rose up between them, led Stroop in.

11

Circles of History, Wheels of Books

THE RAT'S-TAIL of Hiiumaa is Ristnaneem, a long, flat headland reaching off into the sea. Across it, a line of windmills steeple their way far up into the clear blue cathedral of an afternoon sky, their feet secured by piles of stones, their twisted paddles scooping through the breeze that blew its constant way from off the sea. Baron Josef Von Riddarholm watched them from his window, saw them stand as guardsmen to his horizon, had always seen them stand just so, and knew they would stand there still, long after he was gone.

He was thinking of his most recent letter to Whilbert Stroop, and what he would make of it. He wondered if the man had found even a scrap of Jarl Eriksson and his library, if he had already tired of the apparently impossible task he had been set, if he would even consider his latest insane request. He picked idly at the signet ring that held his seal, the tiny blue scriblets of wax that still clung to it, even as he clung to his island. He felt the unrest all around him, gnawing at the edges of Hiiumaa, the soft, insistent tap of it, as if there were beetles running the length of the ground just below his feet, the tap, tap, tapping of them spelling out the death-watch song that only he could hear. The animal mutilations had been bad enough: the lamb scoured of its flesh, the severed cat's head nailed to the door of one of his work barns. It had made him sick, seeing the fur spiked and hard with blackened blood, its white-furred tongue protruding, its eyes a mean slit of gold like an angry goat, the trails of blood departing from it like a river delta that would never find its sea.

Worse had followed a few weeks later, with the pig being found down at the harbour, its intestines wound around a windlass, guts disgorged from its belly, its feed of the day before a green and stinking slime where its stomach had been split in two by a knife, the scrawl of chalk upon the flagstones that had been mostly worn away by the boatmen shuffling here and there, as they wondered what to do, but which looked afterwards a little like the haft of a sword.

And as if all that had not been bad enough, as if every tongue was not already wagging and talking discontent, there had been the disaster of the *Pihkva*, and ever since the constant talk of pirates in these waters, tales of bucca-neers firing on merchant traders, of mysterious lights in the night trying to lure ships onto the rocks. If it carried on like this, trade with the mainland would wither and cease and leave them dead in the water, and then what would happen to them all? Everyone was looking to him, estate owner, employer, and the only law they had, and Joseph Von Riddarholm had absolutely no idea what to do. He had never been a leader, had been content to let things go the way they always had. Had only once tried to break the chain

and do things his own way, when he had signed up a commis-
sion in the Russian Army and been sent to the war in
Greece. He remembered the windmills they had there, small
and cobbed and whitewashed over, truncated towers squat-
ting in the dusty yellow earth, the paddles no more than
sticks with sails of cloth sewn down upon their lengths,
threaded through by ropes. He remembered the horrid
prickle of heat, the harsh sunlight upon his skin, the stink
and sweat of his own body, his own claustrophobic little
war. He creased his shoulders to remember the skinny dust
that had settled upon his clothes and skin and boots, the
constant irritation of tiny flies that had clustered about his
head and underneath the brim and collar of his hat, the
crawl of them upon his neck, in the corners of his eyes.
Felt again the futility of his efforts, the insignificance of the
establishment of the Septinsular Republic, the scrapping of
the larger powers over the bones of the Ionian Islands. Just
as they did over Saaremaa. For them, it had been between
the French, the Turks and the Russians. For him, it was the
Russians and the Swedes constantly trying to lower the yolk
upon his shoulders. And if all that had happened these past
few months escalated, if the piracy continued, if unrest
continued to grow, then it was only a matter of time before
one or other of those greater powers stepped right in and
took over, just as they had done so many times before. If
that happened, Saaremaa and all its islands would lose their
independence once more, and he would lose the print shops
and presses of which he was so proud, and other men would
lose their rights to farm and fish for their own families, and
in their own ways.

His eyes glanced back across the familiar line of windmills, saw the purple run of sunset begin to grow across the sky, the mist beginning to unravel over the edges of the cliffs. He remembered standing here just like this that bad morning back in April, with the frost-fields flowing away from his windows, the forests of pine and oak and holly and birch, that squirm of men coming up the track towards him from the wreck of the *Pihkva*, like the worm comes from the apple.

A breeze lifted off the sea and drew away the clouds, revealed the coin of the moon, the wink of Venus at its side, and he knew from their positions what month it was, and what day. And he knew without having to consult the telescope in the eastern tower, or the almanacs and books of constellations scattered about its feet, that the precession of equinoxes had almost turned its circle, and soon would come the day when the earth was furthest in its orbit from the sun, a cold day, the aphelion, when the planet hung for a moment at the furthest edge of its ellipse and was alone in the vastness of space. Some day, he thought, it would lose its orbit, spin out just an inch, and never find its way back.

Stroop stepped over the threshold and into a hall so filled with light, the roof might have been levered off and left him standing there, uncovered, beneath an open sky.

'My God!' he murmured, and the wall-eyed man lifted his eye briefly in exasperation, the other still staring at the door through which they had passed.

'Quite,' he said shortly, had long ago given up the wonder of walking into this place, the two huge lime-kilning towers

now topped over with glass and pierced through with
windows, saw only the long torture of the stairs he would
have to climb to deliver this man's message and his name,
wanted only to subside back down to the lower quarters dug
below the earth, and the pint of porter and pair of slippers
he had warming on the stove, hoped the latter wouldn't singe
with the heat before he could manage to retrieve them.

'Wait here,' he added unnecessarily, knew this man would
wait as long as needed and hardly notice, had seen the same
reaction a hundred times, and was bored by it.

'Always the same,' he grumbled as he lifted his legs to the
stair, was already counting in his head the ninety-nine steps
he would have to climb to reach the director's door. Ninety-
bloody-nine, he thought, as he always did. Couldn't fathom
a man who had to live halfway up a tower like a tree creeper,
instead of doing the sensible thing, like he would have done,
and building an office down below. Shook his head slowly
as he rounded the first bend of the ever-tightening spiral
that made up the right-hand staircase to the upper floors,
saw the man whose name he had already forgotten cricking
his neck in disbelief, his legs taking him first one way and
then another across the marble and granite floor, noted the
sharp fragments of feldspar and mica that winked up at him
with unhidden malice, tried to blind his progress, made more
difficult his climb. He couldn't stop his lazy eye from gazing
back down behind him, narrowed the other to concentrate
his vision, wondered if he was the only man in the world to
see things as they really were, the left divided from the right,
the things that mattered from those that didn't, decency to
one side, dross-heap the other. Would not have appreciated

93

being told that the only other creatures to spy life such a way were a few birds and fish, and most of the insects to which he was likened by his workmates.

The man whose name he had forgotten as he rode his ninety-and-nine steps had come to rest in the middle of the twin atrium, below the division of the staircases, which twisted off to one side and the other like the insides of snail shells. Between them stood a great machine like a water wheel, encased in two sleeves of wood, banded by rims of brass. It was operated by a treadle, as Stroop soon discovered, having sat at the seat that was placed before it, the leather upholstered arms worn into cushions by the thousands of elbows that must have rested there before his own.

'But this is marvellous!' Stroop couldn't help speaking out loud, didn't even notice the echo of his voice bouncing from wall to wall, could only sit, pushing his feet one by one upon the treadle as if he were in some kind of paddle boat. Of course the chair didn't move, as might have happened with such a boat, but instead, the wheel he sat before slowly turned, and at each push of the pedals, another lectern presented itself, each holding an upturned book, already opened at the pages from which someone else had read. How many paddles, Stroop thought, and how many books? He'd already been through thirteen at his count, but could not have been sure, had been distracted by the contents of the pages that presented themselves at each turn of the wheel. He found he could brake the machine with ease by placing his hands on the brass rims of the two outside edges, and after having got over the immediate delight of the contraption, had begun to bend over and study the words, examine the prints, read of things he had never read before.

Stroop was not a man easily amazed, had seen huge bells cast in sand and wax and come out humming, had witnessed the autopsy of a half-repeating watch with its intricate entrails of quarter-racks and snails and ratchets and cogs and wheels and springs he would have thought too minuscule for any human hand to have made, had seen the creation of moon-dogs within a glass case. But this machine spoke to Stroop of something else entirely, of having a multiplicity of books at your fingertips without having a desk the size of Cathay, and Whilbert Stroop was truly awed.

He knew that herons sometimes threw sticks into water to attract the fish, and if Painswick was the heron, and this paddle the stick, he could be no better fish, and he could not stop himself from reading on and on: about the origins of ink and the complicated process of extracting lampblack from bark, how the best time to harvest varnish was midsummer, that the Chou Dynasty princes of China had a coffin made when first they ascended the throne, that every year of their reign another layer of lacquer was added to the wood . . .

He was interrupted by someone coming to stand behind him. 'Mr Stroop?'

Stroop did not respond. He wanted to take notes, had already begun to compose them in his head, wanted more than anything to keep flipping through the pages of the book before him, and then the next one, and the next one, until the wheel was fully turned. And then he wanted to reload the lectern paddles and start all over again.

'Mr Stroop.'

The voice was loud and right in his ear, and Stroop begrudgingly turned from his studies, wished he had been at home so that Mabel, or one of the boys, had been able to stop this person ever getting as far as his study door. Realised, with the drowsiness of a dormouse quitting its hibernation, that he was not at his home, and these books were not his own, and that there were other things he was here to do. He took his hands from the wheels and disengaged his feet with difficulty from the treadles.

'Ah, yes, of course,' he said, and pulled himself to standing, put out his hand. 'Whilbert Stroop. Yes, I am he.'

The intruder introduced himself as Charles Quaritch, owner of the Painswick Printworks. He took his visitor back up the ninety-and-nine steps to his office, the wall-eyed man grumbling up behind them with coffee, which slopped from its pot, and softened the biscuits that had been thrown untidily onto a plate beside them.

Having been removed from the distraction of the book wheel, Stroop regained his focus and the reason for his visit. Quaritch read Von Riddarholm's letter and declared himself a personal and professional friend, with whom he had a life-long correspondence, had even been over to Hiiumaa on a visit.

'Wonderful place, Mr Stroop, perhaps even more so than here,' and he smiled to see Stroop raise his eyebrows in some disbelief. 'My grandfather built this place out of an old lime kiln works – hence the towers and the shed – had the wit to erect a new industry out of the old. But Von Riddarholm, well, he is truly a visionary. Here we specialise in creating some of the finest papers and inks in the business, indeed we are quite famous for producing the longest machine-rolled pieces of paper available in this country, as well as the largest. Map-makers flock to our doors.'

Stroop himself was envisioning his own study and the jigsaw of paper-pieces that made up his Sense Map of London. Quaritch was telling him he could create a single piece with which to paper his wall, described the desks they had invented with primed rollers either side, so one single sheet could be wound out from one side and into the other, as a man pleased, to a length of over fifty feet. Stroop was inquisitive, intrigued, could see the use he himself could make of their wares.

It took him quite a while to get on to the subject in hand, to ask about the baron's representative, Jarl Eriksson, who had apparently been in this area prior to his disappearance, and whether or not he had visited.

Quaritch shook his head. 'Sadly, no, though we did expect his arrival some time ago. He had sent word from Stroud that he was on his way.' Quaritch poured out the last of the coffee, regarded with distaste the biscuits, which had sogged and disintegrated upon their plate. 'Von Riddarholm sends out his disciples once a year for a visit, brings us his best creations. He is a marvel at producing miniature books out of all sorts of materials – he has made paper from potato, cabbage, flax, bark of every kind, even straw and silk. His die-casters are the most skilled in Europe, and so far, he has claim to have produced the smallest movable type and printed books with it.'

He got up from his seat, unlocked a small cabinet, revealed several shelves no taller than four inches high, each lined with tiny books. 'All these I have purchased from him over the years, one for each visit, sometimes two, and on one occasion, I succumbed to three.' He twitched his mouth at the memory, made his moustache ends quiver like the tail of a red kite in flight. 'They are, of course, extremely valuable, and the loss of Jarl Eriksson, if indeed he is lost, is incalculable, assuming the little suitcase of his wares has gone with him.'

Stroop narrowed his eyes, rubbed the fingers of his hand against his palm. 'Is it possible Eriksson has absconded? Taken the miniature library as his prize?'

It seemed a possible explanation, one that had not occurred to him before, and had certainly not been mooted by Von Riddarholm. But Quaritch merely relocked his cabinet and sat down again with a small laugh.

'Eriksson? Not he.' He began to clip the end from a cigar, offered one to Stroop who declined, watched as Quaritch lit the stump and held it a while, the blue smoke unfurling from it, filling the room with the strong scent of hay and tobacco. 'No,' he continued, 'Eriksson was solid as they come. He was brought up on Hiiumaa, worked every one of his days, man and boy, for Von Riddarholm. His family is there.' He shook his head again. 'Hiiumaa *is* his family. It is often the way with men from that place.'

Stroop was puzzled, surprised at Quaritch's depth of knowledge. Quaritch smiled, took a long draw at his cigar.

'I have men working here who came from there. Or rather, I had. A few of them arrived soon after '81 when I was just learning the trade from my father.' He tapped the end from his cigar, looked at Stroop through the smoke. 'Hiiumaa has quite a tragic history, although I have benefited from it, I can't deny. The island people are in the main of Swedish extraction, and when the island was ceded to the Russians by the Swedes in one of their interminable wars, the Russians wanted the place vacated to make way for their own citizenry. Of course, given the nature of the industry there, that was all but impossible.'

He stood up, moved to a large framed map of Northern Europe, which took up a great deal of the wall behind Stroop, presumably a demonstration of the great sizes of paper he could produce. Stroop was sitting with his back to the door and the map, and had not seen it there, though now, as he turned in his chair, he was quite struck by it. Quaritch brushed by him, placed his finger on some minuscule spot of land that lay some distance from Sweden inside the Baltic Sea, started to move his finger across its surface, bringing it over the North Sea, past London, vaguely tracing the path that Stroop himself had taken to reach here.

'The old baron argued fiercely that he needed many of the men to work the plants and ink presses and so on, and he won the right to keep a great many of them there. But still, some had to go. Most were relocated to the Russian mainland, but a few of them found their way here, brought signed letters of recommendation.' He moved back to his desk, left his cigar burning into ash, tapped his finger on the wood. 'Of course it was a long time ago now, and we are all so much older. The last of the Hiiumaa men died back in April.' He stretched his neck, moved his head upon it to pull out the creases, lifted his eyes to the ceiling. 'Had his daughter here not so long ago to pick up his effects. Terrible thing, terrible,' he continued, still staring at the blank plaster sky. 'The whole valley was washed out in the floods, both Upper and Lower Slaughter completely gone. And still gone. And so is she, back to Hiiumaa, or so she said.' He shrugged, shook his head to clear out the images.

Like everyone else he had trotted over on his horse as a sightseer to survey the damage, and like everyone else, he hadn't been at all prepared for the devastation he had witnessed, the valley run through by water, and every human habitation scoured from its sides. It had indeed been a terrible thing, and like some of the other wealthy landowners who had visited, he had taken on a few of the men and their families, donated funds to the monastery to mop up those who would inevitably be left.

And so it was that Stroop first heard the story of Griselda and her father, though not their names, at least not then, and found his mind backtracking across the valleys and the seas and tracing the possible steps of Jarl Eriksson to Painswick. Or almost to Painswick, Stroop reminded himself, almost.

And although Charles Quaritch had been nothing but friendly and informative, jovial even, there was something about him that Stroop did not like, the dry sliding of his eyes when he had mentioned the dead workman, the unpleasant lift to his voice as he spoke of the daughter, and the spark in his eye when he had talked of the missing library, which might have been taken for glee.

12

Into the Pike Gut and the Past

After the attack on the *Pihkva* back in April, the crew of the *Osil* had been exuberant and exhilarated. The unexpected ease of the enemy's capture and capitulation had been augmented by the dragging of the *Pihkva*'s holds, giving them grain, guns and spirits, just as Torrensson had promised, and surely that was enough to do any sailor for a while, no matter the circumstances. Torrensson had taken them right back across the bay, knew every current that swirled these islands round, every hook of water and whirlpool that tried to catch them unawares, brought them nose and tail through the sharp teeth of that April gale and into calm, slid them into the Pike Gut Strait on the southernmost tip of Finland.

Almost into Hangö, the Pike Gut lay between the islands of Tullisaan and Kobben, a slack stretch of water used for harbour by thousands of ships over as many years. The rocks that lined the coastlands of the strait were cut about with carvings made by long-gone crews becalmed within its walls, scratching out their names and shields, waiting for a fairer wind, or their enemy to appear at the thin slip of its neck, so they could surge out unseen and attack once more. Hundreds of years and hundreds of men had marked this place of hiding, and the crew of the *Osil* were only the latest to take up its advantage, and lie drunk and cradled within its arms.

Up on deck, one man smoked and sober, lashed by rain and all alone, leant against the *Osil's* railings, uneasy with all that had passed. He had watched the *Pihkva* sink with the same despair any seaman feels when his ship has been blown away beneath him, and seen his crewmates sink beneath the waves. He had been unconvinced by Torrensson's rallying victory speech, had felt unable to celebrate the destruction of a Swedish trading ship that had done them no harm, was wondering what he was doing here at all.

'There are greater things,' Torrensson had called out when they had removed themselves into the safety of the Gut, the wind whistling through the spikes of rock around them, the water deep and slack and calm, 'than the loss of individual ships or lives. We have always fought for other people's countries, to other people's orders, but now it is time to fight for our own! To take back the land that was taken from us! To establish our own safe haven to live out our lives!' It was an honest and upright procedure, Torrensson had told them, and as he said it, the way he said it, the manner in which he had catalogued the wrongs that had been done them, who was there who would not believe him? Every last one of them had been chosen for this task from across the years that Torrensson had spent at sea, captaining his ships again and again to victory through battles most would have thought to have been lost before they started. Who would not be proud to have been picked from amongst so many, and by such a man? And every last one of them had roots here, in these islands, ancestors who had lived and died here, before the great expulsion of '81.

Second Mate Onni Berwald knew the rhetoric of their cause, was one of the few who had actually lived there and remembered the rocks and stones, the fields and bays, was not just another hot-headed descendant of parents or grand-parents expunged from this land. He had been brought up on the tales Torrensson was now so good at telling, of how the islands in their infancy had been a pirate nation, had made themselves strong by attacking before they could be attacked, had scavenged and salvaged whatever came their way, and been feared and admired for their survival and success. He knew all about Torrensson's strongest call upon the past, of the coming of the Brethren of the Sword after the Crusades, and how they had struck a bargain with the islanders, would use the largest of their islands for their retreats, build their forts, strengthen their ranks, be free with their coin, and in return would lend the islands their ferocious protection against invasion, make them safe within their autonomy, allow the swilling in of skill and men from Russia, Finland, and most of all from Sweden, and had given the place a future.

'And who are we, comrades,' Onni could still hear Torrensson's voice booming out like a bittern upon a marsh, 'who are we, but the New Brethren of the Sword? We will give again these islands our own protection, we will be the bulls to the dogs that dare to attack, we will rebuild the old fortifications, we will allow the return of our countrymen who were forced to leave these shores. We will be the engineers of the New and Free Land of Osilia!'

Everyone had hurrahed and shouted, hammered their hands against the deckhousing of the boat that bore their name and hope, stamped their feet, powered out the old sea dogs' shanties that sung of their strong veins that ran with salt and tar instead of blood, their skin being more resilient than the canvas strapped to their masts to catch the wind, their bodies harder than the wood upon which they sailed.

They would take their temporary haven here, shouted Torrensson to his applauding audience, their brandy-soaked faces shining up at him like beacons, would set forth like hounds after hares from this place to harry and pursue any ships that passed the islands by, sowing instability and mistrust upon the waters, make the islanders long for a New Brethren to come to them and take command.

But Onni Berwald had not sung nor stamped nor shouted. He had thought instead of his brother, Eyvind, out there somewhere on Hiiumaa, and wished to God he had stopped to listen to what he had said those several months before, wished he could feel the drums rolling within him that drove the hearts of these other men, felt instead a hard pain within his ribs, and the hollow wash of brack within his stomach, had watched the *Pihkva* with a silent sickness, felt as if he too had been scuppered when finally she went down.

Stroop was having his own second thoughts, specifically about Charles Quaritch, owner of the Painswick Printworks, even as the man led the way back down the tower steps, gave Stroop the generous offer of a couple of horses to get him on his way back to Bradford-on-Avon and the canal boat that would take him home.

'I'm sorry you've had a wasted journey,' Quaritch said, his face creased in puzzlement, reminding Stroop of a pine cone that has closed itself up against the rain. 'Maybe Eriksson decided on a visit to Gloucester, or even Wales. We're not so far from the border here, and you know what those Welshmen are like. They've got a hatred for us English, no matter how much they need our trade.'

Stroop was tempted to point out that Jarl Eriksson was about as unEnglish as you could get without changing the colour of his skin, but kept his silence. Other men's prejudices had always fascinated him and he wondered what Quaritch would have made of Isaac the bargeman, who was blacker than the coal he carried, thought probably he'd brand him just as treacherous, if not more so, than the Welsh.

'Still,' Quaritch continued talking down the long flight of stairs, 'take the horses by all means. Leave them with the ostlers at Stroud – you can't miss them. They're just inside the town walls, and know me well. Or take them on down to Bradford and send word. I'll have them picked up in a few days.'

Stroop got the strong impression that Quaritch was anxious to be rid of him, or more likely of his questions, decided to take the man up on his offer, but had a couple of places he meant to go to first, though didn't mention it.

Down in the hallway, Quaritch offered his hand and Stroop took it, thanked him, spared a brief, envious glance at the book wheel, thought he might try to acquire one when he got home. What a surprise that would be for Mabel, he thought, was already anticipating the admiration and amazement on her face when he brought her into his study to see it, was already trying to think who he might ask to make one, the doors he would have to have removed just to get the thing inside his house. Or better still, perhaps he should have the craftsman construct it directly where it would stand.

'Well, thank you again,' he managed to say, as Quaritch waved him back into the care of the wall-eyed man, who had grumbled once again out of his slippers and put on his clogs, received his orders to take the visitor to the stables, and have him fitted out with whatever he needed.

Jack and Thomas were unsurprisingly already inhabiting the stables when he got there, and were delighted to find out about the new travelling arrangements.

'We've things to tell you,' Jack whispered to Stroop as he approached, unaware that he had never been able to whisper, and never would.

'Later, Jack,' Thomas said, and winked at Stroop as he hoisted him from the mounting-block onto the horse.

Stroop had never liked horses, and this one was huge. He was immensely grateful when Thomas leapt up behind him, hands sneaking around his waist to take the reins, saw that he had already expertly strapped their two bags behind Jack, and within minutes, they found themselves being led across the yard, the two gates opening up like the wings of a swan as it tucked its head below water, closing behind them immediately they had taken their exit.

Charles Quaritch reclimbed his ninety-and-nine steps, and now stood looking down on Stroop's departure from one of the small windows that had been pricked into the fabric of the old lime kiln towers. He stood with his hands behind his back, the cold stub of his cigar clenched between his teeth. Of course he should have expected Von Riddarholm to do something to locate his missing scout, but had been surprised at the lengths to which he had obviously gone. He didn't know what had happened to Jarl Eriksson, assumed he had gone the way of many, attacked and robbed and left for dead by footpads or the other gangs of thieves that roamed the tracks that threaded across England. Wondered if perhaps he shouldn't have had the wit to have arranged it himself. But he had never seen himself as a murderer, even after the mishap with Kustin Liit, and again after the problems with Kustin's daughter visiting, even though he knew the woman had been bound to turn up eventually, especially after the flood.

Yet still he had to wonder about that. What had happened to the daughter and the two men he had sent to find her? Surely she couldn't have fought them off, and surely they couldn't have lost her. He knew it had been snowing hard that afternoon, had been snowing since a week or so before the flood, and then again after. Knew also that it had been the heavy falling of the snow and its sudden melting with that false spring that caused the flood in the first place. And still he wondered. If his men had found her and her book, why hadn't they returned? And what of Kustin's little book? Maybe it had been nothing after all, maybe his men had gone a little too far with the girl and got scared and run. Maybe the book was nothing more than it said on the cover, whatever that might have been. But where else was there for Kustin to have made his notes and findings, hidden his secrets? Quaritch had turned over every piece of paper he could find in Kustin's desk after he had died, had searched his quarters top to bottom, with no result. But if the old inksman really had achieved what Quaritch suspected him of – no, Quaritch corrected himself, what he *knew* he had achieved – then he must have left the details of his experiments somewhere. And the only place he had looked, and yet not understood, was that little book with all its scribblings in some foreign language. Kustin's language. But he had been the last of the men of Hiiumaa to be working here, and there was no one else he could have called on who would have understood the least jot of it. Except perhaps Jarl Eriksson, which was precisely why he hadn't mentioned his visit to anyone, not to Von Riddarholm in his letters, nor to the man Stroop. Because if Kustin Liit had passed on his secrets, then it must have been to Eriksson. Quaritch knew they always had a while to sit and talk on Eriksson's sporadic visits, drinking that foul stink of pine-needle tea that seemed to remind them both of home. But with Kustin gone, and Eriksson disappeared, well, the secret had gone with one or both, and if Quaritch didn't have it, at least no one else did either. Not even the daughter.

He remembered that time well. The snow had started falling again, and he could still hear that slow pounding in his ears that had been the flood sweeping down the next valley, though he hadn't known it then for what it was, had taken it for thunder like everyone else. And then the following afternoon she had come here in her tattered skirts, weighed down with enough mud to make it hardly worth her wearing, and must certainly have made the walking hard. She had asked to see him, given the foreman her father's name, explained the circumstances, how everything had gone with the water and she had nothing, only whatever little her father had left to her, and that she had sore need of it now. And he had bade the wall-eyed foremen bring her up the steps and entertained her here, in this very office. Given her the remnants of her father's life: a small box, which Quaritch had already unlocked and been through, and contained nothing more than a couple of old pebbles looking like black glass, a lock of hair, a few beads of amber in which the bodies of insects had been preserved. He had handled these last with some disgust, could not understand why anyone would keep such things. He understood amber itself, of course. Exuded resins were the baseline for many inks, and amber was only a resin, ancient and hardened perhaps, but a resin all the same. But what the use was of keeping it when it had been adulterated by flies or wasps he couldn't comprehend at all. He had never liked flying things, disliked the bats that routinely roosted in the upper reaches of the second tower into which he rarely went, always gagged at the smell of them, which seemed to permeate the walls and drift down into the rooms he occasionally had to visit, housing the racks of wine he kept for special occasions, and the guestrooms for the visiting buyers, whom he preferred to keep at a distance even if he had no choice for the sake of business but to put them up. Didn't even like birds, except when they were on his plate.

He had dropped those amber beads back into the little box and locked it right back up, handed it over to Griselda without a word. And he had also cashed in the balance of her father's pocket book, in which was recorded all the monies he had earned and saved, and even though it had been a pretty amount, guilt had made him add a little more. He had thought then about Kustin Liit and where he had come from, and why he had come, and about all the long years the man had worked in this place for his father and then for him, and it had occurred to him that apart from visiting his daughter over at Lower Slaughter, the man had never left here, at least to his knowledge. Kustin Liit had never gone to Stroud, like all the other workers every now and then, to experience the town or buy gifts or women or whatever else working men chose to do with their money. Instead, he had spent all his spare time in his workshop, at his desk. And it was this fact more than any other that convinced Charles Quaritch that Kustin Liit had finally gained his goal, and perfected the ink that could be used in the presses to print out golden letters, which could have made Charles Quaritch richer than he could have supposed possible, and more importantly, brought the prestige that would make him the foremost printer in the land.

And that brought Quaritch right back to the puzzle of these past few weeks. Where exactly was it Kustin had written down all that he had learnt and done? There had only been the book. And Quaritch had meant to keep it, decipher it by whatever means, no matter how long it took him. But then came the flood, which in turn had brought Griselda, and she had known at once that what he tried to give her was certainly not her father's.

'This is the wrong book,' she had said when he had handed over her father's belongings, had hoped the flash of coins would be enough to distract her from the substituted book. Had sought to persuade her things were otherwise.

'I assure you,' he had replied, 'this is the only one we found in his quarters.'

But then he had seen, just as suddenly as she had, for he had left the evidence lying quite openly on a small desk that lay below the window, cursed himself for his idiocy in leaving it there: Kustin Liit's little book split open along the spine where Quaritch had hoped to find a hidden spill of paper, had held it up by the open window to catch the light, seeking for hidden signs.

'But that is it,' she had said, quite simply, 'unless you have taken up reading Swedberg in his native language?'

And there it was. What could he do? He had blustered, said it had been found on the workroom floor and he hadn't known what it was or to whom it belonged. Even she had realised how weak was the argument, and had tossed back onto the desk the small book of psalms he had substituted in her father's belongings.

'You have mistaken it,' she had said. 'I know that book. He read it to me every day we were coming in on our way to here.'

He had winced at her use of English, had almost corrected her grammar, but knew already that he was caught, and that she knew, of course she did, that the book he had tried to give her was not her father's, and that her father's was lying there on the desk by the window. Perhaps if it had been a Latin version of the text, he could have bluffed it out, but in Swedish? Or at least so he assumed it must have been, for he didn't understand it, and she so obviously did. There was no other course then but to give it to her, and he was still chiding himself that he had not hidden it in his desk before she came, would certainly have done so had he not been so intent upon it, upon the scribbled notes in its margins – so many notes, so many entries, so many allusions to chemical formulae, that he had been so absolutely sure he was on the right track that he had quite simply forgotten to put the thing away before she came to him.

And then she had it, her father's book and all that it contained, and she had continued with her tale of calamity and how she meant to go back to her father's home. To Hiiumaa. Of course, he thought, where else would she go? Both she and her father. And that same anger had come over him as when he had confronted Kustin in his workshop and done what he had never thought he would have been capable of doing. But if Kustin really had perfected that ink, then by rights it belonged to his employer for twenty-odd years, and that meant none other than Charles Quaritch, and so, after Griselda had left, he had made his plans.

Quaritch watched as Stroop climbed the mounting-block as if it were the gallows, saw the small boy tipping his master up into the horse's saddle and skipping up lightly behind him. Saw the second boy get himself ready on the grey. Remembered the woman Griselda leaving, just as Stroop was doing now, except that then it had been snow and her own two feet and his burning need to get back hold of that little book. And now, where was it? Quaritch didn't know, imagined his men fleeing from her corpse, and the pages of such promise rotting somewhere beneath the snow.

He remembered something he had read the day before on the pages of the book wheel that had so delighted the stranger Stroop, that so extraordinary was the quality of some ancient Chinese inks that you could soak a page in water for several days, and yet still the words and lines and pictures would remain. He was sick with it, felt it deep within his body, as if a hornet had burrowed its way inside him and made a nest within his bowels. He would never know the secret that Kustin Liit discovered, and the knowledge of his ignorance was enough to make his hands shake where they were braced against the sill. The only thing that gave him the slightest cheer was that one way or another, the thing was lost, as must be Griselda, and with her he knew the whole family of Liits had been eradicated from English soil. And good riddance.

In fact, at almost that exact same moment, Griselda had not long passed the boundary stones of London town, and would soon be hurrying her last few miles down to the docks at Purfleet where she had been directed. Soon she would secure her ticket to board the ship that would take her to the Baltic, would check every few minutes that it was still tucked safe away under the strap-line of her dress. Several times she would turn and look back towards London, would see the smoke curling up from countless houses and factories only to be bent back towards the roofs from which it had come, settling a dirty fog upon the tiles and wooden beams and thatches, try to sift itself up the sides of steeples and towers only to be forced back again, unable to escape the heavy air that caught the heat, encouraged the stink of mud and rotting leaves and ordure that clung to her boots and skirts and the dirt-ridden skin of her legs. She would look further, try to catch a last glimpse of the wide-open fields and rolling hills through which she had passed, but would see only the brown scum of the Thames overrun with the haphazard higgle of boats and sails, and the scumbles and shambles of the city that crowded alongside its banks, as anxious and needful of it as flies are of a corpse. And she would wonder then if this marvellous city of London would ever experience the treachery of its river as she had done of hers, and what would happen if the waters one day rose up against all those who sucked their living from its edges, sweeping the lice from its back with its fury and self-cleansing revenge.

13

Passages, and the Way that Some Men Pass

STROOP HAD SETTLED in an ill-fitting way into the horse's sway. He wasn't particularly comfortable, and he was far higher above the ground than he would have liked, but at least with Thomas having squirmed around him and in front, he was feeling reasonably safe, free to look at the land through which they were passing. He wanted to thank Thomas for waiting until they were out of eyeshot of the printworks before taking the lead, but knew it was unnecessary, had already decided that he would never again take a case that involved prolonged horse-riding, preferred his days of foot leather expended upon the streets of London town. He had begun to survey the green of unfolding horizons, the gentle ease of hills to left and right, the copses of cobs, the may trees so frothing with blossom, their branches could not be seen, the hesitant lace of the elderflowers beginning to unfold from their tiny green buds. He saw the low purple of heather rolling away over a length of moor, spotted with tufts of cotton grass growing like small, soft-backed sheep wherever a spring or burn must lie beneath.

'You know the man with the suitcase?' It was Thomas, craning his neck far to one side so Stroop could catch his words. Stroop refocused, remembered Jack had said before that they had learnt something, felt a certain pride that when the two of them had followed the men and the postman's baggage off into the big barn, they hadn't needed telling to do a bit of talking and prying and poking with gentle questions. 'Well,' Thomas continued, as Stroop knew he would, 'he was at the printworks.'

Stroop was not as surprised as he might have been if he had not already met Charles Quaritch, had already known the man was hiding something, particularly after he had seen his little locked-up library, each miniature book tagged on its shelf with a tiny label. All except one.

'Ah,' was all Stroop managed as the horse hit a pothole, regained its step, noticed that Thomas rode the stumble as Stroop could never have done, felt a sharp pain in his buttock bone, remembered the hard driving over the ridge of Black Fell the year before, and the month of ache and pain that had followed.

'We knew you'd want us to ask,' continued Thomas, and Stroop smiled, thought maybe this was how a father would feel when he saw his sons do things the same way he would have done them, a strange lift to his heart that made him sit a little taller. 'Well,' Thomas had nowhere near finished his narrative, was only just getting started, 'the man with the suitcase did come here, a couple of weeks before the big flood, or so one of the workmen said.' He waited to see if Stroop knew about the flood. Stroop's silence told Thomas that he did. 'Apparently he came every year, about the same time, but this visit everything was different.'

Stroop's knees tightened on the saddle, felt the faint tingling that comes when your head has already made a small leap without letting you know yet to what and from where.

'Every time else he'd gone straight to visit old Quaritch in his tower, and then down to the printworks to sit and talk with some old pal. But this time he did it all the other way round.' Thomas took a breath, and Stroop took advantage.

'Let me guess,' said Stroop, his heart beating a little faster than he thought was probably healthy on such a big horse, 'he visited a man who came from Hiiumaa.'

'That's it!' Thomas happily supplied. 'Old mates, the workman said, from way back ago. And he sometimes collected a letter to take back with him.'

'And this year?' Stroop asked, though he was pretty sure he already knew the answer.

'Oh, yes,' replied Thomas, 'this year too. They were chatting for ages, the masher-man said, and Kusty someone or other, which is the inksman's name, gave him not one letter, but two.'

'Ah,' said Stroop as his brain moved its paddle-wheel around and presented another book and another page, didn't even stop to wonder what a masher-man might be nor how Thomas knew this information, 'and the second letter was to the old inksman's daughter?'

Thomas laughed and turned his head back to the track so the sound smudged a little in the oncoming wind, reminded Stroop of a curlew bubbling on the wet fields of spring.

'You know everything, Mr Stroop!' said Thomas without rancour, glad he was here and alive and sitting on top of a horse with a man who might not know a hoof from a hock, but apart from that, knew the entire world.

And Jack apparently knew a few things too, as Stroop saw him pause at the upcoming crossroads, take his horse to the west, knew that, without having to be told, Jack was taking the track to the valley of Lower Slaughter, and however much of it the flood had left behind.

For Oravo Tallista Swan, it seemed that everything he had ever been was left behind. That short journey he had taken with Griselda as they walked from Lower Slaughter to the print-works had been for him an epiphany, the only time in his forty-three years of life that anyone had really talked to him. And that realisation had shaken him right down to the marrow of his bones. He had always been apart, he knew that, had wanted it no different, had been born to it. Had lived with Grandmother Swan since he had been too young to remember any different, had always known she placed the blame of the father onto the shoulders of his son, had never forgiven Jorge Tallista for coming here from God knew where, and taking away her daughter. Oh, he'd done his carpenter's work well and good, with his hard, splinter-scarred hands, but she could not bear to think of those same hands on her daughter's skin, could not stand the shine of his black hair and his eyes the colour of crows, and had never forgiven the daughter for preferring her husband's to her mother's home. Had never forgiven the grandson she was left with, the weekend visit that had turned into a lifetime when the filthy foreigner had finally done his worst, and let her daughter's life freeze right out of her, and then taken his own.

They had been buried outside the churchyard wall, and Oravo had visited once or twice, seen something of his own story in the blank face of the headstone, had often wondered about what else lay buried beneath it, about the life his parents had led together that had brought him into this valley, and among these people. And one day he'd decided he wanted to know more, and had taken the path down by the river towards the miller's, found the ruins of the house in which they had used to live, had found the old shed where Jorge Tallista used to work, where he and his sickness-stricken wife had finally deprived themselves of life.

The roof had been caved in with years of wind and weather, but Oravo had cleared that place out stone by stone, and found his father's old work bench still in place, the clamps and vices rusted into the wood, the tools he had once used still hanging from their nails upon the wall.

He had rebuilt that old work shed, had Oravo, had seemed to understand the way the wood would go and the way a joint should be made and chiselled to take the next, had re-thatched the shed and then the house, had replaced the chairs that had crumbled into pieces by the fireplace, had even found a message of sorts from his departed parents, a sad little sampler that hung in tatters from the wall above the dead and black-eyed hearth, the violets and cornflowers a faded blue about its edges, the few words they housed still legible despite the pull of threads that the wrens and black-birds had taken for their nests: '*Nimas*', it had read, '*Nimas Nimenos*', and a small scribble of half-eaten letters below that must have spelt out his mother's name. As for those other words, he had no idea what they meant, only that for him, they were his father and his mother, and he had carefully taken that tapestry down and detached it from what little of the frame remained between the burrows of the woodworm, and looked at it a long, long time. Then he had rolled it up and stored it in a hollow stalk of fennel hardened with calf's-foot glue, and sealed each end of it with wax. Kept it with him ever since, until he almost forgot that it was there, except for the pat of his hand every morning at the little tubular pocket he had sewn for it in the lining of successive summer and winter coats, checking with some un-understood compulsion that it had not been stolen from him, as they had been, and still remained.

And for Oravo Swan, that had been his life. He had his wood and his linnets and his cockroaches, and the people of the village came to him for this or that and paid their way and talked their tales. But until that walk over the moors after the flood, he had never understood the comfort of companionship, had never even sought out a dog to lie at his feet by day, at his side by night, had always known that he had been born silent and had not screamed despite the slaps upon his baby-bottom, and that he had remained that way ever since, had been made that way by the valley and its people, and been content with it.

Until Griselda. He remembered when she'd first come to the valley as the old baker's assistant, had even passed a few words with her whenever he went to fetch his bread like everyone else. Had felt something for her even then, all those years ago, for the other stranger. But that night and day on the moor had given him something he never knew he missed, and he wanted it again: that listening he had given her, and the unimaginable cracking open of horizons she had given him, though she hardly knew what she had done. The walk across the moors to Painswick, the carving of two sticks to aid her passage across the snow, the giving of something of himself to another – Oravo had never known so small a thing could have such worth, and he craved its continuance.

And so, when he brought her to those great iron gates of Painswick Printworks, and saw her small progress across the cobbled yard, he stayed outside, where he had always been, only this time he waited. Wanted to see a little more of what he couldn't have. And he stayed there with the snow melting through his boots, soaking his rag-tied leggings right up to his knees, crouched himself into a small bivouac of trees that lay away to the left, to see what he might see.

She came back out less than an hour later, far sooner than he might have supposed. She approached the post-carriage that had arrived whilst she was indoors, and he clearly heard her tell the driver to take her on to Gloucester as she was heading to London, heard the man answer just as clearly that he wasn't going that way, and her best path was to get herself back to Stroud and on down to the canal. And as she stepped away, Oravo saw the pale freckles on her pale face, the skin pinched around her cheekbones, the lines that ruled her fore-head where her hair was pulled back into a knot of string, and he felt such a cold sadness grip his throat to see her pick up the two stout sticks that he had carved for her, and off she went, not one look back, not one look around to see if he might still be there.

Yet still he might not have followed her even then, found it difficult for a few minutes to even breathe, surely could not move, had such a deep sense of regret and loss he knew he could not bear for her to see in him, realised with utter dismay that the tears were running down his face and onto his jacket, wetting his hands where he still held the straps of his bag upon his back.

But then those two men came out into the yard and began to lever open the gates with their strong arms, and above the screeching of the iron within its ice-ridden runnels, he heard them talking.

'Just the bag, that's what Quaritch said,' said the first, and the second man laughed.

'Aye, the bag and the book. She'll scream blue murder, you do know that?'

'Not if we quieten her first,' said the first man, 'and, mind, he said not to do anything till she was decent distant.'

'We can't risk losing her,' said the second man, heaving at the gate, making a space large enough to squeeze himself through, began to pull it closed again, even as his companion was still negotiating the small opening.

'Leave it till tomorrow, at least,' said the first man.

'And miss a good night of it? Not likely,' said the second. 'Just let's get on with it. You heard what he said. She's no family, and no one to call for her if she's lost.'

'Just the bag,' whined the first man, 'that's all we need.' And the second man laughed again.

'Aye, right, just the bag.'

And Oravo pulled his back up straight against the tree, felt the rub of his sack against his hump, put one hand to tap at the hidden pocket in his jacket, and the other at the hammer he still had hanging from his belt.

'Aye, that'll be right,' his voice whispered through his throat like a stoat weaving through a rabbit hole, and he felt something snap together in his head, the snick of his shutters that last time he had closed them, the screech of the saw going through the green bole of the storm-felled elm. His thumbs were hooked into his belt, and his fingers trembled on the leather where their tips touched the cold metal of his hammer.

He looked after Griselda, but a swirl of snow lifted all around him, came down from the tree branches like autumn leaves, soughed about him as he came out of his hiding place. He couldn't see her, but could still hear the sound of her sticks lifting and falling as she made her way back down the track, the knock of them against the hidden stones and ruts, the faint splashing of slush melted by the few carriages wheels and horses that had passed by the printworks, going from town to town, village to village. And he could see the large imprints of the two men and their boots, watched them snaking off behind Griselda, started his own snaking off behind them.

The afternoon began to thicken and darken, great piles of heavy clouds seeming to sink out of the sky towards the earth, touching the tops of the low hills, tendrils detaching and creeping down their sides, hanging in the tops of trees, drawn to the river meadows and rolling a line of mist out across them so there was cloud above and cloud below, a calm space lingering between them, already scented with snow. Oravo knew that it would come, as surely Griselda must have done, and thought he might know where she would go. She could not get far, could surely not make the nine or ten miles to Stroud in what little remained of the daylight. Remembered the tumbledown cottage they had passed on their way here, how she had remarked how pretty it must once have been when it still had a door and all its windows; had pointed out the little orchard behind it that was nothing now but a tangle of broken-down branches, had been able to discern the furrows in the small patch of field beside it where potatoes must once have grown.

That was where she would go, thought Oravo, and he was right.

Barely an hour later, with the night only held apart from the earth by the glistening covering of its snow, she cut out from the track and started across to the small tumble of building. The two men went on a way until they passed the corner of the hill, presumably waiting for darkness. That was all right, thought Oravo, and gently took the slope behind them, aimed to come down on them from above, had already stowed his sack under a little pile of snow marked with a cairn-stone for later retrieval, needed only his strong woodman's hands and the hammer that was swinging from his belt.

'This is not right,' thought Eyvind Berwald, who was sitting in his sheep-circle of stones, wishing Onni was here and that he had someone to talk to, someone to think his way out of all that he had seen and done.

He had just heard of the death of the boy Steffan, and his slipping from the rocks; the very day, Eyvind thought, when he had tipped the guts of that excoriated lamb right over the cliff. He couldn't be sure, of course. The bare tangles of the boy's bones had only just been found, almost four months after his disappearance, lodged in the rocks the next bay down; they had only been discovered at all because of the exceptionally low tide, which had revealed rocks normally submerged, made it a day when men would come crawling over them to search more easily for lobster and crab.

Eyvind had heard them from his hidy-hole on the cliffs above, the banging of the wood as they scrambled from their boats, every sound large and loud in the dawn, the fractured talking as they worked, the hearty laughs as one or other of them hoiked out a prize with their fish-baited sticks. The other shouts of surprise, and then dismay, as they had pulled out something else, dislodged something of the boy's bones, his height and youth attested to by the femur that was found, the horror at the finding of his small skull, the peculiar lying of his teeth, with their overbite firmly above the lower jaw, and the two missing molars that one of the men knew to have been pulled when the boy's teeth had grown too fast for his mouth, and pushed the rest of them into a crown at the centre of his jaw. There were no clothes, nor flesh, but the consensus was clear and undisputed: this was Steffan, Tamas Swarthaar's lost son. And the men had collected what they could of the bones, and thrown back every last lobster and crab, knowing no one would ever touch them now, knowing them to have grown fat on human flesh.

Eyvind had wept that morning after he heard them talking, had pieced together the history of Steffan's disappearance, and known he had been the cause of the boy's awful demise.

And then he had done what he had been told by Torrensson never to do, and had approached the village from which the men had come, had lain himself down on the small mound above the graveyard, watched the slope-shouldered father standing to one side while the small coffin was brought up carefully from its grave, the wooden boards already beginning to break into soft splinters, stained a deep, dark brown from the peat in which they had been laid, the solemn lifting out of the stones one by one, and their lighter replacement of bones. His own grandparents were buried in this same soil, though he no longer remembered where, had always been pleased for them that they had been able to remain here where they had been born. Remembered the passing of his own parents in that strange land beyond the Dnieper, where they had been directed to resettle after the expulsion, the final hours of their twin fevers, the constant regret that they were dying far from home. And he thought of Onni out there somewhere on the surrounding seas, and wanted to cry out to him, and confess his sins, and ask for, and be given, his forgiveness.

Instead, Eyvind Berwald returned to his sheepfold and ran his hands through the ashes of his fire, rolled his skin grey amongst the embers as he had been taught to do as a child, when a body was burnt within its circle of stones, and a man could keep a little of his loss between his fingers, rub his skin with the one who was now gone, feel a little less keenly the barrier between the living and the dead.

The breeze caught the scents of creeping thyme and dog-rose scrub that anchored the sand to the dunes far below him, carried the soft sound of cranes and geese fanning their feet in the water of the inland pools, brought the memories of his childhood to him so sudden and sharp that his eyes blurred over with their images. He could feel again his own toes wriggling in the waters of a clear blue afternoon, with Onni still beside him, the excitement they had felt when they had netted up the squid stranded long ago by another exceptionally low tide. Remembered the rare mornings after storms, when they went down to the nooky holes in the rocks and pulled out those strange fish they didn't know the names of, with their spiny fins and jag-toothed jaws; the smells as their mother poached them on the stove, the way they had to scrutinise every mouthful to pick out the sharp spite of their bones. Remembered the long lines of mackerel they used to pull in at summer's end, the fish teeming about the island in silver-green throngs that never seemed diminished, the stink left behind on the beach as they piled the guts out of their catch one by one, the oil of fish-flesh clinging to their clothes and fingers for many days afterwards. Remembered something else, something he didn't want to remember, that just like the dead boy Steffan, he and Onni too had used to scale the cliffs around the bays for eggs. Not these exact same cliffs, of course, for they had lived further down the island then, almost to its other tip, but it was from round about here where his mother had been born, and here where her parents had lived out their days and died.

He tried then to picture the face of Tamas Swarthaar as he had stood by the graveside to give a final goodbye to his lost son, wondered briefly if he might have known Tamas as a boy, knew just as quickly that this couldn't be so, that the man was a good ten years his junior, and that Eyvind and Onni had probably been gone with all the rest before this man, was even knee-high grown.

14

Over Seas and Valleys and Broken Bridges

L IFE ON DECK had not been so very different those many years ago from how it was today, and the morning smelt as every morning had done then, of corn-flour patties frying in fish oil, and the pungent stench of salted cod being grilled upon charcoal fires. It pinched Griselda's nose, woke her within her blanket, gave her the faint but familiar knowledge that she had been here before. She opened her eyes, saw the haze of mist souk along the tops of softly breaking waves, felt the slight heave and give of boat-boards beneath her body, the gentle breathing of a calm and sleeping sea.

She rubbed her eyes, saw the sailors cooking in their half-cut barrels along the deck, smelt the scent of rain-damped straw their fires gave to the warming tar as it sank further into the salt-seeped wood, the damp cling of her clothes and the sourness that emanated from every pore of her skin, the skim of seaweed and the sprinkle of seabirds carried on the ocean back, the salt-sea brine that saturated the air, made it seem to scour her a little cleaner as she breathed it in.

It was all so precisely as it had been before that she could not help but feel the same excitement bubbling up within her as it had done then, that great expanse of sea that promised new and distant shores. For the first time since she had left the wreck of Lower Slaughter, Griselda felt the pulse of life tingling again inside her skin, behind her eyelids, inside her chest. She felt the salt upon her bruises and blisters, the hard crack of her bones, the rat's-nest of her hair, the thin layers of her clothes. Felt there might be healing yet to be had on this journey and a reason for the washing away of her old life, and the possibilities of a new one. She thought of her father, and wished he could have been here with her. Remembered how he had always talked of returning home, had spoken to her about it on her last visit to him back in March; remembered then that he had said he had some work to finish, but when he did, he would make proper plans to come back that very summer, and maybe take her with him. She had prevaricated then, made excuses about how busy she would be now that she had to run the bakery all alone, but that she would think about it, try to find someone to help her out, though she had known that she never would. And then he had up and died only two short weeks before the flood, left her grieving and guilt-stricken that she had not made the effort to visit him one last time, at least left him with the hope they would return soon to Hiiumaa together. Still, she'd been glad for him he'd gone the way he'd always wanted to go, dead as a stone-shot crow with no warning, no time for the lingering farewells he'd always hated. Or so the brief letter from Charles Quaritch had suggested, and so she had supposed.

Quaritch had written nothing in that letter of how things

had really gone; had not mentioned the angry confrontation between himself and her father, followed by the hard punch to Kustin's chest that had sent him staggering backwards towards the stool, which toppled him over, the faltering fall that followed, which cracked his ribs against the corner of his ink bench, the punctured lung that left him gasping for breath, even as his assailant stood over him, still muttering about secret inks and loyalty and recrimination. Had said nothing of the slow drip of mercury from the crucible and the spatter of pigments that had dusted Kustin's skin even as Quaritch had backed away, left him to die alone with no call for help, the strange stains and patterns those pigments had made upon his skin even after he had been discovered by one of his workmates and cleaned up. If she had known all this, she would not have been so puzzled at Charles Quaritch's hurry to hide her father in a box and get him buried so that no one else, especially Kustin's daughter, would ever see the way he had truly gone.

But Griselda knew none of this, and was only now, after his death, beginning to see her father through other people's eyes: his gentle ways, his lack of friends, his reluctance to leave Painswick, always waiting for his daughter to come to him even in those early days after she had found her position at the bakery two valleys over could only ever remember him coming to her once or twice; the devotion to his work, which amounted almost to obsession, the silence he had always kept about his other life, about Hiiumaa, and how little of it he had shared, even with her.

Griselda thought about her father now, but also found herself thinking of another whilst she sat upon that deck, looking

out over the calm, bright morning of the sea, saw the swirling
dimples over to portside, knew it meant a shoal of herring
were rippling and ribboning just beneath the surface, maybe
had a school of cod or porpoise on their tails, making them
jump and dance and weave and dip below the prow of the
boat and on. She found herself looking for Oravo, the strange
humped shadow of his form, saw his profile in every man
that turned the corner of the deck-house, and was strangely
disappointed to find it was not him. She wondered if she
had been wrong, if she had imagined glimpsing him every
now and then as she had crossed the country over from
Painswick to London, had had such a strong sense of him
being somewhere just behind her, somewhere just outside
of reach, but always there. It had been a comfort to her
throughout the five long weeks of travelling it had taken her
to reach Purfleet and this boat that was finally taking her to
her father's home, had developed an odd reliance upon his
unseen presence, found it gave her licence to do what she
was doing, that she was somehow being protected by his
guardianship. She thought hard about that now, and yet was
sure that since she had boarded the boat, she had not seen
him, though she had looked, had cruised it several times over
to see if he was there. Perhaps, she thought, he had been
behind her all the way across England, but was not prepared
to cross the seas to unknown lands. And who could blame
him? Oddly she felt the loss as keenly as she felt her father's;
regretted that there was no one at her side to share this deep
hunger she now felt for her returning. Wondered if perhaps
such a hunger had not always been buried deep inside her,
and whether or not it would have stayed there if the flood

had not stripped away everything of the intervening years, and if perhaps it had been Oravo who had brought it all out of her on their long walk over the moors, the hours and hours she had talked of her long-lost island and mined her memories, if perhaps it had been he, and not she, who had made this absolute decision that she should return.

Above the ruined bakery that had once been Griselda's home stood Stroop and Jack and Thomas, the horses idling, snuffling at the spare grass beside their hoofs. They looked down upon what remained of the valley and the mill, and comparative to what they had already seen, it didn't look too badly – the miller's cottage still had its walls, though much of its roof was missing, and the mill barn didn't look in such bad repair, was at least still standing, which was more than could be said for every other structure that had once sewn itself into the valley and its sides.

On closer inspection, Stroop could see that the wheel was smashed to smithereens and beginning already to rust within its pins, and that though the mill barn still stood erect, there were lines scoured high up upon its sides, spatters of weed and leaf plastered there by the flood and dried out, deep dents where heavier things had been thrust against it and then passed on. He was astounded to estimate their height at a full fifteen feet above the ground, could also now see that the furthest corner of the barn, which must have taken the brunt of the oncoming flood, had been cruelly dinted, the boards cracked and splintered, a few bare bones of the underlying piling stones revealed, the uneasy tilt of a supporting beam leaning far too low somewhere beneath. He had already been told that the building was insecure, that the first strong winds of autumn would most likely set the whole thing tumbling to the ground, and everything left inside would be reduced to rubble and dust. Not that there was much inside. The villagers had already been down the valley sides with fine and flanked precision, retrieving everything that was of value, fetching up every last pot and pan that they could find, anything that might be useful to whatever life they might be able to salvage for themselves, and all the grain the miller had managed to secure.

Stroop was already in possession of the bare facts before he had come here, having first gone to the monastery, where Jack and Thomas's sources up at Painswick had told them the remnants of Upper and Lower Slaughter had washed up after the flood. Most had already left, dispersing themselves about the county, some to relatives, others to the nearest towns to try to find work, the few who had refused to leave the valley they had been born to still labouring to rebuild their homes, trying to reclaim something of their ravaged fields and pastures, though they had no animal to work them, and no seed anyway to throw into the drills.

Stroop had wondered at this behaviour, why more would not have stayed to at least attempt to regain what they had lost, until he had actually come here. Only then had he understood the futility of that task, had seen the narrowness of the valley floor, and the shallow level that lay to either side of the river that ran through its centre. So benign had that sparkle of water looked that he had struggled to understand how it could so suddenly have risen up and destroyed the people who had depended on it for hundreds of years, thought surely this must have happened before, and if so, why hadn't everyone already rebuilt their houses back from the flood plain, or moved away the first time it had happened, and never come back?

It was the abbot at the monastery who enlightened him.

'This house of worship has been here for almost three hundred years,' Stroop had been told, 'and never in all that time has such an event been recorded.' The abbot had shaken his head. 'It was such a mild winter, such a sudden spring. We had potatoes coming up in February, peas and beans in March. It was unprecedented, and we all bowed our heads and gave our thanks to God for the good season to come.' He'd sighed then, opened a large ledger lying on his desk. 'We keep records of rainfall and notations of the weather. It was a custom introduced by one Brother Rufus back in 1621. He was a man of advanced ideas, and studied different methods of farming and fertilisation, improved the yields of almost every crop he studied. We still employ his methods, and are well known for our early sprouting vegetables and the abundance of our crops.'

He had moved the book across the desk to Stroop, and Stroop had seen the meticulous rows and lines of figures, admired their neatness, but made little of them.

'Look at the latest entries on the next page,' advised the abbot, and Stroop had flipped the page and looked, seen that rainfall had been high in January, February and March, and the small notations on the opposite pages that indicated the height and growth of certain crops. Saw the next entries, which indicated that April had brought an exceptional rise in temperature, at least until the second week. And then the storms had hit, the snow falling almost daily until the twentieth, when again the temperature had risen to unprecedented heights. He had his finger on the page, was moving it down, day by day, the abbot interpreting what he was seeing, though Stroop had already guessed. 'So much snow,' the abbot had sighed, 'so much snow lying on high ground, and then the thaw. The rivers were already high, and when the snow melted so suddenly and the winds . . . well, you know what happened.'

And so Stroop did, had already witnessed its effects as they rode over the ridge of the valley, had seen the entire lack of farms and houses he knew would have been there a few short months before, seen the fields that hemmed them scoured of topsoil, still littered with branches and the wasted bones of trees and animals, the carcasses of houses that had been stripped of roofs and walls, everything they had once contained turned inside out or taken away, or left damaged beyond repair or salvage. The only building that appeared untouched was the church of Lower Slaughter, but when he had asked about that he had been told that despite its calling, it had not been spared, had been filled right up to its knees with silt, that the pews had all but disappeared beneath the mud.

'We lost our verger in there,' the abbot had said, 'we found him a few days later, lodged behind the altar.' He had stopped then, closed his eyes. Remembered the bringing out of Verger Adamus, and the awful way he had been found, with his mouth and eyes all filled with silt and the only way he had been seen being the tips of his fingers protruding from the mud, and the top of the soiled silver monstrance he had been clutching in his hands.

★　　★　　★

They stood for a few minutes on that ridge, Jack and Stroop and Thomas, thinking about the verger and the other twenty-seven men and women who had been swept away or killed by falling timbers, tumbling masonry, tree-boles lashing their vicious way down with the water, the slides of mud that had come gushing down the sides of the hills above their homes, burying several children and the goats and sheep they had been calling home. They knew also about the miller, who had apparently survived the flood, but hanged himself soon after in the mill barn, an empty bottle at his feet, all the usable grain being piled up first in handy sacks beside the door. And they also knew from the abbot that the missing Eriksson and his suitcase had been to the monastery, had told the abbot he had come from Stroud, and before that from Painswick Printworks; had asked specifically for directions to the bakery, which lay on the opposite side of the river from the mill, and had gone back out into the storm despite being encouraged to stay.

'He had an errand,' said the abbot simply, 'and he was adamant. Said he had a message that must be delivered. There was a fearful wind blowing, but the snow had stopped, and we had no knowledge then of what would happen, so off he went. He can't have been two hours out before the flood struck, and I confess I never wondered about him before now. Possibly he never carried on down the valley when the weather deteriorated. He certainly cannot have made it to the bakery . . .' The abbot had stopped then, looked at Stroop, taken back the ledger of weathers, which had been kept for more than a hundred and fifty years, and Stroop had known what he was thinking.

'I fear your task will end most unhappily, Mr Stroop, for surely if he has been missing these last two months, then the storm must have taken him as it did so many others, and he is lost.'

Stroop thought on these last few words, and knew that most probably the abbott was right, and that Jarl Eriksson was no more. But now, as he stood above the wreckage of the millpond and saw the layout of the valley, and considered the time it had taken for them to reach it, he thought that perhaps the man with the suitcase might just have made it to the mill. The wind had been behind him, and the going easy with the snow melting from the ground. He wondered just how far the man had got after all. And so he went down over the ridge, sliding on his heels, Thomas streaking ahead of him as if it were a day for adventure, Jack staying up atop with the horses. And Stroop wondered about Jarl Eriksson, and what it was that had been so important that he had struck out into that storm to try to reach Griselda, for certainly it was she he had sought to find, thought it could only be the letter he had already collected from Kustin Liit, his old friend from Hiiumaa, and that whatever was in that letter had caused both him and Kustin much concern.

Stroop was beginning to form a theory, and not a nice one; had not foreseen that tracking a missing library might throw up so much dust and soil, so many things from a past he did not understand. Yet he understood this: that the man with the suitcase had visited his old friend and countryman, the inksman at Painswick Printworks, and that Charles Quaritch had lied about his visit; and that that same inksman had given Eriksson two letters, one of which Stroop knew to be for his daughter who had lived in the now ruined valley of Slaughter, and that the inksman, her father, had died very soon after Eriksson's visit. He also knew that though Eriksson had left the printworks with the letter for Kustin's daughter, he had gone first to Stroud to conclude some business, or so Thomas's masher-man had said, and that after a space of one or two weeks, he had then come here, asked directions at the monastery, and left its safety almost straight away, striking out into a storm he could surely have waited out for the couple of days it might take to pass, and yet he had left anyway. And then had come the flood, and that was the last anyone had heard of Jarl Eriksson and his Travelling Library, and the letters given him by the inksman, Kustin Liit, that he had been so anxious to deliver.

Stroop managed to assemble all these facts and still retain them whilst he scrambled without grace down the ruined hillside towards what was left of the old bakery. Thomas had somehow got twenty yards before him, and now had a large medallion of Lower Slaughter embedded into the backside of his trousers. Mabel would not have been pleased, and as Stroop thought of her, he wished she had been here alongside him, discussing what he had learnt, sliding down the hillside with him, scraping up her own little patch of Slaughter. Wondered if, even now, she were on her way back to London, hated to think she might get there before him, and find the house in Eggmonde Street empty and cold.

Just then, he reached the bottom of the valley, heard a few indistinguishable shouts from up above and turned to look back up at Jack, saw him waving his arms, trying to whistle by putting his fingers into the corners of his mouth as he had seen Thomas do, smiled because he knew Jack would never learn to make that piercing whistle Thomas had perfected, and waved back to signal he was safe, then turned away to look at the ravaged contours of what had once been the millpond, saw that the bridge between the bakery and the mill was entirely gone, only a few upstanding timbers either side spelling out what once must have spanned between them.

Stroop made his way to the small pier of splintered planks that was all that was left of the bridge, surveyed the wreckage of the bakery buildings to his left, the still extant edifice of the mill on the other side of the river to his right. He tried to envisage the waters rising to such a height that they had taken this place without an exhalation, and failed. It was Thomas, who started to drag a fallen timber across the weir, watched as it slipped into the millpond pool, who gave him his advantage.

'It wouldn't take much to do, Mr Stroop,' said Thomas, always cheerful, always looking for the bright side of things, never wanting to think back on the bad side of life that he had left behind. Stroop could not help but imagine that other river, that other bridge, underneath which Thomas had once lived, at least occasionally, and that other boy he had never met, but with whom Thomas had spent his early years. Toby, Stroop remembered, that was the boy's name. Toby, who had been taken from that bridge where he and Thomas had once slept, snatched up from right in front of Thomas's eyes, and never returned.

Thomas, however, seemed unaffected, was already trying

to figure a way over to the other side, was pulling snagged pieces of branches from the bank and out of the millpond, intent on his project of getting a way from one side to the other. Stroop though, stood motionless. From where he was, next to the empty husk of the bakery, he could see that the river wound a way round to the left, over the stone weirs to spread its width, went off into a bank of willow copses that stood to either side of the valley. They were all torn up now, that much was plain to see, their top branches still hung with roots and pieces of sacking that must have come from the villages up the river. Stroop wondered about that bend in the river, saw from where the old bridge must have stood between the bakery and the mill that the river must have coursed down over this weir and spread its tide out so much further. He remembered the height of the scour-lines he had seen on the mill barn's sides, moved his eyes up the sides of the valley where it narrowed briefly, the alder copses still clinging by their roots though their necks had been torn down by the floodwaters, the hook of the river where a tributary came down from the hill a few hundred yards away from them before spreading out to their right into a wide expanse of fields.

'Thomas!' he shouted, and Thomas immediately abandoned his beaver-like intentions, was standing within seconds at Stroop's side.

'Go down this bank, Thomas,' Stroop said, pointing at the place where the river had culled several feet from the valley side as it had turned its corner. 'Go all the way down to where you see that cutting.' He pointed to the place where a thin stream broke down from the valley above, taking its own toll of the hillside, wearing a deep gouge into the banks marked by a line of rushes at its base, the spray of stunted alders down its sides. 'I need you to get along above the tree line to where that stream comes down.' He was busy calculating the height of the flood waters, their fifteen feet above the present stasis, plus the several yards more where the water must have been skewed to one side as the valley narrowed and the river turned just as the tributary joined it, where the waters must have been pushed up briefly into the stream's incline before falling back down to the main banks of the river.

Thomas did as he was told, took a few moments to decide his path, nipped up behind the fallen stones of the bakery and hugged the side of the hill a few yards up from the sprays of willow copse, found a slip of earth that resembled a sheep trail pulled loose by the storm, a thin few inches of soil that were free of bracken and bramble and soft-skidding heather, hopped over mud-holes where the water had found a new way up from beneath the hillside, where the flood had cleared away the stones of ages and released the springs that had been searching for their release. He dodged the fallen logs and trees that had been pulled out from their roots and littered the banks at awkward angles, or coming to rest on the lean give of the willows, took his way past the skins of animals tethered to their branches like tents, crabbed a careful way across the screes of stones that had slipped down the hillside, rinsed and graded according to their size, waiting for the fine grit on the surface to be nudged back into movement by the finest touch.

Several times Stroop caught his breath as Thomas lost his

footing, started a slow skid downwards to the bank until he found a solid rock to brace his foot, had to claw his way back up on hands and knees.

It took him almost half an hour, but finally he got there, and Stroop put up his hands to shade his eyes from the sun that of a sudden had been liberated from a small grey thicket of clouds, saw Thomas wave briefly before disappearing into the gully made by the falling burn, knew his skinny arms were pulling themselves up the banks of the tributary to reach the place marked by the highest of the flood lines, would soon be searching the thickets of tangled debris as he had been told to do.

He jumped like a jackdaw to find Jack coming flailing down the hillside towards him in his own special way, completely on his backside, mud kicking up from where his hands and boots had been spread out to brake him, bumping over the stones like a hiccup that was hurtling towards its own ejection. Stroop put out his arms, caught Jack before he went sliding on down towards the river and impaled himself on the few posts that were left of the bridge.

'Mr Stroop!' He hardly had breath to say it, was flinging out one hand, despite Stroop's desperate hold to prevent him going further. 'Mr Stroop!' he tried again.

But before Jack had time to say another word, Thomas had reappeared from the gully, had put his fingers to the sides of his mouth and split the failing afternoon the whole way through with the kind of ear-shredding whistle that Jack could only dream of.

PART 2

HIIUMAA, AND ALL WHO WOULD SOON ARRIVE UPON HER SHORES

1

A Place of Trees-Chapels
and Discoveries

THE TREE-CHAPEL glade was as perfect in the green and orange of summer evening as Griselda had ever remembered. It was the second week of June, and the sun still hung like a moon in the western sky, its soft, cool light playing through the trees a few calm hours before midnight. Clouds of gnats circled lazily in the pine branches, and the mole-crickets had surfaced from their burrows and, maybe expecting darkness and finding none, had straddled the air with their strident churring, frogs singing out sporadically from the lake-side that lay somewhere beyond the line of trees. The great boulder gleamed red at the centre of the glade, the inscribed names of the island's ancestors catching shadows where they had been etched into its surface, the soft sounds of birds still whirring amongst the leaves of the trees.

Griselda stood beside the stone, swaying slightly with her tiredness and content, had landed on Hiiumaa only hours before, disembarked from the boat at a pier she did not recall at all, nor the tall white stanchion of a half-built lighthouse that had stood its guard. Still, she had known where she was well enough, and had not needed directions, just placed her weary, blistered feet upon the track that would take her back to the village she had left when she was a child, could not believe she had forgotten so many details of a place so beautiful and so right that it seemed to her that the soil itself was hugging at her boots to welcome her home.

Above her, the circlet of chapels threaded through the trees like a wreath, so much more astonishing than she remembered, so much more sacred. She saw the ancient, twisting trunks of chestnuts carved with steps into the spirals of their bark, the conical hoods of chapels made from ever-decreasing circles of wooden slats to form their roofs, the oaks and yews that had been hollowed by their age, doors chapped out within them so that a man might enter, kneel at the small altars chiselled into the hardwood of their centres, the runs of boardwalks supported by branches and lengths of rope that went from one tree to another, places on the bark worn smooth by hundreds of years of hands leaning upon them, ledges cut into the barks of beeches to house the tiered lines of candles, which shook and quivered with the few flames that had been lit, even though the night was light as snow and only lasted the few hours after midnight before the world turned again upon its axis, and brought another morning so swiftly, the night had barely begun.

She raised one hand up to her forehead and down and over, made the habitual sign of the cross and bent her knee towards the stone. She did not remember performing this act of reverence before, yet felt no surprise that there was some small resonance of her childhood still within her. Had felt it with every wave that had brought her nearer to this island, with every glimpse of rock and bay, with every step up from the boat's landing, every inhalation that was laden with this island's salt and sand.

My island, thought Griselda, my own island. And she took a few steps forward, opened up her father's knapsack, which she had strung about her neck, removed the short, sharp mason's knife that had been in the little cache of possessions he had left her, and set its blade against the stone.

Out in the Pike Gut, the *Osil* was at ease, the men seemingly happy at their rest. The action of the past few months had been productive, if sporadic, and they had several times boarded, though not sunk, other merchant vessels passing from Estonia to Sweden or back again, had increased the rumours that the waters around the islands of Saaremaa were no longer safe, that piracy was on the increase, and that the threat of attack might soon overcome the rewards of any trade with the islands at all.

Onni Berwald was still there, though he carried out his orders without conviction. He didn't know it, but there was one other besides himself who was no longer so easy with their apparent calling, and that was Captain Gunar Torrensson himself.

Torrensson had spent so long curdling the milk for his rebellion, skimming off those who had risen to the top, preparing himself for this one war above all the others that he had fought, that he no longer knew how to stop. But he had also known for some time now how specious were his arguments, how appalling might be the ends to which he had for so long devoted his attentions, had noted the increase of foreign activity in the area, the battles fought between the English, Swedes and Russians in the waters of the Baltic, the dragging in of others, even the Danes, all threatening to blow all his plans out of the water. He tried to cling to his history of Hiiumaa, which had always been the spur that drove him on. He had spent his whole life being swapped from one army to another, first for Sweden, and then against it; now for Russia, then back for Sweden once more, whichever his masters told him. He had based his whole campaign upon this infidelity to his origins, and sought only to find something that would keep him true, had thought that in the re-formation of the Brethren of the Sword, he would find it. But he was not the only surviving captain of so many wars for nothing, and he understood strategy and planning, and recognised that his own was very close to being undermined.

He thought of Onni Berwald, and the many nights he had seen him stand apart upon the deck, away from the crowing and carousing of his crewmates. It had made him think more and more of Eyvind, Onni's brother, all alone now on Hiiumaa, and Torrensson wondered how sound his judgement of that man had been. Eyvind didn't know much, but he knew enough, and times were becoming more hazardous than even Gunar Torrensson had factored in. The *Osil's* piratic forays had been more successful than he had ever hoped – perhaps too much so. On a brief, incognito visit to Tallinn to garner what he could from his many sources, he had discovered that the English were becoming a little too interested in his activities, were planning their own incursions into these waters, had their own schemes to hatch against the Russians and the Swedes, and would not tolerate interference. If the *Osil* came up against a British man-of-war, that would be the end of everything, bar a handful of splinters upon the waves. Not that the English cared a penny for the islands, not even enough to learn their names, but they had always supposed, in their varied battles, that the waters surrounding them were to be considered neutral, which was, of course, to their advantage; and if that status quo was threatened, the English were not averse to taking drastic action, like placing a seaworthy mobile garrison upon one of the islands, for example. And that was something that Torrensson didn't want, didn't want at all.

Time, he thought, was playing against him, and in such a situation he was going to have to do what any general would do in such circumstances, and that was to eliminate the weakest link before it had time to betray him, and attack the threat before the threat had time to attack him. And Torrensson knew such a time had come and he needed to consolidate his forces, tie up a few loose ends, and tie them up himself. The time, Gunar thought, was upon him, and it wouldn't be that much longer before he could complete his task. And so he made his preparations, and as evening folded into night, he lowered down a boat, and slipped himself away from the *Osil*.

As Gunar Torrensson departed the *Osil*, so too was Mabel leaving, indeed had already left. She'd been on the barge from Astonishment barely an hour when it was stopped and she was hopped on to a carriage that had taken her directly to Carlisle. From here, another short journey had taken her to the docks and deposited her on a packet boat that sailed the country round and round, and landed her the next day, sick with worry and anticipation, in somewhere called Bristol, although it looked exactly the same, if bigger and more frightening, as the port from which she had just come.

A lone man was set to guard her and her baggage amongst the terrifying hurly-burly of the docks, who kept telling her in his almost unrecognisable accent that she should stay there, and wait. And so she did, stayed just where she was told for several hours, too frightened to move away from her guard, too fascinated to notice too much the passage of time. And then with no apparent signal or warning, the man who had been sat on her baggage all this time, apparently asleep, suddenly came to life, hauled everything bar Mabel onto his shoulder and beckoned her with him, Mabel scrambling to keep up.

She felt like an ant in a chicken yard as she ran after him, searching for his strong shoulders and threadbare cap amongst the many, many others, the noise rolling against her like boulders in a fast-moving stream. How he managed to find his route was a mystery, but he threaded his way onto a ship that seemed to Mabel to be falling apart at the seams. The crew were scurrying all about the boards, pouring pots of tar into cracks and crevices, raising and lowering sails, doing a hundred other things she found completely unfathomable. Her guide took her up the steep gangplank, and to a cabin that was little more than a garden shed deposited upon the deck, and put her luggage down.

'Good voyage, miss,' he said, and then he turned and was gone. Nothing more. No waiting for a coin, no words of where she should go or what she should do, whether she needed to have some kind of ticket. Nothing. The tears came up like a serpent within her throat, and she wished she were home again in London, or better, that she had never left at all.

She was restless as she waited for who knew what, sat on the rickety board that passed for a bed, then stood, then sat, smelt things she had never smelt before, which left her feeling nauseous, decided she needed air, tied her hat fast against her head and ventured to open the planks of the door, and walked a few yards out onto the deck, clutching at the rusting railings, ruining the gloves that Violena had given her as she left. Men were winding ropes and lowering great loads and crates into the holds, and though Mabel looked hard, not once did she see anyone who looked remotely like another passenger, and she had an acute anxiety that she would be set adrift upon the seas with no name and no ticket and no one to tell her where she was going or why she was there.

And then it was that she looked across the frightening bustle of the docks, the great forest of masts, which looked like birches stripped for winter, and found something at last upon which to latch her eyes. There was something familiar there, amongst it all, something she couldn't quite make out and yet which gave her comfort. Something that looked exactly like Mr Stroop on a very bad day, leaning against a crate as if he were a broken walking stick, two figures lighting around him like jumping beans.

Could it be? she thought. But how could it? And yet, and yet, the more she looked, the more she thought it was so: it was Jack and Thomas, and Mr Stroop, and for a few moments, Mabel stood looking, trying not to blink, afraid that if she did, she would find them gone.

There was another person upon a different boat who had watched and wondered whether what he saw was real or no, and that was Isaac, the bargeman. He had been surprised enough that Stroop and his boys had actually turned up when and where they'd said they would be, ready for their return trip to London, happy for them that they appeared to have achieved their goal. He was less happy that barely had they set their feet upon his barge, when a huddle of horses had come beating along the towpath and assailed them, a stern grey man, all decked out in some kind of impressive livery, stopping them as they were about to cast away. Isaac recognised with ease that these were port men, men who usually came to rattle their swords and muskets, throwing their weight about your boat as if it were their own, question whatever it was you had on board, slap warrants on whatever they deemed to be inappropriate cargo, caused their own trouble, demanded money just because of who they were and where they happened to alight.

But there was none of that this time. There was only a letter put into the passenger Stroop's hands, which he looked at a few times over, must have read it skin from skin and word for word at least three times, and then turned to Isaac, asked him to delay his throwing out of the ropes and their imminent departure. And Isaac knew then that he would not get his passage back to London in the company of Jack and Thomas and their Mr Stroop, and he felt such a hard knot in his throat that he could hardly bear it. Couldn't begin to say what it would have meant to him to have that silly, simple boy by his side at the tiller for just a few more days, that somehow he represented the whole world of wife and sons and family that had been denied him all these lost, long years. He was ashamed to feel the tears begin to prickle at his eyes, and the burn of regret within his throat.

Stroop took the boys to one side, spoke first with them and then with the grey man who stood like a pillar beside his horse upon the towpath. Then told Isaac he was sorry, that there had been an urgent change of plans, paid him anyway, despite Isaac's protestations. Stroop and his boys stepped up from his barge and were hoisted onto the backs of the grey men's horses, and – here was what he could hardly believe – one of them had slipped himself off again, come jumping back onto the barge, making it shake and shiver. It was Jack, and he had come right up to Isaac and stood before him, solemnly taken the carved coal talisman from his neck and put it around Isaac's own.

'For health and luck,' Jack said, 'just like you told me. It's brought me loads already, so fair do's we share it round.'

Isaac blinked so hard he had to screw up his eyes, couldn't speak for a moment, coughed briefly. Then he regained himself and tousled Jack's hair.

'Thank you kindly for that, young sir,' he managed, and then he held up a finger, dipped back briefly under the canvas of the deck and brought out the little figure he had been carving all the while he had been waiting for their return. 'And this is for you, that your life may be the longest and healthiest and happiest any man has ever seen.' And he had opened his palm, revealed the small black pendant, shiny and smooth: two small boys standing side by side, each with an arm around the other's neck.

'It's me and Thomas!' Jack shouted in delight. 'We're proper brothers now, aren't we, Mr Isaac?'

And all Isaac could reply was a small, quiet, 'Yes, Jack, yes, you are.'

From Isaac's barge, the stiffly uniformed men jogged Stroop and the boys right back down the track from which they had just come. And all the while, Stroop was fighting furiously with himself, the one half battling against the other. The one half telling him to go with the baron's impassioned plea that Stroop should proceed to Hiiumaa, with or without the missing library or news of Jarl Eriksson, that other things were going on of which he had need of Stroop, and the other half that told him he should just throw the whole thing up and go home. The boys, of course, were boys, and had opted for adventure and unknown lands, had no idea the dread Stroop held of such unknown places and the ways that had to be taken to get there.

He thought also of Mabel, and knew she would already be on her way back to London, just because he had asked her. Found it hard to bear that she would arrive at a home without anyone to greet her, that not even Bindlestiff would be by the stove to snuffle at her feet, and felt an overwhelming guilt that he knew he was about to succumb to his curiosity yet again, and that the offer of a berth to the unknown land of Hiiumaa and its troubles would entice him away against his better judgement, and against his need to see her again.

And so, all the while they followed the road from Bradford-on-Avon into Bristol, that guilt rode Stroop like an angry weasel upon his back. He tried to shift his insecurities once they came into the huggermugger of the docks, immediately thrust a hastily scrawled note into one of the accompanying men's hands, told him it needed to be sent without delay to London, tried to shift his eyes up amongst the impossible shuffling of the sails, seeking out the one they had been told to find with the Swedish ensign flying high upon its brow. They ploughed through what seemed like a foreverment of crowds and stevedores and people pushing here and there and at them back and forth, were at last told to stop while the final arrangements were agreed upon. And then Stroop felt a sudden thud to his heart and a tightening of his throat; thought he recognised one small figure leaning alone against one of the deck-rails, took such a sudden intake of breath that he almost fell. Then Jack was jumping up beside him, shouting loud enough to split his eardrums, and Stroop felt as if something inside him had suddenly snapped like a band that had thudded him against a wall and brought him back to life.

'It's Mabel!' Jack shouted. 'I can see Mabel!' And Stroop's skin began to sing and dance because he knew that surely Jack was right, and that he saw the same slight figure just as Jack did, and there could be no doubting it. It was Mabel, and though Stroop didn't know how or why she had got here, he knew that she was there all the same and had seen them too, and was waving and waving and waving, like it was the last thing in the world that she had left to do.

2

Death, and Reunion

Gunar Torrensson had lowered the small barque down into the evening and rowed it alone towards the shore. He had told the few men who knew he was going that things were moving faster than he supposed and he had urgent need of speaking to Eyvind Berwald, his man upon the island. He could see the dark shine of the *Osil's* sails disappearing behind a reef, where they would lie at anchor and await his return. He had told no one of his real reason for this embarkation, would never mention the tremor he felt go through his whole body when he first put his feet upon the sands of Hiiumaa, and ran the grains of its sands through his fingers. Would never tell anyone how he had come across the bay towards the marked stone he and Eyvind had agreed upon to leave messages and the occasional sack of apparently ship-wrecked supplies; that he hadn't even bothered looking, had gone instead straight up the hard push of cliff, heading for the place he knew his man had been encamped these past few months, searching for the small corral of stones, the telltale signs of shelter a man might have made. Would never have told anyone either of the sudden intoxicating rush he had felt finally to be upon this land, this soil, his renewed conviction that the New Brethren must succeed no matter the cost, that more than anything he needed now a place he could call his own, be able to throw off the fickleness and shillyshallying of other men's wars, be able to command his own army in the defence of his own chosen land.

He crept instead like a wolf across the moors, took in the scent of it, already felt as if it was his own, this little piece of world that had been made in his own likeness, waiting, waiting, just for him.

Eyvind Berwald was thinking his own thoughts, conjuring memories mostly long forgotten. He had been eighteen or so when he'd had to leave Hiiumaa with his family, and was in his mid-forties now by his reckoning. He had lived a long life for a soldier and was happy for it, happier still to have been able to keep his younger brother, Onni, by his side and safe. More grateful that no matter the circumstances, he had been allowed a brief chance to return. One thing he did regret was the putting onto the fire too many of the old broom branches he had spent so long collecting, worried that the too-dense smoke might be seen, or someone notice the acrid, cat's-piss smell of their branches, their arms grown too quick and green in an early spring, stopped up again as a second winter took hold and the ends dried and withered away.

He heard a small step somewhere out on the moor as if sheep were foraging gently amongst the heather, and was glad for their company despite his worries, and the comfort of the softly smoking fire. By habit, he checked again the bruise his knife had made that first foray out, had gained a certain satisfaction in maintaining its existence ever since by his poking and prodding, sometimes thumping at it with a sharpened stone, just to keep it there. It had become his own meagre atonement for the sacrifices he had made to the cause he no longer believed in but could not fail, not for his own sake, but for fear his defection would have bad consequences for his brother who was still on board the *Osil*. But mostly it was for the death of the boy Steffan that he grieved, and for which he blamed himself, and for which he knew there could be no true atonement.

Eyvind was wrong about that, for his atonement was now upon him with the garrotte slipping silently about his neck and tightening before he had time to realise what was happening, dragging him back against the wall of the abandoned sheep byre, set his arms and legs kicking against the old stones, clambering heels sending small eruptions of ash and ember up from the edges of the fire, the thin strength of the wire causing his blood to start its course down his bared-back neck, just as the cat's blood had taken its uneven delta down the boards of Von Riddarholm's barn.

Eyvind did not comprehend immediately what was happening, felt only his head being overfilled of a sudden with the deep dark wave that is every sailor's dread, the fear of drowning turning his whole body to water, the horror of being swallowed up by the lonely night of some vast ocean, the terror at dying with no one else's hand upon his own, the small blink of the claustrophobic sky bearing down upon him like the nail

of a coffin; but within half a second he knew the awful stricture at his neck for what it was, caused his thoughts to split
and splay for lack of oxygen, knew only the crack of his own
bones as his eyes no longer saw anything but the blood that
filled them, the last desperate scrabbling for a glimpse of the
sun, another tug of air, tried to call out, make out Onni's name,
but saw only Steffan's bones beating down upon him, tried to
stop his struggling, wanted to embrace some kind of salvation
yet felt the pain and flex of his body as it fought on despite
him, the push of his lungs like overblown toad-throats breaking
against his ribs, the tingling in his fingers and toes as if the fish
and crabs were already nibbling at his skin, the prickle of starfish
and urchins rasping their slow way across his body, the grit of
sand in his mouth and his limbs as he slowly subsided to the
bottom of his life's sea, the bloody weep of his eyes and the
taste of it in his mouth, the final blink of phosphorescent green
that might have been that boy's vengeful spirit, or the slick-by
of a ghost-fish, or the salute of a sun as it slipped down the
horizon, promising that for Eyvind, it would never rise again.

Torrensson pulled at the garrotte again and again, tightened it until the wire dug deep into Eyvind's skin. He did
not know he could be so angry, and yet anger had been his
overwhelming emotion as he had slipped the wire over
Eyvind Berwald's head and pulled and pulled and pulled.
And when it was done, he sat back against his side of the
wall and fought for breath, removed himself from what he
had done, as he had always been able to do, got his breathing
back to normal, extracted his garrotte and cleaned the blood
off upon the heather, and came back around the wall of the
sheep byre and began his search.

Torrensson looked through every pocket on Eyvind Berwald's body, even the thin wallet he'd tied below his shirt, found in it only a few coins. He searched further then, put his hand behind every loose stone in the byre walls and pulled them down, still could not find what he was looking for. Was disturbed to hear someone coming up the short tug of the cliff, his short hard breaths carried on the wind, and suddenly, immediately, Torrensson ceased his search and looked up to where that other man suddenly emerged and stood upon the cliff's edge, hands braced against his thighs as he looked back the way both he and Torrensson had come.

Torrensson knew this meant trouble, that the man must have seen the boat Torrensson had left beached upon the shore, would have recognised it for what it was, a two-man coble lowered from a ship, would maybe wonder why the coble was there but not the boat, for the *Osil* was out at anchor and hidden, and the evening mists were rising from the seas. Yet even as Torrensson watched him, the man abruptly turned his face towards the moors, put his hand up to his eyes, and Torrensson could see the shape of him then, the strange hump between his shoulders, the oddness of his clothes, which were not those of any normal islander.

Torrensson also knew that if he could see this man, then the man must just as well be able to see him, and that he himself was not a man easily mistaken, with his black bear of a beard and the stature that would intimidate most men, just as it had intimidated, and now killed, Eyvind Berwald. He smiled grimly as he recalled Eyvind coming to him with his half-baked plans of dates and mutilations, had known then he was a weak one, knew also what one weak man

160

with his doubts could do to another. Had once seen a man
line up three trees in a forest, gone at them with his axe in
just such a way that when the first one fell, it took the second
with it, and the second one took the third. That was what
would happen the moment Eyvind Berwald fell, and the first
man he took with him would be his brother, Onni, and then
Onni would take another with him and another after that.
And so he had let Eyvind think he had made his own way
out of Torrensson's rebellion with his plan, had even thought
the plan might after all have its uses, knew the value of unset-
tling the populace at the basest level, had applauded the idea
of the Fourteen Helpers as Eyvind had shown him his list,
expounded the undercurrent of disquiet he could sow upon
the island, make Torrensson's final execution of his scheme
so much the easier.

And yet it hadn't changed the fact that Eyvind was their
weakest link, and the time to get rid of him was now. The
only thing Torrensson needed from Eyvind's cooling body
was the list of saints and days, the scrawls Eyvind had put
beside their names as Torrensson had helped him refine the
plan, expounded it out afterwards to his faithful men, incor-
porating the structure of the Fourteen Helpers into the cause
of the Brethren. But he still hadn't found that list when he
spied that other man coming over the cliff.

He's found a friend, Torrensson thought immediately on
seeing the stranger. Of all the men I have recruited, only
Onni and Eyvind actually used to live here, and he has weakened, and put himself in contact with someone he used to
know.

At first Torrensson swore with all his anger, and then he

stepped over Eyvind's body and vaulted the wall of the sheep byre, took just a moment to watch the man who was coming over the cliff towards him and fix his shape and form within his mind, knew he didn't have much time, and that the night was almost down, and that now he would have to go a circuitous route back down to the bay and the boat and out to the *Osil*.

But then Torrensson had another thought. One man down, he calculated, and what more harm to do in another?

What Gunar Torrensson had no way of knowing was that the man who was coming over the cliff was Oravo Swan, and that he had breathed only one short hour of Hiiumaa's air, and saw nothing as he stood there by the edge of the cliff, except the sea and the mist and the plantain pollen that had yellowed his boots, was instead wondering at the flash of pink as the burnet moths took up from the asters in the evening light, and the litter of abandoned sheepfolds sprinkled along the furthest edges of the cliff where the winter gales had gradually shorn away its edges, left the sheepfolds too close to the drop to be safe for the sheep, had to hold his hands up against the sun to see anything at all and, only looking for somewhere he too could hide himself, had not seen Torrensson at all.

It had taken Oravo a while to get here, was almost two weeks behind Griselda and her landing. By the time he had reached Purfleet his money was all gone, and though he had tried to wangle a way on board any ship going Griselda's way by offering his skills, the only one that would take him had been going a much more meandering route across the sea and islands to Hiiumaa.

He had followed Griselda for so long and felt so close at only his one pace behind her that he ached to see her sailing off without him and his protection, felt an unexpected wrench at being so far away from her and for he did not know how long. He had cursed every port his boat had tarried at, felt sick with worry every day that she had gone forward and he lagged behind. He had spoken to no one who was not necessary to his work on the voyage over, hardly understood them anyway with their few words of English, and his own words spoken in an accent they did not understand. But they admired Oravo's easy, workman's hands, and the way he had looked over the timbers he had been shown, selected several for his purpose, passed the test or trap they had laid for him in that selection, and afterwards spent as little time as possible in his company, preferred to play at cards while Oravo went about the work that should have been their own, spent much longer playing cards and drinking than they had ever done on any other voyage, and thanked him for it with a few vague waves of their arms.

Alone on board, Oravo had rediscovered something of the same deep peace he had always felt when picking out the tools that he would need to do his work, and the biting rhythm of the saw, the regular push of plane and rasp, the gradual shaping of a piece of wood until it fit its right purpose. He had always thought how much simpler life would be if people could be shaped and shaved in just this way, made to join and cleave the niches that were made for them, wondered if perhaps he could not carve himself into the right and correct configuration, and knew that this was why he had followed Griselda all this way, just for the chance of it, the faint hope that he could slide himself inside her life like a bolt within its lock.

When they finally reached Hiiumaa, Oravo had disembarked with the rest as if he had a place to go, had itched with curiosity, wanted to know where Griselda was and in which places she had stood as a child, what bay it was where the sand shrimps had hatched and jumped over her feet, made her so frightened to step on them that she had stopped where she stood for half an hour before someone came to rescue her; where the caves were that she had sworn had been filled with the songs of whales that made your whole body sing to hear them, the places where men had died trying to follow the smugglers' paths into the cliffs. But most of all, he wanted to see the tree-chapel glade that she had so vividly described, could almost feel the Stone of Ancestors at its centre beneath his fingers. Knew also that this was no time to reveal himself to her, that such a thing would only give her fright, that he would need to wait and hide himself, try to think of some reasonable explanation of why he had come here on her heels.

As the quay began to empty, he saw the way that everyone was heading, and took the opposite path, went away from the harbour and the lighthouse and the track that he guessed must go up to the nearest village, went instead over the headland, towards the bay. He had shrugged down upon the stones and sand that swam at the edges of the softly breaking waters, noted with some interest the piles of driftwood that littered its tidemark, the lines of rocks that striated the bay, riding out in jagged angles from the beach, the spilt bones of a boat caught upon their reefs like some gigantic walrus, bleached and splintered, the thin passage of flat water at the furthest end, making an inlet from sea to bay that might allow a rowing boat taken carefully, saw just such a one drawn up upon the sand.

He could make out a rough pathway zigzagging up the squared sandstone blocks of the cliff, the yellow-and-pink pockets of rockrose and rocket, the prickly sprawl of salt-wort and pennycress that marked a spring of water coming up from somewhere deep within the stone. Without knowing it, he took the same path that Eyvind Berwald had taken that first time he had been landed here, the same path Gunar Torrensson had taken a few hours since, pulled himself up by the same handholds, came to the same expanse of tussocky moor that met him at the sandstone's edge, stood in almost the same place that Eyvind had once done, caught his breath, holding one hand across his brow to shield his vision from the sun, saw the calmness of the sea before, the slow undulation of it below him, as if some unseen hand were stroking it from beneath, saw the soft tendrils of mist as they rose like feather-down from the gentle roll of waves upon its surface.

He had no idea that a man lay newly garrotted within one of the broken-down sheepfolds scattered all about him, nor that another man was watching him even now, a man who might have come from another world, a man who was already planning how to dispatch Oravo into the next.

3

Comfort and Confession

'I HAVE BEEN rather short in my explanations,' Baron Josef Von Riddarholm was saying – a bit of an understatement in anyone's estimation, thought Stroop.

He still had not recovered from the shock of the voyage to which he had so recklessly agreed, had landed on Hiiumaa barely an hour since, still felt the ground rocking beneath his feet, his stomach twisted within him as if it had been drawn through a mangle. He recalled the vivid fear that had come over him to watch the vast blue strikes of lightning that had hit at the water's surface not two hundred yards distant from the ship-rails, the way the sea had trembled as if some kraken had just awoken, saw again the brief phosphorescent flash of fish against the ship's side before they turned belly up and died, the shockwave hitting the boards like a hammer to a knee-bone, making it jerk fiercely first to one side and then the other. Overhead came a growl of thunder so loud and low you could hear it thrumming through the boards below your feet, the strange fresh tingle he could smell upon the air, the eerie lack of wind, as if the world had hesitated for just a moment before snapping shut its jaws.

Jack and Thomas, of course, had no such ominous trepidations, were running up and down the deck yelling like screech owls, tumbling over with the lurch of the ship, rolling over and over before tugging themselves up by one another's sleeves and carrying on with their inexplicable race. Stroop's heart was beating in his throat with the worry, convinced the next strike would have at their masts, send the boys rolling over the edges, could still see the balls of St Elmo's fire at the sails, was terrified the men already in the rigging would burn up like moths in a flame.

And then Mabel moved up close beside him, her hat battened down upon her head so he could see only the tip of her nose twitching briefly, and then the storm clouds moved on and over them so swiftly that its next strike came a quarter-mile distant towards the east, seemed to be leaping faster and faster across the surface of the sea in its blue-tipped, seven-league boots. Only then came the huge surging tumbrel of wind rolling right against them, sending the ship into a ghastly dance, which had them hauling and clawing at every surface, Jack and Thomas suddenly there and laughing beside him, everything unsecured tumbling all about them, clattering against the winch reels and the decking, slipping through the rails and out across the surface of the sea. Stroop felt only the wind in his mouth stealing his shouts of caution, the rain battering against his face, Mabel's hand still steady upon his own. And out of all that, he suddenly felt his own small laughter gurgle up within him, that they were standing there all together, falling, hauling themselves upright, falling down again, his fear abating as quickly as did the storm.

'No notebook, Mr Stroop?' Mabel asked as the storm

moved on and they found their feet, stood looking out across the now-dead stretch of water that lay all about them, England somewhere to their left, Denmark somewhere towards the right.

'Maybe later,' he said, his voice still shaky, feeling her cold hand press against his own, glad beyond reckoning that she would be there to help him, realised that without her and Jack and Thomas he would be so far diminished that all the Sense Maps in all the world would make no sense at all.

'I have been rather short in my explanations,' the baron was still saying, Stroop trying to blink away the journey that had brought them here, landed them upon these alien shores. They'd hardly had time to realise where they were, had been led so quickly down the gangplank, into a pony trap and brought up to the manor house, which grew like a solid, square boulder of stone and wood from out the ground, with the single aberration of one corner tower being built much taller than the rest. The whole place was austere and formidable, the room they were in spacious and uncluttered, sparsely laid out with carved wooden furniture of monumental proportions. The baron had greeted them personally, shaken Stroop's hand, bowed low to Mabel. He had then suggested – rather shortly, Stroop had thought – that the children and Mabel be taken off and shown their rooms, while he and Stroop had a quiet word. It was the last thing Stroop had wanted, had felt pale and worn as driftwood, but allowed himself to be led away into this vast cavern of a room. The baron had apologised profusely for Stroop's discomfort, made him sit, brought him a vast globe of a glass awash with brandy, at which Stroop could not help but suck and sip; and only then, when his body had settled back into a steady breathing, into the stillness of a world that did not move beneath his feet, only then did Stroop notice that his hand still clutched at the strap of a small suitcase, and that the baron's eyes could not help themselves, but had fixed upon it like an owl that has spied his mouse in the vast, dark field below his wings, waiting for his moment to swoop out of the night and take it for his own.

Stroop took another, slower sip of brandy, then gently untangled his hand and pushed the battered case towards Von Riddarholm.

'I have no idea if this is what you wanted me to find,' said Stroop, with some inaccuracy. He didn't know at all if this was really Jarl Eriksson's missing miniature library, assumed in fact quite the opposite – that the luck that had gone into its finding was incompatible with its sure recovery. Remembered being back in the valley of Lower Slaughter, and at the monastery, and the confirmation of what Stroop had assumed: that Jarl Eriksson had indeed set off to Griselda's house, and must have been caught up in the catastrophic storm and flood that had decimated the valley and all that lived within it. He had thought then that the chances of anyone recovering him or his suitcase ever again were negligible. Either one could have been taken many miles down the river on its bore, or washed up on the banks scoured several times over by desperate villagers. The case might have been broached by the brunt of the angry water, its seals burst open, its precious contents soaked into scum. But as Stroop had stood on the abandoned pilings of the millpond bridge that morning, he had seen what very few others would have seen. He had noted the width of the water and the height of its detritus, had realised that the washing away of the bakery bridge and buildings would have stumbled and slowed the waters for just a few moments, maybe long enough to push the smallest of the debris out towards its edges, had seen the crevice where the river would have risen up to meet its tributary.

It had been the slimmest of chances for such an object to land and lodge, slimmer yet that Jarl Eriksson could have been supposed to be walking near the bridge at that time, and yet, as Thomas had discovered as he tore his shirt and scraped his knees scrambling through the scrub of willows and alder that lined the ascent of the crevice, there had been just the wink of a possibility that with the huge influx of bakery-building beams and bricks and the collapsing of its walls, some such thing might have been thrown above the height of the roaring thunder of the waters and caught in the scroggle of branches and bramble and thickets of sloes that lay at the topmost height of the storm surge.

The suitcase was an object supremely well made for its purpose, an outer casing of strong, light metal, a thin inner skin of leather soaked with wax, and another even thinner, inner lining of metal. It was sealed as well as any casket made to be dropped into the sea and still be proofed from water, more airtight than an embalmer's coffin. And like a coffin, the walls inside were softened with velvet, each tiny book caught into its compartment by a strong silk ribbon.

And against all the odds, there it had been, and Thomas had found it, just as Stroop had seen it landing in the landscape of his mind with its little lines of calculation and perspective, load and lift. It was battered and pitted, each of its corners dinted into uneven curves, and its handle was entirely missing, yet still the locks had held and the sealed sides were unbroken. Thomas had dragged it out from amongst the scattered heaps of reeds and rags and broken-bottomed pots, and brought it out triumphant.

Even then Stroop had not been certain he had the right case, despite Thomas's whistle splitting down the valley. All the way over to Hiiumaa, Thomas had begged to be allowed to practise his lock-picking skills, which admittedly were pitiful despite his constant attempts, but Stroop had forbade him. Had surmised that the cogs and pins would be overwhelmingly compromised by rust and sand and mud, and that short of having at the thing with a hammer and chisel, there would be no way in. And this Stroop absolutely would not do, not even to assuage his own doubts, knew enough of those tiny books to realise that if this really were the right case, and the books were really still inside it and intact, then the moment the case was opened, they might yet need a specialised hand to save them.

Stroop hadn't been sure, not at all, that this battered suitcase was the one he had been seeking, not until this very moment, when he began carefully disengaging the rope strap from about his wrist, saw the gentle greed with which Von Riddarholm took it from his hands and the reverence with which he placed it like a new-laid egg upon the table, watched him stroke its surface, his fingers exploring the locks, and then, just as Stroop had done, he drew back. Left the case between them waiting, closed up like a clam.

★   ★   ★

The same evening Thomas had found the case in the cold neck of the slaughtered valley, Oravo Swan was curling himself up against his first night on the unknown island he had taken so long to find. He shivered inside his shirt, his skin dampened by his weeks at sea, hugging his arms against his chest to try to fight the cold that came at him, despite the balmy warmth of the night. He wished he had not used up the last of his tinderbox supplies on the long way across England, tried to remember each town and trail through which he had followed Griselda, the hammering of his heart the few times he thought he had lost her: that time she had taken a ride in a haywain going south, just as the rains had tumbled out of the sky and soaked up the trails of the horses' hoofs with mud; his luck at having been offered his own ride soon after because of that same downpour; his catching her up at the farm that had given her a room for the night, the night he had spent there tucked underneath a sodden hayrick, until he spied her again in the morning.

She had been shy of lifts up until that point, and he guessed that the money she had hoped to collect from her father's inheritance had either been slight, or that she was saving it, knowing she would need to eke it out, would certainly need it to buy her ticket to Hiiumaa, and to support herself once she got there, maybe even to get herself back to Lower Slaughter, if things didn't work out as she hoped. Most of the long way she had taken on foot, and all of that way he had followed her. Several times he had had to ask about the woman with the plaits and the strange accent, and each time someone had remembered, recognised her own speech in his, and was quick to volunteer her direction. After that, there had been only that one last scare when she had passed the twenty-mile boundary stone to London, and bought her passage on a barge to take her straight through the city and down to Purfleet, the place she had already told him she had landed as a child, and intended to retrace her steps and take a ship over to Hiiumaa. But Oravo had not stuck to her like a burr all this way to lose her now, and he had spent his last few coins hiring a horse, trailed her as best he could along the towpath, seen the barge land her only a few miles short of Purfleet.

It had seemed a wonder to him then that he could have followed her so far and long without losing her, or without her realising his pursuit. Yet now that he was actually here upon her island, the place whose name he still could not properly pronounce, he supposed it had not been so difficult after all. He remembered all the hares he had coursed over the hills back home, using nothing but his feet and the knowledge that wherever he had upped them, they would run far and jagged, but always return to the point from which they had been startled; and he remembered all the many times he had tracked a fox by its spoor when it had been several nights scraping at his linnet cages, how he had managed with ease to trail the animal the several miles back to its earth, and stopped it up, gathered its spraint as he had passed it and laid for it a different trail once it had managed to dig itself out again. And he thanked God for the perseverance such pursuits had given him.

Now that he was here in Hiiumaa he had different worries, wasn't sure if he would ever have the strength to put himself before her, and even if he did, how he could explain his presence here at all, at least in a way that would not frighten her, would not make her turn away from him and tell him to be on his way.

He shivered again, felt his wet clothes like a cloud against his skin, thought the sun would stay awake here for ever, but at last, growing close to midnight, it sank, and straight away the wind rose up from the sea, and the waves began to rise and crash against the shins of the cliff, and the mist rolled in and scrolled itself over the land like a bird settling upon its nest. Oravo felt his jaws becoming numb with the cold, tried to remember where it was he had seen that thin chimney of smoke arising, which sheep byre it had been coming from, did not want company, but realised he needed it, or at least the heat such company and its fire could give him. He looked around him, saw only the velvet-black dark of the night. He squinted his eyes, saw a thin draw of mist pull back towards the edges of the cliff, the first sight of starlight picking out the ghostly pools of cotton grass and the pale outlines of its scut-ended flowers. And then he caught it, just a glimmer of an ember rising up into early morning, a brief flickering of red in its thin column of smoke, and he eased himself up slowly, creaked his legs in that direction, fixed his vision on the spot from which it had come, began stumbling a rough path across the ankle-tripping heather the long five hundred yards towards its source. The moon came out briefly, allowed him to see the pale skin of stones and then closed again, so he had to feel his way about the wall to find the entrance, saw the curlicue of smoke rising up from a meagre fire, and a man, obviously sleeping, leaning up against the furthest wall, dark head on his darker chest.

Oravo tried not to wake the man, noted instead the piles of brush and dead bracken swept into rough heaps ready for burning, used his hands to capture them, throw them onto the dying fire. He tried to make as little noise as possible, but was still surprised that the man did not stir, knew from his own hard travelling that a lone man sleeps light, is wary of bandits and footpads, thought perhaps the man was drunk or that, in these parts, no such threats were in existence. He didn't much care either way, was pleased the man stayed with his eyes closed, threw a few more handfuls of tinder onto the mound of ashes, and a few strong planks of driftwood, hoped his unknown benefactor would at least be pleased his fire had not died and that someone had stoked it into morning, that Oravo wouldn't wake to a vicious hangover staring him in the face, a sharp knife at his ribs. But ultimately, he was too weary to worry about tomorrow, more tired than he could ever remember being, so he gave the fire one last poke and tidy, then curled his body about its edges, and fell swiftly into sleep.

Oravo Swan dreamt of things he would rather have forgotten. The warmth of this summer night and its fire slipped away from him, and he was as cold as the snow that had been falling then. He saw himself standing all alone in the middle of this flat landscape, the vast expanse of sky that seemed to come right down around him like a bell jar, tethering its edges to the circling horizon like a goatskin to a drum.

Somewhere in his dream, his head knew he was here in Hiiumaa, lying by someone else's fire, but a vast shame began

175

to overwhelm him – not so much at what he had done, but for the ease with which he had done it. He could see himself following those two men from out of Painswick, could feel the damp coming through his trousers as he had slithered down the smallness of that hill towards them without their knowing, had already seen their careless fire in the nook of the cottage that had been tumbled down by a century of wind and rain, the cottage that was not a half-mile distant from the one in which he knew Griselda slept, so close that he could almost smell the cinders that his own fire had made the night before when he had been with her, when an ember had jumped up and out at her as he toasted his stale hunks of bread upon its flames, singed a single curl of her hair back to its stem. He felt again the subtle creep of his feet through the snow that seemed to know his purpose, made no warning crisp or crack, gave only a soft sighing as he took his passage. Remembered the way he had waited, crouched up against that small hedge of quince, which had outgrown its useful-ness by fifty years but had once marked the boundary of a small garden, how he had wondered then if perhaps he should not have gone instead to her, knew also that he would never have had the words to say what it was that he had over-heard, that she would never have believed him anyway, and would not have understood why he had come. And so instead he had come creeping, creeping, over the snow towards where her ambushers were waiting out their night. Had known that sooner or later, one or other of them would make his way behind the wall to release the urgent spill brought on by the wine they had been drinking. Had pushed himself down into the quince and snow and made himself invisible, had waited, waited. And waiting was something Oravo had always been good at. Seemed to have been waiting his whole life: waiting for Grandmother Swan to tell him exactly what had happened to his parents, though she never did; waiting for one of the tight-lipped villagers to spill out the reason for their hostility to a boy who didn't understand; waiting for a reason to speak to Griselda, even after she had married the baker's boy; waiting for the waters of the flood to sweep everything away and give him the chance to start again, to leave his old life behind him and cross the seas, to climb his way into this new one.

Even in his dream he knew now where he was, saw himself standing again on the short stubby cliffs of Hiiumaa, the white sheet of the sun flat and bright between the broken-down sheepfolds, then saw that landscape fold back into that other white expanse outside Painswick, the grey shadow of the first man as he turned about the wall, and the hammer in his own hand as he swung it hard and swift, the rough push of his arm that brought the man face down into the snow, watched the black spray of blood as he had hefted down that hammer until he was certain there was nothing left in his head to break, and that the man's life had sunk back into the earth from which it had come. Oravo had breathed then, hard but quietly, quietly; sucked the cold air over his teeth until they stung, knew the second man would not be long in coming, must have heard something from his niche behind the wall not five yards distant, or else would soon get lonely in his drinking and come looking. And sure enough he did, and Oravo had been ready. He'd pushed himself out from the shadow of the gable wall and caught the second man square in the face with his hammer, watched his fall into the snow and the kick of his beetle legs, heard the crack of bone that he didn't think he would ever be able to forget, and the dark stare of that man's eyes coming up alive and upon him as he lay there on the snow, the glint of them as they caught the dim light of the fire as they both fell beyond the boundary of the wall, and then the way Oravo had turned the other man's face into the snow and held him down, held him down until he would never get up again.

Oravo had fallen backwards onto his heels then, the wet snow seeping into his coat, the tears running down his cheeks, his neck, at what he had done. And then the snow had begun to fall again upon him, cooled the burn of bile within his throat and the awful racing of his heart, saw it begin to bury what he had done, as if God had seen and understood, and that his safekeeping of Griselda had been sanctioned and, maybe, forgiven.

4

Boxes Opened, Boxes Closed

MABEL COULD HARDLY believe where she was, was having difficulty equating the distances and journeys that had brought them all to here, was slightly put out that now they were finally on Hiiumaa, she and Jack and Thomas had been immediately sidelined and shown to their rooms. Of all of them, she thought, Stroop had been the one to take the voyage badly, and if anybody needed rest, it was surely him. Still, she thought again, it had been an extraordinary courtesy and kindness their unknown host had taken even to get her here, and she could not be more glad for that.

Thomas and Jack, of course, immediately ignored the fact that they had been given separate quarters, instead invaded the room that lay next to Mabel's and began dragging in some mattress from another room so that they could be together. Not many minutes later, they were back by Mabel's side, jumping up and down upon her bed while she tried to take off her hat and boots, straighten the damp folds from her dress. She threw the boys out eventually, so that she could change out of crease and crumple, and into another dress that had not been so tired out by all the days of travelling.

She could still hear Jack and Thomas laughing and shouting in the next-door room, imagined them hanging themselves out of the large windows they would no doubt have opened, pointing down at the bay that lay below them, whistling at the birds, which seemed to float in great wheels above the sea, could only hope they wouldn't fall and break their necks in their enthusiasm.

She sat on the edge of her own bed for a few moments and closed her eyes, could not believe that only a few days before she had felt that she would never see any of them again, lay down on the bed a while and thought herself asleep, wondered if she was only dreaming, and that in reality she was still at Astonishment Hall. And then she heard a soft foot-fall, opened her eyes, saw Stroop standing embarrassed at her doorway. She smiled up at him, had not spoken to him much on the voyage over, had known how sick he felt, how much he hated having people near him when he was ill, and how much he missed his home, and yet would never say it.

'It's so good to have you with us again,' Stroop said, speaking so quietly she hardly heard him, and then she was up and off the bed in her stockinged feet, and her arms were about his waist and she couldn't get out a single word, just lay her head upon his shoulder, her hair scraggled with salt and wind and smelling of the sea, and he placed a gentle hand upon it, as it nested there beneath his chin. After a few moments, he prised her gently from him, said that she should gather the boys and come down, that the suitcase was about to be opened.

Mabel needed no more encouragement. She had spent as

much time on the voyage as she could opening up Violena's 'Crate Provided for Adventurers', as she proudly found the label to have been presented; had found it packed with books on miniature libraries, the processes of printing, the strange geography and history of the island archipelago of Saaremaa. Mabel had used her travelling time well, reading and absorbing everything she could, finding out about the place in which she now found herself, although she did not understand exactly why. She had tried at first to talk to Stroop on the voyage over, to discuss things as they had always done, but he had been distant and pale, had left her to her learning, which made her all the more diligent in her reading and the making of her notes. She understood Stroop's dislocation, had felt the same at Astonishment Hall, and more so now that they were here in such a distant land, where no amount of Sense Maps could help them. Yet still she had a perfect faith in Stroop and what was filed away in different maps, in different drawers, inside his head, and knew that whatever was coming, he would find the answers as he had always done.

A small while later, and they were all composed and better dressed, apart from Jack, who never looked anything other than a roving scarecrow, no matter what you put his arms and legs into. It was evening, almost nine, and yet the sky outside was clear as morning, the sun still high and bright, shining down through the thin mist that had unfurled from the sea and folded across the land like a ghost, bringing with it the cold chill of an incoming tide. A fire had been lit in the fireplace, which was as enormous as everything else in this straight-walled casket the baron called a home.

They had eaten well from a long table laid out with different kinds of breads and cheeses, fiery-pickled fish, beef sliced thin as leaves and curled onto shredded potatoes, which had been crisped with some strange kind of stringy cheese; there was watered beer and milk for the boys, a sweet, fruity wine for everyone else. Mabel, Jack and Thomas now sat dwarfed on a huge cushioned sofa that might have been hewn for a giant. None of their feet touched the ground, not even the long spindles Jack had for legs, his heels tapping out an arrhythmic beat upon the back-boards. Stroop was better off, had been given a ringside seat beside Von Riddarholm, the table holding the case lying between them, Von Riddarholm's fingers twitching slightly as they lay in his lap, still not really believing that Jarl Eriksson's suitcase had been returned to him, and yet had not a doubt that this was it.

He had known it the moment he saw it strapped to Stroop's wrist as he dismounted from the pony-trap, had barely been able to stop himself snatching it up there and then and running off with it to break the secret of its seals. But he also knew, just as this Stroop must have done, that there was a right way to do things, had admired immensely the restraint Stroop had found to not just take up some implement and break the thing open the moment he had found it. The baron had taken strength from his visitor's restraint, adopted the same poise of purpose, tried to hold back the need he felt to break open that suitcase's bounds, had had to clasp his hands tight behind his back every second he had spoken to this Whilbert Stroop, just to keep them from snatching up the treasure the man had brought him, had almost been about to prevaricate when Stroop had said he had to have his family down here when they finally opened the suitcase, that they had been as instrumental to its finding as had he.

And now here they were, and Josef Von Riddarholm could feel the blood pounding in his ears and breaking in his heart like a wave upon a shore. He couldn't even say the word, just gave a nod, and one of his men came forward as instructed, bearing a set of keys in his hand.

Stroop already knew that Von Riddarholm must hold duplicates keys for each of his Travelling Libraries, knew also that in the circumstances, any keys to this particular one would be useless, and so they proved to be. Apparently Von Riddarholm had assumed the same, and once the keys had been ground several times within the locks to no avail, another man was motioned forward, who unfurled a roll of tools, took his time selecting a thin, flat-bladed chisel, slid it gently along the sealed edges of the box until it came to rest below the first of the three locks. It was to their advantage that the two halves of the library only overlapped by a thin layer of metal, held closed and tight by the complicated barrels behind. The man placed his chisel with exquisite care, tapped it gently several times with a wooden mallet, shifting it to one side and the other until he heard some sign of the lock's position within the seal. Satisfied he had finally placed it where it was needed, he hit the chisel-end smartly with the mallet, once, twice, and again and again, until finally they all heard the thin screech of metal giving somewhere within. The man repeated the process with the second lock, and then the third, until finally he picked out another tool, skinny as a scalpel though much wider, slid it between the edges, and breached the seal. Josef stood up so suddenly the workman hardly had time to withdraw his tool before Von Riddarholm was placing his hands tenderly upon Jarl Eriksson's Travelling Library, and slowly, slowly, lifted the lid.

Seven days earlier, Oravo Swan had made his own discoveries, and found his own box, though had not opened it. He had woken up in the sparse cold light of dawn, and discovered the companion whose fire he had made use of the previous night. He was about to voice his thanks, throw more tinder onto the dying embers, but instead found his feet scuffling up below him, throwing him back upon his heels, cutting his hands on the sharp stalks of last year's broken bracken as he scrambled back until he hit the hard side of the byre, his breath coming fast and shallow. The man was there all right, lying against the opposite wall, his head tugged up against the stones, leaning too heavily to one side, his ear almost touching his shoulder. There was a thin black striation about his neck, from which blue bruises bulged, and there was dried blood where the man had clawed at his throat, deep dark gouges where his nails had dug hard into his skin. That the man was dead there was no doubting. Oravo saw things he couldn't have seen in the brief dark of the night before: that there had been a shelter roughly built just to the dead man's side, collapsed now where his arms must have flailed and knocked out the supporting branches as he died. He noticed too that the dead man's pockets had been turned inside out, and that some loose rocks had been prised from the wall and lay scattered about him. Oravo understood that murder was before him, recognised the signs of struggle and search, and that what had happened here had not happened that long before he reached this place, and the thought made him sweat all the more, despite the dampness of the mist. He saw that though the man's belly was swollen, there had not been enough time for it to rupture and release its gas. Had many times come across dead sheep or goats, seen the stomach rise so high the legs were pushed out at the four corners like a blown bagpipe, knew well enough the smell that came from guts rotting within a body before the skin split from side to side and released what it could into the air.

And there was something else he saw, something that perhaps only he, or someone like him, might have recognised, for he had the very same thing tucked and carried in his pocket since he was young: a short length of fennel stalk lying discarded a few yards from the man's side, crushed as if it had been stepped upon, but from where Oravo sat against his wall, he could see the end had been sealed with wax, just like his own. He was sweating badly, felt the shock leaking out of his body, wetting the shirt that had only just dried upon his back, making his palms itch. He calmed himself a few moments while he pondered what to do, felt guilt enough that he had already done two men to death, both in his recent dream and in reality, that he had left them to rot where they lay, didn't think he could bear that responsibility again, thought he had enough accusing faces staring out at him from the pantheon that moved constantly across the frieze of his dreams, didn't want to add another one.

Carefully he lifted himself up and got himself to standing, went across to the dead man, felt the rising temperature within his chest as if his heart were burning slowly deep inside him, and picked up the fennel stalk box, lifted off one end of the seal with his thumbnail, saw a roll of paper hidden within, just like his own, and pushed the wax down again. He didn't want to look at it now. Knew anyway it would not be in any language he would understand, but knew he could not leave it here where some stray gull or crow might swoop down and carry it away. He looked up then, saw the haze of mist beginning to break and shift, reveal the clear blue sky that was waiting above him, saw the lazy drift of sea birds circling high above, the way they seemed to stretch the fingers of their feathers, knew they were eagles of some kind, thought perhaps they already knew what awaited them down below. The buzzards would not be far behind, and soon this man's innards would be tugged from out his carcass, a garrulous racketeering of rooks picking at the scraps, vying for their place at the feast. He knew all too well the places they would seek first to devour, the soft parts of a body, be it rabbit, fox, sheep or man: the eyeballs, lips, the ears, and rectum.

Oravo had no idea what time it was, felt parted from the passage of the sun, knew that had he been at home, a quick glance at sky and shadow would have been enough, did not feel able to just up and leave. He took a few more deep-held breaths, wondered how it was that on this island of paper and ink, at least as Griselda had described it, there were no note-books growing from out the ground, or sheets of paper ready to be found in every spiderweb that had spread across the stumps of heather and sedge during the past few hours of his sleeping. Wondered what he could do to tell this man's tale without revealing anything of himself to anyone. And then he remembered something he had in his backpack – the small map he had of his own valley, one of the few things he had found in his parents' house that hadn't been eaten by damp or mice, curled in an old tea tin in one of the kitchen drawers, itself half wrenched from its runners with all the rest. He had often wondered how his father had come by that map that led to Lower Slaughter, who had given it to him, and why.

Oravo tried to stop his mind from wandering, realised he was doing anything but look upon the body of the man whose fire he had usurped, which had given him so much comfort on his first night in this foreign land, had seemed to him a welcome to his new home. And he knew something else, knew that this truly would be his home, and that he would never leave it and return to the old country and its valley. And so the idea came to him, and he began to rummage in his bag for the small stubs of carpenter's pencil he always carried with him, sat himself back against the rock and began properly to think. He needed to compose a message and get it to civilisation, he needed to get it right, without the use of words he knew would not be understood. He took his time to draw a brief map on the back of the other, had already marked this place with a cross, and written out the single word he thought might be recognised . . . and then something happened that was so unexpected, Oravo dropped the pencil and a sound came out of his throat like an oyster-catcher warning an intruder from its nest – a sharp, high dik-dik-dik that repeats over and over and does not cease until the intruder has gone on his way.

Up from the bay had come Gunar Torrensson, up the cliff and across the moor. From the first moment he had seen Oravo the evening before, he had made several assumptions: that this man must be a friend of Eyvind and was on his way to visit him, and that he would find his dead friend's body, but that by then the night would be upon him, and he would not be able to move until the dawn; also that he, Torrensson, had not been able to find Eyvind's list, so there was the possibility that he had already passed it on to this stranger, and that whoever he was, he needed to be stopped. From that moment until this, Torrensson's mind had been writhing like a nest of newborn rats, but now he had no doubt at all about what he must do. And so, after leaving Eyvind to his own dark night of the soul, he had gone that long circuitous way over the moor, and returned via the bay to the cliff and clawed his way back up the scrag-end of path they had all taken before, had laid himself flat and uncomfortable on the wind-spooled scrubs of juniper that lined the edges of the cliff, watched for the hunchback through his eyeglass the whole night through.

It had taken a while to spot him, and Torrensson had just begun to fear he was already too late when he had seen him as he stood up from another of the tumbled-down byres, maybe five hundred yards to the left of Eyvind's, and tidily gone behind the wall a way to take a piss, had seemed to scroll his shoulders, maybe to ease the bunched fist that grew out between them, maybe because his neck was stiff.

Torrensson had watched the man relieve himself slowly and without concern, seen him take himself up around the stones, scrunching himself up against the small rising of the wind, and taken himself toward Eyvind and his fire as if this had all along been his plan.

And so Torrensson had waited out the night where he lay, waiting until early light, when he scrolled himself out, crawled with the thin line of dawn advancing across the moors.

5

Openings, and Ice Houses

JOSEF VON RIDDARHOLM lifted the broken eggshell of the lid and held his breath, hands trembling as he eased one edge up from the other. This was just the way the Travelling Library had always been meant to be seen, its base upon the surface of someone's desk, the top half lifted slow and gentle, the gradual revelation of its interior world, the buckled-in books within their small compartments, the luxuriant purple satin of the interior, the flash of gold as each small binding caught the ambient light. He saw it now as others had always seen it, as he had never done before.

Not one drop of water had seeped from without into that case, and everything appeared to be as it should be, apart from the unsubtle cracking open of its locks, and the few books missing that Eriksson must have sold upon his travels. The workman, having done his job, withdrew, seemed completely disinterested in what his endeavours had revealed, pleased only that he had completed his task to satisfaction. Josef did not notice one way or the other, was unaware of anything at that moment except the tremble of his fingers against the two sides of Jarl Eriksson's Travelling Library, did not even register that Stroop had approached and now stood at his side, that Jack and Mabel and Thomas had vacated the discomfort of their enormous seat and were crowding at his elbows.

Josef lifted the lid until it lay at right angles to its base, the hidden interior hinges taking its weight, apparently unhindered by the terrifying journey they had undertaken, only to be brought back to this place of origin.

'It's perfect,' Josef breathed, 'still perfect. I cannot believe it!' And then he undid one of the silken ribbons, released a single tiny volume from its velvet prison: a copy of *The Conjuror's Handbook* by a man who had taken London by storm ten years before. He flicked its untouched pages between his fingers, saw the tumbling of acrobats, the slack-wire antics of a man who had balanced unnamed contraptions from his hands as he walked unaided across a wire slung thirty feet above the stage, the gathering of dwarfs and giants far below his feet; the illustrations of the bees that had been taught to fly through hoops and into hooded tunnels on command; the woman who could fold herself into a box almost as small as the Travelling Library. Josef took up first one book and then another from its silken rope, placed each and every one upon the table beside the violated case after he had checked it carefully for damage, murmuring to himself as each succeeding one was placed upon the pile of its peers.

'This is the one we made from hemp paper, and here's the showcase for the ink that Blauenstauer invented. He told me it wouldn't fade and I didn't believe him! And here is Illi's typeface, and Volgov's thumb Bible, and, my God, I never thought I'd see it again, the *Home Encyclopaedia* in English, the only one we ever made . . .'

As each tiny volume passed through his fingers, so it was taken up by one or other of his visitors. He chided absent-mindedly, told them not to pick up anything if their hands were dirty or greasy from their dinner, but he wasn't really looking, was far too focused on his own task of examining the delights he had not set eyes on for six months, had already imagined its destruction at the hands of bandits who did not know what they had found and used it to keep their fires burning, or the sinking of it with some barge, Jarl Eriksson eaten by the fishes, the stinking waters of a sewage-drenched river taking the Travelling Library and its secret pleasures out with it into the merciless sea.

When he had taken his last ecstatic examination of the books in the no-longer-missing library, Baron Von Riddarholm finally turned to Stroop, grabbed up his hand and shook it so hard Stroop's finger-bones grated together until he winced.

'Thank you, sir,' the baron repeated several times. 'Thank you again and again. I never thought it. I never thought it was possible.'

And Stroop had to agree, for neither had he. He had to admit to himself that it had not his skill at detection that had led him to this suitcase and thence to here, but that it had been luck: bad luck on Jarl Eriksson's part that he must have been near the bridge or even crossing it when the flood came crashing down the valley; good luck on Stroop's part to have made a fairly accurate guess of the way the waters might have taken him once they'd struck, and better luck still that he had Thomas and his staunch ability to scramble through places where other people could not have gone, having spent his previous pre-Stroop life wriggling in and out of market-stalls, sifting through alleys and other people's bins and outhouses, hiding under bridges, in hedges, in stinking sheds. None of this had Thomas's limbs forgotten, retained those years as traces in the way his muscles moved, the slipping between things like a lizard between the stones of its pool. And delighted as Stroop was that he had found Eriksson's suitcase, and amazed as he was at its contents, he could not also help thinking about those other things the baron had told him, and the real reason for bringing him to these shores.

Dik-dik-dik. Oravo felt the sharp high pain in his throat, and heard the small sounds trying to escape him. He couldn't understand what was happening. Only moments before, he had been scribbling with his little stub of pencil, vaguely distracted by the gentle noises of the moor awakening, and how different those noises were to home: the soft shushing sounds of sedge and asphodel moving in the slight but insistent breeze, the small sucks of water between the reeds, the larks that seemed to rise up all at once from their nests of cloudberry and low-lying broom, a few egg-heavy grouse grumbling from their mat-grass nests. He heard so many new sounds as the morning trembled itself into waking that he was not able to distinguish the steps of another man approaching quietly, nor hear him crouch his way through the tussocks, his tunic and trousers already soaked with the peat-brown water that stained and sustained the roots of the heathers and the bilberry.

For Torrensson, it seemed that life had always been like this, belly-down upon some foe-ridden shore, waking bent and stiff and slow, always constant in his creep and creep towards his hidden enemy. Not even the ants that coursed sleepily from the stones of the byre were disturbed by his low shadow, and Oravo had barely finished scribbling on his piece of paper before the noose was let down over his head and Torrensson caught it tight and tighter between his hands, listening with satisfaction to the shrill sounds of protest escaping from Oravo's throat.

It was late when at last all the books had been replaced within their case, each one carefully checked and caressed by Von Riddarholm, less carefully by the other. Jack and Thomas had been restless during this long adulation, had long ago wandered over to the large, wide windows, the depths of their sills scattered over with cushions so the two of them could kneel together side by side and gaze out over this unknown land. For both of them, this was far more exciting than examining a load of books that were mostly too tiny to pick up, let alone read. Instead, they stuck their noses to the glass, which had thickened and pooled towards its feet, gave everything outside a slight stretch from the pull of ages. It didn't matter to them: what they saw was weird enough anyway for them not to notice. There were three windows to choose from, and they chose the one to the east and the view over the long, shingled curl of Ristnaneem. They could see quite clearly the five windmills that strode across the land like giants, their sails turning as the wind came off the sea. And there was so much sea. It was like being adrift upon a vast boat, and they talked in low voices about what it would be like to drag up the vast anchor that must be tethering the island down, and set off with the wind behind them to who knew where. And there was so much down there to explore! Pockets of forest hemmed in by odd-shaped fields growing odd-looking plants, a particular wood that lay not that far below where they sat, the huge boulder they could make out at its centre, glowing red with the strange orange light that made the tree-bark, and even the stone, seem alive. And it was eerie enough itself that the sun should still be shining so late, gave everything a kind of graveyard hush, made you want to breathe a little quieter in case it heard you, decide to take umbrage and slip away. It was as if everything was awake and yet asleep at the same time, the soft murmur of insects you couldn't see, the occasional churr of a nightjar, or a blackbird courting too early and maybe realising, and stopping mid-song. Soon there were no colours, only the kind of bluey grey the grass goes when a will-o'-the-wisp is your only light, and the faint feeling that the ground itself was getting ready to turn over beneath your feet.

Jack and Thomas were entranced, had never seen such a landscape, could hardly wait to fling themselves out into the morning and the landslides of dunes they had seen from their upstairs window, slide down them towards a hundred different undiscovered bays, throw themselves into the subdued turquoise colour of the sea that only comes when it is calm and resting, run and shout and throw echoes through the arch and crouch of rocks that have been a thousand years in their sculpting, the caves that lay in wait just for them, hiding the spilt bones of mariners long lost within their echoey hold.

Stroop was otherwise engaged. Was so enchanted by the miniature library that he barely registered the boys had somehow sifted themselves away. Mabel saw their sneak and stealth – of course she had – smiled to watch the slouch of their conspiracy upon the wide seats of the sashes. Part of her wanted to sneak off with them, see what they could see, take part in their games of pirates or explorers or whatever else it was they imagined in this strange place. And it *was* strange, she knew they would all agree about that. She had never been anywhere like it, had known only Epping on the one hand, her little part of Bexleyheath on the other, and of course, later there was Astonishment Hall, which although astonishing, was so in quite a different way to this.

It occurred to her far sooner than to Stroop that whatever investigation they undertook here would be hampered by the conflict of language. It had been bad enough over at Astonishment, where everyone spoke with a dialect far different from her own, often professed they could not under-stand a word she said when she asked for various things down at the stores. But unlike Stroop, she had read about these islands on her voyage over, scoured from cover to cover the books that Violena had so helpfully supplied her with, had studied their history, stumbling over their odd, double-vowelled names. Wondered if anyone would remember that eccentric explorer Weeems, to whom those books had first belonged, two of which had been written by Weeems himself. From these last, she knew that language would not be such a problem as she had first imagined, that all the island children were required to go to school, at least until the age of twelve, after which they were expected to find a trade, and that whilst at school, English and Russian were mandatory, as well as Swedish, which was their natural tongue.

But none of this concerned her a jot now, for this Baron Von Riddarholm had just explained again to Stroop the real reason for his invitation to his home, was already leading them to the door, had not even bothered to apologise for the lateness of the hour, maybe thought that just because the sun still shone, it was still day, ignored the clocks that struck eleven as they passed the huge curve of the wooden staircase. Mabel thought it strange that a man should have so many clocks upon his walls, all striking out the hour at slightly different times so that the whole way down the corridor they were accompanied by their almost midnight chorus. She wondered if she would be able to hear them from her bed, grimaced a little to think that they would wake her every hour, striking themselves through her dreams. She saw Von Riddarholm's back disappearing down the hallway, saw the stride of purpose as he went on ahead, seemed to think that whatever needed to be done could not wait until morning. She felt the tingle of dread running through her to know where they were going, remembered the cold of Dismal Cobbett's makeshift mortuary back in London, yet would not be left behind. Thomas and Jack were a crowding comfort at her back, had left their window eyrie when Von Riddarholm had at last abandoned his little books and begun to tell Stroop all that had been happening in more detail.

Mabel wasn't sure what to make of this man who was as intense and coiled as one of his watch springs, a jack-in-the-box that has been locked up far too long inside its wooden cask. He paid little attention to Mabel, though plainly he had gone to great lengths to get her here, always telling his tale directly, and only, to Stroop, his English a little too formal, a little too plain and clipped, squaring words that should have been full and round. But what he had told Stroop was this: a week or so ago, they had found the body of a man up in one of the abandoned sheepfolds on the moors above the cliffs. That in itself would not have been of much interest, for many was the man the world over who had died on a cold night by watching too diligently at his sheep, or sleeping too deeply having drunk too hard and too often. But this was different. Nobody had sheep in those parts for fear of losing them over the cliffs, also it was midsummer and not cold; worse was that nobody had any idea who the dead man was, and many had looked. More peculiar still was that they had only found out about the body at all because the old priest had found a note sketchily written and tacked to the church door describing briefly where it was to be found, a faint scribble of a map marked with an X. And it had not been a natural death, that much was plain; so unusual in fact, that the baron had ordered the corpse be brought down from the moors and stored in one of the island's ice houses, had placed it in one of the rooms usually reserved for the autumnal catches of herring, packed in ice. No one wanted him there – for who wants to give home to a murdered corpse? – and now none of the fishermen would set foot within a hundred yards of the place.

Yet, as Von Riddarholm explained, it seemed worse somehow to bury such a man in a wooden box in an unmarked grave outside the churchyard walls. And outside the churchyard walls it would have to be, for no one knew the state of the man's soul, shriven or otherwise, and everyone knew a bad corpse could contaminate the good, just like one fish badly gutted would spoil the barrel. On the other hand, it might be that the man had died a martyr's death, or been a passing innocent who deserved better than to have his bones rot in unconsecrated ground and be denied the resurrection. And so instead, his body now lay within its frozen blocks in the ice house, awaiting judgement, as a prisoner would within his cell.

Had that been all, it would have been enough. But there was more. The note that had been tacked to the church door by a couple of spikes of blackthorn, had a single word upon it written in English. And it had been this more than anything else – certainly more than any worry about the murdered man's soul – that had prompted Von Riddarholm's precipitous note over to England to intercept Stroop, wherever he might be, and bring him back to here.

And so they now found themselves wound out across the grass before the manor house, a frenzy of larks still skittering out their songs against the pale grey sky, lines of swallows twittering on the ropes of the laundry greens, on the frames of the cold houses and hot houses that grew within them their exotic plants.

Stroop shivered as he crossed the dew-pricked lawns, did not like that the trees of the forest were so close to him, saw the menace of their strong trunks but not the things that must lie hidden between and beyond them, the only dark things in a night that was too light. He knew about the places where the sun still shone too late, of course he did, had often wondered how it would feel to walk through a stillness that was neither night nor day. Had always thought it would have a hint of menace, as if the natural order of things had been overturned, and he was right. He didn't like it, had passed through that cacophonous noise of late-striking clocks as he went by the stairwell, felt his body tire at just the thought of the hour, been deceived by his eyes as they had come out into a night that was still day, his body confused and disoriented as though he was at fault instead of everything else about him. He could hear strange grunts coming from somewhere deep inside the forest, could not imagine what could make such sounds, recognised the thin sweep and pipe of bats above him, could see their quick, black forms rush around the tops of the trees, heard frogs or toads croaking somewhere not so far away. It made him shiver to think that so much else was alive so close to where he was walking, and yet he did not know exactly what or where they were. He was briefly heartened by Jack and Thomas squabbling somewhere close behind his back, talking about their Coprological Museum, and how much they would be able to add to it after their planned forages of the following day. Stroop had the feeling that time was being sucked away from him, and that he would be stranded like a piece of bladderwrack on some uncommon tide. And then he felt Mabel's soft hand at his elbow.

'What on earth's a Coprological Museum?' she asked, and Stroop could not but smile.

'It's something they've been making for you while you've been away,' he said, and thought he heard her hiccup faintly beside him.

'For me?'

'Don't get too enthusiastic, Mabel,' he managed, 'until you know exactly what it is.'

But they had no time for further talk, had reached the edges of the wood where it met a well-churned track leading back down to the shore, could easily make out the green-shouldered hump of turfed-over bricks that must be the ice house. Von Riddarholm took up a ring of keys from his belt, picked one out the length of a man's hand, slotted it into the lock of a door that had been entirely hewn from a single width of oak, thicker than two men standing side by side together. Stroop knew a thing or two about ice houses, had studied them once a while back, the first time after visiting Dismal Cobbett's mortuary, which had piqued his curiosity about the effects of cold upon the human body, both the living and the dead. Knew, for example, that a man dying of an excess of cold will often feel himself to be hot as a shrimp on a skillet and start to strip off the last vestiges of his clothing even as he died. Thought it strange that one level of a continuum could be so routinely confused for its opposite, that both extremes of heat and cold could produce identical burns upon the skin. Josef Von Riddarholm showed no such fancy, had not let up his pace from the moment he left the manor, had gone straight at the ice house like an arrow to its hole. Stroop knew what he was about to see, and didn't want to. Dead bodies were not something he baulked at, had seen plenty of them in his time and through his occupation, but never had he enjoyed seeing what could happen to human flesh too long left in a river or riven through by an ox-cart, or, as in this case, several days abandoned upon a moor in high summer; thanked God the body would be frozen through by now so at least there would be no smell.

Von Riddarholm took them through the door, and down a long, squat hall that went, by several series of steps, deeper and deeper into the ground. The dark was soon so impenetrable that there was nothing, absolutely nothing, to see, until the baron picked some candles from a niche in the wall, lit first one and then another, handed them back behind him, obviously knew how many there were in his troupe although Stroop too had noted that he had consistently ignored everyone else but him. He wondered briefly why this was, had already assumed there was no wife or children, otherwise they would have met them by now, or at least seen evidence of their presence. He remembered with fondness Mabel's first entering into his home, her desire to please, her brushing down of the slippers he had no idea had ever needed brushing, the trail that Jack and Thomas could make just by passing through one room on their way to another. Had thought at first it would be a serious inconvenience, thought now that there was no other way a life should be.

Stroop took the candle that was passed him, felt them all to be in one of those long, midnight processions that visit the dead at their gravesides on All-Hallows Eve, could smell the yards of earth piled up above him, knew ice houses were often buried deep inside the earth, the easier to retain the kind of cold and grim that only liverworts and moss enjoyed.

Then abruptly, Josef Von Riddarholm opened one of the side doors, started donning the thick leather gloves of an ice worker, took up the screw-headed picks used to bore into the ice, had already pushed one of them into a block and turned it several times when Stroop came up behind him, was just in time to see him pull away the first of the ice blocks to reveal whatever remained of the nameless, murdered man who had been found upon the moor.

6

Balances, Bells, and Bodies

ORAVO HAD NO idea who was attacking him or why, but he was a man who had been attacked his whole life, had been singled out and set upon back in Lower Slaughter for as long as he could remember. Torrensson could not know how seriously he had underestimated his quarry, had no expectation whatsoever that Oravo's free hand would go by reflex to the hammer he kept inside his belt, that he could knock it free with the heel of his hand so quickly, his fingers slipping easily around the handle, that he could bring it up so hard and fast. Torrensson didn't know anything like this could happen, didn't know Oravo Tallista Swan at all. The hammer went back with such force, it broke Torrensson's teeth within his jaws, and loosened his grip on the garrotte. Oravo turned his body slightly now that his neck was almost free, swung the hammer a second time at a higher angle, caught Torrensson this time on the cheek and crushed the bone. Torrensson fell backwards with the blow, howling like a bad wind through the Pike Gut, the blood running down the inside of his throat, the pieces of shattered bone moving as his muscles flexed, the pain appalling. Oravo was hardly better, was still rasping for breath, was not sure whether he could raise his arm for another go.

But Torrensson did not wait for more, knew he could not take the next blow when it came, and turned to run his way across the moors, stumbling, clutching his hands to his broken face, trying to cease the jarring of the splintered teeth and bone. He headed straight for the edge of the cliff, saw the five hundred yards he still had to cover, hoped he could make it, cursed himself for choosing stealth and garrottes instead of the pistol he should have brought, no matter the consequences of the loud report. He wasted no time in glancing back behind him, had been in too many battles to let such a wasted action slow him down, tried instead to listen for footsteps following, had difficulty hearing anything except his blood battering within his ears.

But Oravo Swan didn't follow, could hardly even breathe, was trying to ease the crease that had been made in his windpipe. It took him ten minutes to get enough air inside him to allow a shaky standing to his feet, and even then, his eyesight was slightly blurred, and all he could see of his attacker was his retreating back as he raced erratically towards the cliffs like a saddle-shot stag, hands held up in an awkward position to his face. Oravo watched the man as he reached the cliff, stumbling down the first path he found from its edge. He saw nothing he might recognise later except Torrensson's great hay bale of a beard, black and wiry as the hair on a badger's back.

Griselda had been on Hiiumaa almost a full month, but the weeks had seemed to her like days. She recalled that first evening she had arrived, when she had gone down to the tree-chapel glade and carved her father's name into the stone. Afterwards, she had rested in the shade of the seemingly never-ending evening, leaning against the bole of a great lime, which she thought she remembered having climbed up as a child. She found comfort in its heavy scent and the constant buzzing of flies amongst its flowers, the occasional drip of honeydew from the aphids crowding upon its leaves. She knew that tree was different now from how it had been then, that it held a walkway within its branches that led to the next tree, and the next tree after that. And that it had its own small chapel woven within its branches that she knew had not been there before.

She had been quite alone all that evening through, and had rested, closed her eyes, listened to the sea, which had never been distant since she had landed, heard also the soft sounds of bees and hoverflies moving amongst the corn-flowers and poppies that grew up all around her, and didn't think she had ever felt such utter peace, hadn't even wondered where she might stay for the night, was happy enough to stay just exactly where she was.

But as the sunlight began to fall away, and the mist came sifting down through the crowns of the trees, settled its chill upon her skin, she opened her eyes again and looked around her, and up into the circlet of chapels, settled on first one and then another, her gaze drifting through the mist, finally resting on what looked to be one of the oldest. She seemed to recognise its contours and the sloping shingles of its roof, the spiral steps hewn into the bark of its ancient oak. That one, she decided, and took up her father's bag, stepped across the short, sweet grass of the clearing, and began to climb. It was a bare six feet above the ground, but once up there, she felt like a wren amongst the creepers, had to push a little of the twisted mistletoe roots away from the door to ease it open. Inside it was small and oddly warm, the faint and musky comfort of long-burnt incense, the wood beneath her fingers worn smooth by a hundred years of those who had gone before. She dipped her fingertips into the small stoop and crossed herself, felt the coolness of the water against her forehead, had the overwhelming urge to weep. She went down upon her knees and lowered her head before the tiny altar as the door finally closed its gap behind her, bringing darkness. She knelt a while then, the tears spilling out of her like sap running down from an unplugged sycamore.

She couldn't have known it, but earlier that same night, and not so far away from her in another of the chapels, someone else had been kneeling. Josef Von Riddarholm had looked up at the large painting that served as well as any stained-glass window. It was a copy his mother had commissioned of some old Spanish painting, something to do with the Mons Pietatis, he remembered, the charity she had favoured, devoted to the decent burial of the poorest of the poor, the most diseased of the diseased whom no one else would touch. The darkness of the painted oils reflected its content: the depredations death wrought upon the human form, which were not depicted gently, included rotting coffins and the bodies they contained, right down to the maggots, degloved bones, and beetles. Up above, the scales hung their balance, threatening damnation, or salvation, and only a breath of prayer between the two. His mother had been dead for many years, but like her, he always took comfort rather than fright in this painting, knew that one way or another, every man ended the same way. And like her he read the scrolled-out words that rolled above the balances: *Nimas*, and *Nimenos*; nothing more, she had told him, and nothing less. Sin on the one hand, salvation on the other.

And as Josef had knelt that night he thought about all that had been happening, how the balance of his own world had been disturbed. He thought back to when it seemed it had all started, with that lamb excoriated upon the church steps; then had come the cat's head nailed to the door of one of the printing barns. He still felt the same creep of horror escalating up his arms and around the back of his neck, the sad bravado that had convinced nobody as he sent out the order to have somebody take down the door and burn it, the extravagant sum he had paid the man who had volunteered to do such a thing, the careful watching of the other men who shared the superstitions of so many of the islanders, which he himself had felt prickling like a hedgehog within his belly, the horrid suspicion that this was just a start, and that other things would follow. Which they had.

The next had been the pig, with its guts wound out upon the windlass down at the pier, only a short while back, on the second day of June. Its discovery had left him teetering on some kind of brink that he had never experienced before, and had no idea which side of the chasm he would fall. And that was without the wrecking of the *Pihkva* and the numerous reports of attempted, or actual, piracy about Hiiumaa's immediate shores. It was the same night he had written again to Mr Stroop of London, decided to make his own stand and declare No More.

Griselda had felt no such troubles, nor any qualms at all. She had slept through the few hours of the night on the single wide-beamed pew, listened to the dark owl-wings swoop within the woods about her, the thin peep-peeping of bats in the trees, the strange bubbling she hadn't heard for so many years, but which she knew at once came from the toads upon the wetlands and the lake, the odd squawks of night-stirring birds, and those big beetles whose name she couldn't remember, which made a sound like angry bees when they flew by.

She was woken not long enough later by the sound of voices down in the clearing below her, lay unmoving on her pew for several minutes, trying to understand the words she hadn't heard since she was a child. Her father had spoken a little Swedish to her on their visits, but she was ashamed at how her native tongue had dropped away from her, and pleased at the ease with which it had been replaced, strove now to reclaim the language that had once been her own.

She sat up, stood up, brushed out her skirts, tried to fix the pins back into her hair, neaten the nest of her plaits, and then went to the door and opened it. She saw two old women stooping down by the enormous boulder at the centre of the tree-glade chapel, was surprised it seemed only minutes since she had carved out her father's name. She watched them plucking wild oats out from the grass, talking quietly to one another. The door creaked as she opened it a little more and stepped out further, and the old women both turned and looked up at her, watched her as she stood there a moment, didn't move as she made her awkward, ungraceful way back down the steps. Even then they just stood watching and waiting in the clearing, plainly wondering who she was and what she had been doing in one of their chapels, and so early. And then one of them pointed at her, said something to the other, motioned with her hand to where Griselda waited in her turn at the bottom of the big oak and the steps, feeling embarrassed and yet easy, was about to step forward and try to make herself understood.

And then the most extraordinary thing happened to Griselda, and it was as if some mechanism within her body was suddenly wound and woken. She was still listening to the old women as they talked, but she began to interpret their ticking, organise the sounds into proper words, was able to garner something of what they said – only little bits, only one word here and there, but enough to hear her father's name, and then her own.

'She looks a little like one of the old clan,' one of the women said.

'Don't see hair done much like that, not like we used, and not that colour.'

'What was that family's name? The one with all the freckles?'

'Wasn't it the Liits? But there's nothing left of them now, surely. Hasn't been for years.'

And Griselda almost ran across the tree-chapel glade towards them, bowed a little formally, tried to conjure the old words to her lips, but managed only, 'Griselda. Griselda Liit. Daughter of Kustin.' But that was enough, and the old women wrung their hands together and then took hers to their chests, touched her fingers to their hearts, and Griselda no longer understood a word they said, they were talking so quick and loud, but she managed to lead them to the place on the stone where she had carved out her father's name the night before. And the two of them put their fingertips into the lines of his name, touched their lips to the stone, and Griselda started to cry again, because at last it seemed that someone besides herself remembered all that Kustin had been, and all that she had lost by his passing. And after that, there was no stopping them. The two old women dragged her back into the village, showed her the old Liit house, which looked just as she had remembered. She felt herself regressing to the child she had been when she had left. People came out of their doorways, leaning on brooms, which they happily abandoned after the news was out. And before she knew what was happening, Griselda was being passed from house to house all along the old village street, the old-timers coming out to greet her and embrace her, forcing her to eat and drink things she'd not tasted for so many years.

There was even one shy woman who came out and curt-sied, introduced Griselda to her many children one by one, and then reminded her they had been at school together, spoke to her in halting English, and hugged Griselda to her with such a tight embrace she could hardly breathe. Griselda cried again then, never imagining her homecoming would be quite like this, that there would be people here who would actually remember her, and more so her father, and with such warmth. And she wished he could have lived just a few more months, and that she could have brought him here with her, and not just his name. And she blessed the flood that she had once cursed, and thanked God for this chance that she would never otherwise have taken.

Stroop had seen as much of the murdered man as he wanted. And that the man had been murdered was not in doubt. The thin line about his neck told of taut wire or some thin rope, and the gouge-marks, together with the skin and blood about his nails, made it clear that he had not done this thing himself. This was corroborated by the way in which the man had been found, pulled up and against the stones of the sheep-fold as if a man had come behind him and slipped a garrotte over the wall of the byre. So much was obvious, and Stroop saw now why the baron had sent for him, understood already from Von Riddarholm's exposition of events that there was no law enforcement here as such, that Von Riddarholm himself was Justice as far as anyone ever needed it, which apparently wasn't often. Mostly he presided over neighbourhood disputes, arguments over who had the right to tenant a particular portion of land, or the suing of one family against another for the upkeep of a child born out of wedlock, occasional acrimonious suits about which family member should inherit what another had left upon some sudden demise.

Stroop was surprised to see just how shaken the baron was when he had removed the last block of ice, saw his hands tremble a little even within the large compass of his leather gloves, saw how he averted his eyes and stepped quickly to one side to allow Stroop a better look. He heard Mabel's sharp intake of breath as she came up beside him, and appreciated the fact that she stayed there while he made his examination, even asked if he wanted her to take notes. He was more surprised when Jack came forward, his own little notebook in his hand, and watched him as he quietly, and without comment, drew the dead man's head and the marks upon his neck, even putting a little code next to the hatchings, presumably to indicate the colour of the dead man's bruises and his hair. Stroop remembered all Jack's other drawings for the Coprological Museum, and realised that it had not been just an exercise the boys had undertaken to amuse themselves whilst Mabel was away, but that they had been good at what they had been doing, and diligent. And that right now, Jack's drawing might be the best chance they had of giving this unknown man a name.

They none of them lingered, not once Jack and Stroop were finished, and Von Riddarholm seemed more than eager to replace the ice blocks and lead them all back up into the world. It was almost dark when they resurfaced, and Von Riddarholm seemed relieved this part of his duty was done. He shook Stroop's hand once they'd regained the manor house, and apologised for keeping him up so late. He suggested they should all take their time in the morning before attending breakfast, which would be at any hour of their choosing. Stroop did not demur. He was tired, knew Jack and Thomas and Mabel must be as weary as he was, asked only that the baron have the note that had been pinned to the church door ready in the morning for his inspection. And then they all retired, and no one knew if the clocks on the staircase wall could be heard or not from within their rooms, for half an hour later, they were all asleep and dreamless.

7

Envoys and Testaments

S TROOP HEARD THE ragged chimes of nine o'clock the same
time as did Mabel. Both had been so tired from sea and
sail and the excitement of the suitcase and the ice house that
they had slept without disturbance the whole night through.
Jack and Thomas, on the other hand, had hardly closed their
eyes before they had been up again, woken by the early
dawn, which had spilled so tantalisingly through the open
windows onto their beds. They had long since scrambled
hurriedly back into their clothes and gone down the stairs
and found their way, by sense of smell, to the breakfast room,
where the baron had only moments before taken his own
seat.

Josef creased his brows on first seeing them tumbling into
the dining room just as he was about to spear the tidy curls
of rollmops onto his plate, was unused to anyone being here
with him, let alone two unruly boys.

'Mornin',' Thomas said cheerily and sat down beside the
baron without being asked, dragged his chair so close he was
almost touching Josef's elbow, despite a full two yards of table

available on either side. Jack was too distracted by the silver domes that hid the plates of breakfast foods to do more than nod at his host. He'd barely sat before he stood again, began lifting the lids up one by one. Josef knew the English liked things the English way, had left instructions that porridge and kidneys be laid out alongside his preferred fare.

'Ooh!' Jack said as he lifted up the lid on the porridge, stuck his finger into its solidity and steam. 'Ugh,' he commented, 'this doesn't taste like Mabel's.'

'There's eggs and toast, Jack,' Thomas added helpfully, having lifted up his own lids, but Jack was not to be stopped. He raised his eyebrows at the stuffed mushrooms, plainly having very little idea what they were, and dropped the lid back without ceremony. When he'd finished his ritual of discovery, he started all over again, this time taking a little from each and every platter, setting the strange food with the known ones with rapt concentration upon his plate. Josef tried to ignore them, but Thomas was already asking questions.

'Where's the best places to go?' he asked, as if Josef had already known they had spent a full hour the night before discussing their plans for their upcoming expedition, their as yet uncharted explorations of a foreign land. 'And what's all those funny-looking plants in those fields near the windmills? Or maybe we should go swimming in the lake.' He looked at Jack then, who was still poking tentatively at the mushroom on his plate with his finger, having already decided the kidney smelt of piss and he wasn't going anywhere near it, then started in on the scrambled egg, which was just about the only thing he recognised, except for the porridge, which he wasn't going to eat because he knew that Mabel hadn't made it, and the only porridge he ever ate was hers.

Josef was irritated by their constant barrage of chatter and questions, which didn't seem to require answers, at least not ones they ever waited for. But his English was good, almost fluent, and after a few minutes he found an odd comfort in their presence, a welcome intrusion of normality back into a world he felt was spinning out of control. Yet still he sat stiff backed in his chair, watching those boys eat their eggs and toast with such enthusiasm that he envied them for it, almost laughed out loud when the older one decided to attempt the rollmop of raw fish soused in vinegar, watched him pop it in his mouth and begin to chew, just as he'd seen Josef do, and the comically exaggerated grimace that froze on his face before he gave the baron an apologetic grin, and spat the thing out onto the side of his plate. It made Josef feel slightly ridiculous that, only minutes before, he had been thinking of his observatory and that awful loneliness he had felt as he watched through his glass the recent passing of the aphelion, the slight shift of the stars that he had felt, but could not possibly have seen, the ghastly knowledge of his vulnerability before infinity and that everything secure had been in the act of falling away from him and his tiny world.

And then these boys had come sprawling in without invitation, and he felt invigorated by their joy and unconcern at living, felt a little hope seep in where previously there had been none. Remembered the look on Stroop's face when he had pulled away the final ice block, the immediate revulsion on his face, and then the bloodhound taking over, the way he had leant in far closer to study the corpse than Josef had the stomach to do, and these boys crowding in too, one drawing pictures and the other taking notes, apparently unconcerned by the death that was staring right back at them.

After the rollmop incident, Josef tidied his fork upon his plate, rinsed his fingertips in the little bowl of water that lay next to it, smiled to see Jack watching him intently and copying his actions, ignoring his own bowl and instead leaning over the table to dip his fingers into Josef's, watched him carefully survey for the napkin he had not bothered until then to unroll. He felt an almost uncontrollable urge to lean forward and ruffle the boy's hair, realised suddenly that Jack was a boy, and not the near-man that his body gave the lie to, and was jealous for a moment of Stroop and his little family, and wanted a part of it, or at least to be some part of his own. He no longer wished these boys gone then, nor desired the silence of the star maps he had been about to study, made a decision and cleared his throat.

'Boys,' Josef said, and if Jack and Thomas were startled that this was the first time he had spoken since their arrival at his breakfast table, they did not show it, 'there are some quite wonderful places on this island, and once you've finished eating, why don't we take an hour or two before your Mr Stroop wakes up and we have to get down to some proper work?'

That did it, and it took no more than thirty seconds for them to slurp up their milk, cram a last wedge of buttered soda bread and eggs into their mouths, spilling a scree of crumbs down their fronts, before leaping to their feet and declaring themselves ready. If anyone who knew the Baron Josef Von Riddarholm had seen him at that moment, they would have been astounded by the way he allowed those ragamuffin boys to grasp him by the hands and practically drag him from the room, and would have shaken their heads in amazement as the three of them went down the hallway like a fall of chattering woodcock, and away down the corridor, out into the morning and the sun.

Mabel had been awoken several times over by the loud scatter and squawk of seagull squabs clattering back and forth along the overhead slopes of her roof, with their constant, persistent piping for food.

The first few times, she had tried to roll herself back into a weak morning sleep, closed her eyes, tried to sink back into dream, but it was a battle already lost, and instead she lay on her side a while, and looked out of the window, watched the mist drift up and burn away, revealing a bright expanse of sky in which she saw the slow swirls of black-backs and skuas riding high above the bay. Below them rode the smaller, cruciform bodies of gannets, who suddenly, swiftly, withdrew their wings and plummeted like crossbow bolts from her sight, re-emerging moments later with the flash of sand eels a silver cipher in their beaks. Her body was tired, but the morning pulled her into sitting, drew her from bed to window seat, and for a while she sat there, an eiderdown around her shoulders, glorying in the blue circle of the sea and sky that surrounded her, the low crouch of a hundred islands revealed and hidden as the mist came and went.

When finally she decided to get up properly, she regarded

with distaste the crumple of yesterday's dress where it hung over the bedpost, rummaged through her bags to find a better one, had just fixed the buttons and stays when she heard the excited shout of boys' voices, and would have known them anywhere. She went to the second window in the room and knelt upon the sill-seat, looked out now to the east, saw them running from the trees that bordered the trim grasslands of the manor, saw someone else with them, a tall black streak striding between their darting bodies. She recognised Von Riddarholm with surprise, had thought him so grim and dour the night before, had imagined him a lonely widower who had locked himself away in his towers with his books, felt a small twinge of guilt that she had so misjudged him.

She heard a gentle tapping at her door, knew it would be Stroop and called him in. He looked almost as dishevelled as her discarded dress, and she reminded herself to ask for the use of a flatiron, smiled as he came across the room and looked out across the sea and then at the grass, at Jack and Thomas bowling over it like balls.

'They look happy,' he said.

'Who wouldn't be?' Mabel replied, wished she herself were down there with them, that she had roused herself a little earlier and flung herself out with them into the day. She rolled her shoulders, felt Stroop's cool fingers briefly touch the back of her neck.

'Did you sleep well?' he asked, but Mabel did not reply. She turned and smiled up at him, kissed him quickly on the cheek, then ducked from the seat and went across to her satchel.

'There's loads I've still not told you,' she said, withdrawing a large notebook, beckoned him over to the boudoir, which was the only table in the room, dragging over a second small stool, which had been placed, for some unknown reason, at the base of her bed. They smiled at each other in the mirror for a moment, didn't need to say again how pleased they were at being all together.

'Aha,' said Stroop delightedly as Mabel flipped open the book, 'notes! Just what a man needs for breakfast.'

Mabel ignored him, concentrated on finding her place in the book. 'Just a few things to let you know about before we go down and meet the baron. Did you get to read much about Hiiumaa before you left?' Stroop raised his eyebrows, reminded her that their information-gathering in London had been primarily about miniature libraries rather than the place from which those libraries had come.

'Did you read any of the books I gave you on the boat?' Mabel persisted, although she already knew how sick he had been on the journey over, and raised a finger before he could speak. 'I'll give you a brief history so you're at least a little prepared. Weeems was here, do you remember I told you that?'

Stroop said he did, had indeed not been too surprised. Halliday Weeems was an explorer, and had travelled all over the globe, amassing an extraordinary library of curios and books and housing them all in the even more extraordinary Astonishment Hall.

'He even wrote a couple of small pamphlets about this place. Violena found them for me, and quite a lot else besides. Shall I begin?'

Stroop nodded, though heard his stomach beginning to grumble, wanted some strong, sweet tea to settle it down and start his day as he was accustomed. It seemed so much longer ago than the eight or nine days since they had been at home in London, with the kettle always on the stove, the tea or the coffee pot always brewing, but now that Mabel was back with them, those days didn't feel quite so lonely and outstrung as they had done before.

'Go on,' was all that Stroop replied.

'It won't take long,' said Mabel, apparently reading his mind, 'then food and tea, or maybe they have coffee, but it's best to be prepared.'

And so she gave him a small history of these islands, thought to have arisen from the sea maybe ten thousand years before, called Eysyla in the Scandinavian sagas, and known as Sarma or Osilia in the earliest records.

'Of course,' Mabel added, 'those names referred to the whole island nation, and there are many islands, though only three main ones which hold most of the population. Every island has different names and differing spellings, depending on when they're being referred to, and by whom. The most common current name for the whole archipelago is Saaremaa, which is also the name of the principal inhabited island. The other two largest islands are Muhu and this one, Hiiumaa. Their histories are very similar: settled early on, significant populations from the thirteenth century. Several were taken over by the German Order of Knights, who at that time owned much of Livonia and Courland, but who are usually referred to in the records, at least the ones Weeems came across, as the Brethren of the Sword.

'They built forts and strongholds on the islands, particularly Muhu and Hiiumaa, which gave the islands prosperity and protection, and a certain amount of autonomy.' Stroop was listening intently, and making his own notes from Mabel's. He put a particular mark by this reference because it was one he had come across before, though not with such benign connotations. He said nothing, though, and let Mabel move on. 'Before the arrival of the Brethren, the islands had more or less been seen as a nation of pirates, taking advantage of the fact that they were on the direct route between Scandinavia and the Eastern European countries. The Brethren managed to give the islanders the security they needed, turned the pirates into traders, and very successful ones too. They even gave them back the name of Osilia, as in the ancient times.'

Stroop was remembering a different kind of history, which had started when he had done some research into the medical procedures carried out during the crusades, the appalling injuries suffered by men and horses, and the brutality of the treatments bullied out on both. He'd been intrigued by the Hospitaller Orders, ostensibly set up to care for pilgrims and fighters in the Holy Land, who yet diverted from their charitable and monkish vows, and became more and more militant the longer they remained in Outremer. He'd become particularly fascinated by the Teutonic Order, who began as a hospital for German crusaders in 1189, and suffered massive military defeat in 1210. So much, so usual, Stroop had thought, until he discovered that they had then been withdrawn from the Holy Land and sent instead to fight the pagans in Prussian lands. He had been astounded that there had still been pagan tribes so

220

late into the centuries, and more astonished still that a military arm of crusaders had been sent off to subdue them by whatever means. There had been no gentle infiltration by missionaries converting men by dint of deed and example and belief. Instead there had come an army out of Prussia of disciplined and war-bloodied men, slaughtering a way right through to the shores of the Baltic Sea. *Schwart-brüder*, was the name he had come across for them, another being the Brothers of the Cross and the Sword. There had been no hospitalling left about them then, had become only a vicious arrowhead, which brought death or dominion and sometimes outright slavery to the natives of whichever land they passed through.

He truly doubted things had been so much different when they'd finally reached these islands, and found nothing more before them to go on conquering but the wide and open seas, would not have built their forts and barricades to give the islanders protection, but to cast over them their shadow, and that whatever name they'd allowed the islands to call themselves didn't matter a jot.

He hardly heard Mabel's next little piece of history, which was a tangle of ownership and wars, of the Swedes taking the islands over, and then the Danes, and then the Swedes again; of the Great Northern War of the 1720s, which left them belonging to the Russians. It was only when he heard her mention a particular date that he looked up again.

'. . . in 1781,' Mabel was saying, 'when thousands of Hiiumaa's Swedes were deported by Russian edict to the shores of the Dnieper.' She struggled over the foreign-sounding names of the villages that had been entirely emptied. 'Kidaste,' she said, 'and Mudaste and Malvaste; and afterwards, Estonians were brought in to take their place.'

'Ah, yes,' said Stroop, interrupting her for the first time, 'I know about that.' And something other than hunger began to wobble in his belly and his chest. He began to see a pattern in all that Mabel had been telling him, and all the baron had told and shown him the night before. Stroop couldn't put his finger out and trace where each thread led, but he knew without doubt that somehow everything was connected, and that even the seemingly inconsequential roads from Lower Slaughter and from Painswick led inextricably to here.

Josef Von Riddarholm could not remember the last time he had visited the meteorite lake, but now that he was here, he found it extraordinary that he had not come more often. The smell of pine resin was so strong that he had to close his eyes and breathe it in again and again, wanted to fill his lungs with the scent so that he would not forget it. Pine pitch was the very essence of what his family had built up on Hiiumaa, the lampblack made from it being the basis of every ink they used, of every kind of ink ever invented here or anywhere else. A long list of the other ingredients needed scrolled across his mind: the oils for steeping the lampblack, the glues for fixing, the stupendous range of ground barks and aromatic plants, of horn, lichen, even of pearls, that added colour, lustre, scent and permanence. He recalled the paper-weight in his study, a long hexagonal tablet of lacquered Chinese ink that came from the Cave of a Thousand Buddhas, and was many hundreds, probably thousands, of years old;

the gilded dragons and characters alive upon its back, the smoothness of its surface below his fingers, the many names the Chinese had for ink: black metal, dark incense, smoky jade, and best of all, the one that was inscribed onto his own little block of his industry's history: the Envoy of the Black Pine.

His reverence was disturbed by Jack and Thomas racing back along the path. They had taken it upon themselves to run the lake around, had left him sitting at the water's edge, thinking how still and black it was, how smooth, how like his block of ancient Chinese ink. He watched a flight of geese whiffling down to land, hesitate in the air above the lake and change their minds, take off to find another stretch of calm water, the slight ripple of fish descending from the noise the boys were making, heard a whirr of dragonflies take up early from the reeds that grew about the lakeside, not waiting the few more minutes of sun to dry their wings as they would have preferred, the abrupt cessation of a wood-pecker's frenzied tapping at some nearby tree. A second later, the boys came into view, skidding along the rough path.

'How long, do you think?' panted Thomas as he crunched to a halt a couple of yards short of where the baron sat, sending up a scrum of crushed pine needles and leaves.

Jack came up behind him, thumping into Thomas, gasping, laughing. 'Five minutes! Five minutes, I'm sure it wasn't any more!'

Thomas put out his hand, and patted Jack on the shoulder. 'A little bit longer, I should say,' he said, 'we did run all the way round. What do you think, Mr B?'

Josef had never been addressed in such a way in all his

life, and took a couple of moments to realise he had been spoken to, had a sudden brief memory of racing around the lake himself as a lad, and clocking it at fourteen minutes and fifteen seconds and how proud of that time he had been.

'Oh,' he replied vaguely, 'ten minutes?'

'Ten minutes! It's a record!' shouted Jack. 'Oooh, look at that!' he said, forgetting his victory as soon as it was done, pointing at a thin blue waft of damselflies as they took up in a cloud from a wavering brown bank of velvet bulrush heads. Von Riddarholm watched with an odd kind of pride as the two boys sped off to examine this new departure, smiled as they were immediately rediverted by the discovery of several small toads crouched in the mud at the bulrushes' feet, found himself looking around at this place he had thought he had known so well, felt a small *frisson* of wonder that he was seeing it all anew; felt an awful guilt that for so long he had neglected to walk along its ways, had chosen instead to seek his own obscure enjoyment in the cold black paths of his duties, and the tracks of distant stars across the night-time sky.

After Stroop's small revelation, he had another one directly upon its heels. Mabel was startled when he stood up suddenly and cursed.

'My God!' he exclaimed. 'How could I have been so stupid? Too busy looking at those blasted books . . .'

And then he left the room without looking back, apparently no longer bothered with getting breakfast or even tea, Mabel trailing down the staircase in his wake, neither of them even registering the noisy ticking of all the clocks, their thin arms clicking up another notch and making the tiny coglet noises that announced that the ones that were able were about to strike the quarter-hour.

Stroop went straight to the room where he knew the Travelling Library to have been left the night before, and tugged open the door with such impatience it scraped its protest hard against the floor. He was relieved to find the case still where it had stood, and straight away went to it and lifted the lockless lid, ignored the familiar twitching of his fingers at the sight of all those tiny tomes. Instead he eyed the shelves that separated the three perfect layers of little books, discerned the tiny squares that had been inlaid inside each one. He pushed it, and out came the first of the drawers he knew must be there, just a millimetre or so, just enough for Stroop to get his finger below it and pull it properly out. A single slender book almost the exact size of the drawer lay within, and carefully Stroop tipped it out and laid it on his palm.

It was Jarl Eriksson's ledger, and though the details of purchase and sale were all in Swedish, Stroop recognised without difficulty most of the names and dates; saw that Painswick had indeed been on his itinerary, and that not only had Eriksson met with Charles Quaritch, but that Quaritch had made a purchase. Stroop remembered his own visit to Painswick, and how Quaritch had shown him the small library of miniature books in his study, how he had gently fingered the last Lilliputian volume in line, even as he was denying to Stroop's face that Eriksson had ever been there several weeks before.

Stroop looked more carefully at the ledger, at its next entry, deciphered it concerned some kind of business with a paper merchant in Stroud, the short, impatient logging of dates with nothing entered beside them, guessed that Eriksson had been delayed within that town for several days for whatever reason. And then came the final entry: the visit to the monastery at Upper Slaughter, a brief scrawl and a date, an entry unfinished, no doubt intended to be properly written up on his return. But Jarl Eriksson had not returned; instead he had written down the name of Kustin Liit's daughter, before going out into that terrible storm to find her, on some deeply personal errand. He was struck with a terrible poignancy that the name of Griselda had been the last word Eriksson ever wrote.

Stroop put the ledger down on the table, and looked a little closer at the Travelling Library. He saw what he had not seen before, that the third layer of books was only half filled, that Eriksson had obviously made some sales, and that one of those had been without doubt to Charles Quaritch. Then he shifted his attention back to the task in hand, and depressed the release for the second drawer, uncovering now two unopened and undelivered letters, knowing before looking at them to whom they would be addressed. One would be to that same Griselda Liit, Kustin's daughter and last remaining relative, and the other would be to the Baron Josef Von Riddarholm on the island of Hiiumaa. Neither did he need to open them to know that they had been written by Griselda's father, and had been given to Eriksson only days before Kustin Liit had died. Stroop did not force the seals – knew the words they protected would be in a language he did not understand – only turned them gently over in his hands, was intrigued to view the signet pattern in the wax, which was of a hedgehog spiked with apples. He knew from his earlier studies in London that this must be a printer's mark, and an uncommon one. He had seen many other types, sometimes on the signboards outside bookmakers and print shops, other times hidden within the watermarks of their paper to state the ownership of their wares. He recalled several such signs: a tiger's roaring head, a grasshopper, a pigeon, a cradle, the emblem of three arrows. He made a small mental scribble to enquire as to the baron's own, but had a feeling he already knew. It would be the hedgehog, the spikes maybe representing all the different islands, each protecting the other as the animal rolled itself into a ball, the apples representing the fruits of their labours.

He laid the letters aside and moved his fingers to the second shelf, the last two drawers. The first held writing implements, seals and inkpots, all cushioned in tiny velvet compartments to keep them still. In the second was a curled sheaf of blank writing paper, and another couple of sheets rolled tightly together, tied with a small green ribbon. There was no seal here to break, and Stroop pulled at the ribbon, let it fall back into the drawer as he unscrolled the papers. It was the last will and testament of Kustin Liit, one in English, the other, presumably, in Swedish, and Stroop knew then that he had not been the only one to suspect Charles Quaritch's smooth exterior: that it was just like the moss that grows too thick upon a branch, the wood beneath being rotten. For why else should Kustin Liit have feared to leave such a document within reach of his employer? Only that he did not trust him, and did not trust him to pass on his possessions to his daughter, as few as they were: the monies left in his passbook as held by the Printworks; a small box of personal effects, which had belonged to Griselda's mother; and a book. Kustin Liit had been most insistent about this book, had written out its author and its title, added that his own name was inscribed upon the inside cover, and that whatever else Griselda took away with her, she should take this.

And that was all. Nothing left of Kustin Liit in this world apart from these few words, and his daughter, and his book. Stroop thought about that book, and about its author, Swedberg. Something about the name was familiar but he couldn't quite place it, and he glanced for inspiration about the room. He had seen nothing of it the night before except that stubborn nut of a suitcase closed upon the table, where it now stood open. The walls of the room were lined with glass cases from floor to ceiling, and each contained numerous glass shelves laid out with a thousand exhibits, accompanied by their carefully scripted labels: ingots of hardened ink from all over the world, from China to India, Japan to Korea, some square, others heptagonal, cylindrical or octagonal, some in liquid form kept in lacquered boxes, others in small holders made from horn or ivory or scrimshawed tusks, or resting as flakes, or carefully hewn into decorated blocks. There were scribed examples of different types of inks on different types of papers, deepest blacks to finest sepia, like those made out of octopus ink, some red as desert sand, or blue as Derbyshire John just like the vase he had at home, or the softest orange of a hunter's moon.

Other shelves were filled by the various implements used for writing: quills cut from feathers, curls of papyri, styli carved from the strong midrib of some exotic leaf, a whole host of brushes of which the smallest seemed to be single-haired, and the largest, the width of his fist, and for the moment Stroop forgot the suitcase and its books and letters and last wills and testaments, did not even notice that Mabel had just entered and was standing somewhere by the door, bearing the tea and toast he had been dreaming about not so long ago. What he could not miss was the sally of loud shouts and cries proceeding from outside the windows, and he moved himself away from the cases, caught a brief image of himself trapped within the glass, of Mabel, a small green ghost behind him, her face a disc that seemed to rest for a moment upon his shoulder.

'I've brought vittals,' the ghost said brightly, and carried in her tray, rested it down on the table beside the suitcase, casting her eyes to the contents within, and at the opened drawers that had until now been hidden. But Stroop had already moved on to something else, and Mabel wondered for a moment what a child's top might look like in human form, and if perhaps it would not look just like him.

8

Swedish Mystics and their Gold

O RAVO SWAN SAT a long while in his sheep byre after
Torrensson had disappeared over the cliff. For the first
hour or so he just sat there, kept touching his hand to his
throat, felt the two soft swells of bruise begin to puff up
from below his skin, the fine fresh line of blood that divided
them, thought of the old miller back in the valley and the
way the man had begun to unwind the rope from around
his waist. Oravo knew that he was feeling only an inch of
the old man's yard of pain, a splinter of the unutterable
sadness that must have overtaken him in those last few
moments his boots stood upon the earth, wondered if it
was possible for a whole lifetime of memories to have been
squeezed into however many seconds it must have taken
between the tying of the rope about his neck, and the final
leap and twitch of his life. And on thinking of such things,
something broke at the back of his throat, and Oravo
Tallista Swan did what he had never done before. A single
sob escaped him, a sound so uninvited and unwitnessed
that it felt as if the world had folded down around him

to stifle him, as an oyster moves and closes itself around its pearl.

Stroop finally consented to sit down at the table that still held the remains of the morning's breakfast, and drink some of the tea that Mabel had stoically brought back with her and placed in front of him. It was stewed, and the scrambled eggs and toast he was eating were cold. He hardly noticed, was far too intent on talking things out with Von Riddarholm, who had just returned with the boys, telling him of the hidden compartments of the suitcase, so much more secret than the little shelves of books.

Von Riddarholm looked grave and slightly anxious; was ashamed he had not thought to delve into those small compartments, had been so concerned with the safety of his merchandise that it had not even occurred to him to look for the last documented moments of Jarl Eriksson's life. He thought quietly now of that man who had worked so stalwartly for his father, and then for himself, for over forty years; chided himself that he had not thought to do what this man Stroop had done.

'Plainly he was in contact with Kustin Liit,' Stroop was saying, 'and had been friends with him for a long time.'

'Yes, yes,' Von Riddarholm agreed, and knew that of course they had been, that he had received several communiqués from Kustin via Eriksson, particularly these past few years, and on one particular subject. Kustin had often written of coming home, the only thing stopping him being his daughter. He had wanted more than anything to bring her with him, have enough income to support her and her family if and when they all returned.

'Chrystomation, he called it,' muttered Von Riddarholm, had to repeat himself when everyone, including Jack and Thomas, who were tucking into a second breakfast, minus rollmops, asked him to speak up. 'Chrystomation,' repeated Von Riddarholm, 'it was a process Kustin was trying to perfect. Something no one has ever done before, nor even got close to, not even the Chinese. For hundreds and hundreds of years people have been using gold to embellish printed works, but always the gold has had to be applied by hand, either as gilt or leaf. Kustin had been working for a long time on inventing an ink that could be used to print gold, and not just in specialised hand-operated presses, but in our most advanced mechanised machines. Capable of being done with the same ease with which we print blues and reds and so on. If he had achieved it, well, it would have been the wonder of the modern world . . .'

Von Riddarholm let his eyes wander off to the window. He could still see the deep, dark waters of the meteorite lake, could see his whole life passing across its surface like a shadow, still hearing the excited shouts of Jack and Thomas as they discovered it for themselves, wondered if he should not have found himself a wife, had children, done other things . . .

And then Stroop spoke. 'Chrystomation,' he said simply. 'I am certain he finally perfected the process, or at least thought he had.'

The words were so direct and simple that for a moment Von Riddarholm could not move. His eyes lifted momentarily from his imagining of the lake up towards a flat blue sky, could clearly see the high clouds sifting above in unfelt breezes, strange landscapes shifting into towers and minarets, ships into rivers, unknown visages fading into the familiar – Jarl Eriksson's, for example, and maybe even the face of Kustin Liit, whose features he knew he should remember, but could not quite grasp.

'He invented it?' Von Riddarholm repeated, felt as if he were plummeting back to earth as suddenly as had done the meteorite that first had formed the lake. He turned upon Stroop, and found his voice a whisper. 'What do you mean? How can he have done it? And how can you possibly know?'

And then Stroop had taken them all back into the glass-lined room, and picked up the documents that were in a language other than his own, though he had already divined their meaning, put them into the hands that they were meant for, saw Von Riddarholm's own hands shaking slightly as they took them, his fingertips purpling as the blood within him fevered at just the thought.

'My God, my God!' Baron Von Riddarholm was almost shouting as he read the letters through. 'I can't believe it! He did it! I can't believe he did it!' His voice seemed to have risen from the dead, had taken on some new texture it had never had before, a strange lilt that was entirely alien to the English words he was now using.

Josef had to sit down. He had the letters Kustin Liit had given to Jarl Eriksson resting in his lap, his hands fluttering over them like swallows returning for the summer, eager to find their homes. Could not let them go, would not let them go.

233

'He wrote to me at the beginning of the year,' Josef said excitedly, 'he said then he had been working on the ink, and was close. But I never thought! I never thought!'

He didn't have to say any more. They all knew what he had thought: that Kustin Liit's hints of the invention of Chrystomation had been nothing more than the deluded desires of an old man to return to his homeland with his head held high. That he had given hints of its progress over the years via Eriksson, but that nothing would ever come from the old exile, nor of his dreams to come home.

Von Riddarholm was shaking his head, and his brow had creased over as he at last began to understand the several things that Stroop had already surmised: that Kustin Liit truly had perfected his Chrystomation process, or thought he had, and that he had committed this process to paper in some form that was not immediately recognisable.

'But where is it?' asked the baron, having read the few documents Stroop had laid to his care. 'I don't understand. There must be another secret drawer, another letter . . .'

'I don't believe so,' said Stroop, and he looked over at Mabel, saw the unwavering trust in her eyes that at times alarmed him, and at others only reassured. 'I believe Kustin Liit had known for some time how close he was to perfecting his process, and I also believe that he feared it would be taken from him.' Stroop did not add his own suspicions of Charles Quaritch at this moment, nor the unease that had struck him on discovering the suddenness of Kustin Liit's death and burial. That was something he would need to pursue later, but now there were matters more immediately important to do and say. 'Above all, I believe Kustin Liit wished to pass on to his daughter the secrets of Chrystomation, and that he wished her to bring them here if he could not do so himself. And,' Stroop concluded dramatically, 'I believe she has done exactly that and is already here, on Hiiumaa.'

Stroop was right about that, though quite wrong in his reasoning. When he'd seen the note tacked to the church door that Von Riddarholm had left out for him as he had asked the night before, he'd seen, like everyone else, the crude map that had led to the discovery of the man who now lay white and wasted in the ice house. Like them, he had also seen the word spelled out in English next to the small cross that had marked the place where his body had been found: 'HERE'. Unlike the others, though, he had turned that tattered piece of paper over, and seen the faint sketch of another map contorted by age and fold, and recognised the contours and rises and scatters of little houses that had once made up the hamlet of Lower Slaughter.

He'd been at first astounded by the coincidence, though on further reflection, it did not seem quite so bizarre. The flood had devastated Griselda's valley; her father had just died; quite probably he had already expressed to her his wishes to return to Hiiumaa and, having neither home nor family left, she had come here in his stead. How she had come upon the murdered man, and why the man had been murdered was not yet something Stroop comprehended, but perhaps the small map of her valley back in England had been the very one that her father had possessed, one of the few things she had brought with her, though why she had brought it,

235

again he did not understand. But how else to explain its presence on the church door?

Stroop had no idea at that time of the existence of Oravo Swan, nor what he had been through, though he, and the rest of the island, was soon to know.

Oravo had cried that morning, and was ashamed of it, had wiped his face so fiercely with his hands he felt like he had been scraped over by a tanner's comb, had been glad of the discomfort, that it had woken him from his few moments of weakness. It hadn't taken him long after that to decide what to do. He had gone over the note he had started to write on the only piece of paper he had to hand, and then had taken his way out over the moors in the direction of what he thought might be the village that Griselda had set off for, taken his guidance from the coastal path he had come by, and the small stump of unfinished lighthouse he could just see as he managed to get himself to the top of a small knoll. It was hard going, and he had difficulty catching his breath, felt as if the garrotte were still around his throat, that the air had thickened around him, that he had to fight every step of the way to push himself on. The day had seemed interminable, and he had no idea how long it had taken him to reach the rough track that took him finally towards some kind of settlement, hadn't realised he had in fact fallen several times, and that he had slept where he lay for a few hours, had no idea that the day had slipped into night, so light was it.

He had found the church isolated in its field of burial, a strangely square wooden building, painted white, the colour peeling from the tired boards. He'd only known it for a church by the lych-gate and the graveyards that lay about it, cobbed in by walls of stone. And then at last he had done what he had come to do, had tacked his message to the door with the blackthorn spikes he had torn from a hedgerow passed not long before. There had been no one about, and though he had already made up his mind to head for the village, any village, find Griselda and tell her all that had happened, he found himself completely disoriented, had no idea where he was, nor that his windpipe had swollen within his throat, the internal bruises almost occluding the passage of air and oxygen to his lungs and blood. He had been so dizzy he had no longer been able to understand the difference between left and right, east and west, north and south, had headed without realising it back up the track along which he had spent the last few hours stumbling, trying to gain his bearings, failing, until finally his body began to dip and sway, and the sack that had lain alongside his hump between his shoulder blades, swung right around with his erratic movements, the weight of it becoming too heavy for him to bear, until at last it dragged him down, and he fell with it to the ground.

And so had lain Oravo Swan, face down amidst the ruts and pits and weathered pebble-stones of the track that he had tried so hard to gain, with no one to know who he was or what he had survived, and no one to even wonder where he had now gone.

Griselda had been almost two weeks drunk, not so much with the alcohol with which she had been plied ever since her return, but with the constant welcome that had received her, and the reiteration again and again of her story and her father's story, the descriptions of her travels to and from their homeland, his life at Painswick, hers in Lower Slaughter, and of the flood that had taken her from one home and brought her to another. She had been passed from family to family, from one house to the next, each one eager to hear her tales again at first-hand.

She had not been the only one to return since the expulsions, but she was amongst the few who had been old enough when she left for some to remember still her name and her face, and those too of her father. She was proud, and a little ashamed, that Kustin Liit had been so well regarded and that she had not known it, was saddened and simultaneously overjoyed to meet the few older women who had attended her mother's death. It made her realise that she had not thought of her mother in as long as she could remember, that always for her it had been Griselda and her father, and that long travail across the English countryside, his letter of recommendation tucked inside his pocket, his inability to find the place to which they seemed always to have been heading, until finally they arrived at Painswick and their journey's end.

Of her mother, there was very little left to her. She had died before Griselda was old enough to be able to recall her face, having fallen to some fever. And yet these people remembered her quite clearly, and one woman even took Griselda to the stone in the tree-chapel glade, pointed out her mother's name carved high upon its surface. 'Kala Anna Liit,' she read, '1752–1773.' Griselda stood there before that name and crossed herself, thought she saw something of her father in those neatly chiselled and squared-off letters, felt such sadness when she placed her fingers to those last few lines of her mother's life and wished she had thought to look for them sooner, that she had placed her father's name beside them. She swore that her own name would be there instead, and regretted that she had no daughter of her own to come and place her fingers here when she herself was gone, and know she too had a history. And for that, and for her father and for the mother she had never known, Griselda knelt before her island's stone, and wept.

On hearing Stroop's assured assumption that Kustin Liit's daughter was already upon the island, Von Riddarholm cursed quietly and thumped the table with his fist, set the dishes rattling within their silver lids, apologised immediately and tried to explain.

A couple of months earlier, he told them, he had sent out specific instructions to every elder of every village that he should be alerted to the arrival of any strangers, or of any unusual occurrence.

'What with the cat's head,' he went on, 'and the pig and the *Pihkva* – well, there has been a certain amount of unrest upon the island. And then the murder—'

Stroop interrupted. 'Excuse me, Baron. The cat's head? The pig? The, er, the . . .' he stumbled over the foreign word.

'*Pihkva*,' Josef supplied, and sighed deeply. 'It was not just for the delivery of the suitcase I brought you here,' he smiled weakly, knew Stroop already knew as much. 'There have been other things going on as well, aside from the murder.'

And so, at Stroop's interrogations, he told them all he knew about the mutilated animals, starting with the excoriated lamb back in February, and the cat's head and the pig. There had been a dog too – he'd forgotten about that, though it was the most recent. The poor thing had been strung up by its hind legs in the tree-chapel glade, and its throat cut. Just thinking about that pool of blood, with all the flies that settled and rose like a swarm of summer ants, had brought the acid to his throat; remembered how the villagers had insisted on cutting it down and burning its body to cleanse the chapel glade of its desecration. Had assumed, like everyone else, that it had been a rogue dog that had been found at the lambs or the hens, and a summary, if cruel, kind of justice meted out, though no one could understand why it should have been done in such a sacred place, and no one had admitted doing it, or came forward to claim the dog's body for their own.

Stroop shook his head at this new information, recognised some kind of escalation in the way things had gone, struggled to find some kind of meaning to such strange events, to piece it together with the spiderweb of paths from Painswick and Lower Slaughter.

'And the *Pihkva*?' he asked, finally getting his tongue around the word, and Josef explained about the storm and the setting of the false lights, and the luring in of the *Pihkva* to its ambush, when it had been set upon and robbed and left to be smashed upon the rocks in the bay beyond the lighthouse.

'And when did this happen exactly?' asked Stroop. He had asked about the other days, when the animals had been found, but the baron had been vague, had apparently made no particular note of when exactly they had occurred. But Josef knew about the *Pihkva* all right, and answered without hesitation.

'The night of April the twenty-third,' Josef replied, and Stroop flicked his fingernails together, closed his eyes, tried to find the rhythm in this apparently random string of events, between the things that had happened over in England to Jarl Eriksson, Kustin and Griselda, and those that had been happening here. Nothing was clear yet, but he was aware of some vague notion pushing at his mind, some starting point from which he could make his way; felt like a mariner who has watched the sky for many nights and seen only cloud and darkness, has just begun to notice a slight shift to the mist, a glimpse of the smallest pinpricks of stars that will tell him his way. He saw again the seal that Kustin Liit had set into the wax of his letters, as if the earth were the hedgehog, and the apples the constellations radiating out from the tips of its elongated quills.

'Mr Stroop?' It was Mabel. She had placed her hand upon his arm, and was shaking him gently, until he opened his eyes, saw Jack and Thomas prodding cautiously at the last few bits of food on their plates, daring each other to be the first to eat what they could not name; saw Josef drumming his fingers impatiently a hair's-breadth from the table surface so as not to make any noise; saw Mabel watching him anxiously, knew she wanted answers too, had been disturbed by the cat's head and the pig, and especially the dog. Knew she would have been thinking of old Bindlestiff, and how he was getting on without them. Quite well, Stroop thought, given a fire to lie by and a bit of food and the occasional

warm stroking of his ancient, moth-eaten fur by the neigh-
bour to whom they had entrusted the old dog's care.

His mind was working away like one of the clocks upon
the staircase wall, slotting things in here and other things in
there, creating small maps within his head. He thought he
was beginning to find a little reason in all that had been
happening, as if he had been playing hopscotch in the dark
only to wake and find all the squares scattered in a circle
about him, their numbers scrawled, but indistinct, waiting to
be put back in their proper order.

'One thing,' Stroop asked, opening his eyes and fixing them
upon Von Riddarholm, 'just one thing more for the moment.
Who is Swedberg?'

Von Riddarholm was surprised, did not at first understand
the question, was searching through the names of all the
villagers on his islands.

'He is an author, I believe?' Stroop prompted.

'Swedberg,' Von Riddarholm murmured slowly, 'Swedberg?'
And then he had it, though why it might be important he
couldn't think. He had not read through Kustin's last will
and testament as thoroughly as he might have done, had been
too focused on the Chrystomation process to look too hard
for anything else. He scoured through his early learning,
through his literature, and found some kind of answer.

'There is a philosopher called Swedberg,' he began with
some hesitation, 'you probably know him as Swedenborg.'
And of course Stroop did know, and knew now why the
name had tickled him, had read something of the same man
not so long ago, when a minor furore had been stirred up
in London. Swedenborg had died there some thirty or so

years before, but only a few months back, some of his followers had decided to set up a church in his name. From what Stroop remembered, Swedenborg had been at first an engineer, a mineralogist, who had travelled widely, had then had some religious experience that turned him into a full-time theologian and mystic, had given up the stones of the earth for the words of God. Very big in Sweden, Josef informed him, and hence, Stroop now concluded, very big in Hiiumaa.

'Could that explain Kustin Liit's attachment to his book?' he wondered out loud. It didn't seem particularly likely, at least not to the extent implied in his will. And yet Kustin Liit had been so absolutely adamant that the book went to Griselda, and more specifically, that it be the very book of Swedberg that Kustin had owned for many years, had even gone so far as to describe that book in detail, right down to his own inscription, in the extremely unlikely situation, Stroop now concluded, that a substitution was attempted.

'Maybe he wrote his ink stuff in it,' piped up Jack, and Josef swivelled his head around like a mantis upon his neck to look at the boy. 'I mean,' Jack went on, 'if he didn't want the Painswick man to get it, maybe he wrote stuff in some kind of code on the back page or something.'

Of course! thought Stroop and Mabel and Josef all at the same moment, though Jack was supremely unaware of his revelatory statement, was intent only on picking the cheese out from a pinwheel of ham.

'I like codes,' he added, and there was not a one amongst them who disagreed. Codes, they all thought. Kustin Liit was a printer, and all good printsmen know their codes.

Josef was already calling in his men-at-arms and began to give out instructions, but Stroop halted him, estimating that if Griselda had left her valley immediately after the flood and then gone on to Painswick to collect her father's belongings, she could have been here in Hiiumaa for several weeks by now, and yet no one had bothered to inform Von Riddarholm of her return.

'She would not have been viewed as a stranger,' Stroop added, 'merely as one who had returned. And most certainly, she would have tried to return to the very village her father left. Do you not have records?'

Josef did, and immediately sent for the demographic logs that had been made at the time of the expulsions, when each family had solemnly written down their names and the places of their birth and residence, having even at the time of their leaving the faint hope of their return, wanted to be able to reclaim their family homes and the land they had once worked. Within minutes of looking, Josef discovered that the Liits had originally lived in one of the several villages from which his main workforce were drawn, the closest one, in fact, to the tree-chapel glade, quite near Kopu, which he could almost see from the highest window in the highest tower of his manor house. He was impatient once his men had been sent out to that village. He read Jarl Eriksson's little ledger of itinerary and sales, translating for Stroop all the parts he was not able to understand. Von Riddarholm was shaking his head sadly.

'It's all here,' he told Stroop. 'Eriksson tells us plainly that on his last visit to Painswick Kustin told him he had perfected his process. And worse,' Von Riddarholm sighed a little, 'Kustin told him that he thought he had been discovered, and that the poor man was in fear for his life.' He stabbed at the tiny pages with his fingers, laid down the magnifying glass he had been using to read it. 'It is all true. He writes that Liit was concerned that Quaritch would not release him, would not allow him to return here to his home with such a great invention. I can hardly believe it.' There was a smoulder of anger to his voice, the kind that lingers in the embers and makes you believe the fire has almost died, before flaring up and burning down the house. 'I have had that man Quaritch here in Hiiumaa, in my home.' He jumped up suddenly, unable to wait any longer, having already decided to change into his riding gear and go to fetch this Griselda as quick as he was able. Kustin Liit's daughter. And Kustin's little book.

He was interrupted by an urgent tapping at the door.

'At last,' he breathed, thinking she had already been located and that she was already here at his very door. But he was disappointed. A manservant poked his head into the room and spoke to his master in Swedish. Josef swore – at least that's how it seemed to Stroop and Mabel, though neither of them could understand the words. They exchanged glances, wondered what was going on, Mabel fearing it was some other animal strung out by its guts to hang and die in the afternoon, Stroop hoping to God it wasn't another man dead and blocked in ice, awaiting his perusal. But it was neither. Josef dismissed the servant, turned back to them all, an expression of thunder upon his face. He saw Mabel's concerned eyes looking back at him, the thin figure of Stroop stooping slightly where he had too suddenly stood up at the intrusion. Saw Jack and Thomas at the other end of the long room, apparently playing marbles with some of the rounded pebbles they had found by the lakeside, and with which they had been so fascinated, resembling as they did some kind of smoked glass.

'My apologies,' Josef said, and laid his hand across his heart. 'It has been a quite unusual morning, and I have just had yet more news.' His eyes met Stroop's but he seemed to recall himself, shifted his gaze briefly to Mabel before turning back to Stroop, including her, however slightly, in his conversation. 'Following my earlier orders, no matter how late they are in coming, a stranger has been discovered, over at the Widow Vedrukha's, which is not so very far from the church where we found the note.' He coughed gently, lowered his voice; maybe, thought Mabel afterwards, didn't want Jack to hear. 'She has a softness to her head, and apparently introduced this stranger as her brother when a village elder came to visit and found him chopping at her wood. But she has no brother, nor ever had.' He went to the door then, opened it full wide and went to leave. 'I must take some men with me to the widow's house, see who he is and what he is doing here. He has a bandage, so I am told, about his neck.' He gave Stroop another hard look, and added briefly. 'I have given instructions that the woman Griselda be brought here directly to you when we have found her.' He clicked his heels in a military salute. 'Do not let her leave until I am returned.'

9

The Glorious Stag Arises

O RAVO WAS ENTIRELY unaware of the woman poking at him with the tip of her boot when she found him lying face down in the dirt at the place where her own rough track met the slightly less rough track that led down to the church. She had been on her way there to pray as she did every morning, rising with the blackbirds and the wrens to which she was not unlike, setting off as soon as the light was grey enough for her to pick out her way. She had taken the same route there and back every day for almost forty years, though she hardly knew how to count them, had no idea how long those years had been, still thought of herself as thirty-five, still waiting for her man to return from the wars which seemed to have been going on for ever, waited for him to give her again the children that had already died and been so long buried she didn't even remember the names they had so briefly held.

She saw the man lying there, his breath making the small puddle about his face bubble where the water touched one corner of his lips. At first she thought he was a boulder, thought she must have mistaken her path in the dirty streaks of dawn that were trying to push away the mist, but soon enough she saw him for what he was, crossed herself, placed her two hands over her heart and thanked God that he had brought her brother home and almost to her door. It was an odd thing that she forgot her husband and the children, so long vanished from her life, rolled their little bodies up into one and made them into a man who had never existed. Odder still that she had absolutely no doubt, on seeing Oravo's body, that this was that brother finally returned.

She might have been old, but was still strong from heaving straw-ricks on her back, and hauling sheep and goats up above the slaughtering block, axing wood and digging up peat for the fire. She didn't even turn the stranger over to check his face, but ran straight back up the track like a whippet after a hare and hauled the flat-bodied cart out of the barn, loaded it with two short lengths of plank and a piece of rope, pushed it quickly before her back down the track. It took her a while to set the planks against the side of the cart, keep them steady with clods of earth and stones so that she could drag the unconscious man up by the ropes she had tied so laboriously beneath his armpits. But she managed it, and hauled him on, and pushed the cart back up the small hill with no hesitation, her breath coming so quick and fast it seemed to her as if her whole body suddenly came alive and young again, gave her the strength she needed finally to bring her lost family back to where they had always belonged.

She dragged her unconscious bundle into the small tumble of wood and turf that was her cottage, rolled him out onto

248

the shallow earthen niche dug into the wall that made her bed, spent her time constantly warming water and soaking compresses for his throat and head, dripping thin barley gruel into his mouth, though most of it ended fouling yet more of his mud-drenched shirt. And she thanked God over and over and over that He had finally answered her prayers and brought her kith and kin back into her fold.

It was the old priest who finally alerted someone to her lack of attendance at his early morning Masses, and sent a boy off with a message for someone to check on her, fearing the worst, and that reality had at last broken through the armour of her grief, and wrung out what little remained of life and sanity from her tired heart. About that he was wrong, and by the time Ilves, the head man in the nearest village to her isolated home, received the priest's message, and sighed his way out of his slippers, put on his boots and went to check, he was amazed to find the widow up and sprightly, garrulous to the extreme. She insisted he come in and sat him down and took off his boots, gave him several glasses of home-brewed barley vodka, talked non-stop about the brother who had at last returned with all his tales of war and heroism and capture and escape.

'Twenty years he has been held in the prison camps up by Archangel,' she sighed with a certainty Ilves found himself almost believing as she refilled his cup yet again, and then her own. He couldn't imagine where she had heard of anywhere called Archangel, but was lulled by the drink, relieved not to find her wrinkled up like some old shrew, decomposing on her own floor, had let her go on. 'Twenty years! Imagine.'

And they both shook their heads, she at the unimaginable hardships she believed her brother to have endured, Ilves
at the extremes to which the woman had descended into
her madness. And then he heard a sound, thought at first it
must be some woodpecker hammering out his heart in the
little copse of trees out back, listened again, and this time
was not mistaken, knew without a doubt it was the sound
of an axe splitting wood. He jumped up then, went through
the door and walked the small way up the neglected garden,
forgetting for the moment he was not wearing his boots,
poked his head out just clear of the barn, and saw a real live
man send the axe down again and again upon the tree stump,
splitting logs into perfect wedges as easy as cutting up a
truckle of cheese. He felt his heart then jumping hard within
his throat, almost tripped as he ran his way back into the
widow's shack and made his apologies, pleaded urgent business, shoved his feet inside his boots without doing up the
laces, said he would be back soon, and, with a flourish of
which he was still proud, said the village would hold a surprise
welcome-home party for her brother, and that she must not
say a word. She had put her finger to her lips and smiled.

'Hush,' she said, and Ilves nodded, skidded his way back
down the track, thanked God he had walked the way to
enjoy the day and not brought the pony, hoped that the
stranger had not heard his arrival or seen his sudden departure, felt a little guilt that perhaps he was leaving the widow
all alone with a murderer, knew also that if murderer he was,
he would be gone quicker than a stoat down a rabbit hole
if he had even a suspicion that anyone knew he was there.

★   ★   ★

Griselda was lifting water from the village well, looked down into the deep tunnel of water that spooled out of the bedrock and threaded its way from the meteorite lake, formed an underground stream along whose buried depths small wells had been dug, strung out across the island like the circles of sand a lugworm leaves behind as it curls its way beneath the tide line, saw her own reflection, pale and rippling on the surface of the dark water as she pulled up the bucket, had the fleeting sensation that everything that had happened the past few months had been but illusion, and that she was still looking into that other mirror as she passed it on the miller's wall, felt the dampness of the flood all around her, the smell of rot and mould and things destroyed. She heard someone call her name and brought the bucket splashing back over the well rim, did not feel alarm until she saw who it was who was calling: two men, armed with swords and pistols, heavy boots clumping over the packed earth that made up the village street.

'Griselda Liit,' they were calling, 'daughter of Kustin. Griselda Liit, daughter of Kustin.'

They were not asking, they were demanding, and the few men and women who were not out at work in the fields or at the print barns fluttered from their doorways and watched. One or two made their way towards her and stood anxiously by the well, hovered behind her shoulders. Helle, the woman who had remembered Griselda from her schooldays, ran swiftly from her house straight towards her, abandoning her small children as they clustered about her porch, poking at the earth with the chickens, took a tight hold of Griselda's hand and stood like a wall beside her. And without being told, these men knew right enough which one was the woman they sought, read with ease the way the rest of them moved, the quick flick of their eyes, the way the woman Helle clutched at Griselda's hand where she stood by the well, where she still stood, her heart thumping, her hand shaking as she put down the bucket, unhooked it from the well-cord.

'I am Griselda Liit,' she said, the words feeling strange upon her lips as if she had only just realised herself who she was. She freed her hand from Helle's, patted the other woman's arm and took a pace forward, saw the two men advance, seemed to take an age to reach her. But when they did, they did not draw their weapons nor clap her in irons for some unfathomable reason, but both bowed short and brief, one even touching his hand to his cap.

'Please come with us, miss. The baron wants to see you, and says you've to bring your father's book.'

Griselda tried to hide her astonishment, but did not have to go any distance to retrieve it, tucked as it was in the small band she had tied about her waist, had not left it for a moment since she had departed Painswick, since that small argument she had had with Quaritch about its provenance, remembered the greed in his eyes as he had looked at it open faced upon the desk by the window, the unwillingness with which he had parted from it. And she had no fear, only the feeling that something was unfolding, and that she was a part of it, and that her father was somewhere close beside her; felt for just a moment the scratch of his old and stubbled face against her cheek.

★   ★   ★

Gunar Torrensson had lost two teeth to Oravo's hammer, and a third one shattered and broken. Throughout his long career of soldiering, he'd been many times wounded, had been slashed by swords and bayonets upon his arms and back, had grapeshot scars scattered like pox burns across his stomach, and a dent in his chest where he had been hammered to the deck by a piece of fallen rigging; but the pain of that one tooth broken and split was too much for him to bear, and after a week of clove oil and strong vodka, he finally marched his way down to the surgeon's cabin, took up a pair of pliers and ripped the trunk of it from his jaw with his own two hands. Every man on board ship heard the awful howling that came from out his mouth with that tooth, stopped at their cards or their caulking, the spoon or the bottle halfway to their lips, parted quickly from his path as he came back out towards the deck, fearing him as he climbed the steps that led above the wheelhouse, the blood still coursing down his chin.

They had been back in the Pike Gut, had spent their days riding every now and then off the coast of Hiiumaa, attacking boats that were not so greatly armoured, then back again into their hiding within the mists, anchored behind the uninhabited spills of reef and boulder, the gulls clammering about them, the small, round heads of seals bobbing and nosing at the waste that drained from their scuppers.

And then their captain had suddenly disembarked and taken himself all alone over to Hiiumaa. The crew had been jittery until he had returned, and even more so once he had. Straight away they had retreated to the Pike Gut, had been talking in low voices ever since, wondering at the inactivity, had been told to spend their days scrubbing decks and cleaning weapons, replacing frayed guide-lines, damaged sheets. They all recognised the patterns of this tidying up, this getting ready, this honing of a blade before the battle, but still they were puzzled at the timing, and worried that ever since Torrensson had returned on board, no one seemed to have seen him for the best part of a week.

It had made them twitchy, this sudden disappearance from their midst. They knew he was a captain like no other, a man who never ate alone in his cabin but always at the galley tables with his crew, a man who spat in the face of every enemy he had ever been put against, and always come out the better. He had never been sickened nor significantly weakened by any of his many wounds, and so the shock had been all the more profound when he finally did come out of his cabin, and they could all see for themselves that great black bruise stretch a gangrenous sunset across his face, one cheek swollen up like a toad, as if he were holding a musket ball within his mouth. No one knew what had happened to him over on Hiiumaa, or even why he had gone there, and certainly not why he had hidden away for a week once he had returned. But everyone knew that roaring for his own the morning he had gone below decks and re-emerged with the blood all down his chin, the bloody pliers still held in his hand, and were terrified when he came striding out upon the decks and up the steps and stood like a great black monolith above them, the bruises livid across his face, casting him in shadow, his words slurred by the injuries to his jaw, yet unmistakable in their strength.

'The time, my friends, is upon us!' He poured out his anger upon his crew like a storm of burning ash running down a mountain, his voice bursting from him like the rolling of a drum. 'There are things that have happened over on Hiiumaa, and we can no longer wait for Eustace and his day, but must take up his sword and wield it as our own.' His men looked at one another, and up at Torrensson, knew all about St Eustace, and why their final attack had been planned for his feast day. He had been a hunter and a Roman soldier, and then one day had had a vision of the cross within the antlers of a stag and converted, and been exiled and reduced to penury for that choice. But he had risen up again and returned to lead his own army in a glorious, victorious campaign, just as they would do. That he had been later roasted alive in a brazen ox with all his family, was neither here nor there. For them, he was the greatest of the Fourteen Helpers, and Torrensson the stag of their revelation, the man who had enlisted them to his cause and made it their own, given them a goal and a future, and a sure promise of return to the land they too had been exiled from, and that they would be the men to free it and subdue it, would ever afterwards call it their own.

Torrensson stood there far above his men, and felt nothing but contempt. Rhetoric, he thought, as did all good leaders, was such a fine thing. Make of it a ring of gold, and you can lead the fiercest bull by its nose, take it wherever you would, make it do whatever you chose. He spat some blood from the corner of his mouth, and turned away from his men, saw the sun as round and low in the sky as a cannonball just fired, and the small and distant shadow on the sea that he knew to be Hiiumaa, and took an oath beneath his breath that if he could not have it, he would find instead some way to utterly destroy it.

10

The Widow and the Watermarks

ORAVO WAS CHOPPING wood, had taken to the woman's axe with ease, felt the long years of usage smooth beneath his fingers, enjoyed some kind of rightness with the world as he brought that axe up over his shoulders and down again, the blade splitting the wood exactly on the grain. He had no other way to thank this woman who had cared for him for he knew not how long.

He awoke one night, looked out of a small window and saw the thin black line of moor outside, and up above a sprinkle of stars. They reminded him of Griselda and her freckles, wondered for an instant if he were not still in that ruined cottage where he had spent the night with her by his side, could still smell for a moment the faint toasting of the bread upon the fire, hear the softness of her voice as she spoke her secret memories of the land that had been lost to her. It was only for a moment, and too soon he realised he was somewhere else entirely, heard the faint snore and whistle of someone sleeping nearby, saw the old woman tucked up like a bracket-form on the rag-rug by the fire. The fire was almost at its end and it reminded him of something, though he could not place it. So many fires, he thought, and all going out.

He tried to move then, felt a stricture about his windpipe as if he were caught in some shepherd's crook, put up his hand and touched the damp cloth of a compress against his throat, tried to cry out, but the only sound that came was the thin skreeking he had once heard from a vole just hefted into the air by the talons of a sparrowhawk, felt himself spinning high up above his own life, wondered if he would ever get down again and feel the earth beneath his feet, the wood below his fingers. He touched his pocket then as he always did on waking, and was comforted to feel the old cylinder of his past still there, but was troubled to feel its twin beside it. Could not remember what it was or where it had come from. He felt the heaviness in his head and lungs, tried to turn himself a little more onto his side so he could see the window a little clearer, saw instead a brief splutter of embers in the fireplace, saw in them the yellow halo of daffodils as he handed them over to Griselda, felt sleep rush over him as a wave upon the incoming tide, saw her pale speckled hand take the flowers, but this time she remained by the door, and the door stayed open.

After Josef's departure, Stroop and Mabel stayed at the table, Stroop pouring himself more coffee, Mabel savouring another glass of the smooth, round-flavoured chocolate drink she had not tasted before, knew she wanted to taste again. They discussed the case in logical fashion, trying to order all the events and make sense of what was happening here on

Hiiumaa and what had already happened over at Lower Slaughter. Neither of them was in any doubt that these two separate sets of events had somehow collided.

The first precipitation had come with Kustin Liit over at Painswick, and the fact that he had discovered some miraculous new form of ink; secondly had come Quaritch's discovery of this invention, or at least his suspicions that such a momentous thing had taken place; next had come Jarl Eriksson's visit to Kustin at the printworks, and Kustin's handing over of the letters and the declarations of his intended will should anything happen to him. Next came the fact that something *had* happened to him, and that Kustin Liit had died, most probably before his time. There was some discussion between the two of them as to the details of this latter event: could he have died a natural, if unexpected, death? Or had Charles Quaritch lost his patience with the man who had worked for him for so many faithful years, and yet desired to take away with him his most valuable invention? It was a moot point, and something they could not know, although Stroop suspected the worst. He could not quite see Quaritch deliberately stabbing or beating a man to death with his own two hands, wondered if he had employed someone else to do it, or if they had simply argued and Kustin Liit's heart had seized up within him like a bud that refuses to open and face the shock of spring.

Either way, it was not in dispute that the man had died. And very soon after, maybe a week, maybe a little more, Eriksson had gone to the valley of Lower Slaughter to deliver his letter to Griselda, and had been caught up in the catastrophic flood that had swept away Griselda's village, and presumably him too, parting him from the Travelling Library, which Thomas had later found.

Griselda, meanwhile, had lost everything in the flood apart from her life, and had left the valley and made her way to Painswick and Charles Quaritch, recovered whatever her father had left her, including the small book in which Quaritch, and now Stroop and Mabel, suspected he had secreted the recipe for an ink that could revolutionise the printing world.

And then there were the animals, and Mabel voiced what both of them were thinking.

'What on earth can the killing of these animals possibly have to do with Kustin Liit or his daughter, or the Travelling Library, come to that?'

Stroop was silent, didn't know, had already tried to lay the time-line out before him. There had been the lamb some-time back in February, the severed cat's head in May, the gutted pig in June, and again, not two weeks after, if Josef's recollection could be trusted, the dog in the tree-chapel. And he thought about that tree-chapel, wanted to go and see it for himself, but there was something else nagging at him, something about the flood in Lower Slaughter and the piracy of the *Pihkva*. Both had happened within a week of each other, and he could not shake the thought that they were in some way linked, though how that could be he could not fathom.

He was interrupted at that moment by someone knocking on the door.

'Come,' he said, hoping the person on the other side would understand the word, which obviously they did, for the door opened, and two men stepped inside, and behind them came a woman notable for the scatter of freckles about her face and wrists. Griselda Liit, Stroop thought immediately, and was not mistaken. She stepped into the room, made what was half a curtsy and half a bow, then straightened herself, came towards Stroop with her hand extended.

'Baron Von Riddarholm?' she asked, and revealed what she was holding, held it out towards him. It was a book, quite small, not much bigger than her palm, and Stroop knew, without having to ask, that this was Kustin's book, and he felt a small rush of heat to his face as he took it from her.

The murderer was not hard to capture, indeed he walked quite freely towards them, his hand upon the bandage about his throat. He did not speak, and Von Riddarholm wondered if perhaps he was unable to even if he wanted, if the bandage would not preclude such a thing. It was the Widow Vedrukha who was the problem, had heard them coming up the track from the church even before they turned onto the path that took them to her door, had sworn at her supposed brother, trying to force him back into the barn, had still been shoving last year's mouldy straw bales haphazardly to one side in an effort to hide him. But when they came, he appeared more relieved than anything else, pulled at the bandage that strode his throat, undid it, and let it drop to the floor. The only resistance he showed was when the widow tried to hurl herself across the barn floor and into one of Von Riddarholm's men, and that man pushed out his hand, and swatted her to the ground, her thin bones grating and creaking as she hit the corn-dusted floor.

'No need for that,' the murderer croaked out and came

towards them, ignored the swords and pistols brandished, picked the widow up and set her on her feet, held her behind him, a mountain hiding a deer from the oncoming storm.

Von Riddarholm was astounded for several reasons: first, that the man spoke English, secondly that his now naked throat plainly showed the yellow of old bruises rising above and below a thin line that he had seen before, and thirdly because the man stood there solid before him, one hand holding back the spitting widow, the other held up in a gesture that could only mean surrender.

'Who are you?' Josef asked in the same tongue the man had employed.

For a few moments the stranger said nothing, plainly surprised to be addressed in his own language, allowed the widow to take advantage of his momentary stupor and come ducking underneath his arm. She ran straight at Von Riddarholm like an arrow loosed, started hammering at his chest with her fists, continued going at it even whilst one of his men plucked her off him easier than picking a lady-bird from a leaf, held her at arm's length, still pummelling with futile anger at the air.

'You'll not take him!' she began to scream. 'Twenty years he's been away and more! Twenty years in those camps! You'll not have him, I say, you'll not!' And then the woman suddenly collapsed, crumpled to her feet without hope, as the tube nest of the caddis fly cannot survive without its occupant, and all the grains fall back undone to the riverbed from which they have come.

★   ★   ★

Griselda had known that it would all come to this, that somehow everything would fall back on to the little book her father had carried all those years. Remembered his reading it out loud to her as they travelled over those fields and roads that were then so foreign, the strange way people had watched them as they went, the long, long time it had taken them to reach Painswick and for her father to resume the job he had been born to. She knew there was a secret in that book the moment she had set eyes upon Charles Quaritch, and now here was someone else scouring at its pages, and she wanted to stop him, to shout out that it was sacred to her, that she had already had the mad thought of burying it somewhere within the circle of grass that surrounded the big ancestral stone. He was not even Von Riddarholm, but an English man named Stroop, and despite his soft and reassuring manner, she watched him closely as he held that little book up to the light, fingering its pages one by one, felt as if her father were being violated, that she had betrayed him, that perhaps the secrets those pages apparently held should always remain hidden. And then the man Stroop spoke again, and she no longer had any idea what was going on.

'Aha!' he said. 'I see it!' and he placed Griselda's father's book down upon the desk and took up the sharp knife that she saw must have been waiting.

'No!' she cried out uselessly, but the man Stroop ignored her, took up the blade and began to cut the bindings clear.

'The watermarks,' he said mysteriously, 'it's all in the watermarks.'

11

Lower Slaughter Reunited

IT WAS HARD to say who was the more surprised when
Oravo and Griselda finally came face to face. They both
stood immobilised when Oravo was first brought into that
room, where Stroop was busy butchering Kustin's book, and
Mabel trying to calm Griselda, who had at first tried to intervene, now had stopped and let instead the large tears cascade
unstoppered down her cheeks, making her skin translucent,
and the sprinkle of red freckles all the more distinct.

The excitement brought Thomas and Jack up from the
other end of the room, and both clustered around Griselda,
seeing her obvious distress, Jack taking her hand and stroking
it, Thomas trying to tip a chair beneath her in case she should
fall. It was an awful thing for her to see Stroop dissecting
her father's book, slicing through the tendoned threads that
held the pages all together, could not understand why he
was doing what he was doing.

Only later was it explained, after the hardly less shocking
introduction of Oravo into the room. He was preceded by
Von Riddarholm, who had abandoned the protective

custody of his men, was talking to Stroop even as he entered, Oravo hanging behind him like a man already spent. But when Oravo saw the woman standing there, slightly to one side, the boy clutching at her hand, the light of the orange sun catching her hair to flame, the tears that were running like a fountain down her face, he thought the wire had been placed once again around his throat and he could not breathe, put his hand there to check it, felt the hard fast pulse of blood beneath his skin and almost stumbled. Von Riddarholm turned swiftly at the noise, caught the man's elbow, pulled him in, stopped his own talking when he saw the small, sharp knife in Stroop's hand, the bend of his back down towards the desk, the small book with the pages being fluttered one by one from its spine by his fingers. And for a few moments, no one spoke, and nothing moved, except for Stroop, who was carefully sorting through the leftovers and pickings of the book he had dismembered, taking out first one leaf, and then another, and another.

It took several glasses of strong wine to bring everyone back to order and all ideas were pooled into the fold.

Griselda's tears finally ceased, and Oravo Tallista Swan was properly introduced, and the two of them stood apart from one another for a few moments after his name was spoken. Oravo, unable to move, felt like a taper was burning deep within him to see Griselda there, afraid to meet her eyes, ashamed that his hands were shivering like a wasp's nest that had been disturbed beneath his skin. He still did not move when she started the few steps towards him, saw the concern in her eyes as she noticed the unhealed ravage that ringed his neck, the bruises on his face, thought his heart might beat itself to death when she placed her hand upon his arm and spoke to him.

'Welcome, Oravo. I knew you would come.'

He moved slightly then, felt his whole body rocking gently as if a wind had caught him, felt ridiculous and red and brutish standing there beside her, unable to do anything but stare at her hand where it lay upon the mud and blood that caked his sleeve. And then the situation moved on without him, and she took him to a chair and pushed him down, sat silently beside him, and a small boy rushed over with a bottle, which he uncorked with his teeth, and another older boy produced glasses so pure and pristine and lined with gold at their rims, Oravo feared he would crush the one offered him with his large workman's hands, but swallowed what was given him without question, and then another, and another. He felt as if the day were breaking somewhere deep within his bones and that at last the sun he had waited for his whole life had suddenly risen up from the dark horizon.

Von Riddarholm, on the other hand, forgot everything and everyone around him when he saw the slaughter of the little book upon his desk, knew without asking that this was Kustin Liit's, and that the woman must be his daughter and that Stroop had figured out what no one else had been able to do.

'You've found it?' he asked, unaware that he had spoken in Swedish, and yet still Stroop had understood.

'I've found it,' said Stroop, and he picked up one of the several pages he had separated from the rest of Swedenborg's *Arcana Coelestia*, wished he had the use of the light-box he had

had at Astonishment Hall, asked instead for someone to fetch him a couple of blocks of wood and a piece of glass, some candles, preferably low and shielded. Josef shouted for his men, who still waited at the door in case of trouble, harried them into finding the objects Stroop required, fidgeted incessantly for the several minutes they took to supply them, swallowed several glasses of wine in his waiting, tried to listen to what Stroop was saying but found it impossible to concentrate. *He did it,* was all he could think, repeated over and over like the over-wound watch whose hands constantly went back to the minute that has just passed. *He did it. Kustin really did it.*

Stroop himself was occupied with studying the little book. He was not able to understand a word of it, but was fascinated by the tiny marginalia written on almost every page, wondered if there was any meaning to it, or if Kustin Liit had fabricated every scribble and scrawl to throw off anyone who might look, who might seek, but would not find. He tried to explain to Von Riddarholm and the collected company what Kustin Liit had done.

'He was a printsman and an inksman,' he was saying, 'knew every little intricacy of how a book is made. The history of binding itself is quite fascinating. There's split-binding and flat-back case binding, amongst many others, and much argument about the use of various cords, whether of linen or hemp or silk.'

He was interrupted by Mabel bringing him a glass of wine, speaking the few words needed to get him back on track, to tell them what they all wanted to hear. 'How did he do it, Mr Stroop?'

'Ah, yes,' said Stroop, lifting his finger, waving away the wine, and so he explained.

Kustin Liit had been a man surrounded by books his whole life and steeped in their making and manufacture. He had a secret, and he wanted that secret hidden, did not want it to be obvious to anyone, except to himself and those closest to him. He had given explicit instructions in his letters and testament that this particular copy of Swedenborg's *Arcana* be handed on to Griselda if, and after, he died. That he had not expected to die quite so suddenly was plain from another letter he had sent to Josef Von Riddarholm several months before, requesting leave to return to Hiiumaa. That expectation was not quite so assured in the last letter written to Von Riddarholm, which the latter had not received, at least not until the recovery of the miniature library and the letter's release from the hidden drawers, which would have been delivered by Eriksson, had he not perished in the flood. Since its discovery, Von Riddarholm had read it through and translated it for Stroop. In it, Kustin stated unequivocally that he had achieved his greatest aim, and perfected what he called his Chrystomation Process. And in that same letter, he stated categorically that he had written down the recipe for his Golden Ink in his little book. The same book in which Charles Quaritch had taken so much interest, and which Griselda had had so much difficulty getting from his grasp. After such a tale, Stroop had concluded that the secret was not in the pages or the marginalia, neither on the flyleaf nor scattered throughout the text, nor in the notes that jotted every margin. So, where else then to look?

Stroop had done his research, and knew his history of

paper and how it was made, knew of its raw ingredients and what it could be made from, be it rags or bamboo or bone. He knew how the desired constituents were treated, how they were pounded into a certain consistency onto which a fine mesh frame was lowered. The mixture dried, the frame was raised, the thin layer that formed upon it was the paper from which every page was made. And if you were clever, and had the time and inclination, you could weave a pattern into that wire frame, and when the paper was removed, that pattern would remain imprinted upon the paper, invisible unless you held that paper to the light. And this was exactly what Kustin Liit had done.

Like Quaritch, Stroop had at first been distracted by the foreign words he did not understand, thought there might be a system to the underlinings and asterixes indicating hidden meanings, had been further misled by the code-like markings in every margin of every page of that book. But unlike Quaritch, Stroop dismissed the obvious, had spent his time flicking illiterate through its pages, noticed after the fourth or fifth time that several of the pages were of a slightly different consistency than the rest, then saw the small dribble of glue that exuded from the top and bottom of the back fly leaf, had looked closer, poked at it with his thumbnail, knew with certainty that this was not old and mellowed glue and was of a different composition from the rest. And it was then that he had held those pages up to the light that streamed through the windows, and seen the faint symbols marked beneath the printed lines of text. Had realised how Kustin Liit had hidden his secret, and marvelled at how long it must have taken him, and the extreme lengths to which he had gone, how Kustin Liit must have taken apart his little book, splitting the spine from the binding by removing the back fly leaf and slicing through the cords and glue that held them, had then removed several non-consecutive pages, replaced them with ones of his own making, carefully reproducing the typeset and every word that had been on the original pages, adding more notes and markings to match the rest. Looking closely at these replacement pages, Stroop could see the typeface was very slightly different in formation – a longer tail to the Ys, a tighter tucking of the curve that made the Gs, a minor displacement of the dots above the Is. It seemed an extraordinary thing for Kustin Liit to have done, to have made the paper with its watermarks, reprinted it, repaginated the book, rebound it, replaced the back fly leaf with another, and reset the glue within its spine. And even more extraordinary to consider what it now contained, which was something of far more value than the inscrutable theology that Emanuel Swedenborg had dreamt up fifty years before.

The makeshift light-box was now assembled and the candles lit below the glass. One by one, Stroop gently placed the pages upon its surface, and Kustin Liit's Chrystomation Process was finally revealed.

For Stroop and Mabel and Griselda, it was a disappointment when the underlit script was finally discernible beneath the heavier lines of type, written as it was in some symbolic inksman's language they could not understand. But for Von Riddarholm it was a revelation akin to Swedenborg's own, and he saw the percentages, processes and ingredients clearly apparent, understood immediately the printsman's shorthand, and as he looked at each page as it was placed before him, his stern lips first parted, then smiled, then at last he laughed out loud, started scribbling feverishly on a notepad Stroop had placed beside him, watched as Kustin's miracle of Chrystomation was translated into lines and words, into formulae, and laid its genius bare.

And there were more revelations to come, which seemed to everyone, apart from Von Riddarholm, to have much more import. Oravo was silent throughout the light-box show, did not want to move or hardly breathe in case his very own miracle should be shattered like ice below an ox hoof, the pool it shielded shown to be nothing more than the muddy water he had always known. He hardly noticed the two boys, who had shown such interest at first in the little book, then been bored by their incomprehension, coming back to him when Griselda and the others trickled away to take their own turn. They started telling him their tales of piracy and mutilated animals, and the dead man they had seen not so long ago in the ice house, who had been murdered up on the moor, who had bruises about his neck just as did Oravo. One of these boys, whose name he thought might have been Jack, even produced a notebook, thrust a sketch of the murdered man beneath his nose. And Oravo recognised that face immediately from the sheepfold, struggled to recall how long ago it had been, but could not. Remembered only waking that night in the widow's house, the cylinder of fennel that was not his own, lying within his pocket. He knew that what the boys had told him had some meaning, had some bearing on whatever else seemed to be whirling down about him on this strangest of nights, but he failed to find it. Instead he extracted the dried stalk he had found near the murdered man, gave it to the smaller boy, who was sitting somewhere near his feet, the other one having elected to throw a scatter of small glass pebbles about the floor, was busy dividing them into two opposing armies, trying to decide which one would win. Oravo put his hand to his throat, knew that though the bruises had subsided, the memory of them still lay within his fingers, looked at Griselda, where she now sat at the table, saw the way her face with the freckles looked just like the eggs his linnets used to lay, wished the hump between his shoulder blades would go the way the bruises had gone and start to disappear, knew that it would not, that it would only grow and grow like an unwanted child who would never be born, would always be a gargoyle clinging to his back, and that she would never want him, that no one would ever want him. That not even his parents had been concerned enough to stay for him, that Grandmother Swan had despised both him and them for just that reason, that he was a lone man and a lost one, and would always be so.

Thomas took the fennel-stalk box from the stranger's hand when he offered it, moved it several times around within his own. Had the sense that this silent man was deeply, deeply sad and troubled, and understood it. Remembered the horrid abandonment he had felt when Toby had been snatched from him below that London bridge and never been returned, recalled the semi-eaten apple that he had gnawed down to the core, left it tooth-carved at its centre and no more, waiting to give the perfectly divided half of it to his friend. Remembered also, and did not want to, the way they had found Mabel's family, all dead and garrotted to their chairs,

271

saw the thin line at the stranger's throat and knew he had been through something similar, and yet had survived, as he and Jack and Mabel had all done. And so Thomas pushed forward with the gift the man had given him, knew it was something more than just a tube waxed off at either end, thrust it at Mr Stroop where he was now standing, his arms neatly tucked behind his back, watching Von Riddarholm watching the glass and the papers lifting slightly from its surface with the heat of the candles beneath.

'It's his,' Thomas whispered conspiratorially, nodding towards Oravo. 'I think he found it somewhere, and I think it might be important.'

And so it was.

12

The List of Days

OUT IN THE Pike Gut, Gunar Torrensson's blood had boiled itself dry beneath his skin. His stomach felt bad, as if he had eaten rotten meat, or the weevils in the ship's biscuits were eating through his stomach walls. He couldn't rest, kept going over and over his newly edited plan, looking for mistakes and pitfalls, though could find none. The pain in his face and jaw seemed to have lessened now that he had made his decision, and the swelling had at last gone down. He no longer cared about Eyvind and his little list of days, no longer gave a curse if anyone discovered it and discerned its meaning, if anyone figured out that the crossed swords next to Eustace meant the day was coming for the dawn of the New Brethren. He no longer cared about the Brethren, no longer cared about anything except taking the prize he had suffered so hard and planned so long to gain.

He would twist the situation as he had always done, had already rallied the troops, replaced the name of Eustace with St Marina, tugged a little harder on that golden ring, could already hear the hammering of hoofs at his back, had always known that they would follow wherever he would lead.

Stroop took the slim tube from Thomas's hand, unplugged the wax end with his knife, pinched out the thinly rolled scroll of paper, and pulled it open. It was obviously some kind of list, and though an obsessive compiler of lists himself, Stroop could make no more of it than that. Every letter, every word, was foreign to him. It could have been in Swedish, or even Cyrillic, though even of that Stroop hadn't been sure, so cursive was the handwriting.

'Von Riddarholm,' he called, but Von Riddarholm stayed where he was, still at the light-box, still constantly shifting his eyes from Kustin's pages to the notes he was jotting down to one side, still glorying in the discovery, the candles of the light-box making of his face a map of contours and dips and rises in the dim light of the room.

Mabel and Griselda had moved away, were talking quietly at another table, sitting in unconscious imitation of one another, ankles crossed, arms held down upon their skirts, fingers skimming the thin stalks of their almost empty glasses.

It took Stroop several prompts to get Josef to look up. His eyes were unfocused, still saw the symbols jumping up at him from the final page, wanted to get everything down and right, and start at once on the Chrystomation Process, accumulate the correct ingredients at their right strength, the exact oils at the exact degree of viscidity and temperature, fingers itching to replicate the experiment, call out his most experienced inksmen and get them started, had already decided he would call the new ink 'Liit's Metallurgica', had seen straight away, no doubt as Liit had intended, that the process could be adapted for metals other than gold, was already planning in his head the introduction of these extraordinary new inks and the new miniature books he would soon be creating, and how he would go about it, was thinking he should recall all his present out-of-country representatives, wondering how long it would take him to get some brand-new, top-of-the-line titles printed to showcase this unique invention, and which titles they should be . . .

Von Riddarholm finally heard Stroop's voice, heard the insistence of it more than the words. Eventually, and with some reluctance, he folded Kustin's pages carefully within his own notes so as not to crease them, and tucked them away into his innermost jacket pocket and buttoned it up, jealous even now that no one else should see them save himself.

'I hope you can read this,' Stroop was saying as he put the new piece of paper in Josef's hand, had already spoken to Oravo about where and when he found it. 'I think it is a matter of some urgency to uncover what it says. It seems most probable it belonged to your ice-house man, and, judging by what Mr Swan here has told us, his murderer was very keen to find it.'

He nodded at Oravo, had listened intently to the man's brief telling of his tale, had had to use persistent and prescient questioning to pull the memories from him, Oravo finding the details only now coming back to him as he spoke of them out loud: his finding of the body, his noticing that several stones had been lifted down from the wall, the little shelter rifled, the pockets of the murdered man's clothes turned inside out, the latter fact that Stroop himself had observed upon his viewing of the corpse within the ice house. They'd both seen also that the fennel tube seemed to have been stamped on, meaning that even if the searcher had seen it, he had not known it for what it was. Oravo had been very reticent about the end part of his story, and his own near-garrotting, but Stroop had got out of him what he had already begun to suspect: that it was Oravo, and not Griselda, who had pinned that note to the church door. But when Stroop asked him about the other map on the underside of that note, the map of Lower Slaughter and its environs, Oravo had become confused, found mincemeat in his head instead of memory. Just like Jack, Stroop had thought, and wondered about the way the human mind carried out its workings, and how it chose that some things should remain and others be quite forgotten, how entire days or even years could be mislaid for some unspecified interval, or even erased as cleanly as rain washes chalk from a slate.

Josef too puzzled at Oravo and his narrative when finally he heard it, mostly for the way he had gone after disembarking from the ship; could not understand why he hadn't gone straight-away to the village and the woman he had so plainly followed here, had taken instead an opposite and difficult path, gone over the lighthouse headland and across the long stretch of the bay and the rocks that were the very reason the lighthouse was being built, saw its clear, blue lagoon of water beckoning harbour, and the thin teeth of the reef that lay not two yards beneath its surface, sharp spires and underwater pinnacles, which had ruined many more ships than just the *Pihkva*, although the *Pihkva* was the only one he knew of to have been lured there deliberately to be wrecked.

He thought also how odd it was that a man from so far away could have happened upon another, murdered man his first night here, and then almost been murdered himself. But Von Riddarholm said none of this, had other things upon his mind. He read through the paper that Oravo had found up in the sheepfold, translated for Stroop the scribbles that were written there in an odd combination of Russian and Swedish, mouthed out the months and the saints' names that stood beside them, but did not understand anything of their meaning. Was surprised when the girl Mabel interrupted him part-way through his litany, said she was familiar with the Intercession of the Fourteen Helpers and added the days of the months that were missing from his list: 3 February, she had said, St Blaise; 23 April, St George; 8 May, St Acacius; 2 June, St Erasmus; 15 June, St Vitus, or St Elmo as he was otherwise known. She had also put something else together before the rest of them, having grown up with these saints and their stories, knew that St Blaise was represented by two crossed candles or an iron comb, that Acacius had been beheaded, that Erasmus had been martyred on a windlass, that St Vitus had for his emblem either a cockerel, or, more tellingly, a dog.

Von Riddarholm felt the familiar sinking of inadequacy then, realising he should have seen the patterns of mutilations for himself, remembered the old priest muttering something about St Blaise and his iron comb. Stroop tried to ease his guilt by pointing out a possible secondary symbolism, that each of the animals was connected to the emblems used by printers: the tiger's head, the iron comb, the black dog; but even Josef thought such a thing so coincidental as to be hardly worth mentioning, knew the girl had the right of it, though he had no notion of what it meant.

Oddly, he found himself thinking of Jarl Eriksson and the way he must have died with that great boil of water bearing down upon him, bristling with tree trunks and detritus, and whether he had watched it come, his eyes wide open, waiting for eternity to take him, and thought most probably he had. That he had faced his death as he had faced his life: his never-lessening enthusiasm for every trip Von Riddarholm sent him on, his expectations growing with each new contact made, his loyalty, his fealty to his family and his land. And Josef also realised, with something like despair, that Jarl Eriksson had never been disappointed, that of all the men he had ever met, Eriksson had probably been the happiest, and suddenly it seemed a crueller thing because of it for him to have lost his life too early, and in such a way.

Mabel interrupted his introspection. She took out a note-book from her pocket and started flipping through it, making Josef wonder idly if possession of such a book was a pre-requisite for joining this strangest of families, stopped his thoughts in pure shock at what the girl said next.

'Look,' she said, and stabbed a finger at the open page, trying to remember all that she had previously read of Hiiumaa and that island's history, and get it right. 'The Great Uprising,' Mabel said, 'the one back in the 1200s, when the islanders fought off their enemies and claimed sovereignty and independence. They called it St George's Night, and we all know what happened on his feast day.'

'I don't understand,' Griselda said, and she truly didn't, and nor did anyone else, though Stroop was beginning to get some inkling.

Oravo started at Griselda's voice, had had no interest at all in what had been going on, not even in the fennel box and what it had contained, was only glad to be rid of it. He had retreated into his own small world of thoughts like an anemone that withdraws its arms from the waters, waits for the tide to turn and make everything all right again, make his world the way it had once been, was finding this new one too strange and too frightening, did not know what to do with all the feelings that were bubbling out of him as if a keystone had been lifted and a whole lifetime of emotions suddenly released, threatening to destroy him as the flood had done to Lower Slaughter, drowning him from the inside out.

Stroop's mind was all the while ticking and whirring. He grasped now what Mabel had been getting at, that the Fourteen Helpers and their fourteen days had taken on a new significance. He looked over at her, saw her nod slightly and smile, knew they were both remembering their conversation that morning when they had talked about the ancient order of the Brethren of the Sword.

'It seems to me,' Stroop said calmly, 'that someone is employing the schedule of the Fourteen Helpers to carry out their scheme.'

Von Riddarholm was looking out of the window at the line of windmills striding across the headland of Ristnaneem. He didn't turn, didn't interrupt, just let Stroop go on.

'Someone who knows quite well the history of your island, who knows all about the ancient order of the Brethern of the Sword, and the uprising of St George's night, and the reputation of the old Osilia for piracy and theft.' Von Riddarholm still didn't move, had too much going on inside his head, was still trying to assimilate everything that had happened, felt it was all happening too fast and he had nowhere to put all the extra information.

'I think,' Stroop continued, 'that these people want us to believe they are some kind of reincarnated New Order, New Brethren. I think that all the animal mutilations on all the feast days were meant to give a message, were intended to induce a climate of suspicion and unease, augmented exponentially by the wrecking of the *Pihkva* and all the little acts of piracy that have abounded since that time.'

And at last something stirred within Von Riddarholm, and he recalled again the coming of the shipwrecked sailors to his house.

'By Christ,' he said quietly, 'he told me. Anto Juusa told me.' He turned and faced Stroop then. 'Freedom to Osilia.' He spoke the words almost to himself. 'Juusa told me that's what the wreckers' captain said to him before he left the *Pihkva*. He told me, and I did not understand.'

He understood well enough now, though, and saw the entire history of Hiiumaa unrolling like a carpet below his feet, saw its patterns and its weave, felt as if he had suddenly stepped inside a pageant he had known, and yet been ignorant of, his whole life.

13

How Eyvind Was Almost Given Back his Name

IT WAS NIGHT, though hardly dark, the mist breathing itself
in from the long rolls of an incoming tide, settling itself
in silent spectres about the canopy, wisping amongst the tree-
chapels, sidling down the roof-tiles whose summer warmth
sent it straight away to water soon as it had touched, driplets
collecting amongst the eaves like iridescent swallows, pittering
and mizzling through the air. The great boulder at the centre
of the tree-chapel glade glowed a russet amber as the sun
began to tilt and set, sent its last rays slowly burning through
the mist, drew short lines of rainbows shimmering between
the tall legs of the trees, made the people gathered down
below them feel there must be another world out there,
somewhere within the forest, just out of reach.

It was several days since that last talking up at the manor
house, several days in which so much had to be done, and
some of it already achieved.

Stroop had been insistent then on two things: first, that
the man in the ice house be identified, for Stroop was sure
he must have come from these islands, had been the beetle

in the bee-house able to disguise himself sufficiently well not to be spotted carrying out the orders he had been given – namely the sacrificing of the animals upon the saints' right days; secondly, Stroop had urged Von Riddarholm to gather as many of the islanders as possible, and explain to them all that had passed, and what had been happening on Hiiumaa these past few months.

'If I am right,' he said, 'then there is some campaign ongoing which has your island in its sights. Hiiumaa is advantageously placed for trade, and comparatively prosperous, primarily because of your printworks. If someone wanted to overtake it, there are many from whom he could have picked his army. Think how many villages were depopulated in 1781, and how many families there are out there who must have sons still bitter at that expulsion. Who better to recruit into this new order of his brethren? And how better to proceed than to appeal to justice and a loyalty to the land of their parents' birth? I know that so far nobody has been able to identify your ice-house man, but how hard have you tried? He is of an age to have been born and grown up here. Could you not send for any people who still remain here, who came originally from those depopulated villages?'

Josef was agitated to the point of numbness by Stroop's suggestion of an armed and outright attack against Hiiumaa, was unwilling at first to believe that island men – men who had been born here, or had family born here – could even imagine to do such things. And yet, and yet, there had seemed no other coherent explanation, at least none that he could find, and he had thought again about exile and the bitterness it could bring; thought of men like Kustin Liit, thirty years departed from Hiiumaa, who still felt such attachment to his homeland that he had been prepared to forsake everything in his new world just for the possibility of returning to the old.

And so he did as Stroop suggested, and called out for his men, organised them into teams, had them riding over the tracks and moors of Hiiumaa to bring back representatives from every village and township who were of the old stock, who might remember. The operation had taken several days, and a storage barn had to be cleared for their accommodation, but at last there was one man who had come from the island's most southerly end, who had viewed the man in the ice house, and seen past the rigid casement of his hair and the blueness of his lips, the frozen slack about his cheekbones, the eyelids that had been pulled down to hide the stare of death.

'It's one of the Berwald boys,' he said. 'Can't be sure which one. Could be Onni, could be Eyvind. Used to ride with them way back when, before they got thrown out with the rest. Heard later they'd gone soldiering, though couldn't swear to it. But it's one of them, I'm sure enough of that.'

Von Riddarholm had not really expected such an outcome, had in fact prayed for quite the opposite, wanted something to be said or done that would squash Stroop's theories, make laughter of his fears, lessen the likelihood of his grave predictions coming true. But with the naming of the Berwald brother, one of those predictions had already come to pass, and Josef could now see no other way but to act upon the other.

★   ★   ★

And so his islanders were gathered now within the tree-chapel glade, the mist a wreath and wraith about the tree-tops, cooling their skin, pattering droplets down upon and all around them. Von Riddarholm could feel his heart beating, his blood like a charge of cavalry men beneath his skin. He began to ascend the steps that had been carved into the trunk of a huge holm oak, his hands pulling him up and clear, started to make his way across the boarded walkways slung between the trees, beneath their great green canopy, already knew the best place from which to be seen and heard was outside the Spanish chapel built by his mother, and slung into the branches of the oldest lime, felt the stickiness of the honeydew on the planks beneath his feet, the small crawl of somnolent lady-birds that had slipped down from the aphid feast upon its leaves, and knew he was almost there.

Everything felt so calm and right that he could hardly bring himself to speak the words he had come to say. Could hear the waters folding in and out of the reefs and rocks that hemmed his island's shores, wondered if Stroop could have been mistaken, if there was nothing out there except the kittiwakes and cormorants nodding on their ledges, the fulmars stretching out their long grey wings across the sea. He thought of the small boy who had fallen from the cliffs some time back in February, and how his family had had to bury a coffin full of stones before his body had been found, how they'd then had to drag that same coffin back out of the earth and rebury it with what little was left of him, thought of the band of outlaws who now threatened his island, and that they were doing the same: dragging Hiiumaa's past out of its grave, and wondered if, once exhumed, it could be so easily reburied as had been the boy.

Josef could feel the great bole of the lime at his back, the hundreds of years that had gone into its growing, the painting that it hid within its chapel of decomposing bodies, and balances that weighed out every man's rights and wrongs. He took strength from it as he looked down on all those people staring right back at him, swore he would repair his own balance and that of his island, and began to speak.

'We have three days,' Von Riddarholm was shouting out from his stanchion in the branches of the lime tree; had picked his spot well, was easily seen by all who were gathered beneath, their faces upturned like spoon-backs towards him, fogbows dancing slowly as the sun began to sink below its horizon. He told them all, held nothing back, did as Stroop had suggested, gave them the knowledge they might need to combat all that was to come.

'The twentieth of July is the feast day of St Margaret, and if the pattern follows through, we can expect another dead animal, another decapitation.' Josef swallowed hard as he spoke these words, saw the cat's head being nailed again to the barn door, transmogrified it in his mind to that of a man, maybe even his own. 'Three days,' he went on, 'our enemies are trying to foment unrest and insurrection, to unsettle our heels from our porch, to force us into disarray so we will not be ready. But we will!' He heard his voice crack slightly, had rehearsed his words so many times he thought they would come out of his mouth smooth as cotton from a reel, but now that he was here, seeing the moon-pale faces down

285

below him, the anxious lines and shadows on every one, he felt that old familiar hammering within his chest, remembered that old soldier back in Greece and his small time of war, how he had pushed his own guts back into his belly, felt again the taste of that man's blood in his mouth as he tried to help, but could not, and failed. Swore he would not fail again. 'We must be on our guard,' he continued, 'any strangers must be sought out and brought to me. They may be entirely innocent,' and with this he glanced his eyes amongst the throng, sought out Griselda, and Stroop and his little family, found them standing at the edges of the gathering, out beside the big stone, had already informed the populace who these people were so that they might know them. 'You must report any animal that goes missing, any strange behaviour you might observe.'

He explained again that the man in the ice house had been identified as one of the Berwald family originating from the other end of the island, that most probably it had been he who had carried out the previous animal attacks, but that obviously now he was dead some other would have come to take his place, maybe even the man who had been his murderer, though no one yet knew why. Josef had been inclined towards Stroop's suggestion that the Berwald brother, once actually back upon Hiiumaa, had begun to weaken in his plan, maybe even threatened to derail it completely. Either way, it meant that whoever was sent next in his place would certainly not be made with the same weakness sewn into his skin and bones.

'Do not be fooled,' Josef was still shouting, his voice growing hoarser and yet the stronger for it, 'this is not an end, only a beginning. At some point in the following months, we must expect to be attacked directly.'

Instantly a wave murmured about the glade as men and women turned towards their neighbours, drew in a breath, let out a sigh. Josef had expected this, and waited, but only for a moment, then held up his hands, remembered Stroop pointing out the crossed swords by St Eustace in September, but would put no store by this, wanted his people to be ready.

'We do not know when or how, but we know that the threat of this attack is real, and though I will do everything in my power to prevent it, we must be ready for it, if and when it comes!'

He thumped his hands back down upon the wood of the railing, wishing they made a louder sound, a rallying-call to battle, but they had not. The mist had dampened the wood, like everything else, hushed the sound, and there was nothing except his own voice hanging there amongst the enclosure of branch and chapel. But Josef was not dampened, had already decided that the answer was not to enlist the aid of the Russians or the Swedes, would not give them any excuse to set up a garrison upon his island and take it over, trample the islanders' rights beneath their feet. Instead he appealed to his captivated audience.

'Every man who has a weapon must be ready to take up arms!' The words sounded like a challenge, rang about the woods like a bell. 'Every man who ever cared about his home-land and his family must follow when I give command! We will not cower like rabbits in a burrow waiting for the smoke to bring us out, nor will we fear the strike of the ferret set at our doors; we must seek the traitors out before they attack again, and we have reason to believe that they are ship-bound, and almost at our shores!'

This last exhortation was taken solely from Stroop's assumptions. He had wanted, and succeeded, in getting Von Riddarholm to take up some command and spell out to his island people the only plan they had come up with. There was a trade ship down in harbour at nearby Körgessaare, which had been docked for several days, waiting for repairs and the uploading of a shipment of ponies bound for the Russian mainland. Instead, it had been decided, the boat would be boarded and crewed by the islanders themselves, with whatever weapons they could muster. They would take the old cannons that had been rusting at the quayside for God knew how long, and would clean them out, make them serviceable, and remount them. They would not stand idle to be invaded, but would attack the attackers. They would take out every boat they could, and patrol their own borders and be ready. Whatever was coming, Stroop had told Von Riddarholm, would certainly head for his own manor house, the pivotal control point of the island, the old stronghold of the original Brethren, and many times rebuilt and strengthened since those times.

Josef figured there were only three or four bays upon which the insurgents could land to be within easy reach of the manor house, and the islanders must be ready and waiting for them, lookouts needed to be set both day and night. Every head man from every village must go back and recruit as many other men and weapons as they could muster, take up guard upon the headlands above those bays, and others be stationed at the manor house in case of the worst. As soon as they could, they would sail that boat out of Körgessaare and go hunting for the men who were threatening their island and their very way of life.

As Von Riddarholm was shouting out these new instructions, he could feel the lifeblood of his island's history running out with every word he spoke, just as the meteorite lake ran below the very soil beneath his feet to feed the villages' wells and fields. He thought of that lake now, and of its deep, dark silence, the hidden fish that sometimes shivered up towards its surface, the dragonflies that lurched their uneven ways across its banks, the cranes and swans that paddled in its shallows; thought of the time he had spent there only a week or so before with Stroop's boys, wanted to be able to take his own boys there, wondered for only the second time in many years why he had never sought a woman out to sit with him upon its banks, why he had ever thought the dark light of the skies could suffice for his companionship. He also knew it had been that going away to war that had done such dreams to death, that like Oravo's hump, he had things about him he could not, would not share; that he had been a coward and a failure then, had come crawling home with the false lies of victory upon his lips, and could not bear for anyone to get close enough to him to learn the truth. Yet still he thought of the English woman, who was not English but came from here, and her freckled, speckled skin; wondered if, when everything was over, there might not still be some chance for him to go forward, recapture everything he thought had been lost to him.

Josef was as wrong about this as he was wrong about so

many other things; that both Mabel and Stroop, as well as the old priest with his hands like stunted blackthorn hedges, had all been wrong as well would be of no comfort.

'St Margaret,' Mabel had told them, 'feast day in July. Virgin martyr, known as Marina in the East. Very important in Russia as the woman who looked after sailors and the waters through which they must pass. Feast day, the twentieth of July.'

It was such a small mistake, only a few days' slippage between two long divergent liturgies, between the eastern and the western, between the one that celebrated the same saint, as Mabel had assumed, upon the twentieth, and the other, Russian way that celebrated three days earlier, on the seventeenth.

And it was the night of the seventeenth right now, and the *Osil* lay at anchor, lights extinguished, not five hundred yards from the unfinished lighthouse of Hiiumaa, manoeuvred behind the rocky outcrop on which Eyvind Berwald had so unwillingly set out the lights that Steffan's father had thought he had seen and then dismissed, the very first light that had lured the *Pihkva* towards its death. And at the very moment Von Riddarholm had gone out to address his gathered islanders in the tree-chapel glade, Torrensson had given the order for the landing boats to be lowered, had already begun to shinny down the ropes into the first of them, ready to lead his men to shore. And while Von Riddarholm was shouting out his three-day warning, the New Brethren, with their newly sharpened swords, were already starting their creeping out and past the headland, across the same short stretch of crowberry and stunted juniper the men of the

Pihkva had come over several months before, and by the time Von Riddarholm was giving out his orders about the ship down at Körgessaare, Torrensson's men had already breached the baron's home, were already claiming the Brethren's oldest stronghold for their own, slitting the throats of the two men who were still there, though not to guard it; were only game-keepers waiting at their posts, ready to set out into the night to trap the weasels or other vermin that had been eating at the young pheasants, having dug a hole beneath their protective nets.

14

From the Pike Gut to the Glade

V ON RIDDARHOLM STOPPED speaking, and for a few moments all that could be heard was the mist drizzling down from the trees, the lapping of the waves in the bays that surrounded them, the slight rustling of clothes and feet as women drew closer to their men, and families came together, frightened by the words that they had heard.

Not so far from them, up at the manor house, up in the tower where Von Riddarholm had stood not so long ago worrying about the earth being at its furthest point from the sun, there stood Gunar Torrensson, gazing out of the large windows at the dark tracts of land and sea all about him, knowing nothing of equinoxes nor aphelions, yet understanding that same dislocation from time and life that Von Riddarholm had so keenly felt.

Everything, Torrensson was thinking, had been far too easy, much too simple: from the swinging down of the boats to their sailing undisturbed into the belly of the bay beyond the lighthouse. They had seen no one as they had come across the moor, not a single farmer in his fields nor a fisherman docking his boat or cleaning his nets. Not a light in any of the print barns, nor one man straggling across the land in the evening light to home. There had been no one at all. Torrensson had been at first surprised, and then angered to find the manor house empty and undefended, his men swarming in like hornets with no one to fight, was suspicious of this empty land, was already beginning to wonder if they had stepped right into someone else's trap.

He looked out now at the perfect compass of his view, and knew he had been right about Eyvind Berwald and his treachery, and that the New Brethren must already have been betrayed by one of their own. He ran his tongue over the craters in his mouth left by his missing teeth, one hand clenched around the hilt of his sword, the other about the bandoliers that crossed his chest from shoulder to belt, holding his pistols and his ammunition. He closed his eyes briefly, tried to calm himself against this unseen complication of simplicity, had been in many other battles and at far worse odds. Knew that even if the islanders had already been warned by Berwald, there had been no sign of foreign warships coming to their aid, that all they had for defence was them-selves, and that he, Torrensson, was already garrisoned in their stronghold. And so he stood there, trying to convince himself that he who had the stronghold had Osilia, but remained all the while unconvinced and troubled.

He winced suddenly as the pain from his cracked cheek-bone shot him through as he flexed his jaw, still felt that hammer at his teeth and the black swelling it had caused that he could even now feel lying dormant just below the skin, felt the rage rise up again within him like a fruit about to burst its skin, threw his shoulder at the large telescope and rocked it off its cradle, caught it up like a cannon and hurled it through the largest of the turret windows, shattering the glass, felt the scratch and splinter of it on his skin, could no longer stop the anger boiling out of him, let out a long, long roar sustained by all the rage that had been within him, the sound of it echoing across the island, carried by the breeze that roamed its way beneath the mist, spread it out as far and wide as it could reach, and bore the bellow of it on its back as the waters of an estuary roar down to meet its tide.

They heard it clearly in the tree-chapel glade, that animal howl that came at them through the silence and the falling night, and though no one knew what it was that could have made it, they knew well enough from where it had come, and looked towards the square-shouldered block of the manor house upon its knoll, and the panic came down upon them like rain from a clear blue sky, and they realised that all that had been told to them was true, and that the warnings they had been given had come too late, and that the worst was already here and happening, and that their guns were lying dirty and useless in their houses, the gunpowder dampening in their outhouses and sheds.

Mabel clutched at Stroop's sleeve just as Steffan had tried to hang on to that precipice when the rock doves had up and scattered about him, her bones shrinking beneath her skin, and Griselda stood like a sundial gnomon lost at midnight, saw only Oravo's strong hand reaching out to take her own in his, and let it be taken, felt him heave her to his chest, the fast beating of his heart against her neck where he had lowered his head to her shoulder, thought about the flowers he had given her, and how strong they must have been to push their blades out of the ground even when the snow was falling, uncaring that there might be worse to come, and came anyway.

And Josef Von Riddarholm held his stance, his hands upon the boughs that formed the railings about the Spanish chapel and its painting, sticky with the honeydew and the sweat and fear that surged through his body, felt a prickling upon his skin as if those flies from Greece had somehow found him even here, felt them settling again between his neck and collar, clustering against the corners of his eyes, obscuring his vision. And yet somehow, somewhere, he found it in him to respond and give answer to that awful howling, knowing, as everyone else must have done, that it meant the wolf was already on the fold.

'They are here!' he cried. 'They are here and at the manor house! Everybody back to the village, and to arms!'

It was a confused following, Von Riddarholm swinging himself down without grace through the trap door in the walkway, clutching at the amputated stumps of branches, stopped only from breaking both his ankles by a surge of men who hurried forwards, caught his legs and brought him safely down. He was still shouting as he forced his way through the already dispersing crowd, ran with them down the path that led between the forest and the fields, past the bulky outlines of the print barns and the workshops, felt the beat of every heart that was at his back, the heat of his skin beneath the coolness of the mist, the hardness of the ground beneath his feet, and on he ran, and on, and behind him came the men and women of Hiiumaa, breathing hard, forcing themselves to recognise this new reality, that they were about to be called upon to fight, and maybe die, to protect their homes.

The only one who did not follow was Oravo Swan. He had held Griselda so tightly to him that she had had to beat a fist upon his chest for her release, but still he could not let her go, grasped at her hands with the force of seaweed cemented to its anchor and its stone.

'Oravo.' She spoke barely above a whisper, was still finding it hard to get her breath, found her own heart pounding within her at the fierceness of his embrace, could feel the racing of his blood beneath the fingers that still held her own. 'We must go,' she finally managed, 'we must follow to the village.' Had already started moving, trying to drag him with her, felt as if she were pulling at an oak-root set deep within its hole of centuries. She had stopped then, an arm's pace from him, saw the rough set of his face, his hair dampened to his brow, found that for the first time since she had known him he was staring right at her, right into her eyes, felt her own blink against his gaze, the strength of his grip, the resoluteness she saw burning deep within them.

'No,' he said, 'I will not go.'

And they stood there with the mist all about them, and beyond them the trees and the chapels, and beside them the huge ancestral stone, which had dulled into shadow. And she knew then what he was going to do, and her throat constricted, forced the blood into her cheeks, made her freckles glow like fireflies.

'Come with me,' she said, although she already knew that

he would not, felt his hands gently release her own, stroking her skin with his thumbs as he withdrew.

'You go on,' he answered. 'There's things I have to do.' And Griselda said not another word, watched him turn away from her, the dark hump of his back disappearing into mist, the hard running of his boots barely heard as he rounded the stone, knew that he was headed for the manor house.

'Oh God,' she murmured quietly as she watched him go, 'oh the Lord my God, protect him.' And she crossed herself, called on every saint in every chapel that the tree-glade caught within its arms, and then she too turned and swiftly ran her way across the grass, tried to catch a glimpse of the disappearing villagers, saw them not, but knew where they were headed and which way to go.

No one noticed that Jack and Thomas were not with them, had been bored by the Swedish speech they could not understand, had climbed the nearest ladder, followed the scents of moss and damp and leaves, and the warm day's resin running out from the pitch-holes in the pines and the forest all around them. Up they went, and then further, right up into the Eyrie, the highest and smallest of all the chapels, perched like an owl between the top-most branches of a chestnut, hidden by the fronds of its fingered leaves, making of it a secret place, a quiet place. A perfect place for Jack and Thomas.

They heard the roar as everyone else did, but it was muted by the drawing closed of the tendril-knotted door, heard more clearly the down-below shouts of panic, made their way out of the chapel a few moments later, then down from the chestnut and its branches, descended to the lower deck of the chapel glade; but all they found when they got there was the emptiness of the mist grown down to the ground, thin limbs dancing like spectres, and the pale edges of the sky disappearing as the night began its slow roll across the sky, and all they saw of the people who had been gathered there was one man running hard and untidy like a crab, recognised Oravo by his hump, saw that he was headed back towards the manor house. They jumped the last few feet towards the dew-drenched ground, and followed.

Torrensson's men did as they were told, swept every room and every outhouse, captured without difficulty the only other few men within the compound, not counting the ones who they had already split ear from ear. There was a cook who had been skinning a haunch of venison hanging in the pantry, and some rudimentary kind of butler shining up some glasses with the silken gloves he wore upon his hands, and a solitary stable-boy who had tried to hide himself within a rick of hay.

Torrensson knew his men were disappointed not to have found more men to fight now that their blood was up and their sword hands ringing with expectation; had expected some kind of army to set themselves against, found nothing to challenge them, only bare rooms, old men, and piss-scared boys.

They too had heard Torrensson's roar of anger bursting from him like a gale-force wind tunnelled between two cliffs of stone, had heard that similar sound not long before, when he had pulled his own tooth from out his broken jaw, and sent them scurrying across the decks after he had given his orders, that they were going straight away to the Finnish port of Turku to pick up supplies and arms, had made them swing the *Osil* out of the Pike Gut and start out to cross a sea of storm and waves with the wind running badly to beam, Torrensson knowing which way the wind would blow itself between reefs and islands that scattered the tip of Finland, steered them through the eddies and the maelstroms, the small waterspout that had sent a swarm of shrimps down upon their decks. They had all known then that there had been a change within Torrensson, that whatever had happened to him alone that night upon Hiiumaa had wound him tight and tighter, like the string upon a bow that is ready to loose its arrow. A few of the crew had murmured discontent about this precipitate action, and the abandoning of their carefully laid out calendar of the Brethren and the Fourteen Saints, but once they had reached Turku and started loading the final crates of ammunition, their sinews too had begun to twist and harden, and they felt that familiar tingling that comes before a battle, the jittery strength it gave their every movement, the mixture it made of them that comes from excitement, and of fear.

Gunar Torrensson heard his men below him, swaggering through the manor house, scouring every room, and gazed out of his tower towards the tree-chapel glade, saw the huge shape of the unmoved boulder, as if it too stood against him. Saw something else, saw a single man break cover and run directly at this house and his insurrection, recognised the hunched knuckle that lay between that man's shoulders as he was briefly silhouetted against the stone and the very last of the light. He pressed his eyeglass to his face, felt the ring of it sinking into the bruises about his cheek, and focused on that man and his hump, and wished he had his own hammer that he could swing out into the night, and crush him dead.

The villages closest to the tree-chapel glade were in chaos. There were three of them clustered down below the wind-mills, all small, all the inhabitants being employed one way or another by Von Riddarholm and his inks and papers and print shops. More confused were the incomers who had been summoned from the rest of the island in the attempt to iden-tify the ice-house man. They went first one way and then another, kept shouting out their family names so relatives could come and claim them, give them shelter, and any weapons they might have. Within a quarter hour of the crowd's arrival at the nearest village, everyone had dissolved like blood in water into various houses and barns, and for a few moments, Stroop and Mabel stood alone and adrift upon the damp soil of the street.

'Where's Jack and Thomas?' Mabel was frantic, couldn't remember seeing either of them in the glade after the first few minutes of standing with them by the stone, certainly didn't remember seeing them in the tide of people that had swept the two of them to here. Stroop tried to think of re-assuring things to say, tried to remember when he had last seen them both, had a feeling they had scampered up one of the tree-chapel ladders not too long after Von Riddarholm had started speaking, and could not blame them. Had known what the man was going to say, had of course discussed it with him, but, like Jack and Thomas, couldn't understand a word of it when it came. Had only grasped Von Riddarholm's gestures and the crowd's reactions, assumed Josef had said what had been agreed upon, wondered if he had gone overboard and said more, but had no way to be sure.

'They'll be fine,' he said, though felt a horrid familiar prickling in his belly. 'They'll just have gone off exploring. They can't possibly have missed us. They'll be here in a little while.'

But Mabel would not be quieted, went from one house to the next with her imperfect Swedish tongue, began to run back up the street towards the tree-chapel glade, came across Griselda slumped against the village well, weeping. Mabel was so panicked she didn't notice for a moment the other woman's distress, asked several times if she had seen Jack and Thomas before realising that Griselda was sobbing so hard she could hardly breathe, and then Mabel went down on her knees beside her and took her shoulders, and pulled the other woman to her. And all Griselda knew then was that there was only one thing in the world that she now wanted, that she wanted other arms around her, and prayed and prayed that Oravo, even with his hump, would come back, and would come back to her.

Torrensson descended from his tower and his rage, put himself in order and gathered his men about him in the stone-paved hall where the earlier Brethren had once brought their horses in to safety. The feeding troughs were still in evidence, long oblong basins dug into the walls, hooks above and below for tying up reins or hanging bags of barley and of oats. Most were obscured now by what, to Torrensson, was an unnerving mix of library and museum, old machines gathered against the walls like giant spiders, obsolete printing presses serving as tables for cabinets holding shelves of out-dated lines of typeface, bookcases growing up between them, guarding their ancient domain.

He found himself a platform on one of the paper-rolling mills, swept the cabinets from its surface, the glass crashing and splintering to the stone floor, the jumbled letters spilling from their forms and scattering off like mice into shadow and gloom. Torrensson leapt up and rattled his sword at his men, drew the gleaming yard of it from its scabbard and held it high above his head, symbol of their junta and new dominion.

He had spent a small while up in the tower after the thunder of rage and impotency had passed through him and moved on. Felt calmer now, felt the call to action, the urge to fight and win so strong in him that it seemed to oil his bones, numb the pain, narrow his vision, and all he saw now was the island as an enemy that he must quell and make his own.

He fired his men up with a speech on duty and the liber-ation of their homeland, the parallels that existed between the Old Order of the Brethren and the new one they would soon be bringing to this land, told them to commandeer every source of food and drink they could find, to draw closed the huge doors that were the only way of entry or egress from the courtyard, that they were now so near their goal that no one could hope to stop them. Proved himself still to be a leader of men. Had the cook dragged before him to spill out the secrets of the manor house's layout, before Torrensson's sword spilt out the man's guts. Thereafter, he sent men to the ice house to raid the wine and root cellars, told them to bring in as much as they could as quick as they could, whatever was there – dried barrels of fish, potatoes, sacks of rye and barley flour, kegs of beer, spirits, and wine. Knew his men needed to be commanded and kept busy, sent others off to fetch every tool and weapon they could find; had them lay out stocks of wood and pitch along the roofs and turrets, wished he were closer to the print barns, and the vats of oil and barrels of pine tar kept there for the ink making. He remembered the smell of them from his brief time here as a boy when he had been brought over from Sweden to visit his mother's folk, how his uncle had ridden him across this island, swatting at the robber flies with their black and dangly legs, astonished at the dragonflies and swallows that skimmed across the dark unblinking eye of the lake, the tingle of the scent of resin being drained from the pines, the piling of wood into the kilns, the slow, dark treacle of the pitch as it was released. He knew again the strange wonder of this place and his wanting to belong to it, the years that followed of his apprenticeship upon the boats that plied its shores, just to be near it. The yearning he had felt ever since that first visit, to return. The knowledge that now he had returned, he would not be cheated of his victory, and that however things went, he would not leave, hoped only that if it ended badly, someone would heed the instructions he had sewn into the lining of every coat he had ever worn in every battle, that when he died, someone would bring him here and bury him in the tree-chapel glade, carve his name out on that enormous boulder, so that finally he would belong.

He deliberately told his men to go at the wine and brandy, have a night of it but make sure they were ready, positioned strong men upon the roofs and turrets, felt sure though that the villagers would muster no attack until dawn, wanted these few short hours to find that man he had seen scuttling away from the tree-chapel glade, tried to think himself into his shoes, thought he might have had the answer when the stable-boy was finally found and brought before him, smelling of fear and urine just like a rabbit within the jaws of a fox. And then the boy had told him something that might give him his advantage: somewhere beneath the houses, he said, were tunnels running below the earth, though he could not, or would not say where, even when Torrensson's sword began its final striking through the air and took the boy's head off at its stalk, felt the warm blood spray across his face, tasted it in his ruined mouth, and exulted in it.

15

The Coming of the
New Brethren

THE VILLAGE MEN were gathered, had come at last to order,
the panic of their families and kinsmen quelled, Von
Riddarholm's leadership coming to the fore. Every pony and
cart was gathered, every woman and child being stacked upon
them with a few belongings; the first had left already, heading
off along the rough tracks into the twilight to be as far distant
as they could get with the small patch of dim light that was
left them, everyone looking to the west and the roll of night,
which was growing too fast across the sea, devouring the
mists, blinding them to the outside world, coming down
upon them like a great, dark bowl.

Von Riddarholm had sent off scouts, and the first returned
within the hour with the news that the manor house had
indeed been overrun, and all the horses taken from the stables
and brought into the courtyard, the huge oak doors pulled
to and barred.

Others took longer to return, had been sent to check out
the bays for the insurgents' ship; none had found it, but one
boy reported that seven or eight boats had been brought up

onto the bay beyond the lighthouse, dragged through the tide-line and the detritus that was all that was left of the wrecking of the *Pihkva* three months before.

'So,' said Von Riddarholm to the men he had gathered about him, 'eight boats, a maximum of fifteen to each one, makes one hundred men, maybe one hundred and twenty. We know they have occupied the manor house, we know they will be well armed, we know they have brought the horses from the stables into the courtyard.'

Stroop was standing at the edge of this gathering, Mabel slightly behind him, having refused to leave Griselda, though agitated more than she could say about what had happened to Jack and Thomas, and where they might be now, and if they were safe. Stroop was thinking about the horses, and why the New Brethren, as he found it easiest to call them, had rallied them inside their stronghold. He had a sudden terrifying vision of them racing down upon the villages in the pre-dawn light, swords drawn, firebrands flying into thatch and barn. He tried to reason with himself, thought that more probably they would be used later on in the campaign, to ride out and subdue the smaller villages one by one, was trying to figure out a way to help Von Riddarholm help this island, stop any slaughter before it began.

His first thoughts were of negotiation and barter, his second that this would be of no use, that this incursion must have been years in the making, and that if the New Brethren had come this far, they would not be stopped in their mission by a few words softly spoken, had obviously no plans to retreat, had left their boats in plain sight where they must have known they would be burnt the moment they were discovered. Von Riddarholm indeed had already given such an order. And then he thought of burning and of boats and the ship already berthed in Körgessaare. And suddenly Stroop found a plan already formed in his mind, and thrust himself forward through the crowd, punched his way the last few yards and grabbed at Von Riddarholm's elbow. He was pushed off first once, then twice, felt Von Riddarholm's body shaking with either anger, resolution or fear, still shouting out what must be done, ordering his island men to gather at specific places, prepare their arms, be ready to attack the moment dawn struck a line across the horizon, brought the breezes in from the sea and set the windmills turning.

Oravo had placed himself well, was hidden behind a hedge of quickthorn that had blown its flowers and was beginning already to bud green clusters of unripe berries, had a clear view of the manor, the ice house and the drying lawns that ran between them, had seen the lines of men shuttling between the two, carrying what they could.

He'd no clear idea what he would do, knew only that he must do something; knew that by the time the villagers had been calmed and readied, their time for attack would be long past. Had spent his several days up at the manor house wandering amongst its rooms and grounds, going down to the lake and the tree-chapel glade, around the stables and the outbuildings, the dairy and the workshops used by the carpenters and blacksmiths. And he knew there was one way into the manor house that did not require a door: that there was a short tunnel kept open between the wood stores in the carpentry shed to the cellar beneath the kitchens, so that all waste timber could be taken from the one place to the other, to feed the manor's fires. Knew there was no time to waste trying to be understood by people who could never understand him, that even people who spoke his own language had never understood him, and that things would be no different now. Still a stranger, as he had always been. Except perhaps to Griselda, he thought, and just the possibility of such a thing gave him the burn of strength and hope, felt her heart beating against his chest as if she had left an imprint of herself within his skin, knew that he would fight and die to have that one chance of feeling it again, would prove himself to be a better man than he had ever been, would make himself worthy. He nearly jumped out of his skin when someone touched him lightly on the elbow, his hand already at his belt.

'What's going on?' said Jack, and Oravo narrowly missed his head as he swung the hammer wide, and dropped it just in time into the leaf litter at his feet.

'The lighthouses,' Stroop was shouting at Von Riddarholm, having finally managed to get his attention, found himself upon the makeshift stage of straw bales in the barn they had all crowded into, 'we need to send men to the lighthouses! Get every last one of them lit with fires, even if they're not ready!'

Von Riddarholm had been so intent upon his scheme to get his men into units and armed that he had forgotten the bigger plan. Felt that balance in the Spanish chapel swing once more against him, couldn't believe he hadn't thought of something so obvious. But he didn't have time for recrimination or regret, remembered the schemata for all the various lighthouses being built around Hiiumaa's shores, and a few of the older ones that were inland and on high ground.

Stroop was still yelling in his ear, 'Get every last one of them lit; there are trading ships out there, English ships, Swedish and Russian warships, you don't need to take these men to war!'

And he was right, and Von Riddarholm was wrong, and he was suddenly so overwhelmed with the same nausea and guilt he had had in Greece at sending men into futile battle that he could not speak. But Stroop was there at his elbow, telling him what to say, and the words came out of him in the language of his island men, and he held up his arms and shouted out: 'Get yourselves into groups by family: the Ligis, Saskas, Uinos, Janssons, Mandels, Selirands . . .'

And so Stroop gave out his instructions, and Von Riddarholm translated: each family to each lighthouse, and never mind that some of them weren't yet finished. Even if they had to burn every lighthouse down to its foundations, it would be a small price to pay. Take any horse or any pony and get to each and every one, take every piece of firewood, every barrel of oil from the print barns, and set Hiiumaa burning up in the dark seas like a torch: bring in the sharks, let them be the ones to clear out the invaders, and afterwards, what would be would be, and most probably would be no different than it was before.

'One more thing,' Stroop was saying, 'the ship down at Körgessaare, get it launched or get it burnt, but do not leave it for anyone's escape.'

'You can't be here,' Oravo was saying to Jack and Thomas, hoped they would just go away, didn't know Jack and Thomas at all. He wasn't used to speaking, every word coming out of him like a grudge.

'But something's going on,' Thomas countered.

'And where's Mabel and Mr Stroop?' Jack added, pushing his way beneath Oravo's arm, felt its immovability like an iron bolt that has been many winters rusting.

'You can't be here,' Oravo repeated. 'What are you doing here?'

Thomas and Jack didn't rightly know what to say.

'We followed you,' said Jack, hoping it was the right answer, added again, 'Where's Mabel and Mr Stroop?'

Oravo heaved a sigh from somewhere deep inside his chest. Wasn't sure how to proceed, had already decided what he was going to do. Knew that all the villagers had scudded back to base, that they would be preparing arms, would maybe try to storm the manor house, that the only advantage they had was that he was here already, waiting to burrow beneath the enemy like a beetle into bark. What he certainly didn't want was a couple of boys hanging around him, like the miller's rope about his waist he thought, but didn't say, waiting to trip him up or get him hanged.

'They've gone back to the village with the rest of them,' he finally managed. 'They'll be waiting for you. Why don't you go and join them?'

'But what are you going to do, Mister?' one of them asked. It was the tall, gangly one, the one who had thrown out a battlefield with a handful of stones. Oravo had a sudden vision of those stones, and saw himself the fox against the geese, knew that if the game was played right, then occasionally, just occasionally, the fox could win.

'I've things to do,' Oravo said, 'and you're not a part of it. Get back to your Mr Stroop and leave me alone.'

'But we can help,' offered Thomas brightly, 'just tell us what to do.'

Oravo weighed up a couple of things in his mind, tapped automatically at the fennel tube in his pocket as if it would bring him luck. Caught a sudden glimpse of the little carving one of the boys had around his neck, which looked like two people twined together. Oravo and Griselda, he thought, and could hardly bear that such an impossible thing might actually be within his grasp, and would leave nothing undone no matter the cost, if only to close his hand upon it.

The men had been sent, and the lighthouses lit, and back up in his tower, Torrensson saw the brief flares of them where the night clouds had rolled over the island, watched with disbelief as the lanterns took hold like enormous brands, calling out to ships other than his own. He felt nothing, only the calmness that always overtook him in the midst of battle, the only aim being to survive and overcome. He understood he had been pre-empted, and that his own secondary plan of attack, which had been to set the forests burning, bring the islanders to their knees, would now only aid his enemy, and was oddly glad of it, had never wanted anyway to destroy this place, had only wanted to possess it, wondered if his men so long gathered would defend this citadel as he had asked them to, felt the creep of the damp night and inaction in his bones, knew it would be creeping just so into every one of them as well. He must gather his men again soon and set his own fires burning within them. But before that, there was one thing he needed to do, and knew that the time for it would be soon, had already set himself to watching the night-time through from his tower and seen the humpbacked man slide into deepest shadow behind the carpenter's shed. And he had known his plan then, and that he would be able to scupper it, that the stable-boy had babbled out all he needed to know before Torrensson had sliced him off from his life. He smiled a little, and rolled his shoulders. Got himself ready for his final fight.

He didn't know that one of the men he had sent across to the ice house had been Onni Berwald, nor that Onni had found his murdered brother within its walls, that Onni had guessed who had done this thing, and when, and why.

And would not have cared even if he did.

Oravo had tried his best to rid himself of the two boys, but they had clung to him like tics, and eventually he knew he would have to take them with him, at least part of the way. They took their passage across the laundry greens and behind the orchard hedges, came out behind the stables where the carpenters' sheds were sited, Oravo going first, then a few minutes later beckoning the boys in after him. Then he opened the flaps built into the outside walls, which could be propped to let out the dust, or closed against the wind when it blew in against them. And he was glad now these boys were with him, had seen that the courtyard had been snapped shut like a badger trap, barred by the huge oak doors, and that the only way into the carpentry shed now was through these flaps. What he had forgotten was how small they were, and how much time it might have taken him and his tools to enlarge them. Instead, he now heaved Thomas up on his shoulders and sent him flying through the hole as Jack held the dust-flap open, told Thomas to pass him through a saw, described the one he wanted and where it was. Even in the pitch-dark of the shed, Thomas found what he had been asked to find within a minute and handed it out.

It would have taken other men a long, long time to saw a hole through the frames from flap to flap big enough to let a grown man to pass, but not Oravo, who knew every piece of wood by its knot and grain, and where the dowels would be to hold them, and how to keep the saw's teeth from screaming and grating against the grain, and had the strength to see the job through. It took him maybe five minutes before he had weakened the wood sufficiently, Jack jiggling so hard at his back that eventually Oravo tossed him through the now half-kicked-out entrance towards Thomas, telling them to find a candle or a lamp and get it lit. Then he finished his sawing and his splitting and his kicking-in of the planks, and crawled his frame in to join them.

Once inside the wood shed, Oravo surveyed the tools upon the walls and picked out several short-handled axes, kept two himself, gave one each to Jack and Thomas, tucked a few sharp chisels into his work-belt and several of the long spikes used for hammering into logs to aid their splitting. Then he heaved up the trap door that led down to the tunnel, pushed past the trolley that was half filled with offcuts, ready to be sent along its rails towards the kitchen, took the lamp he had been given and bent himself down, went as fast as his crouch would allow him, Thomas and Jack scampering and tripping at his heels.

Onni Berwald didn't think he had ever been so shocked. He had been sent to the ice house with a small contingent of the crew, had left the others to the pilfering their few months of piracy had hardened them to, heard them laughing as they set off rolling barrels across the grass and back up to the manor house. But he had been curious, had seen turfed stores like these when he had first arrived on the shores of the Dnieper, mysterious humps that had been dug back into hillsides, in which were stored the harvests that would see them through to spring, knew that very often there were deeper chambers near the back where other, more valuable things, might be hidden. And so he had ventured a little further than the others, pushed open the thick door at the back of the main storeroom, felt the air become cold and still and chill, saw several chambers going off to left and right, could make out the flattened shapes of oddly human-looking carcasses: pigs already skinned and dressed, halves of cattle and deer, some huge fish, gutted but still whole, probably sturgeon.

And then he saw something else entirely, saw the blue of his lamp shining through the ice blocks, the holes where the screw-picks had been applied, the slight misfitting of the ice bricks that had obviously been removed and replaced many times over, and quite recently. Had seen such things before in those other ice houses, in that other country, when a body had died too far into winter to be buried in the frozen ground, and needed to be stored until the spring, when the ground would be soft enough to dig a hole and lower it in. And so he had put on the leather gauntlets that still hung wet from their hook, and picked up a set of ice screws, and begun to pull away the blocks.

16

The Trap-Door Spider
Meets its Mate

V on Riddarholm was anxious; more than that, he was
  terrified, though he tried not to show it, felt Stroop's
hand upon his arm willing him to be calm. Knew it had been
only a few hours since they had fled from the tree-chapel
glade, and only two since he had sent for the lighthouses to
be lit. He worried that the men would run out of fuel, that
the lights would die out one by one before any passing
lookouts even saw them, heard Stroop prompting him to
send out other men after the first with extra barrels of pitch
and oils from the print barns, and wished he had thought
of so obvious a solution. He felt useless and incompetent,
and hated more than anything to be waiting for other ships,
other nations, to come to his island's defence.

'Surely we can do something,' he heard himself saying,
despised the heightened edge to his voice that meant he had
no idea what.

'We can only wait,' Stroop had said, ever calm by his
side, though surely he could not have been quite so serene
as he seemed. Von Riddarholm looked out into the gloom

of the barn and the uselessness of the straw bales, its lack of fighting men, thought perhaps he should have stuck to his first instincts and flung them all up at the manor house when he'd had the chance, knew also the futility of this gesture and that Stroop's plan was undoubtedly the better. He saw the small, still pietà of Griselda and Mabel, the girl comforting the woman, knew his brief dream of having the freckled woman by his side would never be, wondered how he had ever thought it could be so. He thought of something else then, something he should have thought of earlier, cursed himself for not having the wit to ask.

'Jack and Thomas,' he said, 'where are Jack and Thomas?'

And when Stroop shook his head, said he didn't know, only then did Josef Von Riddarholm truly understand the cost of all the small wars he had lived through and the one he was living through now, and something kicked inside his gut as if that old soldier who had died pushing his own intestines back into his stomach was somewhere deep inside him, trying to claw his way out. Something snapped inside his head and heart, and his whole life's balance swung and tipped, and Von Riddarholm leapt down from his hay bale without another word, and set his foot towards the door.

They were in the underbelly of the kitchens, getting ready to push the trap door up above their heads and fly out. Oravo had put his fingers to his lips, and so Jack and Thomas had stayed helpless in that tunnel. There was the soft sound of someone moving above them, and then nothing. Several minutes Oravo made them wait in that dank undercroft, and then he levelled his fingers at them, signalled a one, a two and a three, and they had understood that he was going to open the door on the three and that they should follow. Oravo had other ideas. Had already planned to be up and out the hole and lock it from the kitchen side so the two boys could not get out, had been expecting a band of marauders to be waiting on the other side, found instead only one man, sitting on a stool with his head down, his elbows shaking on his knees.

He was so surprised he forgot to throw the pins on the trap door, and Jack and Thomas were up and out quick as worms from rain-drenched soil. Oravo withdrew a chisel with one hand and his axe with the other, but the man in the kitchen never moved, did not even register their arrival. Oravo kept his axe high as he closed the few yards that separated them, but could see the unnatural way the man held his body, the small convulsions that seemed to move through him like waves through the sea, his hands drawn up tight against his face. Oravo hesitated as he heard the sounds that came from out behind those hands, saw that they were wet, and was horrified to see that it was tears that coursed out from between the stranger's fingers.

The setting fire to the ship in the harbour of Körgessaare had been a masterstroke. The boards had been only recently careened, caulked and retarred, and when the news had been made known to the few citizens of that port, all the men and boys came running back out of their houses carrying lamps and candles and burning brands, and launched the bottles and jars they had brought over in the coracles as they came up about the ship, set her going on every side, surrounding her with a circlet of flames that grew and joined and provoked a sound of wind and orange light rippling across the calm waters of the harbour, sent up great screes of burning embers into the night sky.

There were three ships at anchor within sight of the islands: a merchant barque, which had set sail from the Åland Islands the day before; a Danish schooner on its way to trade in Riga; and an English thirty-two-gun frigate, the *Cerberus*, a day ahead of the rest of her squadron, heading for the Gulf of Finland to engage with the Russians at Fredericksham.

Up in the crow's-nest, the lookout boys saw the small dots of lights glowing far across the sea as the night pushed away the mist and made the fires seem brighter, and by the time the ship in Körgessaare took hold, the captain and the first mate were already on deck with telescopes, did not understand the burning of the lighthouses, but knew a ship on fire when they saw one, and the *Cerberus* had already lifted anchor, and men were running across her decks and scattered throughout her rigging like dawn-alerted crows, releasing or refurling sails, whatever would give them speed, and behind them the wind blew down from Finland and pushed them on, set the flames of Hiiumaa flickering and running high, and soon all the men from every village on every island in sight of the coast of Ristnaneem were hurrying down to their own harbours, worrying at their boats, making them ready, cursing the darkness that prevented them from setting off that very minute, spent useless hours stamping their feet along the shoreline, hands held up against their eyes, watching and waiting, waiting and watching for that thin line of light upon the horizon that was the harbinger of dawn.

★ ★ ★

'He's crying,' said Jack.

'Shush!' warned Thomas, his hand sweating on the handle of his axe, unsure if he could actually use it, remembered other heads and other weapons, other blood. Oravo had no such qualms, but had lowered his axe, though still clutched the chisel before him, motioned Thomas to go stand by the door that led into the main hallway, and Jack to the other one leading out to the path that went down to the ice house. But as Jack passed the crying man to reach the door, the man's hand shot out and caught Jack by the elbow. Jack was so surprised he dropped his axe, but Oravo was over the flagstones and had his chisel at the stranger's throat even as he croaked out a single word, which though in Swedish, quite obviously meant 'No'. Blood was already trickling from the man's skin from where the chisel had pierced it, when Jack gently put his hand out to Oravo's and drew it back.

'It's all right,' he said, though whether to Oravo or the stranger, no one could have been sure. But Jack had seen that man's face and the grief in his eyes as he'd lowered his hands and, slow as he was, already understood what he meant by that one word, and that he had seen the man in the ice house and somehow known him, and didn't want anyone else to have to suffer seeing him there, didn't know they already knew his face and almost his name. Jack took out his notebook and opened it to the sketch above which he had had Thomas carefully spell out the name as he had heard it.

'Bear-vald,' said Jack slowly, and held his sketch out to the stranger on his seat.

And that man looked at it only for a moment, a fresh line

of tears overspilling his eyes, wetting his cheeks. '*Eyvind*,' he said, '*broor*.'

And Jack reached out his hand and beckoned Thomas to his side. 'Brother,' he said, pointing first to himself and then to Thomas and back again.

The strange man understood, set his fingers to the sketch, then held his hand against his own chest. 'Bro-thorr,' he repeated with some difficulty, 'Eyvind,' he said again, nodding at the notebook. 'Onni,' he said, tapping his hand against his heart. And then the door from the hallway was flung open and a man stood tall and large within its frame, the tangle of his beard black and hard against his broken cheekbone, the purpled yellow flesh slightly puffed above it, the dark crescent of his mouth opening in an odd sort of smile, showing the blacker gaps where his teeth used to be.

For a few ticks of the clocks that worked on unperturbed in the hallway, fixed and serene in their stairwell, no one moved. Torrensson recognised both Onni and Oravo, had guessed Oravo's path here having found out about the tunnel's end, and watched and waited in his tower, ready to descend at just this moment; had no idea about the boys. Oravo recognised Torrensson from the moors, from his bulk and his beard and his bruises, and Onni saw the captain he had followed for so many years, and saw also the man who had slain his brother. Jack and Thomas had no idea really who anyone was at all.

Then Oravo let fly his axe, sent it spinning through the air straight at Torrensson's head; Torrensson ducked into the kitchen as the axe split straight into the wood of the door and stuck there, closing it once again from the hall. Torrensson yanked it free, tossed it from one hand to the other, settled it in his right, then Onni was up and off his stool, roaring across the floor like a horizontal tornado, pushing the table over as he passed it by, head lowered, hand going to the knife he kept at his belt.

'No!' shouted Jack, but couldn't move, had Oravo's strong bolt of an arm shoving him backwards, pinning him against the wall, keeping him immobile, and then one of the spike pins was out of Oravo's jacket pocket and flying through the air, caught Torrensson askance upon the shoulder, fell clattering to the stone of the floor just as Onni reached him, head down like a bull, thundering into Torrensson's stomach, sending him back and up against the squared stone of the massive sink. Torrensson raised the axe and brought it down, but the force of the stone on one side and Onni on the other had winded him, and the blade thumped uselessly down on Onni's back without force, could not get past the leather of his jerkin. Torrensson recouped, threw Onni back against the floor, where he stumbled against the overturned table, caught the back of his knee against the table's leg and fell heavily. Torrensson was on him in a moment, and this time there was force behind that axe and the blade, and though Onni turned his head, the axe took off his ear and the skin of his neck, sent blood spraying up and out, momentarily slicking Torrensson's hand upon the axe handle, forcing him to take another grip, held his other arm against Onni Berwald's throat and lifted the axe to strike again. Jack slumped suddenly to the floor as Oravo released him, made a noise like a stag in rut as he took the few paces across the floor, stepped onto the back of the table where the underlying struts would give him grip, hefted out another log-spike, sent it down with all his force onto Torrensson's uplifted arm. It was not much of a blow without a hammer behind it, but it was enough to make Torrensson release the axe, and it fell blade down, catching Onni's elbow. Then the two of them were rolling over from the table to the floor, each one grabbing for the other's throat and Oravo could hear that there were other men coming, could hear their shouts and heavy footfalls running down the corridors and stairs, knew there was not much time, fumbled at his belt for his hammer, grasped for another chisel but could make no hit at the men writhing beneath him like snakes uncovered by a stone, could not get a clear aim to strike. And then another form was up and behind them, and another axe was coming down, and Thomas slammed his blade down onto Torrensson's spine and there was so much blood come pouring out that everybody stopped – everyone except Onni Berwald, who took his moment, thrust Torrensson up and over onto his side so that the axe handle scraped against the stone, and sat astride him, his strong sailorman's hands encircling Torrensson's throat, tightening their grip, and no matter that Torrensson's fingers were clawing at Onni's face and that the blood was coursing from his ear and neck, Onni kept on tightening, and Torrensson began to gasp, his breath whistling within his lungs, and Oravo still heard those footsteps and those feet coming quicker, coming closer, and he turned away, grabbed Thomas roughly by the arm that had swung the axe, dragged him away from where he stood apparently unable to move, his eyes fixed upon the blood, shouted for Jack to open the trap door, bundled Thomas up beneath one arm and threw him down into the tunnel, pushed Jack down after him, leapt in behind them, barely missing Thomas's head with his boots as he landed and hauled the trap door closed, threw the bolts, only then beginning to breathe again, could still hear Onni up above him grunting with the effort of squeezing the life out of a man who did not want to let it go, didn't know it could take so long for a man to die, nor make so terrible a noise with no air left within his lungs.

There were other sounds that came at them as they stumbled back along the tunnel, noises that were muffled by the three yards of earth that separated that world from their own; but they could make out one man's voice and his shouting, and knew it was Von Riddarholm, screaming out some battle cry as his feet thudded hard across the lawns above them, crossing the dark tunnel that kept them safe, a few men of the village somewhere at his back, Von Riddarholm snatching up some of the small boulders that lined his driveway and hurling them through the windows of his rooms, smashing a way back into his home, striking left and right with the scythe-blade shortened off from its handle by his stamping at it, having set it between two strong stones. He must have known he could not win, that the men inside would overcome him in a moment, but Von Riddarholm did not care. He had about him the air of the soldier he had never quite been before, and although he did not know it, he was not by then alone, for the fighting men of the *Cerberus* had already hauled into harbour and disembarked, understood the brief, insistent barks of the men who had set the ship in its harbour all aflame, and gone running without further question up to the manor house, muskets and pistols already primed, well trained to do battle at a moment's notice, had taken on bigger targets than a load of marauding pirates who had stepped so far over the lines of mutiny and insurrection that no solider nor sailor from any army in any land would allow them to go further.

They converged on the manor house to find the windows broken and Von Riddarholm screaming at the gates, his men lighting the way with burning brands, the door to the kitchen already half hacked open by Von Riddarholm's broken scythe. They poured into the kitchen after him, found a band of men pulling Onni Berwald off their captain, who was apparently still alive, despite the axe that had split his spine, and his face being the colour of bletted berries, his tongue hanging out of him like an ox that has been hung too long upon its hook.

It all went very quickly after that, the New Brethren with their swords and guns being no match for the well-armed men of the *Cerberus*, who stormed the manor house with as much ease as the New Brethren had done earlier, jumping through the broken doors and windows, setting the court-yard barricades burning, blasting through the great oak doors with the cannons they had dragged up from the harbour on their carts, swarming into the fortress and courtyard at every point of entry. A handful of the young bloods of the Brethren fought on, but their resistance was chaotic, desultory and futile with no captain to lead them and no one to remind them of the piles of tinder and pitch held upon the roofs to pour down on their enemies, nor of the horses made ready inside the compound for a quick escape. Some of the older ones were too drunk to even realise what was happening as the ideals of the New Osilia were blown to bits around them, and soon laid down their arms and called for surrender, even as others of their brethren went on fighting uselessly around them, every last one of them, without mercy, being cut down.

Dawn bled over the island and every man upon it, brought the smell of damp ash and burning tar and spent gunpowder, and the sweat and blood of men, some alive, some dead, many dying. The ship set alight in the harbour down at Körgessaare was smouldering still, sinking slowly into the brine, every inch sending out another black rainbow across the water, staining the stones of the quay with the horrid, greasy residue of another ship gone down, coating the pier arms with the successive lines of its demise as the tide went on and lowered, as it had always done.

Torrenson died almost as soon as Onni was pulled off him, only two breaths left within his lungs, and without Torrensson, there was no army and no New Brethren, only a band of desperadoes who had once been valiant in their soldiering and sailoring, but who had succumbed to the rhetoric of power and new beginnings, and found themselves disintegrated into a band of pirates ready to kill their own. Those who had not been slain up at the manor house were herded into the holds of the *Cerberus* and sailed away with Von Riddarholm's blessing, the English eager to be on their way to proper fights, proper battles in proper wars. The last of the New Brethren were swiftly executed and thrown overboard as the *Cerberus* passed into what they thought of as international waters, where the sea that once sluiced the

islands of Saaremaa swept into the Gulf of Finland, their
bodies left to fatten the fish that grow there big as men. The
only one of them who did not die in either place, in either
way, was Onni Berwald, his death coming later, slower, his
blood poisoned by the edge of Gunar Torrensson's blade,
his neck growing mottled and dark beneath his missing ear,
his skin growing loose about his bones, his organs failing
one by one until he and his brother were both taken down
to the graveyard and buried, the one on top of the other,
with no one to put their names upon the stone.

That first morning after the battle also brought a flotilla of
other men from other islands who had set out for Hiiumaa
as soon as they were able, landing on every available beach
and shore, swilling their way through the villages and tracks
that led towards Ristnaneem, greedy for news, alarmed and
angered by this attack on the strongest of their islands. They
sought out any relatives they could find and offered help and
succour, went later to the manor house and pledged any aid
that might be needed, every last one of them signing a charter
swearing their allegiance to Saaremaa or Osilia, or whatever
else they chose to call their island land. And as the news
spiralled out to all the other islands, to Prangli and Piirisaar,
to Kihnu and Kassari, to Abruka and Vislandi, other men came
and also signed or made their mark, swore they would not
allow such things to happen again. And for all that the New
Brethren had wanted their New Osilia, it seemed it had been
found under someone else's flag, and Von Riddarholm felt the
islands invigorated and strengthened and newly bonded, shaken
at last from the complacency and inertia with which they had

always greeted yet another war being fought about their shores, without their giving any intervention or consent.

Von Riddarholm himself bore his own wounds with shy pride, would gaze every night at the undressing of his scar that looked like a melted aubergine upon his thigh where a musket ball had shattered his bone, did not mind that his leg would always be slightly bent, and that every time he took a walk around the meteorite lake, which he would often do, that he would need the companionship of a stick, and would never run it round again like Jack and Thomas had done, as he had done in his childhood. He knew that he had earned his wound and his place upon his land, and earned it well.

Throughout it all, throughout all the fear and the fighting, he had kept safe within his buttoned pocket Kustin Liit's little formulae, just as he had placed it there that night when Whilbert Stroop had discovered it. Within weeks of the island resettling itself back upon its haunches, regaining its ancient rhythms, he had launched himself and his inksmen into its successful re-creation, had made yet more astonishing books that would be placed in every one of his Travelling Libraries, regretted only that Jarl Eriksson would not be among the men who would take the miracle of Litt's Metalurgical Inks out into the world, had already settled a percentage of the monies it would earn onto the island's newest inhabitants, Griselda, Kustin's daughter, and Oravo Swan.

It had taken Thomas longer than most to recover, not so much from the ankle he had broken when Oravo had thrown him down into the tunnel, had not even felt the break of his bones as he ran with the others, had felt nothing at all since the wielding of his axe, saw nothing except the bringing down of its blade, and the terrible amount of blood it had engendered, the sticky warmth of it soaking into his boots and skin, and the awful sound the axe had made as it hit the bone, could still feel the judder of its impact ripping up through his elbow to his shoulder and on into his neck; still saw himself standing there, the dreadful, conspiratorial wink of the light upon the axe blade in its wound. Thomas had not even realised he had been hurt, had only felt Oravo pushing him onwards through the tunnel, seen the small bright light of Jack's candle flickering wildly as they went back along the way that they had come. It was only when they'd finally reached the tree–chapel glade that they'd stopped to take a breath, that the pain had finally bit through him and he had cried out and looked down at his ankle, saw the horrid puffball of it swelling beneath his skin. Oravo had said nothing, had just picked Thomas up and placed him gently over his shoulder as if he weighed no more than a bag of feathers.

Thomas had lain there with his head resting on Oravo's hump, and thought of Mabel and Mr Stroop, and wondered where on earth they were, hoped more than anything he had ever wished for that they were all right. He had longed so much to see them that it hurt, almost more than his broken ankle, though he knew already he would never be able to tell them everything, not even to Mabel. There would be many bad nights and many bad dreams to follow that would find him back within that kitchen, his arm still striking through the air, the sound of his axe hitting Torrenson's bone, the feel of that blow still reverberating within his bones, the smell of blood so strong within his throat and nose that he could taste it, that strange immobility that had come over him before Oravo had swept him up and thrown him down the hole, that weirdest of feelings Thomas had had then, that he wanted to do it all again.

As for Oravo, once he had deposited Thomas and Jack back where they belonged, he felt so acutely tired he could barely stand, was embarrassed by the gratitude shown by the man Stroop. He whispered off towards the tree-glade and stood instead alone and immobile before that huge and immeasurable stone, watching as dawn began its slow ascendant arc across the sky, the shadows moving across the face of that great boulder, shifting all its colours from blue to red. He heard her coming then, knew it without turning, thought he would always know her by her stepping and wondered if there would ever come a time when he could turn and stand and gaze upon her, and tell her truthfully about his tracking her across all England, and how he had killed for her and her father's little book.

Griselda saw Oravo Swan standing there beside the stone into which both her mother and her father's names were now inscribed. He did not move, though surely he must have heard her coming, came so close he must have felt her near him. She looked up at him then, and saw his eyes were closed, and heard his breath coming quicker. She didn't say anything, just moved against him, took his hand inside her own and lifted it to her lips, kissed it gently, knew she would never kiss another man if it could not be him.

Marriages, Homecomings, and Death

IT WAS ALMOST two weeks later, and deep into the night, the mist keeping the island of Hiiumaa close within its hold. Everyone was exhausted, happy, and not a little drunk. Mabel was smiling broadly as Jack told her once again how he had fallen into the lake that morning, had been trying to climb a semi-submerged tree trunk to reach the crane's nest slumped so ungraciously at its end, wanted to get a few feathers for his collection, had already shown her his drawings and explained the Coprological Museum to her, and all the specimens gathered here and at home that awaited her approval.

She looked up to see Thomas sitting quietly in a large armchair, his splinted foot held before him on a stool, Stroop on another chair beside him, reading to him from some book.

She had worried for Thomas the first few days after the island's insurrection had been vanquished. He had been so quiet and withdrawn, had said nothing of what had happened up at the manor house that night, though Jack had boasted endlessly of Thomas's famous axe-strike. His excuse upon being questioned had always been the same – that his ankle was painful and was bothering him, and that anyway he could not remember much. She had not pushed him, knew there was some deeper wound, some other pain that he was feeling. Knew they had all seen their fair share of death and dying, and that to deal it out yourself must be something else entirely.

She was glad though, of this past day, that had seen him happy and laughing as Jack tried to haul him up by a rope into the tree-chapel for the wedding, Thomas banging against the branches and throwing pine cones up at Jack as he swung unprotected below him this way and that, before Oravo had come to his rescue and reeled him in. Knew that if anyone could heal those wounds, it would be Jack, and Mr Stroop.

It had been a good day, and a right ending, thought Mabel, and had been immensely grateful to the old priest that he had speeded up the usual reading of the bans so that the months had been made into weeks, and she could be Griselda's bridesmaid before they left. And then there was the even better news – that they were leaving, and leaving altogether, and that tomorrow they would be sailing off for home, and nothing, thought Mabel, could be righter than that.

Had Oravo Swan known what Mabel was thinking at that moment, he would surely have disagreed, was so overwhelmed with happiness at his own right way of being. He was up in one of the tower rooms, Griselda sitting by his side. They had left the gathering only half an hour earlier, the island men slapping at his shoulder and winking, offering several dozen bottles by the neck as he passed them by, should he have need of them. But he hadn't, and had barely touched a drop the whole day through, apart from the interminable toasting, didn't want to miss a single moment of this most extraordinary day, couldn't imagine being more intoxicated than he already was, with Griselda, as his wife, sitting by his side.

They were on the window seats looking out onto the dark back of the sea, a sliver of moonlight tracking a ripple across its surface, the mist seeming to have lifted just a moment for this very purpose, saw the fires of the light-house by the headland bay, which had been lit again this night, not for warning, but for them and their celebration. Neither one of them could have asked for more. Or almost. For there was one question of Oravo Griselda needed to ask, but had not until now dared. She squeezed Oravo's arm as she broke their silence.

'Why the Spanish chapel?' she said, knew they had looked at every one of the tree-chapels, and that Oravo had been insistent on the Spanish one the very moment they had ducked their heads below its door, even before they had walked its short, dank aisle or talked about its shortcomings or its advantages. She had not been able to understand why he wanted to be married beneath that picture, with its mouldering bodies and the balance that swung above them like a threat, but had been happy enough, at his insistence, to acquiesce.

Still, though, Griselda was curious, and knew, as she looked up at his face, that there would be a lifetime of wanting to know, and a lifetime in which to find out. Unexpectedly she saw that Oravo was smiling, saw the outline of his face and the hump she now loved and could not imagine him without, and the soft shadows of the half-full moon lighting up his face, saw that it was strong as the cliffs below them, and wondered how she had never noticed such a thing before.

He reached his hand into his jacket, took out a small tube, and passed it to her.

'It was my parents',' he said simply, 'and like so many things, I never knew what it meant until I came here.'

She looked up at him briefly, then down at the little phial of fennel, prised her nail beneath the wax and pulled it open, extracted a small piece of linen from its depths.

'What does it mean?' she asked, not recognising the words that had been embroidered there as she unrolled it.

'*Nimas, Nimenos*,' Oravo said, and saw again the sampler where it had hung upon the wall of that cottage for all those years both before, and after, his parents had died, the one he had found when he had claimed their cottage for his own; the little piece of them that he had taken with him wherever he went, though, like Griselda, never understanding. Not until he had seen those same words in that painting in the Spanish chapel, written beneath those scales that signified the worth of every man's life.

'It's Spanish,' he said, 'like my father.' And it was the first time he had ever said those words out loud, and the last. It was something only for him, and now for her, it was his past and his isolation, and what had brought them both indirectly to this place and together, and, for him at least, to such a happiness and completion he'd never known could possibly have existed.

'*Nimas*,' he said again, 'means "nothing more", and *Nimenos* . . .' he began but did not finish, turned suddenly towards Griselda, kissed those lips he had thought about so often, took her beautiful hands in his own, ran his fingers over the wonderful freckles on her wrists and face, let that little fennel tube drop to the floor. Only later did he tell her the rest, that after he had seen those same words in the painting in the chapel, he had sought out Mr Stroop, asked him to find out what they meant. And Stroop had searched Von Riddarholm's library and soon enough found it out, and that the words were Spanish and gave him at last the meaning to the only words his parents ever left him.

Nimas, Nimenos, he told Griselda: nothing more, and nothing less. And he told her also how he had finally understood his parents and his past, and why they had chosen to abandon him, follow one another into death; knew now that Grandmother Swan and all those other villagers had been right, and that now he had found Griselda, he would do the same thing as had his parents done, would choose to go whatever way it was that she would take him, even into death, and leave behind him anything that might stand in his way.

Stroop too had found meaning in those words, and found comfort in the rightness of the patterns he had discovered that had led him all the way from London to Lower Slaughter, and then to Painswick and beyond, to here. Oddly, he found himself thinking of Isaac the bargeman, and the disappointment that had been so obvious upon his face as they had taken their abrupt departure towards Bristol, and to Mabel, and Hiiumaa. It had been such a fleeting glimpse, but Stroop had recognised it well, and all the losses and years that had gone into its making. He remembered the horror and despair he had felt that night he thought Jack and Thomas might have been taken from him, when he had stood nevertheless in apparent calmness by Von Riddarholm's side, giving out his orders, feeling all the while that black maelstrom growing inside his chest, getting wider and more powerful with every minute that passed with all the worry of where they were and what might be happening to them, had wanted more than anything to go running after them, no matter how useless might be the task, had thought briefly that if he should never see them again, he would go back to that black lake within the forest and throw himself in. He remembered also the relief that had flooded through him when he had seen them again, as strong, if not stronger, than the flood that must have taken Lower Slaughter, and his complete inability to express his gratitude to the man who had delivered them, had been able to do nothing for Oravo but shake his hand, nod his head at Jack and Thomas as if they had been away only an instant.

And then there was home. It was all that he could think about now, all he had thought about since the dawning of the day that had brought an end to his latest task, could hardly believe it had all started out as a pleasant diversion to find a missing library and the man who carried it, had begun just as something to take all their minds away from that other missing person of the time, which had been Mabel, who was now back with them as strong as she had ever been. Mabel and Stroop, he thought, Jack and Thomas. The only other thing he wanted now was home, to be able to create his own little island of lists and books and keep his family safe within it.

Stroop had kicked his heels the last two weeks leading up to the wedding, had spent his time perusing the glories of

Von Riddarholm's many, many miniature books, and the ordinary-sized ones in his library, most of which Stroop could not even understand. He had helped repair the damage done to the collections strewn and stamped on by Gunar Torrensson and his men, had regretted, with Von Riddarholm, how men could do such things.

And then at last had come the wedding between Griselda Liit and Oravo Swan, and it had been wonderful, or so everyone told him, for he had spent most of it sitting quietly in his room, often with Thomas by his side, who seemed as keen as he was to get home and have done with foreign places and people they didn't really know, wanted to be back in his familiar surroundings doing familiar things, had pined as Stroop had done, for his study and his Sense Maps and his ledgers, and his own bed.

And after it was done, so came the long-anticipated return, and they suffered the belly-swilling voyage from those islands of the Baltic and across the North Sea and up the Thames and onto the trap they had engaged to take them the last tortuous miles back to Bexleyheath. And when finally they disembarked for the last time, their legs folding beneath them with tiredness, when they were finally back in front of the home they had missed so much, Stroop and Mabel had just stood there, allowing the coachman to throw down their bags with abandon, stuttered into movement only when Mabel's chest from Astonishment Hall landed with a crash at their feet, and one side splintered open, letting out a scatter of books, only then had Stroop and Mabel looked at each other and smiled.

Jack had already catapulted from his seat and lifted Thomas

and his broken ankle none too gently down, and together they hobbled off to the next-door house to collect Bindlestiff, happy, and shouting out his name. But there had been no Bindlestiff to collect, for the old dog had curled up and died while they were gone, and there was nothing left of him, not even the old nest of blankets in which he had lived his last two years beside their fire, for they had all been burnt along with Bindlestiff's cold body in their own back garden. And all they had left of him was a small grey circle in the grass and a patch of dew-damped ash.

It leeched all the happiness and gaiety of their return right out of them. Mabel and Jack spent that first night crying quietly together, neither one of them able to comfort the other, and Stroop could not settle in his study, lost the thrill he had anticipated for so long to see the books and maps and ledgers he was ashamed to have missed so much.

Thomas took it hardest, clumping his way up the stairs with his wooden-jacketed leg, then lay on his back on his bed, the tears running from the corners of his eyes and down into the pillow, chest heaving with silent sobs. He stared up at the peeling yellow of the ceiling, but did not see it; saw only that axe hefting itself down again and again on Torrensson's back, knew that it was the same night that old Bindlestiff must have breathed his last, and breathed it alone. Could hardly bear that he would not run his hand through the smelly, moth-eaten fur just one last time, that the old dog had died on his own by someone else's fire; had an awful, secret guilt that somehow he was to blame for his dying, that when his axe had come down, it had come down not on Torrensson, but on Bindlestiff.

337

It was many hours later that Stroop climbed the stairs behind him, pulled up the rickety old chair from the rickety old table by the window, sat himself down upon it beside the bed, and took Thomas's hand in his own.

'It's no one's fault,' Stroop said. 'Everyone and everything has their time of dying.'

Thomas continued with his silent crying, and Stroop felt his own sadness brim up within him and almost over-flow. He understood now Josef's wild running up to the manor house with his useless blunted scythe, his fierce defiance of the enemy that was attacking his island and his home.

'We're a family now, Thomas,' Stroop said, 'and you will never be on your own, whatever happens.'

And only then did Thomas turn his body slightly towards Stroop, his splint creaking faintly as he rested his cheek upon Stroop's hand where it clasped his own, and finally, slowly, managed to sink into sleep.

He dreamt then of that deep, dark lake on Hiiumaa, and the polished black rocks that lined its sides, saw the big ances-tral stone glowing red with the sunset, and all the hundreds of years and hundreds of hands that had scrawled their people's names upon its surface, and the great line of windmills that still guarded the shores of Ristnaneem. He saw himself there again and felt its safety and its peace and the cool mists rolling in from the sea. Felt Stroop and Mabel and Jack standing somewhere close beside him, though he could not see their faces.

It was a dream he was to have often, and it saddened him that whenever he was in that place of dreaming he always felt the draw to stay for ever by those deep, dark waters, and yet it gladdened him, on waking, that he never did. And that Stroop and Jack and Mabel really were somewhere near beside him, and that, unlike Bindlestiff, would never leave.

Historical Note

Big APOLOGIES TO Upper and Lower Slaughter, which are
still extant, and for the liberties I have taken with their
geography, as with Painswick's. To the islands of Saaremaa I
have been truer, and have tried to get their historical back-
ground right, including the coming of the Brethren of the
Sword, and the expulsions of 1781. I have, though, compounded
several features on to Hiiumaa that by rights belong to other
of the islands, the great erratic boulders, and the meteorite
lake, being the most important. As to the windmills, there are
many still there on the islands to be seen, as well as the lighthouses, both inland and on the coastal reefs. There are also
many woods, but sadly no tree-chapel glades, which I have
made up, though there are chapels in trees in other places,
one of the most famous being the Chêne Millénaire of
Allouville in Normandy.

The Pike Gut Strait, though, is real enough and as
described, and Emanuel Swedenborg a now well-known
author and quasi-theologian/mystic who died in London in
1772. The *Cerberus* was an actual ship and its actions against

340

the Russians as described, except they took place exactly a year after they happen here, in 1809. As for St Margaret/ Marina, her feast day really does shift between the Orthodox and Western canonical calendars, and the Fourteen Helpers are still regularly asked for their intercession.